NOT
TOO
COCKSURE

THE TRUTH FROM THE DARK SIDE OF THE BRIGHT LIGHTS

Marc freden

NOT TOO COCKSURE

THE TRUTH FROM THE DARK SIDE OF THE BRIGHT LIGHTS

SUNSTONE
PRESS

SANTA FE

Sunstone books may be purchased for educational, business, or sales promotional use.
For information please write: Special Markets Department, Sunstone Press,
P.O. Box 2321, Santa Fe, New Mexico 87504-2321.
Cover design › James Messer
Book design › Vicki Ahl
Body typeface › Cambria
Printed on acid-free paper
∞
eBook 978-1-61139-357-6

Library of Congress Cataloging-in-Publication Data

Freden, Marc, 1962-
  Not too cocksure : the truth from the dark side of the bright lights : a novel / by Marc
Freden.
    pages cm
  ISBN 978-1-63293-049-1 (softcover : alk. paper)
  1. Reporters and reporting--Fiction. 2. Celebrities--Fiction. I. Title.
PS3606.R42958N68 2015
813'.6--dc23
                              2014044946

WWW.SUNSTONEPRESS.COM
SUNSTONE PRESS / POST OFFICE BOX 2321 / SANTA FE, NM 87504-2321 /USA
(505) 988-4418 / ORDERS ONLY (800) 243-5644 / FAX (505) 988-1025

To Hollywood:

Thank you for the confessions unmade, the scandals not spoken about and the secrets untold. . . all so I can.

Marc

Prologue

H e had to take a piss. But that was going to be awkward, as he would have to leave the darkened confines of his little cubby on the basement level of the Dreamland Spa.

The Dreamland Spa, off Vine Street in Hollywood, is an institution for horny men to get laid, no questions asked. It is a three-story sextorium complete with workout equipment, sauna, showers and Jacuzzi, even a snack bar—all the trappings of a spa but none of the intent. It is for all intents and purposes a fuck den.

Bathhouses are no longer taboo and visiting them is no longer the social scourge it was when AIDS was understood to be a pandemic and not, as now, for better or worse, confusingly considered a treatable and maintainable chronic disease. Still, the place is dotted with the prerequisite signs alluding to the notion of no unsafe sex or public displays of public sexual activity will be permitted. Ha! But what goes on behind the doors of the sixty odd cubicles that line the darkened maze of hallways is obvious.

His door is open, just enough to invite in the passerby, without having to actually communicate. "Hi," would be enough, or a subtle nod of acceptance, and then it's on. He keeps the lights low as to not be too obvious, at least that is his excuse. What he really wants is to not be recognized but that is another issue all together.

He peeks out just to see if the hallway is clear. He really needs to take that piss. Wrapping a towel around his naked body, he wishes he wore flip-flops or track shoes instead of boots in which, could be rather clumsy to walk the halls. He is resigned to having to walk barefoot across the crusty industrial carpeting and that will be gross.

Stepping out into the light and walking with purpose, he makes his way down the hallway to the open line of urinals by the showers. Privacy is not really an issue at the Dreamland Spa, so being somewhat pee-shy, he had to take a deep breath and relax. It was worth it.

Taking the scenic route back to his room, he winds his way down one dimly lit passageway after another. He passes a man in the doorway, semi erect and looking for company, but turns his head away to indicate he is not interested.

There is a smell to the place, pungent if you really take notice. It is a mix of poppers—amyl nitrate—and lubricant, sweaty men and a damp mildew from open showers and other water-based facilities. There is nothing sexy about the place. It is simply a one-stop shop to take care of business. He chose not to think of the obviousness of the Dreamland Spa, he is more of a romantic at heart—and this place could not be more devoid of romance.

With the entire spa being three floors, he could really browse but he likes to stay confined to the basement and the aisles therein. The basement, with all pun intended, is for the bottoms—those who are more likely to take it than to give it. This isn't always his preference but on this night, he felt he was more likely to see some action if he made himself available. Sometimes, it is better to receive than give.

He darted along in the direction of room seventeen, which has its light on full. The light casts a bright streak out into the dank but adequately lit hallway. The light is begging attention and he glanced in accordingly. There, on what he could only imagine was a three-day bender, is a very sweaty and tweaked acquaintance, Don. Don's eyes are glazed over and it is clear that Don didn't recognize the familiarity of his friend. And that is just fine.

Don glistened from sweat. And that only accentuated his well worked out body. He had seen Don shirtless before, at pool parties in Palm Springs and the usual haunts, but never naked. Through the blush of his embarrassment, he couldn't help but to be impressed with the length and girth of Don's lubed up member, which he continued to stroke, oblivious to whom he was putting on his fruitless show.

Don has been in the throws of what everyone considers the longest midlife crisis known to man. An avid gym goer—but who isn't in Hollywood—he is obsessed with beefing up to a level beyond normal for a man of fortyish years old. Everyone is convinced he must be on 'supplements' to achieve his extraordinary results and those 'supplements' clearly drive his libido to new and dangerous levels. He is notorious for getting tweaked and disappearing for days on end only to be found face down and ass in the air at the Dreamland Spa—exhausted from being used and, most likely, abused by as many a passersby as he could humanly handle.

By day, in the normalcy of his life, Don is a very successful interior designer with a rich and influential clientele base. If those clients could only see him now! Then again, who would care? And, most likely, it would make him a more interesting person. He may have the body of a G.I. Joe but he has the intellect of a Barbie. Let's face it; in Hollywood everyone has a secret.

No one knows that better than Mica—short for Michael. Michael became

Mica when his business career—yes he is in 'The Business'—took off. Mica, is the aforementioned 'he', and 'he' knows he shouldn't be in the Dreamland Spa, for obvious career reasons. But a man has his needs.

Mica Daly—he took his mother's maiden name—lives on the periphery of being famous. His dream of fame developed first during tap dance lessons at Mary Kay's School of Dance and then in regional theater back as a boy growing up in the biggest little state in the union, Rhode Island. True fame is no longer a goal as he has seen what it does to some, being illusive and unfair to many and rewarding to mostly the undeserving. But he is a reporter on the hit daily entertainment news show, *Drop Zone*, for which he makes a good living covering the comings and goings of Hollywood's elite. By proxy, he too is a celebrity of sorts, higher up the pecking order than a local newscaster and about as recognizable as a national nightly news anchor, and that is good enough for him. Still, he is on television, giving him a certain amount of celebrity, and that, unto itself, is a precarious position to be in. There are plenty who can do his job and plenty more who want his job. Being recognized at the Dreamland Spa is a hardly a career forward move.

By now, Don, pushing back the damp sheets, had rolled over on to his stomach and arched his back so as to raise his ass and spread his cheeks. The welcome mat is out. Mica continued down the hall feeling bad for Don and hoped to God that was not his own future.

Mica turned the corner and could see his room in the distance. He wasn't sure if seeing Don didn't ruin his own spa experience. He may not be tweaked or on a bender like his far away friend but he was there to get laid by some stranger and the potential of that suddenly registered as pathetic and cheap rather than fantastical and exotic. Damn!

The ugliness of this momentary thought was shattered by a loud smack sound and Mica turned left to the half opened door and peered around. Two rather hot guys were wrestling as best they could in their confined cubicle. The older of the two, well built with sculptural body hair has clearly gotten the dominant betterment of the skinny, silky smooth, blonde younger one. Both had raging hard-ons as a reward for their effort. The older one caught Mica's eye and nodded his head to invite him in. Mica, feeling a certain stirring down below, sidled in and closed the door behind.

With one quick move, the older guy scooped up the young one, flipped him over and plowed his veiny dick deep into his ass. The acrobatics brought out a gasp in both the young one, for obvious reasons, and a startled Mica. The pounding was fierce.

The gyrating ass of the older man intrigued Mica, who normally didn't particularly get turned on by very hairy men. As the guy pushed forward his ass cheeks squeezed together in muscular symmetry. As he pulled back, his cheeks spread apart and a furry forest emerged. Mica squatted down and leaned toward the pounding flesh and pressed his face along side his manly ass to let the course hair rub against his skin. Almost instinctively, Mica reached up with one hand to run his fingers through the thick bush of his crack. The man is moist with sweat and that is getting Mica hard.

Mica could hear the glottal moans from the man as he threw back his head but couldn't tell if they were the result of Mica's stroking along his ass or a pre-climax warning as he pounded the other guy's ass. Mica felt the slapping of the man's hairy balls against his forearm and could feel their weight. And they felt good.

Mica didn't notice the man's hand reach around and cup the back of Mica's head, gently pushing his face toward his crack. The older guy pulled out of the blonde and bent over, ever so slightly to accommodate Mica's tongue. The blonde flipped over on to his back and quickly swallowed the man's engorged cock. Groans turned to growling as the man got close to his reward.

Mica's towel had slipped away and his cock was pulsing back and forth demanding attention. Mica dare not touch himself, as that was not the moment he wanted to climax. As the man began to glide feverishly in and out of the throat of the blonde, Mica pulled back to watch the scene. He couldn't help notice the raging hard on of the blonde and was secretly hoping the blonde was more versatile in his proclivities and not just a bottom.

With one final grunt, the man unexpectedly slammed his cock down the throat of the blonde, which made him gag it back up and out of his mouth. The result of his efforts oozed over the blonde's face and in his hair. He lay there and took it, licking it off his lips and stroking his own cock. Mica knew the blonde was going to cum and he was disappointed by the thought of that.

Now finished, the older man grabbed his towel and without a word, stepped over Mica, slapping him accidently with his still half erect cock, and left. Mica got a glimpse of his face and, man, is he handsome. He wanted to run after him and get a number but this isn't that kind of place, usually. He'd be lucky, while getting lucky, to even exchange a first name let alone a promise of a more sophisticated meet sometime in the future.

Mica reached up and stroked the blonde who was nearly silent when he came. He bucked a few times and shot all the way up to his chest. He used his free hand to smear the cream across his beautiful skin and then brought the hand up to his mouth to lick what was left. He exhaled in afterglow, took one more lick and without even acknowledging Mica rolled over, got on to all fours and pushed his ass out invitingly. Mica, who was now standing, couldn't believe how wonderfully smooth and clean this blonde is. He rubbed his hand across his waiting and wanting ass. A moment passed and the blonde reached back and gripped Mica's cock, which almost made him cum on the spot. Mica backed away with a smile that said it all.

"You look familiar," the now squinting eyed blonde gurgled. "Are you on television?"

"No and thanks for the offer," he said as he patted the blonde's ass. "This looks great but I think we are looking for the same thing at the moment."

Before any more incriminating post coital chitchat could out Mica, he backed out of the room, leaving the door ajar for the cheek-spread blonde. "Good luck," Mica offered awkwardly and somewhat inappropriately. This guy didn't need any luck, just a condom.

Mica made his way back to his room, his own erection wrapped against his pelvis by the tightly tied towel. He reached for the door and was just about to put the key in the lock when a hand grabbed his ass. Startled he turned around to see the man from four doors down. He really is as handsome as the previous glimpse lead Mica to believe. The man leaned in and planted his lips on Mica. A kiss! It always amazed Mica as to the number of men who wouldn't kiss but would willingly fuck you in ways the Marquis de Sade hadn't thought of. But a kiss? God forbid!

This was not just a kiss. He was aggressive and masculine and drove his tongue in and out of Mica's mouth with lustful purpose. Mica fumbled to get the key in the lock all the while holding up his towel, which had given way between the ass grab and his own cock wanting to spring free. The door flew open and still lip-locked; they fell forward and on to the bed platform.

"I thought you were done for the night," Mica said by way of unnecessary conversation as he noticed the man's swelling cock pressing against him. Mica couldn't help but to reach down and feel it, caress it, pull it closer. As he stroked this fantastic tool, he felt a little droplet of wet form on the tip.

"I carry a blue pill or two for moments like this. I don't get an opportunity like this very often." With that, he rolled Mica over and dug that purposeful tongue between Mica's ass cheeks. Mica writhed with excitement. He knew what he was in for but just didn't want it to be, for once, this impersonal.

"I'm Mica...er...Michael."

"Joe...er...Joseph," he joked back. Mica wasn't so amused. He slid up the back of Mica's body and whispered in his ear. "Don't worry, I know who you are and your secret's safe with me. I have my own too."

Mica flinched at being recognized. This is the last place he wanted to be known to frequent. Not that he was a frequent flier, just when the need arose. And it has been a long time for Mica.

Mica is more career driven than lust driven and finds it hard to date. He is never sure, especially among the gay community, if someone isn't dating him because he has a relatively high profile or because they genuinely like him. And, as such, he takes the easy way out and rarely goes out. That doesn't mean there are no dates, just rarely and nothing very serious. Besides, there is always the Dreamland Spa, when he is ready for *push to come to shove.*

"Ok, share," Mica said.

There was a pause and then, "I'm married...to a woman...*and* I'm a cop. There. See? I have something to hide too."

"So why would you tell me that so quickly...so easily," Mica asked, relaxing as Joe...er...Joseph rubbed his hot dick up and down Mica's ass crack.

"Mutual destruction. I've got something on you and you've got something on me. But don't worry. You may tell things about people for a living; I do not. But remember my name, if you ever need an ally, I am your man. And right now, you are my man."

"Well, let me say for a cop that is one impressive nightstick!" Mica joked.

With that Mica felt a little pressure and then a shove. The shock to his system made him gulp and clench. Joe stopped and allowed Mica to relax. With that Mica knew this guy was more lover than rapist and wished he hadn't told Mica he is married. But the guilt subsided and the rhythm progressed. And very quickly, Mica was doing hard time at the hands of one hot cop.

1

Mica shifted in his seat, day dreaming about the interlude the night before, proud of himself for giving as good as he got. It was a momentary distraction, thinking of the cop's asshole rather than dealing with the assholes in the cars surrounding him along Highland Avenue. The top of Highland is cordoned off for an 'event' while some studio or other raised bleachers and rolled out the red carpet for yet another movie premiere. He would inevitably be standing in front of those bleachers, behind a velvet rope, along that very red carpet come 5:30 this evening. He hadn't been assigned to the 'event' yet but red carpets are his usual shtick so he can rightfully assume the assignment will be his. Fortunately, he's left a suit at the office because he certainly wasn't dressed for a premiere.

He hated the drive to Burbank from his Hancock Park apartment. But then again, Mica hated driving anywhere in Los Angeles. The congestion and arrogance of the road raging people of L.A. is like no other. And even under the best of conditions, it is a miserable experience. Hancock Park is about as centrally located as a neighborhood can be and it still takes an hour or so to get up and over Barham Boulevard and into Burbank, even as early as he has to be in to work.

Most people assume Mica lives in West Hollywood. Doesn't every gay person live in West Hollywood? But that presumption alone is enough of a reason not to live in West Hollywood. When Mica moved to Hancock Park it wasn't as chic as it has become. People simply didn't want to travel east of Fairfax. Why would they? The riots years before had condemned Hancock Park to a dowager no man's land of aging estates and old but dwindling money. Now, with the emergence of the loft scene in downtown Los Angeles, Hancock Park and the en vogue boutiques, restaurants and galleries that line La Brea Avenue are considered the epicenter of the town. New moneyed stars, producers, writers and directors have all found a grandiose lifestyle for what was pennies on the dollar compared to the McMansion palaces of Beverly Hills. When people ask why Mica lives there, he likes to say, "I guess for the same reason Melanie and Antonio Banderas have lived here. Their house is just down the street." Even he knows that is a fairly snotty response considering the Banderas house is a Spanish palazzo and Mica lives in a rent-controlled apartment on the wrong side of La Brea. But it is true; it is down the street.

Not surprisingly, an hour later almost to the minute, Mica swipes his security card at the gate outside the refurbished cement factory in Burbank which now houses the production offices for *Drop Zone*. He slides his car in an open space two down from the boss' Bentley Continental convertible. If she had a dick, the Bentley would be her way of wagging it.

"Where the fuck have you been?" said Lisa at the front desk, who never minced words, which is why the staff alternatively love her and hate her.

"Traffic." Mica offered up as an excuse as if he was suddenly answerable to Lisa.

"Just a warning, she is running around like her hair is on fire...again!" Lisa shrugged and waved Mica on in.

Another hair-on-fire-day is nothing new for Lydia, also known as Labia on a day like today. She may be a cunt but she has earned the title honestly.

Executive producer of *Drop Zone* Lydia Gray is, to say the least, a formidable presence. One tough broad who made it in a man's world, which is something she is quick to point out to anyone who will listen. And to some extent she is right. On the cusp of turning fifty, she is angry that, unlike her counterparts, men, it took her these many decades to make her first million. But now Lydia makes a seven-figure salary—just over seven figures by a margin of chump change, mind you. She did it the old fashioned way, hard work—being a news gypsy and hopping from one local shithole station to another, climbing the ranks of news production the country over until her titles and aggression became legendary. Her take no prisoners approach to journalism was a perfect fit for a new news format, an entertainment/tabloid syndicated series in the nineties called *Hot Type*. Everyone said it was career suicide; that if this series failed, there would be no going back to the legitimacy of local news. Fuck local news and its eighty thousand dollar a year glass ceiling, sweatshop infrastructure. This was her chance for the big time—national syndication.

If there is nothing else remembered about *Hot Type*, it should be noted that under Lydia Gray's watch, stars had to watch out. Their comings and goings wouldn't be just the stuff of headline news; *they* would be dissected until they *made* headline news. Ambush reportage and questionable premises got the show banned from red carpets and movie junkets and forced the show into trolling through garbage cans for salacious tit bits to turn into top news. And it worked. It had all the decadence needed to feed the fetishes of a hungry audience's guilty pleasure for tabloid journalism without them having to be seen buying salacious magazines at the grocery store check out. This was dirty dealing from the comfort of your living room easy chair. Sure there were the lawsuits and the occasional need to recant, but the initial accusation was planted in the hearts and minds of Americans and so what *Hot Type* spewed, audiences ate up.

It was to the shock of many in the industry when Lydia was poached from her lofty perch to create a new industry friendly series, soon to be known as *Drop Zone*—the place where stars can come to tell their side of a salacious story, where uplifting news of Hollywood's good would flourish, where there will never be a negative review, critique, or comment. Really? Lydia Gray, by industry standards, had gone from the witch who wanted the ruby slippers left behind when a house fell on her sister to Glinda the good witch. What gives? Seven figures, that's what gives. A base salary just over a million dollars and quarterly bonuses for ratings bursts was too much for this whore of Hollywood to pass up. She was in the big buck big leagues. Fuck Bakersfield, Spokane, Knoxville, Tampa, Boston and any other local speed bumps she called career stops. She now had a corner office overlooking a legendary studio and a Bentley to get her there.

"She's been looking for you," said show producer B.J. B.J. was also a broad like Lydia who climbed up the ranks, besting her male peers. But unlike Lydia, she didn't have to be a bitch to do it. She is simply smart.

"Me personally?" Mica asked tossing his bag over his cubicle wall—yes cubicle. Only the anchors and upper management get offices; reporters get cubicles.

"You, as in you are part of the bigger team and she wants the entire team in the conference room in three minutes to discuss the lead story." B.J. rolled her eyes as if to say this lead story would have been big in the old days of *Hot Type* but it is hardly the kind of the thing we do at *Drop Zone*."

"What's the story?" Mica asked innocently enough.

"Antonia Guest."

Ugh. Antonia Guest is perpetually in trouble. Why, oh, why are we doing yet another feel good story about such a troubled actress? Why is Amy Winehouse dead and Antonia Guest still alive is baffling to Mica and to anyone else that has to report on her roller coaster of a life?

"Nuff said." Mica rolled his eyes as he walked through the mayhem of the bullpen office—staff on phones, checking leads, furiously typing on computer keyboards, printing scripts, running to edit bays. Speaking of which, Mica needed to check in with his favorite editor, Evol—a chosen name, not a given name.

Evol is 'Love' spelled backwards and to the unsuspecting, she has a disposition to match. Evol is an overly tattooed lesbian who locks herself in the first edit bay and virtually bars reporters and producers inside until she had taken their scripts and raw video and done a visionary first pass as to what she believes the segment should look like. Not everyone is happy with this arrangement but Mica loves her work. She knows his voice and sensibility. And generally what she churns out for Mica makes it to air with very little, if any, changes. Evol makes Mica's life that much easier.

Lydia storms in on heels high enough to defy natural order and an outfit straight off a fashion week runway that cost more than the monthly salaries of three quarters of those sitting in the room. She not only likes the trappings of new wealth but also likes to flaunt the trappings as if to say, "Fuck you. Look at me now." And of course, those demons are simply in her head. For those in the room who worked eighty hours a week with no overtime, all her trappings say is "fuck you" to them.

Strangely she is respected not because she deserves it, which she actually does, but because she is feared and expects it. They don't teach that at Wharton or Harvard Business School. But it plays out here at *Drop Zone*.

"So nice that some of you could join us." Lydia eyeballed a few around the table and settled on Mica. "What were you out getting fucked last night and had to sleep it off?"

"Actually..." Mica has no fear of taking Lydia on and that is why they get along. Although she feels superior to the gays in that she believes her support of the community warrants their subservience, it's her belief that if she hadn't hired Mica, no one would have taken on a mincing fag to be an on-camera reporter. Mica is no mincing fag and she knows it. But in her world all fags are somewhat mincing and therefore beholden to her open mindedness and tolerance. Whatever.

"We don't need to hear your spunk sucking experiences, Mica. We have news to break," she began. Lydia is a walking human resources lawsuit waiting to happen. "Antonia Guest! Lead story! But how do we spin it?"

"What is the *actual* story?" You can always count on B.J. to cut to the quick.

Lydia paused for a moment to look at B.J. who is always chic in a funky way. Lydia could never pull off a natural style, just an off-the-runway look that is never personal, just pricy. B.J. has style. Lydia has money.

In that pause, the new girl, what's-her-name, spoke up. "We've got video in from a stringer that shows Antonia peeling out from a nightclub last night in Hollywood and side swiping a car. The driver is now in the hospital and Antonia denies everything."

Lydia stares at the new girl. I know that look, the new girl—don't bother to learn her name—will be gone by the end of the week. Everyone knows, or had better know, that when Lydia calls a meeting, it is her meeting. The details of whatever the subject matter is must come from Lydia. She is the oracle of *Drop Zone* believing all information comes from her as if she is the only one with sources and resources in this industry. Everyone knows it is bullshit. But that is how you keep your job.

"Lydia," B.J. interjected and broke the momentary tension. "What did you have in mind?"

"Look, we don't need the father. He is just a fright night of a sound bite," she began with that exasperated tone that said we should have come up with the solution. Although everyone, with the exception of the ill-fated new girl, knows that Lydia wants to be the one with all the answers. "I think that we should find at least three people in Antonia's camp who can say that she would never do a thing like that, that she was obviously tired and, for fuck's sake, make sure we find someone who will say on camera that she was clean and sober last night."

There you have it, *Drop Zone* at its best. Make up a premise, pre-write a story, and come up with the corroborating sound bites and video to make it true. Make no mistake; no one is going home with any awards for journalistic integrity for working on this show.

"Mica, there is some fuck off premiere at the Chinese tonight. That is yours as usual. Try to make it entertaining. It is the difference between being the lead story tomorrow or the comedy kicker at the end of the show." Lydia looks at Mica and can't resist, "I know you like it in the end but I am giving you an opportunity to be on the top."

There was a pregnant pause as Mica winked at Lydia. He got that was her idea of affection but in any other company, any other industry, she would have been marched into human resources, fired and handed a lawsuit to be settled later.

"That was a fag joke for all of you sitting there with your mouths open," she announced as she headed for the door. "Now get to work."

No apologies necessary.

Mica certainly isn't looking for apologies. He actually likes his job. He has become very high profile on the show and within the industry thanks to his antics on red carpets and his self-deprecating one-on-one interviews with the stars. The publicists have come to know Mica as a go-to when the stars feel uncomfortable at an event or during an interview. They know that Mica won't do anything to embarrass them or throw a curve ball question into the mix, much in the way the reporters did on *Hot Type*. Because the stars respond to Mica, so to, do the fans of the show.

Mica knows he has a certain amount of job security being the class clown over the other reporters who have to constantly turn shit sandwich stories into delicacies for our saccharine audience. But even Mica knows that if he wants to get ahead, he's going to have to sink his teeth into more meaty stories.

°°°

"Has anyone seen the final attendee list for tonight's premiere," Michelle yelled out to her assistant who had long since left his desk to track down the answers to her previous dozen or so questions. "Does anyone hear me?"

With a nasal twang that defies you to believe she is either Jewish or a New Yorker—neither is true—Michelle Bianco is truly the mouth that roars, inside the office and across the industry. Having finally been promoted to full publicist at the prestigious agency of Regis and Canning after five years of cow-towing to the P.R. brilliance of agency partner and senior publicist, "Big Eddie" Fielding—enormous in physical and industry stature—Michelle has let her very limited powers go to her head. Because hers is a head no longer filled with nagging, née annoying, questions like: Have you run that by Eddie? What does Eddie think? Does Eddie approve this? She can finally think, do and act on her own accord, on behalf of the agency's well-established clientele. Or so she thinks. There are still plenty of eyes watching her. Whippet thin, long black hair and with a Goth-like pastiness to her complexion, she can be as frightening to look at as she can be to deal with. The problem is you never know where you stand with Michelle. One day you are a professional favorite, the next public enemy number one.

With appropriate trepidation, her assistant Dave pokes his head into Michelle's office. "Did you need me?"

"Not as much as you need me," she countered unnecessarily. "Have you got the final list of tonight's attendees?"

He fumbles for a minute with in the filo of papers he is holding and produces one sheet and hands it to her and she begins to scan.

"Bullshit, bullshit, bullshit," she mutters as she goes down the list. Half these people will not be attending tonight. Traditionally a personal assistant RSVP's to these sorts of invitations, the star's name is attached to the official attendee list and some minion from the office inevitably walks the red carpet in his or her stead. Still a smattering of Oscar winners, high profile socialites and the right number of 'IT' couples on the list tells Michelle this will be a P.R. bonanza in terms of media coverage for the night. And that is what it is all about.

"Annnndddd?" Michelle snaps at Dave. Without even needing to hear what she is asking for, he hands over a second list of media outlets attending. There are all the usual suspects. "Who are they sending from *Drop Zone?*"

"Mica Daly."

"Good," she waves Dave in and motions to shut the door. She hasn't even merited an office with a window, yet she sits behind that desk like a queen upon a throne. Dave sits in the uncomfortably low slipper chair in front of her desk—a deliberate design element so that Michelle always sits higher than whoever is in her office.

"Here's my plan. Do you know the shit storm that is about to hit with Antonia Guest?" She doesn't wait for an answer. "Well, everyone is going to run with that story I'm sure!" she spews in that affected way that says she knows everything that is happening in this town and how it will play out. It's an affectation most publicists acquire but it is particularly irritating coming from Michelle.

"So what I want to do is load up Mica with as many good names as we can. *Drop Zone* has this 'feel good' mandate but they are going to have to run with the Antonia story. It goes against what they are trying to do. If we star-pack Mica, that will be their 'feel good' event for tomorrow's show. We may get a good three minutes of air time if we play this right." And she is right. "It is always funny to me how shows like *Drop Zone* think they are in control of the media. Remember this Dave, they are nothing with out access to the stars, the events, the set, you name it...and *we* control the access."

Dave nods.

"Now, do you have my other list?"

"I am working on it."

"Good," she nods, "You know that is our future."

Michelle understands that in order to make a mark in the office, and potentially have a firm of her own one-day, she has to cultivate new talent, faces, and stars of tomorrow. The big names already associated with the agency are looking to the Eddie Fielding's of the office to do their bidding. Michelle Bianco needs newcomers to be beholden to her and her alone. The search is on.

◦ ◦ ◦

Across town on the fourth floor of the Hollywood and Highland complex, the vast and vacuous thirty thousand square foot nightclub being turned into hell—a sort of *Dante's Inferno* themed event for tonight's premiere. Then again what else would you do when the movie is called *The Devil Made Me Do It!* Everyone agrees that is a trite, if not a downright corny title, but the high wattage cast should make this film a sleeper hit of the season. So big money is being poured into this night. From the location of the Chinese Theater—the number one location for the best premieres—to this multi-million dollar shindig being designed by none other than Mighty Oak Productions—the party producers of such prestigious events as both the Oscar and Emmy Governors Balls.

Under the watchful eye of Shari Somerset, the creative genius behind Mighty Oak, the small army of three hundred workers—from florists, to bartenders, waiters, to construction crew, lighting, sound and talent—move in strict and orderly formation. Hers is a well-oiled machine and nothing, not a wilted flower nor limp asparagus appetizer nor off key singer, gets by her. So it is all the more amazing that Chad is pulling off the ultimate sin.

Back in the nearly empty staging area, nestled within the floral arrangements yet to be assigned to tables, Chad Martin—cater waiter and aspiring actor—is urinating. He is pissing right into one of the larger, red rose embedded, topiary centerpieces.

The relief felt good; a good piss always feels good, but the rational even had Chad questioning himself. He is young, twenty-three, so you can excuse the notion of a boyish prank. But that was not the impetus. It is as if Chad chose this, of all moments, to piss on the town, the industry that seems to always be pissing on his dreams.

He was born and raised in Nowhere, USA, the small town boy who's come to the big city with even bigger dreams. Yada. Yada. The town had heard this story since the beginning of the movie industry. He wasn't from a poor family. He wasn't abused. The worst he had going for him was a mild form of dyslexia that made schoolwork difficult and reading for auditions a nightmare. And at twenty-three years young, it is hard to think he has paid any dues. The bottom line is no one is pissing on his dreams. He is simply frustrated. Like the tens of thousands of other hopefuls in this town, with more looks than talent, Chad wants tomorrow to have happened yesterday—it is the entitlement issue of today's generation. No one wants to work for anything; they simply want it handed to them.

Chad does have a work ethic though. He willingly and enthusiastically goes to acting classes, auditions and more auditions—even landing a national commercial, which, when shot, was shelved as the marketing went in another direction. And along the way, he hears the same thing over and over again. "You are a natural. With that face, you were born to be a star." Okay, so when is *that* going to turn into a career.

By the time the piss was over, he felt guilty. But it was too late. One of the Asian flower arrangers had come around the corner as Chad was tapping away the last droplets, tucking in and zipping up. "You pig," she cried. And he knew he was fired. Sure, now he had an anecdote for some late night talk show appearance when he finally hit the big time but right now, right here, he literally pissed away his only source of income.

In the hustle to get him off the floor and out the door before Shari's eagle eye spots the commotion, no one bothered to take back Chad's staff credential for the night's event. He'd be back, but not catering to the stars, walking among them.

2

"Cuba..." Mica forcefully requested a few words with the Oscar winner.

"*Cuba!*"

"*Cuba!*"

The actor didn't hear or chose not to hear Mica's pleas. That is odd and frustrating as they have become red carpet pals over the years and Cuba always provides Mica with an entertaining sound bite.

"Don't worry Mica, I'll get him." said Michelle Bianco. Dressed in the uniform of the red carpet—black—she is on her best behavior. She has three new clients on the red carpet tonight and one is starring in the movie. It is her firm, Regis and Canning, handling the P.R. for this event and even "Big Eddie" Fielding is here to provide a watchful eye over the proceedings. Every time Eddie arrives at an event, Michelle is a different person—professional is the best way to put it. It is almost sickening the way she will kiss up to Eddie and cut off the dick of an errant reporter who is not doing her bidding.

Is it an unusually hot evening on Hollywood Boulevard or is it just that Mica is feeling particularly claustrophobic? These events are never really fun. Reporters from all over the world are sequestered behind a red rope and into a section of approximately three square feet. They share the space with the cameraman, soundman and sometimes a producer, lights and camera equipment. In the adjoining three square feet on either side, the same mash up is happening. And so on down the carpet. Behind that spectacle are the screaming fans drowning out the reporters' questions and the stars' answers. Mica's job is to make people believe events like this are not only fun, but, also glamorous and *the* place to be. They're not.

Mica has come up with a tried and true shtick for the red carpet. He takes the theme of the movie or event, perhaps parodies the title as he has tonight, and asks one question, which everyone can have fun with. Publicists love it because it makes the stars feel comfortable and provides something to have fun with amid the ambush of all of this media. As a result, his segment on *Drop Zone* is one of the most watched and anticipated on the show.

"Cuba," she began as if introductions were necessary. "Surely, you know Mica

Daly from *Drop Zone*? If you could just give him a few moments." Michelle winked and mouthed, "You owe me!"

"Hey man!" Cuba Gooding Jr. gave Mica a big hug and they settled in for the traditional three-question interview. Three questions is a luxury at a star packed premiere like this.

Cue the shtick. "Cuba, what's the one thing that only the devil could make you do?"

Cuba laughed a hearty laugh. "You always kill me with these questions." He stood back to give it a moment's thought. Fortunately, Cuba is a complete professional and wasn't thrown by Mica's distracted gaze. There is a man over Cuba's shoulder, simply standing and watching the interview. Mica is trained to glance around to spot the next potential star interview as they make their way down the carpet, but this man has stopped him dead. He is simply gorgeous and yet a complete nobody.

There's that guy from *Drop Zone* talking to Cuba Gooding Jr., Chad thought to himself making note of the star count all around him. So far no one has looked at his staff credential close enough to bounce him off the red carpet. Genius. Until that happens, Chad Martin is going to enjoy every moment rubbing elbows with the A-List at his first premiere.

Spectrum Studios has pulled out all the stops for this film. Premieres at the Chinese usually mean the studio is investing big in the success of the movie. Word has it cost over one hundred and fifty million dollars to produce and another one hundred million dollars to market. In Hollywood speak, with its shady accounting, this film has to bring in half a billion dollars to be considered a success.

Mica noticed Barry Stegman—the former music mogul turned entrepreneur and powerful founder and head of Spectrum—and his trophy wife, Diandra, as they walked by. He nodded to the media and continued on his way. He is notorious for avoiding interviews. Not one to miss a detail though, he stopped to whisper in the ear of Eddie Fielding which sent Fielding trotting down the carpet to right whatever the wrong may be.

"Mica, I have a favor to ask," Michelle began behind the cupped hand of secrecy.

"Sure."

"I can give you a couple of minutes each with my clients. Can you make sure they all end up in the piece when it airs? They are new clients for the agency and I just want them to feel important."

"No problem," Mica returned and then with all the sincerity Hollywood types can muster he continued. "You know I would do anything for you fine folks at Regis and Canning."

"We have Suzy Chambers here tonight. Trust me when I tell you, she may be a reality television hot property at the moment but we are going to take her career meteoric," Michelle began with her usual salesman pitch verbal strafing. "Rod Stevens is, of course, in the movie so you will want to talk to him. And Sean Jones is over from Europe. He is a new client too but think 'action star'." With that she winked at Mica as if she had just bestowed some vital insider information.

"Again, no problem. But you can do me a favor and make sure we don't miss Jada and Will." He winked back as if to say: I'm not talking to your B-List talent at the expense of missing the A-List stars.

"Of course." There's that Hollywood 'sincerity' again. You could cut it with a knife.

As Michelle darted off to wrangle her cadre of talent, Mica continued with the job at hand. "Rita Wilson, get over here and talk to me. You know I love me some Rita Wilson." Sincerely.

o o o

Chad walked with purpose, somewhat buried in the crowd, after the movie let out and during the long walk up to the fourth floor after-party. He was thinking it has to be a good quarter of a mile from the actual theater to the nightclub where the reception is being held.

As he reached the entrance his first plan was to simply straighten his tie and walk in as if he was an invitee. Hopefully no one would ask to see his ticket.

Plan B was more the reality. As he stepped toward the door, security, an off duty cop who was ruggedly handsome named Joe Tomasso, asked to see the phantom ticket. Chad pulled out his staff catering credential and handed it to the cop at the door.

"I am with the staff." Chad looked directly at him and didn't flinch.

"You should be entering through the staff entrance." The cop could see this technicality was holding up the real attendees from getting in and it wasn't going to be worth making an issue out of which door the staff used. He waved him through with a warning to leave with the staff and not the guests.

Several people passed by the cop when one guest in particular caught his eye, Mica Daly from *Drop Zone*. "Hey there, good to see you again." With that he winked.

"Joe, right?" Mica was startled. This is the cop from Dreamland Spa with the hairy body and huge cock. Mica felt a stirring. "What are you doing here?"

"Thought I would clock some over time. We all do it."

"I am covering the event. My crew should already be inside," Mica began as if he was going to have to talk his way in.

"Got it."

As Mica walked past Joe he couldn't help but to let his hand slide across Joe's crotch area. He could feel Joe ever so subtly stiffen. Joe quickly grabbed Mica's arm and positioned it such a way as keep Mica's hand against his crotch. "If you ever need anything, call. I mean anything." He winked again and handed Mica a card.

Mica felt himself stiffen. "Will do?"

As Mica walked in and observed both the sea of people flooding the club as well as the 'Hell in Hollywood' theme of the room, he couldn't help but to be impressed. He quietly noted to himself, he should pitch a segment to Lydia on Mighty Oak Productions and how they make these incredible events happen. In the meantime he has job to do in covering this event.

As efficient as ever, Michelle Bianco, zeroed in on Mica grabbed him by the arm and led him to where his crew is situated. "You, of course, can stay as long as you would like Mica. But the crew has to be out of here in twenty minutes and can't walk around or leave the designated roped off section. On the platform, you will see the V.I.P. area. Even you aren't allowed in there...sorry!"

Mica was used to being on the periphery of fame—his being just enough of a celebrity to get in the door but not enough to get into the V.I.P. area. But that is the pecking order of Hollywood. Still, it is a big deal having the *Drop Zone* crew inside a party like this. No other program had been allowed in. This is an exclusive look, even from the periphery, at the high end of the high life. And in Mica's world of on-camera celebrity journalists, he is fairly high on the pecking order.

A quick word with Denzel, another kiss on the cheek from Rita Wilson, a positive critique of the movie from Channing and a soliloquy of a sound bite from Tarrentino and Mica wrapped the crew. They had plenty for the segment and Mica had been distracted once again by the good-looking guy staring at Mica and the crew. It is the same guy from the red carpet, only this time he was not simply watching but more like studying Mica.

Mica decided he'd meet the guy and find out just who he is. But just as he started to make his move across the crowded room, two barely twenty-something giggling girls dressed in heels too high and skirts too small ambushed Mica. "We know you are on television," one of the two begins. "My friend here wants to know how to get your job."

Slightly flattered, Mica began to explain how he had gone to college to study journalism and then noticed the blank expressions on the girls' faces. "No," the other jumped in frustrated. "I want your job."

"Oh I see," Mica said. "You don't want a job like mine, you want my job."

She nodded enthusiastically.

"How about I go into the office tomorrow, quit my job and recommend you to take over."

"That would be so cool," she purred.

"Ladies," Mica leaned in as if to whisper some great insider knowledge, "Get the fuck away from me." With that, Mica pushed his way past the two morons and looked in the direction of where the mystery man had been standing. He is gone.

A keen Mighty Oak Productions staffer had spotted Chad Martin then notified Joe, the cop out front. Without much fanfare, Chad had been escorted out the back door, the undignified employee's entrance.

Not being able to locate his mystery man, and a cocktail later, Mica decided to call it a night. He would have to be in the office early to edit this segment and could use a good night's sleep. As he walked out the front door fumbling for his car keys, he felt a body uncomfortably close. "Going somewhere."

"Oh Joe, you scared the shit out of me."

"Where are you going?"

"Home, I'm afraid." Mica shrugged with that 'maybe some other time' gesture.

"I'm officially off duty. Perhaps you could use a police escort."

There is something about this Joe that gets to Mica. Is it that he is turned on by the uniform, the power, and the fact that he is married and unavailable? Whatever it is, it gets Mica hard...very hard. "Perhaps."

Mica started to walk away, turned back and looked at Joe and after a moment's thought, nodded his head to invite him along. There may not be a good night's sleep, but there will be a good reason for it.

3

Albert Switzer is old Hollywood for sure. A product of the latter end of the studio system, "Little Albie Switzer" was a child star of no real consequence. The *Our Gang* kids were virtually a thing of the past by the time he was ready to play in their sandbox. And there were only so many teary eyed orphan types being cast. And as television hit its stride, again, guest spots as the goofy younger brother to the new friend of Gidget or Patty Duke were few and far between.

Still as "Little Albie Switzer" grew up to be Albert he had amassed a reasonable acting nest egg, which, thanks to another child star, Jackie Coogan, that egg had accrued in a trust fund and provided him with the means to purchase outright a small house in Studio City, in the shadow of Universal Studios. He still calls it home.

Everyday he makes the reverse commute over the Hollywood hills to his cramped duplex office in an historic building just down from a favorite meeting haunt, Musso and Frank, the iconic restaurant on Hollywood Boulevard. Thanks to the revitalization of Hollywood, his office location is chic again. But during his moneymaking days as an agent in the 1970s, 80s and into the 90s clients begged him to move to more suitable offices in Beverly Hills and later Century City to attract a more notable or prestigious clientele. Nothing doing. Today, he is thrilled he hung on to his rent-controlled, perfectly located office digs; even if that means he only represents up-and-comers and C-list has-beens.

Coming of age in the 1960s and always a progressive thinker in his own mind, his assistants have always been black. "Give 'em a chance," he'd say. And for the time, he was ahead of the culture.

When the O.J. Simpson trial riveted and divided the city, that was the only time there was tension between the outer reception area and the inner sanctum of his office. He would lock himself behind the glass door and assume his then assistant couldn't hear the television bleating on with endless gavel-to-gavel coverage. Albert didn't believe in O.J.'s innocence, and for the record neither did the assistant, but all Albert could say aloud about the trial was "shame about the wife." On the day O.J. was acquitted Albert gave his assistant the day off with pay, as if he had lost a bet. She quit.

When the riots hit in the 1990s, he offered his house in Studio City to his assistant "for as long as it takes", as if all black people lived in South Central, Los Angeles, the epicenter of the violence. That particular assistant who lived in affluent Westwood, having graduated from UCLA, declined the offer and quit.

"Hard workers," was all he ever said about his past employees.

Today his assistant is also black and is what only can be described as a Godsend. Anthony Wright, stage name Tony, gave up an opportunity to work his way up from the mailroom at one of the 'big' agencies to get in on the ground floor of somewhere he believed he could have a say, make a difference, work his way up faster and better and potentially become an agent/partner. ASA—The Albert Switzer Agency—was legendary if for nothing else than by having to survive as an independent agency for close to five decades in an ever changing, merge-centric, business atmosphere. Anthony had done his homework with the formerly famed, if not fading, Mr. Switzer. He interviewed having known Albert's past achievements in front of the camera and the stars he nurtured along the way. Anthony made suggestions about expansion, new talent, and platforms of opportunity for income such as the internet. Albert isn't narrow minded and understands his scope of ideas may be a tad antiquated. Anthony was not only hired but is also represented by the agency.

It also didn't hurt that Anthony is hot. And when he trolls the nightspots of Hollywood, West Hollywood—yes, Anthony knows how to swing a dick to get business done—and beyond looking for fresh faces and new names, there is no shortage of people who willingly listen to his pitch. That's how they found Chad Bozworth.

Sure he was cocky and arrogant but both Anthony and Albert believed Chad had "IT," the old Hollywood expression for the inexplicable star appeal. If they could wrangle in his attitude and convince him to drop his real last name of Bozworth and stick his first two given names of Chad Martin, they may just have a honest-to-goodness star on their hands.

Chad, for his part, was thrilled to have been 'discovered' like the Lana Turner lore of Hollywood legend suggested. Unlike the late great Lana, he was not sitting at the soda fountain in Hollywood but rather perched on a barstool staring at a be-thonged, semi-erect, male stripper in West Hollywood. But discovered he was.

What Albert and Anthony soon understood about Chad was that he was a go-getter. There is nothing that is going to hold him back. He wants to be a star and will be, and that's that. What can easily be mistaken for arrogance is really self-confidence. They both liked when Chad came in for a meeting. He has one of those thousand watt smiles and can take command of the room by simply walking through the door. And his walking through the door is just what they are waiting for. Chad is uncharacteristically late.

Chad was not only uncharacteristically late but also uncharacteristically hangdog when he eventually walked into the office. "Is something wrong?" Anthony asked, immediately sensing his thousand watts are slightly dimmed.

"I pissed in a flower arrangement the other night at the premiere...well before the premiere actually...and got myself fired from the catering company."

"You did what?" Anthony recoiled just a bit. This is not the Chad Martin he knows.

"I know it was stupid," Chad mumbled. For all his bravado and self-assurance, Chad was still a bit of a boy. He still couldn't get over what he had done, nor why. Frustration, sure, but everyone gets frustrated. And now, worse yet, he is broke and just another out of work actor.

"But, there was an upside!" There is that thousand watts shining brightly once again. "They never took away my staff credential and so I walked that red carpet like I was meant to be there. I even snuck into the after-party. It was so cool."

"Wait'll you walk your own red carpet, son," Albert boomed from inside his office. "You were going to have to cut the cater waiter bullshit anyway. I've got a gig for you."

Anthony followed Chad into Albert's office, notebook in hand. Anthony already knew the broad strokes of the deal about to be explained to Chad but needed, for the record, to hear the details as well. One thing Anthony noticed from early on was that Albert wasn't a detail guy. He loves the idea of making a deal and signing contracts, but the minutia he leaves to Anthony.

"I've got a picture for you." Albert still called movies 'pictures'. "No need for an audition. They took a look at your reel and loved what they saw."

Having clients doing scenes on video and/or compiling film and television clips of their work creates their reel. These reels were an innovation for the agency but a no-brainer for Anthony who had put all the reels up on the agency webpage. All of which belied the old school mentality of auditions and callbacks in Albert's mind. "You gotta see what you see," was Albert's rational. It is not that auditions are a thing of the past but it is far easier to sell a client with a click of the computer mouse. And that, it seems, is all it took to cast Chad Martin in *The Other Brother* for Spectrum Studios, playing, of course, 'the other brother'.

"We're not talking huge dollars here. A good payday for sure but just five figures."

Five figures for the recently retired cater waiter is music to Chad's ears. He had never made that kind of money and he can barely contain his enthusiasm. "When do I start?"

"There are table reads and wardrobe fittings and general pre-production," Albert waved off the details, again. Anthony furiously took notes knowing he would have to follow up on all of these.

Unable to sit still, Chad starts pacing in very small circles in the cramped office. "This is fantastic."

"I have a script for you," Albert says as he tosses the manila envelope across the desk in the general direction of the moving target, Chad. Anthony managed to catch it and hand it over to the star about to be born. Chad tore open the envelope and starts thumbing through the manuscript.

"By the way, do you go to the gym?" Albert asks almost as an aside.

"Of course. Why?"

"There was some talk about you being shirtless," Albert mumbled.

With that Chad pulls his form fitting tee shirt over his head as if he had to prove something. He didn't, the tee shirt was already clinging to his rather defined pectorals. But now shirtless and chiseled, Chad's display caused Anthony to stifle a gasp. Chad is magnificent—a well developed chest, six pack abs and a happy trail of hair from his belly button traveling south below the belt-line of his low-slung jeans.

Anthony sensed that Albert may have skipped yet another detail. "Why would they bring up being shirtless as an issue? It's not even a line item in a contract. Is there something I am missing here?"

Albert grumbled a little and shifted in his chair. "There's a love scene." Both Chad and Anthony leaned in and waited for the other shoe to drop. "There may be some nudity."

"May be?" asked Chad.

"Butt shot or full frontal?" Anthony demanded.

"I don't know. They just wanted to know if you would be comfortable with nudity.

"Fuck that," Chad declared and dropped his pants to the surprise of Albert and Anthony—Anthony the more pleasantly surprised of the two. No underwear made the maneuver quite fast and the reveal spectacular. "I've got nothing to be ashamed of." That is an understatement.

Chad's cock is nothing less than porn star perfect. At seven inches flaccid and three inches around with a large, circumcised, mushroom head, it hangs perfectly between two very smooth low hanging balls.

"You trim, I see," was all Anthony could muster referring to Chad's well- manicured bush. He then crossed his legs as to not embarrass himself with the stirring between his own legs.

"What the hell are you doing?" Albert boomed. "I don't want to see that."

"You aren't the audience," Anthony was quick to point out.

"Exactly," Chad exclaimed with two hands planted squarely on his hips. "I know, and now you know, that I have what it takes to star in this movie."

"Don't start thinking with the wrong head," Albert began with his fatherly tone that said I've been around in this business a long time. "Read the script, we'll set up a meeting with the director and producers...during which you will keep your pants on...and they can make a decision from there."

That fatherly tone always gets to Chad. It reminds him that he still has a thing or two to learn. Humbled, he reached down to pull up his pants.

"On the other hand," Albert began by way of a joke, "I can now see why they call people like you 'cocky'." He winked at Chad and waved him off with a deal as good as done.

o o o

Chad couldn't help but to feel good about himself. A major movie! Well, at least, a low budget movie with a major studio attached. He had been so excited when he left Albert's office he had forgotten to ask who else had been cast. Never mind. Details. Details. His euphoria continued even as he reached his car and noticed a parking ticket on the windshield. It's sixty-eight bucks in Hollywood for an expired meter. That is a lot considering his last paycheck was, in fact, his last paycheck. But even this didn't deter him, quite the opposite; it got him thinking.

I should do something special for myself, he thought to himself. He'd ponder that thought all the way home.

Home for Chad is a decent sized studio apartment on Formosa, just west of La Brea off Sunset, in one of those cheaply constructed but modern looking boxes put up en masse in the 80s and 90s. It consisted of the requisite builders' grade kitchen and bathroom, builder's beige walls and taupe wall-to-wall carpeting that, more than likely, started out a creamy color and has been stained with age and filth. There is a bedroom alcove that, with the help of a room dividing panel screen from Pier 1, provided the semblance of privacy. The balcony looks squarely into the next building across the alley adjoining, so he rarely went out onto it. A second hand couch and dining set more than filled the living area. The big expense, more like extravagance, is the over sized forty two inch flat screen television, which dominates the room but can be easily seen from the couch or the bed. A twofer like that was surely a good investment.

As Chad walked in he peeled off this t-shirt and dropped his pants. He loves to be naked and doesn't particularly care if the neighbor across the alley sees or not. On more than one occasion, he has forgotten he's naked and answered the door much to the surprise of the pizza deliveryman, UPS guy and occasionally the mailman. And once still, when Chad had to sign for a package, the FedEx man whipped out his own package and really delivered. Chad would have no problem with nudity with this film.

He nestled into the corner of his couch and began to read, occasionally stroking his cock. Even he can't resist touching his cock. He knows that in Hollywood a big cock means power and is very happy that genetics served him well. A few strokes later and he figured out his treat. A massage. Not one of those expensive spa treatments but a rub and tug from one of those guys advertising in the back of the local fag rag magazine.

He put down the script carefully and picked up the latest edition of the street handout and flipped right to the back. Money is tight so he settled on Ethan with the smooth torso picture and an eighty-dollar an hour price tag.

By the time Ethan arrived, Chad had finished the manuscript, called Albert to say he was "psyched" and would absolutely "kill this role". No problems with the nudity either, as if that was still an issue in anyone's mind. Chad is now really feeling good about himself and was willing to eat cereal for a week in order to pay for the massage to come. He deserved a treat.

With a knock on the door, Chad reached for his jeans and then thought otherwise. He's gonna see it anyway, Chad thought to himself. So why bother to put them on just to take them off. He had the jeans in his hand as he opens the door.

"Hello, Brian?" Ethan asked not really acknowledging the nakedness before him. "I'm Ethan." 'Brian' was the first name Chad could think of when Ethan asked over the phone. Now that Chad was going to be a movie star, he knew he needed to play the anonymity game. Or so he was convinced.

Chad swung the door open to accommodate the portable but still bulky massage table Ethan has hanging from a flimsy strap off his left shoulder. "Do you need help with that?" Chad asked sympathetically.

"No, you just relax and get ready. Well, I guess you are sort of ready now." They smiled at each other.

Chad went to the refrigerator and got himself a beer, offered one to Ethan who declined as he was setting up the table, and stood back to take a good long look at the masseur from behind.

Ethan arrived in biker shorts and a tank top, so it is easy to get the overall picture right away. He is olive skinned and very smooth—either he waxes or at the least shaves his legs. They glistened from being heavily moisturized. His arms too were smooth and muscular, big biceps. Chad wondered if he was smooth all over.

"Do you work in the nude?"

"If you want me too," Ethan answered coyly.

"Well if I am nude, I think it is only fair," Chad shot back just as coyly. This was nothing more than verbal foreplay.

As Chad got on the table, laying face up so that he could see, Ethan pulled off the top and shorts revealing a completely hairless body. Chad's cock twitched ever so slightly and he rolled over on his stomach as to not pop a woody this early in the proceedings.

"Is there any area of your body that is overly sensitive or you don't want me to work on," Ethan asked in a professional voice.

"No. I like it deep everywhere."

With that, lights were dimmed, a compilation of Indian and Middle Eastern music played softly from the iPod and oils were applied. Instantly Chad began to groan with the soft stroking Ethan put in to his oiling of the body. Chad could tell already this would be money well spent.

Ethan started with his back and stood parallel to Chad's hand. As he kneaded the musculature of Chad's back and side, Ethan's cock ever so subtly rubbed against Chad's upturned hand. Chad instinctively cupped the semi-erect member and Ethan, undaunted, continued to work.

"Nice," Chad mumbled through the muffled padding of the headrest.

Having worked both sides of Chad's back and getting a woody in return, Ethan moved silently to the head of the table and started on Chad's neck. Chad couldn't resist but to lift his head, which brought him squarely in front of Ethan's hard on. This smooth boyish body with the manly cock turned Chad on. Ethan pushed a little closer and Chad delicately stuck out his tongue and gently licked the tip of the head of Ethan's cock. His cock pulsed and Chad pulled away.

"You've got to keep your head down," Ethan scolded playfully.

"Really? Cause I don't think you are keeping your head down." They chuckled.

"All good things come to those who wait," Ethan played.

Hearing that sent a tingle down into Chad's groin; he is getting harder by the moment.

Ethan moved down to his legs, taking long luxurious strokes from Chad's ankles to his upper thigh. The exercise moved higher up the thigh and pressed into his buttocks. Again, Chad moaned and separated his legs so Ethan had better access.

Ethan grabbed the bottle of oil and drizzled some over Chad's butt and inside the crack of his ass. Chad has a hard, worked out, ass and Ethan went through the pretense of deeply massaging both cheeks. From this side position, Chad was able to grab hold of Ethan's cock once again and started stroking—gently but tightly. Ethan had to pull away as to not cum prematurely.

As Ethan worked Chad's cheeks as part of the process, Chad's ass spread apart and Ethan could see the hairless pucker of Chad's asshole. Ethan slid his hand up and down the crack, ever so slightly giving a squeeze to the taint area causing Chad to flinch with excitement. As he drew his hand back up the crack, he applied careful but distinct pressure to the pucker and continued on his way. Back and forth. Back and forth. Chad moaned appreciatively.

With one last stroke, Ethan's hand settled on Chad's asshole and slowly but deliberately, Ethan inserted his well-oiled index finger into Chad's ass.

Chad is no bottom. With a cock like his, why would he bottom? The most he'd ever let anyone do up to this point was to rim him. But this felt good. Ethan was neither forceful nor aggressive. He simply slid his finger in and out pushing just a little further each time. Then he bent over and with both hands spread Chads ass and began licking the area. Ethan's firm tongue darted in and out and he began to alternatively use both his finger and tongue to please Chad. Chad writhed with pleasure. But enough is enough and Chad rolled over revealing his monstrous hard on, a good thirteen inches and five around. Even Ethan was taken aback.

"You want to eat something, eat this," Chad moaned and Ethan didn't need to be asked twice. As Chad lay there, Ethan went down. Ethan is surprisingly good at relaxing his throat and letting most of that big cock slide in and out. Again, Ethan slipped his finger into Chad's now well-oiled hole while he continued to suck. Chad had never felt anything like this before.

Without stopping, Ethan climbed up on to the table, positioned one knee on either side of Chad's face and lowered his own pulsing cock down to and into Chad's mouth. Chad hungrily went to work, loving the sensation of Ethan's hairless pubic area rubbing his face. They bucked together rhythmically for what seemed like an eternity but it was only a few minutes before Chad moaned and thrust his cock further down Ethan's well readied throat and came. Ethan accommodated and gulped the juice.

'Where do you want me to cum," Ethan asked politely as if to point out the faux pas he had just accommodated for Chad.

"Not in my mouth..."

With the Ethan flipped around, straddled Chad's chest and spewed all over Chad's face and neck. Chad lay there as Ethan knelt over and with tiny kisses, licked up the residue.

There was a pause, afterglow, and then Chad made the motions to get up and off the table. There was no conversation other than the exchange of the well-spent eighty-dollar fee. Ethan silently pulled his clothes on and dismantled the table and headed for the door.

"That was great," Chad began to fill the awkward silence. "I'll call you." That was an empty promise, as Chad was never going to call again.

"Thanks, Brian."

With that Ethan left and in the quiet of the room, Chad caught himself, naked and in all his glory, in the mirror. He took a good long look and smiled.

o o o

Naked, as always, Chad walked over to the sliding glass door of his apartment, opened it and slid the screen across. He wanted to get some air in the place; it smelled like sex. Chad has air conditioning but the apartment being so small, the place becomes as cold as a refrigerator very quickly. A little air will do just fine. As he was arranging the screen, he waved over to the neighbor across the alley. He loves to show off and the neighbor loves seeing that big piece of meat.

Chad settled into the far corner of the couch and without really much thought, picked up the television remote and clicked on. White noise. He picked up his script and started to thumb through it again. Reaching a page where he has dialogue, he reached over for a highlighter and started to yellow ink his lines and direction, just to see how much of the script is about him. He'd gotten through a good portion when something caught his ear.

"I'm here at the world premiere of *The Devil Made Me Do It* at the famed Chinese Theater in Hollywood," Mica Daly from *Drop Zone* was reporting from the red carpet. This was the event Chad was fired from being part of and then subsequently crashed.

A quick montage of the stars along the carpet followed Mica's introduction. There was Suzy Chambers—the big-titted television "IT" girl of the moment, Rod Stevens—Chad's latest idea of competition, Sean Jones—the British sensation, and a smattering of bigger Hollywood names: Denzel, Will and Jada, Channing, Uma, Ben and Jennifer, and Cuba.

"I'm here with Cuba Gooding Jr.," Mica went on enthusiastically. "And the question of the night is: What is the one thing only the devil could make you do?"

Before he could answer, Chad paused the television. He could hardly believe his eyes. There over the shoulder of Oscar winner Cuba Gooding Jr. is none other than Chad Martin, standing on the red carpet as if he was meant to be there, watching his 'peers' comings and goings.

"God Fucking Dammit," he shouted. "I am a star!"

He quickly pressed the record button on the remote. He wasn't about to lose this moment. In the days and weeks to come, he would play this segment over and over again—naked, alone, stroking his big dick, repeating his favorite mantra: "You have to visualize to realize."

4

The pool glows in the evening light. It is beautiful the way the bodies' silhouette in the pool light. It wouldn't be a Roger Keenan party without a porn star or two—in this case four—swimming naked in the pool. That's one element that makes his monthly dinner soirees uniquely original and the talk of those in the know. Along with porn stars, there is always a smattering of real stars, plus industry movers and shakers—even the occasional promising up and comers.

His parties are legendary at that fabulous two-story, Mediterranean style house at the base of the Hollywood Hills bordering West Hollywood. The house, built in the 1920s was the former home of some long forgotten silent film star who was the only owner until Roger bought the place in the 80's when she died. Among the 'in' crowd, they like to refer to the house "as that place from *Sunset Boulevard* and, needless to say, Roger has been occasionally and affectionately called "Norma."

Roger Keenan is a long expatriated British import who came to America during the hazy disco days of the late 1970s with a layover in New York City where Studio 54 kept him up all night and white powder kept him up all day. His accent, which he has aggressively held on to for these many years, opened doors and his suave and innovative approach to international marketing quickly gave him a name among entertainment hotshots whose corporate headquarters were in the city and not on the coast. But it wasn't long before Hollywood came calling and he willingly make the leap past the fly-over states and settled nicely into that palazzo on the edge of West Hollywood where his English formality became a hit with laid back Los Angelinos. Everyone wanted to socialize with Roger Keenan.

He is, for the lack of a better a term, a character. Dressed in wildly color-ful clothes—usually madras pants, bright polo or dress shirts with bow ties, his ever present reading glasses perched on the end of his nose and a panama hat to shade his face from the sun. All this color belies his dark side of decadence, which he acts out through his wildly outrageous parties where just about anything goes and everyone knows it and where he shamelessly encourages your every whim. New faces, old stalwarts, A-list, above the line, porn stars and hookers; you name them, and they all could be there. And his parties are both show and business because he has the knack of putting the right people together at the right time. Many a big deal has been made between courses of sex, drugs and anything else that tickles your fancy. But what goes on behind those gates stays behind those gates. Those who talk, are out and those who play, stay.

Roger's is one of those coveted invitations, which are bestowed by way of loyalty and luck. Roger's is a collection of over one hundred diverse and immensely interesting friends—and they are friends, not just clever acquaintances, who would and have been there for Roger on several occasions—which he invites to dinner, monthly, in groups of twenty. The way he picks those twenty is his idea of fun. It's a lottery. He places everyone's name in a bowl and then has an assistant pull out twenty names randomly. Even Roger doesn't know who they are at any one time; it lets him play along with the surprise. Those lucky twenty, ensure the group of dinner guests are never the same group of people month after month. Everyone is thrilled to be invited—never knowing until they arrive just who their dinner mates will be. And those who aren't invited this time are never offended.

On this night, Mica is one of the lucky chosen. Neither the first nor the last to arrive, he decided to take a few moments poolside to watch the motion in the ocean. The pool is cheekily called 'the ocean' because of its enormity. The size of Roman bath and built in a time when money was no object, it would be considered a monumental burden for most homeowners, what with maintenance and the cost of heating it. But to Roger, this is his baby. Roger prefers the birthday suit to the bathing suit and expects guests to adhere. And they do.

Mica recognized three out of four of the porn folk by face and the fourth he would like to know better. Two, Bob and Neal—their real names—are bobbing in the shallow end softly stroking each other's wet bodies while gently kissing. It always intrigues Mica about the life of a porn star. Just how to they achieve romance living and working in a world of constant sex? But these two seem to have something special going on.

On the other side of the pool, Ty, a sinewy black man, has his face buried between the legs of the unknown fourth player who is sitting splay legged on the coping of the ocean's edge. The distinctive tattoo on the side of his thigh and a second on his shoulder indicted to Mica that he had, at least, seen his work even if he couldn't remember his name. So mechanical, this blowjob appeared to Mica. Nevertheless, he is sure they are having fun and who wouldn't with that large porn prick to play with. But compared to the delicacy from the two at the other end of the pool, Mica felt he was watching them work rather than play.

"Magnificent aren't they," Roger spoke from behind Mica.

"Don't you mean fagnificent?" Mica reached back to wrap an arm around Roger and planted a kiss on both cheeks. "Thank you so much for the invite."

"I think you will like who we have coming tonight."

Just then a moan from the side of the pool pierced their conversation and the unnamed porn star shot his load all over Ty's face.

"I already like those cumming tonight," Mica joked nodding over to the antics at poolside.

"I am sure there will be more of that for your enjoyment as the night goes on. There always is."

"That's why you're the perfect host, Norma."

Of course, Roger Keenan is the perfect host. He knows the marketing game like no other. He has amassed quite a tidy fortune working with the studios on creating marketing campaigns—mostly movie posters and movie trailers—for their blockbuster releases. One thing he has learned over the years, when it comes to any movie budgeted at over one hundred million dollars with a marketing budget to match, studios are nervous about their investment despite their outward confidence and bravado. In fact, Roger is responsible for a lot of that bravado. And for that he is given a virtual blank check. He wouldn't say he gouges the studios, but suffice it to say, when you are considered *the* expert in your field, the free marketplace isn't so free for those writing the checks.

"Let's make our way inside and see who else made the lucky draw." Roger put an arm around Mica and led the away from the pool and on into the big house. "I am dying to know who I am dining with."

There was pause and then a warning. "And remember Mica, no names. These parties are for us and not for public consumption. I don't want to be the subject of one of your fun little segments on *Drop Zone*."

Mica agreed, of course, but is a little annoyed not to be trusted completely at this stage. This wasn't the first of these parties he's attended and hopefully wouldn't be the last. But he's built a career on knowing more than he tells.

"Do you like them?" A starlet star of the latest supernatural trilogy interrupted Mica and Roger's moment. No names.

"Darling, good to see you." Roger gave her a kiss.

"Hi Mica," she said leaning to give him a kiss. "Soooo?"

They paused, looked at each other and then back to her.

"My breasts," she announced. "Do you like the new ones?" Without waiting for an answer, "Aren't they so much more natural than the last pair. I am so much happier. And feel them." With that she grabbed a hand from Roger and Mica and placed each on a breast.

"First rule of marketing, know your audience dear," Roger winced. "I couldn't tell you what they are supposed to feel like."

"Then look." Without much concern or discretion, she untied her halter and let them out into the evening's light.

"Well they're certainly symmetrical." Roger continued his witty retort. "But darling, really? On an empty stomach?"

She laughed as Mica helped her tie the halter back up. "You old queen's have no appreciation. Mica knows a good rack when he sees one. Don't you Mica?" It was a rhetorical question as she didn't wait for an answer and leaned in to whisper to Mica. "I even have the feeling back in my nipples."

So far a blowjob show and a titty grab, Mica thought. This is certainly another Roger Keenan evening.

o o o

The dining room is as grandiose as the house itself and overly large a space. Large beamed, vaulted ceilings tented the room with an impressive wrought iron chandelier—bought from some desperate cash poor Spanish aristocrat and brought back after an Ibiza romp—magnificently lights the room in the most flattering combination of pink light bulbs and dimmed wattage.

The dining table is beautifully set with one of the twelve different china patterns Roger has collected. Roger liked having twelve sets of china, one for each of these dinner parties he throws each year. The table itself can seat thirty, which, as Roger points out, is perfect for twenty guests. "Plenty of room to spread out." Of course this also makes for very loud conversations, as people generally have to shout up and down the table to be heard.

No names are given unless they are spoken casually. You are supposed to know who is in the room. This night sitting around the table are: the aforementioned starlet, an Oscar winning director, a soap star, the author, one of West Hollywood's premiere drag queen comedians in full regalia, one of those guys from a defunct boy band who's made a bit of resurgence having come out of the closet, two out of the four still naked porn stars, *the* haute couturier socialite of a certain age and her husband, the gay former studio head, a disco diva, two big money socialites from Texas and San Francisco, a former child star for whom they are talking about making a reality show, three former flames of Roger, Roger himself, Mica and *him*, that guy from the premiere the other evening.

Before dinner was served, a toast. "Does everyone have some champagne?" No one did as if this was a ploy to introduce the waiter staff. The other two porn stars emerged from the bar area with trays of Dom Perignon, dressed in black tie from the waist up and naked from the waist down. Trust Roger to turn a dinner party into a Bacchanal.

"They are Bob and Neal, which happen to be not just names but also verbs in their profession," Roger began as they distributed the champagne. "Some of you may know them by their stage names. But if you need anything, they're here to service...and not for the first time." Chuckles, somewhat awkwardly from the socialites, all around.

"But seriously," he continued 'sincerely', "thank you all for joining this evening. Notice I didn't say coming, that's for later." More chuckles. "As you know the guest list is a random selection of a group I hold near and dear to my heart and even I, until you arrive, don't even know who will be attending. So it is always a pleasant surprise to see great friends and new faces...and some great friends who have new faces." He lifted a glass to toward the distinguished lady from Texas and drew the biggest laugh so far. "So as we start, remember two things, this night is for pure enjoyment and anything goes."

"Would anyone mind," the socialite from San Francisco began hesitantly, "if I changed places with that darling young thing over there? I simply have to catch up with my dear friend from Texas and I don't think I have the lung capacity to talk across the table."

With that the mystery man from the premiere exchanged seats and settled right next to Mica. "I'm Chad, " he introduced himself to Mica with an extended hand.

"Nice to meet you, I'm Mica."

Seeing the interplay, Roger darted around the table and interjected himself into their introductions. "This is perfect. Mica I see you now have been introduced to the perfectly delicious Chad Martin. I am marketing his new movie *The Other Brother* and he is simply going to be a star. He has some assets that really pop on screen."

The reference made Chad blush but is completely lost on Mica.

Sotto voce, Chad leans over to Mica to speak. "I know I am not supposed to say these sorts of things at a party like this but I really like your work."

"Thank you," Mica accepted the compliment with a blush. "I look forward to interviewing you on a red carpet one of these days."

That was music to Chad's ears.

Dinner is served.

° ° °

"What does anyone think about the latest exploits of Antonia Guest?" Roger threw out as a conversation starter. For a man who prides himself on discretion, no one loves a good piece of gossip like Roger.

"She is guilty!" declared the starlet. "I lost a role to her and she should not even be hired in this town after the shit she pulled."

The two socialites leaned in toward each other. "Who is Antonia Guest?"

The director, who hadn't proved to be much of a conversationalist, piped up. "I worked with her once. She was professional on the days that she chose to be professional."

"What does that mean?" the former child star shouted incredulously. "In my day you were professional every day or you were out."

"Exactly," the starlet chimed in.

"I wouldn't give her a contract," the former studio head mumbled. "To much of a risk. I mean, we have to carry insurance on all our cast. Who would insure that mess?"

"I bet Mica knows a thing or two," Roger prodded.

Much gossip was covered over the five courses, catered by the best gay owned restaurant in town, Michael's on La Cienega. Dinner began with mini beef Wellington tarts, along with soup, salad, an entre of duck a l'orange and then, of course, dessert. The chef came out, to the applause of all, and announced that Michael's would be closing on La Cienega and taking over the existing Ovation restaurant in Los Feliz. "The end of an era," the gays at the table bemoaned while the others couldn't have cared less. They didn't understand this announcement is the gay equivalent of when Spago left the Sunset Strip and moved into the old Bistro Gardens in Beverly Hills. Quelle surprise! Quelle damage!

By the time dessert, a creamed confection of a cake, had been served, everyone had been long sated and the cake just sat there until, as only can happen at a Roger Keenan affair, the two table-side porn stars started scooping it up, smearing it on each other and licking it off. This, as if on cue, opened up all kinds of fun opportunities. Before long, the boy band member was playing the baby grand in the living room while the disco diva belted out a medley of some of her bigger hits. The socialites danced like they were back in the heady days of Studio 54. It wasn't long before the starlet joined them only to drop out two songs in when she saw the second waiter masturbating in the chair and thought there may be opportunity for some fun. Fortunately he could keep it up for anyone and proceeded to let her rub her new tits all over his cock.

The drag queen and fashion designer had much to discuss on the couch with a new round of cocktails, while her husband, the former studio head was, in fact, giving head to the second of the waiters in a side vestibule. Meanwhile, Roger was himself trying to encourage action between his two former lovers—wanting them to go upstairs and start and he would join them later.

The cake scene had progressed to all out fucking. The two porn stars had now climbed on to the table, atop the cake and were fucking doggy style. It was clearly Ty's turn to give the no named other what he'd gotten poolside. Grabbing up handfuls of cake and smearing it all over his back, Ty pounded the other's tight ass all while the Oscar winning director, who ate nothing but sniffed his way through the dinner, is circling the table, index finger to thumb and thumb to index finger creating a mock lens, as if he was filming the proceedings. The child star followed the director around the table like a puppy, trying desperately to get him interested in a reality television show idea.

Meanwhile, Chad and Mica, who are both intrigued and somewhat stimulated by the show on the dining table but won't admit to each other their interest, have been deeply engrossed in conversation. "You want to go out by the pool?" Chad suggested. He was getting more and more distracted and he wanted to keep his eyes on the prize, Mica. Mica, who hasn't been flattered by this much attention by a strikingly handsome man in a very long time, grabbed a full bottle of Dom Perignon and two glasses and followed Chad out back. They settle on two adjoining chaise lounges, which they moved to be even closer to each other.

∘ ∘ ∘

"Crazy party, eh?" Chad began.

"They always are."

"Do they always get so...so...playful?" This was all new to Chad.

"Oh yeah. And Roger's aren't the only ones. There's quite a decadent side to Hollywood. It is rumored, and most likely true, that there is a gay web of A-list directors, producers and writers who have even wilder parties with no one over the age of twenty five where hundreds of people have to check their clothes at the door and it is nothing more than an orgy inside. There is a lot of talk that many of the boys are underage. People in this town have to watch out. What is interesting is no one thinks they are being decadent. So when it comes to Roger, this is nothing. It is as if everyone throws parties like this, with guests like these."

Chad and Mica had covered a lot of ground, getting to know each other over dinner. All the basics had been told: childhood, parents, schooling, ambition, dreams and goals. Mica had never been so comfortable in talking about himself. Chad had thought the same. Moreover, both are generally interested in the other.

There was still so much more Mica wanted to know about Chad and yet talking seemed to be over temporarily. They spent quite a while staring at each other. Mica was simply drawn to Chad's crystalline blue eyes, even in the dark of the night, with just the glow of the outdoor fireplace and pool light to illuminate them.

"I have to say this," Mica began almost child-like, "you are beautiful."

"Thank you," Chad whispered and reached out and took Mica's hand.

Mica realized what he said was textbook corny and tried to correct himself. "I mean..."

Chad stopped him mid sentence. "I know what you mean. Look, I look in the mirror and can see that I am attractive. But many people...most people in this town... are attractive. But *attraction* is about the person you are and not the face you carry."

"Profound."

"Does that mean you are attracted to me?" Chad asked teasingly.

Neither said a word but Mica leaned in and they kissed—a slow, gentle kiss of affection rather than lust. And then they kissed again.

When they pulled apart, Chad spoke first. "That was nice."

"So to answer your question, I am attracted to you."

They kissed again.

"Drink?" Mica poured two more glasses of Dom and they instinctively brought them together and clinked. Then Chad began to chuckle.

"What?" asked Mica, concerned something had gone wrong.

"I just didn't think I would meet someone like you."

They kissed again and both took a sip of champagne.

"Hey, I've got an idea. Let's go for a swim."

Mica stammered, "Now? Ah...I don't have a bathing suit with me."

"I was counting on that." With that, Chad pulled off his shirt and in one quick motion pulled down his pants. Mica stifled a gasp at what he saw with a quick sip of champagne. "Come on, don't let me do this alone."

Mica stood and slowly began to unbutton his shirt. Chad began to help. And that gesture alone began to make Mica hard. Oh please don't pop a boner now. How embarrassing, he thought.

They kissed again as Chad undid Mica's belt. Chad could feel Mica's stiffening cock and, rather than embarrass him, gave him a quick peck and dove into the pool. Mica scrambled out of his pants awkwardly and that momentary distraction calmed down his passion. He walked over to the pool's edge, somewhat chilled in the night air. "Is it cold?"

"Get in here you wuss," Chad challenged and splashed him with a handful of water. The pool is heated. Mica jumped in and as he reached the surface made sure he had slid against Chad.

"Meant to tell you before you jumped in," Chad began.

"What?" Mica interrupted nervously.

"Nice cock." With that Chad reached over and gave Mica a playful tug. "In fact nice everything. Nice guy."

Mica has what is considered a swimmer's body—not overly built but taught. He has a dusting of hair on his pectorals and a trail to his bellybutton all of which he keeps trimmed, not shaved. He does like the trimmed feel and takes it to his arms, legs and underarms. Mica was so pleased when someone coined the phrase man-scaping and defined a beauty regimen instead of what he thought to be a fetish. "I like the trimmed thing," Chad declared as he felt along Mica's body, settling his arms around his shoulders and once again kissed.

"What do we do from here?" Mica asked.

"What do you mean?"

"I would like to see you again."

"I would like that too." Chad blushed.

"I am not going to sleep with you tonight," Mica announced.

"Who said I am going to let you," Chad countered defensively.

"What I mean is, I would love to. But I would like to take you on a real date if that is okay."

Again Chad blushed. "That is so nice."

"Then it's a date?"

"It's a date."

With that, they went back to kissing.

High on second floor of the house, while past lovers were maneuvering into a triangle position in the background, Roger Keenan is peering out of the window and looking at the goings on in the pool below. He loves a happy ending.

5

What if I get hard? Chad thought to himself on the long walk from his trailer to the set. He is only dressed in a robe and so far the only one to see him naked is the make-up artist who applied the body paint, a petite little thing with no interest in Chad or his member, just the job at hand.

This is day one of shooting and he is already naked. Everyone involved— the producer, the director and Albert, Chad's agent—thought let's get the awkward scenes out of the way first and free them up to act before personalities, emotions and ego get in the way of the acting. No one bothered to ask Chad if he was comfortable with this plan, which of course he is.

He walked past a myriad of crewmembers, some who nodded, others who said "Hi" and still others who simply ignored the newcomer. Arriving on the set, he wished Mica were here to give him support. He surprisingly had really begun to connect with Mica during the various phone calls they've shared since that night at Roger Keenan's house.

"Hey Chad, good to see you. A newbie and on time, I like that." Chad recognized the director right away, Drew Peters—a man of independent film fame and mainstream curiosity. The buzz is this film is the cross over project he needs to get the big boys looking at him for those big budget, blockbuster, sequels that dominate the summer movie going season. The fact that Spectrum Studios is behind this is a big stepping-stone in that mainstream direction.

The Other Brother is hardly Shakespeare, but respectable enough. The story is your typical boy meets girl, boy falls in love with girl, other brother also falls in love with girl but it is taboo. The girl also has feelings for the other brother. Long story short, the first brother becomes terminally ill and while he needs the support of the girl, he encourages her to turn her affections to the other brother so they will have each other, and the memory of him, to carry on with when he is gone. Selfless, yes, but hardly Oscar worthy material.

The director of photography and the director are huddled together while Chad inspects the set. "Chad, make yourself comfortable, while we wait for the others," Drew shouts across. By 'others', Chad assumes he means his co-stars who were pleasant enough to him during table reads. But on the first day of shooting and being naked may be cause for a different dynamic. "I take that back, Chad, since you are here, lets have you step on set for a lighting test."

Chad having just settled in to his very own director's chair, which he made note to ask to keep when the production is over—got up and walked to the center of the set, unwrapped his robe and threw it back toward his chair. He looks fantastic, in all his naked splendor. And it seemed everyone on set paused, just for a split second, and took in his handsome physique. He is going to be a star, is the collective thought bubble hovering above the heads of one and all.

"Ah, you don't have to disrobe, Chad." Drew raced over with robe in hand. "This is only a test and when we need you to be naked we will close the set with only the necessary crew allowed to be here. To make it more comfortable for all concerned."

"I'm fine," Chad dismissed, put on his robe but didn't tighten the belt. He could already see the power his cock was having on people and he isn't about to put it away at this point.

o o o

Mica, too, had his party pal on his mind. He really did feel a connection, even though he had sworn to himself two things: no twenty-something twinks and no actors! But Chad seems different—determined, ambitious, intelligent and playful—there doesn't appear to be any of the entitlement issues all the young Hollywood hopefuls all exude these days, at least not with him. Sure he has his childish side—he had confessed to pissing in a flower arrangement—but more importantly he booked his first film. He is no longer a wannabe actor; he is a working actor.

Mica is not only intrigued by Chad but his kind—the young, ambitious, hopefuls...tomorrow's stars. "Is there a segment on "fresh faces" we could do on the show?" Mica threw out to Lydia in the privacy of her office.

The office is on the second floor of the renovated factory with an almost floor to ceiling window across one wall which allows her to overlook the bullpen of cubicles below. Like Lydia, the office is decorated rather coldly and impersonally with a sterile glass top desk and the only piece of art being an Andy Warhol like knock-off lithograph image of Lydia.

As they sat, a basket was delivered—some thank you from a studio, agent or manager for some kiss-ass piece on *Drop Zone* featuring their project or client. She never opens them, never looks at them and, God forbid, never shares them. They just pile up around the room until they start to smell and then are thrown out.

Including this one, there are now five in Mica's peripheral vision dotted around the room.

"It's from the studio," her assistant Brad whispered loudly enough to have Mica hear. "They loved the segment on *The Devil Made Me Do It.*"

"They should have sent one to you, Mica," Lydia purred. "But clearly they love me." There's that bitchy alter ego Labia again. She can never miss an opportunity to point out that she is the chief of the operation and for that deserves all the kudos. Lydia and Labia, you never have one without the other.

Lydia, who had been shuffling through papers on her desk and intermittently returning emails the whole time Chad was talking, paused, squinted her eyes a bit and thought about it for a moment. Then she spoke. "This is not some trick you are boning and promised to get on TV is it?"

"Should I be calling human resources?" he half-joked.

"Cute," she fired back.

Not yet, Mica thought. "No Lydia. Jesus Christ, you always go to the ass end of every idea. This is a legitimate segment."

"What made you think of this?"

"I met this guy..."

"AH HA!" she shouted.

"NO. I was at Roger Keenan's house..."

"By the way," she interrupted by way of an aside. "You have got to get me into one of his dinners. I hear they are something else."

Not a chance, Mica thought and continued undaunted. "So I met this young actor who is working on the new Spectrum Studios project. Something called *Another Brother* or *The Only Brother ... The Other Brother,* that's it. Anyway this guy is really handsome and clearly has that star 'IT'. And so I got to thinking about when I was at the premiere of *The Devil Made Me Do It* and how Michelle Bianco from Regis and Canning forced her new client, Suzy Chambers, on me..."

"There is a waste of two tits, putting them in front of you. Great segment by the way," Lydia interjected and pointed to the solo basket again. "Speaking of Michelle Bianco, she called me pushing Suzy as a segment."

"That's what I mean." Mica is getting more excited. He could see behind Lydia's eyes, she is processing this. "I think we could do a great piece, in fact several pieces like a series, called *The Ten Faces You Are Going To Want To Know*...or something like that."

"I like it," she conceded in a surprising nod to not co-opting someone else's idea and making it her own. "I suppose you are thinking you should be the reporter on these segments."

"Lydia we've had this discussion before. I like my job. I like the shtick. But I can do more. I *want* to do more."

"I tell you what, get me ten names and faces that show real promise and not someone you want to suck off and let's see what we can do with it. And by the way, I do think you are capable of doing more than shtick on a red carpet. Show me what you can do and I will give you something with some meat on the bone. God knows you love big meat."

"Thanks," he headed for the door and in a sotto voce voice continued, "Labia!"

"Did you just call me a cunt?" Busted.

"NO, of course not, Lydia."

But if the Labia fits.

o o o

She'd arrived on set with all the graciousness of an actress who believes, and unfortunately is, the biggest name in the cast—unjustifiably regal. Ashley Beckwith is by all accounts a Prima Dona on a mission to become a big star. A former Australian soap opera star, she was a big fish in a small pond down under. When she decided to take on America, she was going to do it the way a star of yesteryear would have— all glamor and glitz. Arriving at premieres and events in stunning evening gowns rather than casual chic, never being seen coming out of yoga class or Starbucks in sweat pants and always courteously available, if not condescending, to the media. Chad seemed impressed by the way she courted attention and, as such, the way she got what she wanted.

"Darling, would you be a dear and get me this..." or "Oh Dear, I wouldn't think of the doing the scene that way..." were little moments during the table reads he found alternatively laughable and endearing. Of course, she hadn't pulled any of that shit with him yet. And it might not be so cute if she does.

"There's my fabulous co-star," she announces and dashes over to give a Chad a 'sincere' air kiss—must not alter the make-up—and a hug. As she approaches she notices Chad cock sticking out from his robe. "Maybe I should have said co-stars!"

The set, as promised, was closed and the skeletal crew assumed their positions as both star and co-star assumed theirs—Ashley under the covers of the bed and Chad in the middle of the set, back to the camera, facing Ashley. They would start with an over the shoulder angle of Chad looking at Ashley's face.

As Ashley is under the covers and all the audience will see are her well-augmented tits, she is wearing a G-string to cover her well talked about box. A starlet with the type of airs she puts on is bound to elicit negative rumors. The rumor *du jour* is there is a sex tape floating around featuring her playing with a legendary actor's prized Oscar. And apparently it is not good enough just to be nominated. What she can do to and for a thirteen-inch statuette is fairly impressive. She should definitely thank the Academy.

Chad was already naked and in place while Ashley was being situated and the sheets draped as how the set designer wanted them. She couldn't take his eyes off his beautiful manhood and he knew it. "You are going to be a star," she mouthed to him as they worked on her positioning.

Once set, the director called for a rehearsal. "And action!" The dialogue began.

"We can't do this," she began.

"He knows there is something between us," Mica returned.

"But I love him."

"And I love you."

The dialogue was trite but there is an almost instant chemistry between Chad and Ashley. It is the stuff of Hollywood legend. Mica walks the few short steps to the bed and leans over to give her a kiss. They kiss hungrily and passionately, more than what the script calls for.

"Cut," the director yells from behind the video monitors. "You two are great. We just have to work on a camera angle."

The problem, it seems, is that when Chad bends over to kiss her, the cheeks of his ass spread ever so slightly but enough to give the impression of an asshole shot. Assholes are for porn. Secondarily, as he turns to kiss her, his cock swings out and it appears as if he is going to titty fuck her. Steamy yes, romantic no. After a few minutes of thinking and rethinking the solution is to have him sit on the side of the bed before he bends to kiss her. Problem solved.

"Back to first positions."

Everyone is in place. "Rolling. And. Action."

They do the scene repeatedly for various reasons and each time Chad stands up from the bed, Ashley finds a way to rub a hand or her forearm or whatever she can manipulate against his penis. And each time he gets a little more swollen.

They film the scene one more time. But at this point, young Chad is reacting like most young twenty something guys. The kissing, the subtle stroking is all too much as he pops an impressive hard on as they kiss. "Cut."

There is a quick scramble to throw the robes over the co-stars.

"I think we should take a break while we review the cuts," the director instructs professionally. "We may have this one in the can already. So we can move on to the reversals." To Chad and Ashley, " We will call you when we need you."

"Sorry about that," Chad mumbled to Ashley as they make their way back to their respective trailers.

"It won't happen again," Ashley began and was quickly interrupted by Chad.

"NO! No...of course not." Chad thought he would quickly whack off in his trailer and pray that would do the trick.

As they arrived at Ashley's trailer first, she silently took him by the hand and led him inside. Without saying a word, she knelt down in front of him, reached up and cupped his smooth shaved balls with one hand, gripped the base of his cock with the other and parted her lips and slid the shaft into her mouth—well, as much of it as she could take. No woman had ever done this to or for Chad in the past and it felt good. Thoughts of Mica flooded his head and blood flooded to his engorged organ. She picked up speed and stroked the shaft as she sucked the head.

She continued to stroke as she looked up, "I don't want to ruin my makeup so I am going to swallow this for you. I don't ordinarily do that." Sure.

He didn't know what to say. He just went with the moment. Several minutes later, and wanting to push his finger in his ass the way the masseur had turned him on to; he came violently in her mouth and down her throat. She gulped like a professional.

"Now, unless you can come twice in a relatively short amount of time, and let me know if you can, that should take care of any embarrassment on the set." With that Ashley opened the door of her trailer and motioned for him to leave. "By the way, I don't fuck my co-stars. So if you had any ideas forget it."

Now there is a line in the sand, Chad thought. Always good to meet a gal with standards. He quickly wrapped his robe around himself and headed out the door. And then it hit him. This is his first day of work on a union film. He officially will be given his SAG—Screen Actors Guild—card and be considered a legitimate working actor. Wow. And oh yeah, he just got a blowjob from Ashley Beckwith. Some day!

o o o

"Michelle? It's Mica Daley from *Drop Zone*." Mica is sitting under his desk as to not be heard on the phone. These cubicles, while just high enough as to not have your office mate stare at you, they do nothing to block out the sound. Mica wanted some privacy before anyone else knew what he is up to. Like any shop in

Hollywood, *Drop Zone* is competitive. Mica is never sure just who might want to steal his idea and make it their own. And he has a lot to prove with Lydia.

"Hello, of course." Michelle, picking up the phone handle and immediately taking Mica off of speakerphone, and in that usual bitchy way she communicates with her underlings, snaps her fingers to her assistant outside and motions to close the door. "Please" is not in her vocabulary for subordinates. "I was going to call you and thank you for the premiere piece."

"Thanks, but no need..."

"Now, what can I do for you?" Michelle likes to cut to the chase if she thinks she is on the hook to return a favor. And small talk is never her style.

"It's what I can do for you, I believe. I am working on a series of segments all about new faces in Hollywood. You know the up and comers you should be looking out for. And, along with Suzy Chambers, who, of course, we will feature in the series, I want to know who else you have that is ready for some heavy promotion."

Michelle fist pumped in the air. "Mica, I think you and I have a lot to talk about."

"Oh..."

"This is completely confidential and off the record," Michelle lowered her voice even though she is alone in a closed office. "I mean it Mica," she threatened.

"Ok..."

"We are working a search as we speak for new talent who is just about to break through." What she isn't telling him, is that *she*, and she alone, is working on this search, for her *own* gain. "Needless to say, I...er...we are looking to represent the next wave of talent. I think we can work together on this. You profile and we represent."

"Sounds fantastic," Mica returned. "I might even have someone in mind already for you. I have some fleshing out of the concept to do first. But I just wanted you in the loop from the start."

"Darling Mica, you are a doll for thinking of me," Michelle purred with that now infamous 'Hollywood sincerity'. "We really must go out for a drink. Let's figure out a date soon."

"Great." That fell on deaf ears as Michelle had already hung up. She'd gotten what she needed.

6

Things have been moving along nicely for Mica and Chad since first meeting at Roger Keenan's party several weeks ago. It's not that there have been quantities of time together—with Mica's erratic reporting assignments and Chad's long days on the set—but their time together has been quality.

They prefer dinners at Mica's place rather than public outings. "Gotta protect my image," Chad would say and Mica would roll his eyes. What image? And when out, their relationship appears to be anything but romantic. Chad is determined to be a star and the whole gay thing doesn't play well with his star dream. Chad had yet to introduce Mica to any other friends, for that matter even mention other friends. In Chad's defense, Mica hadn't really introduced Chad around either. If they do run into someone familiar their introduction of each other always begins with: "this is my friend..."

On this night they decided on something daring, the semblance of a date. They arrived at Michael's on La Cienega at 7:30 for an 8:00 P.M. reservation. That way they could settle in at the bar, have a cocktail and take in the crowd. Michael's closing is just a week or two away while they put the finishing touches on Ovation, the new place in Los Feliz. So the place is packed with last minute, last time reservations.

"It truly will be the end of an era," Mica bemoaned after taking his first sip of a very familiar tasting cocktail. Chad opted for a margarita, on the rocks with Michael's special sea salt rim.

"Spent a lot time here have you?" Chad asked knowing the answer. Mica had already kissed both the owner and the chef, stopped by two tables to say "hello" and waved at miscellaneous people around the room. This has been Mica's place ever since Michael's opened its doors.

Michael Carter, a straight guy who had more than embraced the gay community, had opened Michael's on La Cienega about twelve years ago. Before long, it was the gay destination restaurant for birthdays, dates and celebrations of any sort. The bartenders and waiters are all flirtatious, very hot, wannabe models and actors and, maybe even over the food, are the draw for most of the clientele. Their tight pants and even tighter shirts, thanks to daily gym visits, provided the eye candy while nightly specials, happy hour pricing and half priced Mondays made Michael's quite literally a cheap thrill. It was, and is, at least for another week or two a haven.

Several years ago, Michael had been in a car terrible accident and sold the business to an entrepreneurial couple named Scott and Brian who made Michael's an institution by hosting community fundraisers and branching into the catering business. Now the question looms as to whether there is enough loyalty in a very cynical town to get the gays to drive across Los Angeles to the new location in Los Feliz and make that an equal success.

"If this place is such a success, why close and move?" Chad asked.

"More space and cheaper rent. Pure economics, I hear."

Mica and Chad moved to their table, the coveted first booth with a view of the entire place. Chad seemed a little unnerved by the exposed seating but capitulated to Mica's obvious thrilled expression.

"See that guy over there," Mica discretely pointed to an older man sitting alone against the wall. "That is Bart...oh shit, I can't think of his last name. Anyway he was the president of one of the big three networks and now runs a cable subsidiary. Look at him."

Bart Lewis, a regular a Michael's, has a penchant for sitting alone with a couple of vintage bottles of wine from his own collection and proceeds to have very colorful conversations with the empty seat across from him.

"Creepy," Chad muttered.

"Exactly! And he runs a God damned television network."

"Speaking of networks," Chad began as he signaled the waiter for two more drinks. "I have some news."

"Oh...?"

"I want to wait for the drinks to arrive, so we can have a toast."

"Oh, so it is good news?"

"We'll see," Chad said coyly.

As they spoke, Lance Novak was being escorted to the booth next to theirs. "Hi there," he leaned over to give Mica a hug. "Thanks for giving Antonia Guest a fair segment on the show."

"I didn't know you represented Antonia?" Mica queried.

"We do now." Lance winked and then extended his hand to Chad. "I'm Lance Novak."

"Chad Martin."

"Oh I am so sorry...Lance this is Chad...but I guess you know that already,"

Mica clumsily interjected. "Chad is an up and coming actor on whom we may be doing a piece for *Drop Zone*." That was news to Chad and instantly Mica understood that he might have spoken prematurely. "And Lance here is the hotshot, young Turk, entertainment lawyer with Dunning, Baker and Astin,"

"You're too kind," Lance blushed.

Mica is hardly being too kind. Lance is, in fact, the hotshot at the most prestigious entertainment law firm in town. They handle the biggest names and biggest cases—everything from contract negotiations to divorce litigations—but one of their biggest claims to fame is cleaning up messes. If there is a scandal, they take care of the details. Case in point Antonia Guest and that messy driving debacle several weeks ago. She could have been charged with attempted murder, leaving the scene of an accident, assault with a deadly weapon, drunk driving and a myriad of other things. Thanks to the team at DBA et al, and Lance in particular, she got the usual starlet slap on the hand. She was charged with speeding.

"Perhaps you can negotiate my next contract," Chad held his newly arrived cocktail high as if it were a done deal. Lance and Mica laughed at his naiveté. You have to be considerably further up the food chain to be considered a potential client for Dunning, Baker and Astin.

"You have a contract?" Mica asked teasingly. And Chad raised his eyebrows in return—a tease of his own.

"Hey, you never know," Lance pandered. "Just keep yourself out of trouble. We prefer that people *want* to hire us rather than *have* to hire us. If you know what I mean?" He winked again, "Nice to see you and meet you." With that, Lance made his way to Bart, the television executive, said a quick hello and settled into his booth to join his assembled meal mates.

Refreshed drinks at the ready, Mica is dying to hear Chad's news. "Soooo?"

"What?"

"Oh come on, you have your drink now spill it...the news not the drink!"

"Well, I had an audition today. Actually a call back," Chad began deliberately speaking as if leading Mica down a path. "For a television series!"

"Yes," Mica egged him on.

"It's called *Divas* and I will play the boy toy to a much older woman. She's the cougar on the show."

"Really. That is fantastic. Why am I just hearing about this now?" Mica was a bit disappointed that Chad had kept something as big as a network audition a secret from him.

"I didn't want to jinx it. And I didn't want to have to come back as say 'well there's another role I didn't get'," Chad justified.

"Are you saying you did get the role?"

"It looks good. My agent is working things out as we speak."

Mica can't believe his ears. A network role means a steady paycheck of significant dollars even if it is just a supporting role, plus the recognition factor. He knows Chad has what it takes; he just couldn't believe it is happening so quickly. Mica instinctively leaned over to plant a congratulatory kiss on his 'boyfriend'—though no one had defined their relationship as boyfriends—but Chad pulled back.

"Not here."

Mica pulled back into the booth. He was not prone to public displays of affection either. But this was a special moment, now lost, and the rebuff seemed harsh.

"We've talked about this," Chad reminded Mica. "Neither of us need to walk around like billboards for the gay community. My career is about to take off and I don't want to be known as a gay actor. I want to be an actor. You of all people should understand that, Mica. After hearing the kinds of verbal abuse you take from Lydia."

"That's just Lydia being Labia," Mica justifies.

"That's not the point. She doesn't talk to your straight coworkers the same way."

"That's true."

"I know it is a new world order where people like a gay sitcom star can play a straight guy and cable news anchors can come out of the closet and read the news without losing credibility. But they are still labeled as gay before their titles and I don't want that for myself. I am going to be huge...soon...and I don't want anything in my way."

For a young guy, Chad understands the world around him fairly sensibly. Mica is impressed with his rationale, even if Chad is being a tad melodramatic.

"I will be more than happy running from the box office back into the closet to count my millions than to be standing on a gay pride float, a once but not proud gay out of work actor."

"I get it," Mica obliged. "I was pushed out of the closet professionally and made the best of it. But I wonder sometimes if opportunities weren't there because I am queer. You are at the beginning of a great career. I have no doubt. And you have to manage it the way you see best. I can go along with that. As long as it doesn't come between us."

"Thanks for that." Chad felt a warmth and comfort come over him. He felt his, their, secret is safe with Mica for perhaps the first time. "Now I know you are going to hate me but even this place is a little too 'out' for me. Can we just finish our drinks, go home and really celebrate."

Chad ever so discretely took a hold of Mica's hand and squeezed under the table. Mica likes the fact that Chad is grappling with who he is in the world of what he is about to become. Mica can see a long-term relationship happening—with an older brother, mentor, and sensibility to it. It's just what he's been looking for.

In Chad's mind, on the other hand, he isn't grappling for one moment. It is what he wants that matters most.

"Now what's this about a profile on me for *Drop Zone*?" Chad reminded Mica as he gulped the last of his drink and stood ready to leave.

"If this show comes through, I think you should definitely be one of the subjects of a series I am doing on new faces. But also, I think you might be ready to meet a publicist friend I know. She could really help your career."

Chad is swimming with the news—a movie in the can, a new series, a personal profile on *Drop Zone*, his own publicist—it is all too good to be true. As Mica walked past him on the way to the door, Chad whispered into his ear. "You are good to me and good for me. I want to fuck you when we get home."

The prospect excited Mica even though, and perhaps it is because he was whispering in a loud restaurant, but the offer seemed almost like a threat.

° ° °

Across town, in the dimly lit office of ASA, Albert Switzer's head is spinning. The offer has come in to cast Chad Martin in the new network series *Divas* and the contract is lengthy and confusing. The networks have changed since he booked one of his C-list talents onto an episode of *Murder She Wrote*, *Fantasy Island* or *The Love Boat*. Albert loved those shows—always steady work for his has-been clients. These days the networks know a good thing when they see one and want to tie it up for seasons to come. So the contract is for five years, which should be a good thing. Except this contract is littered with plenty of 'outs'—reasons to fire Chad. It is simple really: start the actor at minimal pay for a newcomer, tie him up for five years with standard but intermittently small pay bumps at the start of each season, with no guarantees that he will be picked up or the character will continue for all five seasons and make it iron clad as to ward off renegotiation. It all seems so one sided. Thank God, Anthony is there to translate the fine print.

"I suggest that we ask for more money to start," Anthony began after pouring through the novella of pages sent from the network's legal team.

"Good, I like that. I say we go from fifteen thousand per episode to twenty thousand," Albert added.

"We need to also ask for a guaranteed number of episodes. Right now he could end up in only one episode a season and he is tied to the show for five seasons," Anthony continued.

Albert wrinkled his brow. "Good catch. Where does it say that?"

Anthony showed him on his well-flagged copy of the contract and continued. "Also pay bumps should not be a percentage but rather a figure. Say next season he jumps to fifty thousand dollars an episode and so on."

"I like it! I like it!" Albert exclaimed. "Anything else?"

"Yes the whole contract should be renegotiated in season three, just to make sure he is not being screwed."

"Screwed? How?"

"What if he is a runaway success or the character is popular and they boost his involvement. Or what if he gets multiple offers because of this exposure. We have to have outs on our side too."

Albert loves the fact that Anthony is so aware of the minutia of the art of the deal. Albert was never a detail guy; it was always about the big picture. He has been wondering if it isn't time to give Anthony some sort of added role, perhaps elevate him to being a full agent.

"I will get these notes all typed up and we can get the revised contract over to the network in the morning. By the way, when are you planning to tell Chad the good news?"

"I figured we could submit our changes to the contract, feel out their response and then deliver the good news along with the bad news."

"Bad news?" Anthony questioned.

"Oh yes, the call came in while you were out at lunch," Albert began sheepishly for not having told Anthony earlier. "They are shelving *The Other Brother.*"

"*What!* Why?" Anthony couldn't believe his ears.

"There is some problem with distribution. There is talk of putting it in turn around but who knows if that will happen."

"You've known this information for eight hours and this is the first I am hearing about it," Anthony is beginning to wonder if Albert is starting to forget things. But that is something he is going to have to deal with later. In the meantime, he feels for Chad. "Chad is going to be so upset."

"Bullshit! He is about to make more money then he's ever made and be seen by more people than would have ever gone to that dick-swinging movie," Albert dismissed. "He is going to be fucking ecstatic."

Anthony would have to give him that. "Divas" are the perfect showcase for Chad. But still, Anthony thought the dick-swinging movie was going to make Chad a star nonetheless. His is quite a dick to swing.

° ° °

"Chamtini?"

Mica walked into the Hollywood regency decorated bedroom with its bold wallpaper and tufted headboard bed and placed the tray on the low cocktail table between the vintage Billy Haines slipper chairs. The gays can, if nothing else, decorate. On the tray is a bottle of Kettle One, chilled bottle of Veuve Cliquot and two extra large martini glasses.

The chamtini was a drink they had made up by chance when they had nearly finished off a bottle of champagne but weren't quite ready to stop drinking. All that was in the house was vodka, which they liberally poured into the last of the champagne at the bottom of their respective glasses. Champagne in lieu of vermouth and the chamtini was born.

"Please!" Chad playfully demanded. He is naked, sprawled across the bed on his stomach with one leg bent upwards ever so teasingly separating the cheeks of his ass, revealing his very smooth crack to Mica.

Mica, for his part, was bent over the table mixing their favorite new celebratory cocktail. Chad could see the goings on from the reflection in the mirror above the bureau across from the bed. To get low enough, Mica spread his legs thus revealing the crack of his ass with its dusting of downy fluff. Both had the same thought. The pop of the champagne cork startled both back to the task at hand. A toast.

Carefully bringing the tray over and setting it on the bedside table, Mica passed a nearly overflowing glass to Chad who quickly sipped to avoid a spill.

"You're not supposed to sip before we toast," Mica chastised playfully, sort of, and tapped him on the ass.

"So what are we toasting?" Chad asked as if he didn't know.

"Well if you remember we created the chamtini to celebrate the end of filming of *The Other Brother*. Now we get to toast you're becoming a big television star on the aptly named series *Divas*. Here's to your on going success."

They clinked, sipped and kissed.

"Our on going success, Mr. Television star yourself." Chad corrected.

"Hardly, but I'll drink to that." With that, Mica hoisted his glass and a large wave of cocktail swelled over the rim of the glass and splashed down on Chad's back. "Don't move. I'll take care of that."

Mica placed his glass carefully back on the table and then crawled in between Chad's legs and began to lick from his shoulder muscles to his tailbone, lapping up the spilled drink. The taste of the vodka and saltiness of Chad's skin is delicious and stimulating. As he moved down toward the top of Chad's ass, Chad accommodatingly spread his legs a little further apart and passed his cocktail back to Mica. Mica knew what to do.

The liquid trailed down the crack of Chad's ass as Mica dribbled just a bit out of the side of the glass, handed the glass back to Chad and then buried his face in his ass. Chad alternatively sipped and moaned. Normally, Mica took to the bottom role and Chad's ass was off limits. But tonight with the mix of cocktail and tongue, Chad is completely into it. And Mica is more than pleased to please. Chad arched his back and positioned himself on his knees and let Mica go to town.

As Mica's tongue darted in and out of that tight hole, he reached up and pulled Chad's hardened cock back through his legs. Licking from the head of that cock to the pulsing asshole and back, repeating and repeating, is sending shivers of delight throughout Chad's body. And the more Chad moaned with pleasure, the harder Mica's cock became.

Mica rolled Chad over and pulled Chad's legs up over his shoulders and leaned in to kiss Chad. They are deep, hungry kisses, each sucking on the other's tongues. When they pulled apart a string of spit kept them connected and Mica dove back in for more. As Mica pressed against Chad, Mica's hard cock settled into the length of Chad's crack. He rhythmically thrust his hips forward and his cock rubbed against Chad's swollen asshole. Would this be the night Chad gives himself up for Mica?

"I want to fuck you," Chad whispered between sucking on Mica's tongue.

"I want to fuck you too." Mica extended his index finger, stuck it inside Chad's mouth to get it well lubricated and then eased it into Chad's swollen and wanting hole. Sliding his finger in and out, with Chad flexing to embrace it, he gently slid the finger out and pushed the head of his cock against the pulsing hole. Again, Chad moaned. He pushed a little further and his head slid in and he rested there so that Chad could relax.

Chad squirmed and pulled away, "I can't."

One day, Mica thought, he'll want my cock.

With a little reconfiguring, they moved into the sixty-nine position and began to mutually suck. Mica tapped a finger lightly on Chad's hole while he slowly stroked

Chad's cock with his tongue. Chad, with no effort at all, swallowed Mica completely and let his tongue dance along the shaft as his lips made a tight grip. Up and down, in and out, their mutual lust heightened.

Mica's head began to drip sweat down on to Chad's crotch and the taste of his flesh with the salty sweat only added to Mica's lust. Chad sensing he didn't want to cum this quickly pulled out and slid Mica down and got a full look at Mica's downy crack and pulsing hole. "My turn," Chad said playfully.

With that, Chad through a pillow down toward Mica's head so he would have something to rest on, got up on his knees, bent over and slid his chamtimi lubed cock inside Mica.

Mica flinched, not ready for that much girth and Chad paused to let Mica get comfortable. "I forget how big you are," Mica muttered through the muffling pillow. "Slowly, do it slowly."

Chad obliged, slowly sliding his cock in and out while sipping on his cocktail. He caught himself in the mirror and the sight of him dominating Mica's ass got him all the more excited. He loved the look of his abdomen muscles flexing as he pushed in and out, harder and harder. Mica moaned the deep moan he utters when Chad hits his stride.

After several minutes, Chad rolled Mica on to his back, never releasing himself from inside and accelerated the pounding. Mica grabbed his own cock and began stroking in rhythm to Chad's thrusting. Chad could tell from Mica's breathing that he was near to release. He pulled out and they stroked together. Within moments they both came. Mica on the flat of his stomach and Chad spewed all the way up to Mica's neck and face.

Mica took his stroking hand and smeared his thick load into his skin and all over his stomach. Chad leaned in and licked from Mica's face and neck. Chad rolled over and lay next to Mica and they panted their exhaustion.

"Can I ask you something?" Mica broke the silence.

"Sure," Chad turned his head to look squarely in Mica's face.

"Why don't you want to get fucked?"

There is a pause and Chad turned away. "I need to feel like the man. Dominant. In control...I guess."

"Do you think I am a big girl for taking it up the ass?" Mica asked, slightly incredulous.

"No not at all. I am not explaining this correctly."

"I know you are very determined and ambitious. And you may have to look like you are in full control when you are out on auditions and whatever. But this, right here, is about letting go and letting me in. This is not a career move."

Nothing comes before my career, Chad thought, especially not a fuck. And then by way of pacifying the situation, Chad turned to Mica. "You never know, one of these days I may surprise you."

"Chamtini?" Mica asked as he noticed Chad was hard again.

7

The usual frenetic morning mayhem is in high gear at the offices of *Drop Zone* and Mica had taken refuge in B.J.'s new office—an office granted to her after a heated moment with Lydia. Recently, during one of her classic Labia incarnations, Lydia went off on B.J. She accused of her of not fully realizing her talents and therefore not doing enough for the show. As a reward or punishment, Lydia handed off a great deal of the day-to-day responsibility to B.J. along with a generous raise for her new-found troubles. B.J., realizing she may actually have the upper hand for a nanosecond, demanded that if she was going to take on more work, she needed a private place to do it. Lydia caved.

Mica liked hiding out in B.J.'s new digs. Evol, the editor, is sequestered behind closed doors of edit bay one working on his latest segment and he knew better than to demand to be in there with her. He wasn't much for small talk with his anchor team—she of the toothy grin and obviously dyed hair, and he of the reputed large dick cockiness, which virtually made him a dick. Besides, B.J. is one of Mica's favorite co-workers at *Drop Zone*—razor sharp and acerbic. She could have Lydia's job, should Lydia ever step down or is struck down with a crowd-pleasing aneurism.

"You are the perfect fag hag. I can tell you anything and you look great on my arm," Mica began.

"Get the fuck over yourself. I am not a fag hag. At worst I am a fruit fly," she said, fluttering her eyes. "But make no mistake, we are friends but your world is not my world," she corrected. No offense taken on either side. This is not the first time they've bantered like this.

Just then B.J. paused from what she was doing, putting the day's show rundown together, and looked squarely at Mica. "Why are you in my office anyway? You have that freshly fucked look about you. Is there something you want to tell me?"

"I found someone." Mica is almost giddy. "At least it feels that way."

"Who? And how long?" B.J. is if nothing else a take no prisoners conversationalist.

"He's an actor."

"Oh God. Didn't we pinky swear over a martini or two that neither of us would ever get caught up with an actor. Is this someone I know?"

"No a newbie...but he is getting some work."

"So what's the attraction here?" she shot back. "Wait, let me guess. He is strikingly handsome with a huge cock?" Mica blushed. "But the bigger question is what does he see in you? A chance to get on television?"

"He doesn't need me for that," Mica confessed. "Besides, can't you be happy for me."

"Well I will say, it is nice to see you getting fucked by some guy rather than being fucked over by some guy," she snickered.

"Cute."

"Okay, so when are we all going out," she intoned an obligation on the horizon.

"Now, that's a good question."

"So what is the problem," she drilled. "I can just tell there is a 'but' dangling out there."

"I am all for being discrete with relationships." Mica exhaled as if he finally had someone to talk to. "But I just get the idea that his career is not only going to be more important that me, but certainly relationships in general."

"Are you telling me that...or trying to explain that to yourself?" Pause. "He's an actor for fuck's sake. What do you expect? Isn't this the very reason we swore we wouldn't go down this path?" She paused to let that sink in. "Now get the fuck out of my office before Labia gets on the warpath looking for this rundown and I find my ass back sharing a cubical with the lovelorn you."

∘ ∘ ∘

Chad is very impressed with the offices at Regis and Canning. He had been used to the cramped, overstuffed, retro office of Albert Switzer and not the glass and ultra-modern spaciousness of this Century City high rise. He feels important just being here. Even the receptionist has a view. He didn't bother to get her name as she was just a minion but then he thought better of it. He figured he would be calling the front desk quite a bit.

"What is your name?" he asked flirtatiously.

"Allie," she whispered coyly.

"I'll have to remember that...if you promise to remember me."

"Michelle is ready for you now," Allie blushed and then instructed Chad where to go.

Mica had orchestrated this meeting with Michelle Bianco and Chad didn't know what to expect. He'd never had a publicist before, never needed to and had been told that the network would handle everything concerning *Divas*, so he wasn't quite sure what this was all about.

Michelle kept her power position behind the desk and was just finishing up a phone call that smacked of being a set up as Chad poked his head in her office. She waved him in as she spoke. Again, Chad is taken by the office space. Even her windowless box impressed him.

"My ten-thirty has just arrived so I have to jump. But suffice it to say, if she is going to wear his clothes, they are going to have to pay an endorsement fee." She hangs up, stands up and reaches her hand forward. "I'm Michelle Bianco."

"Yes...oh...and I am Chad Martin."

They shook hands and Michelle held on just a moment longer than was comfortable. Chad's natural attractiveness and those eyes have already taken her in and she was momentarily thrown off her game. "Where are my manners? Do sit down. Now what can I do for you?"

It is Chad's turn to be thrown, "I am not quite sure."

"That's what I want to hear. Anyone who walks into my office with a preconceived notion of what you expect me to do can turn around and walk right back out of my office," Michelle declared. "I'll tell you what I am going to do for you."

Chad sat back in the chair; instinctively knowing he was in for a long lecture.

"First, we wouldn't be having this meeting if it were not for my good fiend Mica Daly who recommended you highly. And I take recommendations from other professionals very seriously. He obviously sees something promising in you." There is a pause as she thinks for a second. "Just how do *you* know Mica?"

"We met at a party and became friends," Chad explained loosely.

"You're not fucking?" Michelle fired at him jokingly.

Chad clearly is unnerved. "*What?*"

"I get it, you're not. But that is the type of scrutiny a big star has to face. Your private life can be an open book especially with a friendship with someone like Mica. You are guilty by association. And you have to be prepared to be thrown off by the media with questions like that. That's where I come in. I make that kind of stuff stop or I can at least deflect it. And to that point, I guess I should ask...and I am jumping ahead here...but is there anything in your past or present I should know about?"

"No."

As if on cue to her presentation, Michelle got up and came around the desk to sit next to Chad and hold his hand. This is the way she seals the deal, offering to take the young naive client under her protective wing. "Just from this short a conversation, I can tell you have to be groomed and prepped for the world you are about to walk into. Again, that is where I come in."

"Okay," Chad stammered.

"Now, let's talk about your career. Who are you and what have you done?" She already knew the answer to this but wanted to see how he presents himself. Pretty well but unpolished she ascertained as he droned on about his past, his goals and his work on *The Other Brother* and now *Divas*.

"First I want to get you on to some red carpets and magazine covers. We want to establish you as the hot new thing. I can work with the network on some of this but you also have to understand I am working toward your career goals and the network is only going to be interested in what makes that series a success. So there is a lot I want to do to form the bigger picture."

"So you want to represent me?" This is all moving very fast for Chad and even between Michelle's verbal strafing he likes what he is hearing.

"Of course I will take you on. I can sell your looks to a blind audience." She laughed at her own joke and continued. "I going to assume at this point that your talent can match your looks but fuck it, this is Hollywood, a good face trumps talent any day." She smacks him on the knee as if to indicate they are already at a familiar place in their relationship. "By the way, fire your existing agent."

"Albert? Why?"

"You mean Albert who? This guy is a nobody. I had to Google the guy to know who the hell he is. That is not good. You need an agent who, just by naming in him in a meeting, people fear your power. I will set that up for you."

"I don't..."

"You don't get a say. This is what we do here; we make careers at Regis and Canning. The next thing is, I want you to get a good trainer. I see you are in good shape but I want you in great shape. You have a boyishness to you and you need to become a man. Every waking minute that you are not on set, you'd better be in the gym. There is nothing like the paparazzi getting a shirtless shot of you coming out of the gym. Gold."

"I have already done a nude scene."

"Excuse me?"

"In *The Other Brother...*"

"That is not going to happen again without my say so. You have to be careful of that kind of exploitation."

"It's been shelved."

"Thank God!"

"I guess I should ask what is this all going to cost?" he asked cautiously.

"It is not a cost. It is an investment," she lowered her voice to close the deal, 'sincerely'. "Yes there is a retainer but it is what we call the necessary expenditures of doing business in this town. I will send over a contract and it will all take care of itself. Do you have a lawyer?" She rolls her eyes, "Of course you don't. I am going to recommend Lance Novak from Dunning, Baker and Astin."

"I've met him," Chad interjected enthusiastically, finally having something to contribute that she wasn't dictating.

"Great. I bet he liked you!" She winked. "And speaking of that. There will be no love life for you for the conceivable future. We will set up dates and appearances with the right gals. We need you to look like a Hollywood player that all the ladies are swooning over and you have your pick of the litter." She paused, and again with that Hollywood 'sincerity' leaned in. "You know if you are ever stuck for a dinner companion or whatever, I can always make myself available."

Michelle is notorious for hitting on her handsome clients. And her affair with one Oscar nominated Lothario once represented by the firm ended so badly, she almost lost her job. But that doesn't stop her from trying.

Chad is caught between verbal intoxication and being overwhelmed by everything Michelle was spewing forth. He likes what he hears but can't wrap his head around the magnitude of what she is promising. His eyes are beginning to glaze over and Michelle can sense she has done enough for a first meeting.

"Look," she began as she stood, "I know this is a lot to take in. But I think this is going to be a great relationship. You are going to be a big star. There is no doubt. You just have to let me do what I do best." He nods like a child being taught a life lesson. "Now, I have a lunch with Suzy Chambers across town so I have to get a move on."

Michelle escorts Chad to the door and then stops. She's had a brilliant idea. "Let me set you up with Suzy Chambers. Dinner. I'll arrange it and call the paparazzi in to catch you coming and going. Now, there's a headline." She kisses him on the cheek rather inappropriately and sends him out the door with all the confidence that she has her first two clients for what will eventually become Michelle Bianco and Associates.

∘ ∘ ∘

"So I have signed with Regis and Canning," Chad announces to a dumbfounded Anthony. Anthony had just come from the gym across the street and is exhausted. So he was hardly ready for a bombshell like this.

It had taken several days for Chad to process all that was said in that Century

City high rise, which houses the offices of Regis and Canning. After a long conversation with Mica, during which Chad did not go into Michelle's dating policy or the lack there of, and some real soul searching, he believed everything Michelle had told him to be correct and in his best interest. He knew there would be no good time to have a conversation about moving on to a bigger, more prestigious agency, but he felt the best plan of advancement would be a conversation with Anthony.

They sat at the counter off to the side in what is known as 'the big gay coffeehouse' on Santa Monica in West Hollywood. Chad didn't want to meet there—too gay for his new image that will be carefully crafted by Michelle Bianco.

"When did this happen? No, better yet, how did this happen?" Anthony asked between gulps of his Chai iced tea.

"I'm a friend of Mica Daly, the reporter from *Drop Zone*."

"I know who Mica Daly is. And what do you mean you are 'friends'?"

"He's a friend of mine," Chad defended, "I know he is gay but we are just friends. Anyway, he introduced me to Michelle Bianco at Regis and Canning. They have great things planned for me."

"Well, I have to say," Anthony admitted, "this is good news for all that is happening in your career. Have you told Albert yet?"

"Well..."

"You have to tell Albert, Chad," Anthony cautioned. "He is your agent."

"I wanted to run all this by you first."

Just as the intensity was rising, some queen sauntered up and put his arm around Anthony. "Who's your friend?"

"This is..." Anthony began and was cut off by Chad.

"I'm Bob and if you don't mind we are in a bit of an important conversation." In another place, another time, Chad would have been flattered by the attention. But this is the new Chad, the star Chad Martin. The pushy queen sauntered off in a huff.

"Bob?" Anthony questioned with a roll of his eyes.

"Can we go somewhere else?" Chad pleaded.

"We're here now," Anthony dismissed. "Besides I am all sweaty from the gym. But enough of that, why haven't you told Albert."

"It has been suggested," Chad began sheepishly, "that I drop Albert for a bigger agency."

Anthony's jaw dropped. Chad Martin is one of those once in a lifetime clients for an agent like Albert Switzer. Chad has star trajectory and it has been Albert's hard work, or better yet Anthony and Albert's hard work, which has launched Chad on this path. Albert has been feeling energized and rejuvenated because of Chad and the future he has. And there has even been talk of a partnership for Anthony. Chad is a magnet for the agency to attract other potential stars. If he leaves the agency, there may not be an agency and certainly no future for Anthony.

Anthony broke from the haze and shock and grabbed his bag. "I can't talk about this now. Albert has gotten you the two biggest roles of your fledgling nothing of a career. And now when its about to pay off for all of us, you drop the agency. There is something called loyalty, Chad, look it the fuck up if you can spell it. You may be pretty but you are not the brightest bulb if this is the way you are going to treat people who have nothing but your best interests at heart."

Anthony stormed off, somewhat regretting that rant. He knew if Chad was on the fence, he might just have pushed him in the wrong direction. But Anthony is hurt, for Albert and himself.

The attack was just a bit harsh for Chad to take. A tear welled in his eye, which he wiped away with all the determination of wiping away anything that will hold him back. Michelle Bianco could see he is going to be a star and the only way to get to the big time is to play in the big leagues. Little Albie Switzer has never been in the big leagues.

o o o

Across town at Cecconi's on Melrose and Robertson, Lydia pulled up in her prized Bentley and threw the keys at the valet. "If you could just keep that up front," she asked by way of demanding. She wanted everyone to see her enter and exit in a Bentley. What is the point of having one if you can't flaunt it? She is just about ten minutes late for her long overdue dinner with Michelle Bianco. Ten minutes is just enough time for Michelle to fume.

Cecconi's is one of those 'see and be seen', flavor of the month, star havens Lydia loves. This, the third such haven incarnation for this spot, having most notably been Morton's, the sight of Oscar night's biggest star packed party. Despite her being just a television producer and despite the fact that her show is just an entertainment news series, Lydia believes that because she profiles stars, she is equal to them. She couldn't be more wrong. And everyone knows it, except for Lydia. Unfortunately for Lydia, there is not a star to be seen in Cecconi's at the moment— no one for her to accidently bump into.

They air kissed when they arrived and were sat in one of the more desirable tables out front. Lydia, who strangely doesn't drink—a control issue—ordered a sparkling water and Michelle a Manhattan.

"This is lovely," Lydia spoke first.

"And about time," Michelle countered.

These are two broads who act more like two cats, circling and hissing. In any other world they would not even be friends; they are too much alike. But in this world of Hollywood, they need each other to feed their mutual beasts. Lydia needs access to the stars and Michelle needs access to the media. Thus the air kisses and Hollywood 'sincerity'.

"The show looks great, never better." Michelle hoisted her cocktail in a toast.

"Thank you. It's a vision that I've made happen," Lydia accepted selfishly, as if she is a one-man band of a production entity. As Mica put it sarcastically once, Lydia radiates modesty. "But we are always looking for fresh ideas."

"I am glad you said that because your Mica Daly has been a doll lately in talking to me about putting my clients into your 'fresh faces' segments. He's even turned me on to my latest client. So I have put together a short list of clients I can give you immediate access to."

Lydia looked at the list. "Suzy Chambers! Of course we would love to do a piece on Suzy Chambers." She ticked off the next three names with an "Uh-huh." And then, "Who the fuck is Chad Martin?"

"He's my latest. He's just been cast as the hunky boy-toy, playing opposite Gina Hamilton, the cougar in *Divas*." Michelle pulls out her cell phone and shows Lydia the studio approved publicity shot of Chad. "Trust me when I tell you he has star quality and is going to be huge."

"He is gorgeous," Lydia gasps. "I think a set visit to *Divas* is in order." That is music to Michelle's ears. "And you say Mica Daly turned him on to you?"

Lydia's head is beginning to spin, futilely trying to connect the dots between Mica and hunky Chad. Her gaydar is piqued. But before any salacious innuendo could spew forth, Michelle dropped a bomb.

"I am not supposed to say anything," she whispered teasingly. "But I think there is something brewing between Chad and Suzy. I already know they're having dinner together...and well...wouldn't they make the perfect 'IT' couple?"

"Something to keep an eye on," Lydia salivated for a scoop, burying any previous thoughts about Chad and Mica. "How can we get the exclusive on that?"

"Well, I think we are all playing in the same sandbox," Michelle purred. "And I think we can share our toys." They clinked glasses.

And just as Michelle gained the upper hand in this media chess match, in walks her client Sean Jones—the Welsh film star Americans know from a PBS series and period dramas and most recently *The Devil Made Me Do It* and who is currently becoming a sensation playing a comic book hero in a trilogy of movies.

"Sean, darling," Michelle cooed as she called him over. "Surely you know Lydia Gray from *Drop Zone?*" Before anyone can answer, Michelle continued, "if not then shame on me for not putting you two together."

"It is a pleasure Ms. Gray." The words seemed absolutely poetic with that lilting Welsh accent, so hidden on the screen.

"Lydia, please, call me Lydia," she uncharacteristically purred girlishly. "Perhaps we need to do a profile on you Sean. You know the man behind the spandex. Something like that."

He winced undetectably to the women at the table and then smiled. "You will of course have to talk to Michelle here." Michelle relished in the thought of being the star's gatekeeper in the eyes of Lydia Gray.

o o o

Later that evening, Chad and Mica had sex. Loud, angry, sex. Chad had been sitting waiting for Mica, letting Anthony's words churn in his head, frustrating and upsetting him. When Mica walked through the door, without saying a word he pounced, ripping off Mica's shirt and tearing at his pants. Mica went with it.

Still in the living room with his shirt nearly off and his pants around his ankles, Mica was flipped around by Chad and bent over. With spit for lubricant, Chad rammed his cock inside Mica. Mica's screams of pain were muffled by Chad's cupped hand.

"I love you," Chad shouted as he came deep inside Mica and then started to cry. "I love you but I can't."

In the name of love, Mica had been raped. But neither would call it that.

8

Mica has been on plenty of movie and television sets and they are always the same, elaborately decorated and surrounded by what always appears like too many lights and equipment and even more crew sitting around, collecting union checks and doing seemingly nothing. But the set of *Divas* is different. It is mammoth. Seven houses on a purpose built street on the back lot of one of Hollywood's most historic studios. Each house represents the house of a main character and within each house is a fully functional, fully furnished home. No soundstages for this production, rather an actual neighborhood. Impressive, even to the jaded, set weary Mica.

Divas had already premiered to great critical reviews and strong network backing. Three episodes had aired by the time Lydia pulled the trigger and okayed the profile on Chad Martin. Lydia, always the pragmatist, wanted to make sure the show was a hit and that *Drop Zone* wasn't seen shilling for a dud. Michelle Bianco was less than pleased with the delay but knew that delay would mean at least three solid minutes of a profile on the highest rated entertainment show in the world. She greeted Mica on to the set with the full V.I.P. carte blanche, or as much as is within her parameters.

"First we are going to shoot some B-roll," she instructed the crew. "We will have plenty of time to set up for the interview so don't worry about that right at this moment. What is important right now is the scene we are about to shoot. Chad will be shirtless in a pair of swim trunks cleaning the pool." She was almost giddy in describing the scene. "Mica, wait to you see Chad shirtless. This is no eye candy. This is star meat!"

"Really." Mica said. If she only knew.

She flicked her hand in the direction of one house, indicating where the crew should go, " The director of photography is Derek and he knows you are coming. He'll let you know where you can and can't be."

"Do you think I could say hi to Chad before we start," Mica asked Michelle.

"Well I don't ordinarily let reporters meet with the star..." she began.

"Michelle, I knew him before you did. He is your client because of me. I just want to say hi."

"Oh my God, of course Mica." Michelle as of late has been bombarded with requests for interviews. Three episodes into this show and she is handling the on-slaught of demand of a bona fide star in the making. Even by her standards, it has been overwhelming. "You have to forgive me. This is exactly why I wanted to do this earlier. The demand on his time is incredible."

She didn't have to tell Mica how unavailable Chad is becoming. Between shooting and publicity and the bullshit 'dates' he has been going on to create his hunk image, they barely see each other except for an occasional dinner at Mica's place and a hit and run fuck. Although, in that department, Mica is almost more turned on when Chad returns from some made up date, all hot and horny, and they fuck passionately for hours. In that department things have been great. But even that has a 'quality of time over quantity of time' issue since Chad rented that glass walled home in the 'bird streets'—named for different bird species—above Sunset.

"Let me see if he is okay," Michelle cautioned as they approached Chad's trailer. Michelle is one for the melodramatic, especially when she thinks she is in charge on the set.

She knocked. And through the closed door heard, "Come in." She entered and found Chad in nothing but a towel.

"Chad, darling," she planted two kisses, one on each cheek, as she spoke, "I have Mica Daly outside, but if this is not a good time..."

"No, let him come in." With that, Chad leapt to his feet, which loosened his towel and give Michelle a good glance at his ass. He tightened the towel and opened the door for Mica. "Mica, good to see you again. How have you been?"

"Great," Mica returned with an innocuous fist pump.

Chad looked at Michelle and indicated she could leave them alone. Michelle smiled, "of course". And made her way back out of the trailer. As much as Michelle is aware that Mica and Chad knew each other before she and Chad established a professional relationship, she finds it uncomfortable to leave any client alone with a reporter of any sort.

As soon as Michelle stepped out, they kissed. "I wish I had time for you to blow me," Chad whispered hungrily, but both of them knew Chad is not one of those three-minute suck and run kind of guys. Chad has incredible staying power. Chad waved open his towel knowing full well that just the sight of his dick is enough to turn on Mica. "It would be cool to have someone blow me in my own star trailer."

Mica just rolled his eyes. "No thanks, I don't need you ruining *my* makeup!"

There was a pause during which they both stared at each other and then Mica spoke first, "I miss you."

"I know, me too. But just look at all this. It's everything I've dreamed about."

Mica sighed and nodded his approval. He knows that if they stand any chance of staying together, he has to allow for a moment or two of Chad's selfishness. Eventually none of this will seem special, just work, and then Chad will come around.

"Now listen," Mica began, "When we do the interview I am not going to embarrass you or lead you down and uncomfortable path."

"You have to ask me about dating Suzy Chambers," Chad shot back.

Mica is taken aback, he isn't thinking about this made up relationship in terms of 'dating'. "Okay."

The awkwardness of the moment is broken up by a knock on the door. Some production assistant announced that they need Chad on the set and Michelle quickly followed up with, "Mica, we need to let Chad work."

Chad dropped his towel and pulled on a pair of board shorts.

"Aren't you going to put on underwear," Mica asked protectively.

"Nah, I want the camera to see *all* my assets without actually seeing *all* my assets. If you know what I mean."

Unfortunately, Mica knew exactly what he meant and he wasn't sure if he should be proud or jealous.

° ° °

The set visit was a great success. Chad's shirtless scene and his playing around for Mica's camera was great exclusive footage with just enough boyish playfulness and manly sex appeal. The interview went better than even Mica had expected. The two of them acted like old friends and, in no way, indicated there was anything more between them. Mica also interviewed the director, executive producers and even his cougar, co-star, Gina Hamilton, all of whom had nothing but praise for the newcomer Chad's natural abilities and his hunky image.

Michelle Bianco could not have been more pleased, except for the moment after the interview when Mica went up to Chad to allegedly thank him. If she didn't know better, she would swear they were about to kiss. Mica's face was unnaturally close to Chad and from her vantage point it looked like Mica had brushed his hand against Chad's chest.

But she knew better. According to Suzy Chambers, Chad is very into her—information that only made Michelle pang with a little jealousy. She can see herself with Chad and theirs being one of those Hollywood relationships that could actually last—she the brains and he the beauty.

She thought for a moment. If Mica is really interested in Chad that only proves

Chad's wide sexual appeal that will put asses in seats. She is by no means offering up Chad as a gay poster child but what she is quickly realizing is that Chad can't also be locked with Suzy Chambers. He has to play the field and play it big. She'll get to work on that.

∘ ∘ ∘

Lydia, with B.J. just behind her, barged her way into Evol's edit bay—another hair on fire moment. She wants to see the segment on Chad Martin and moreover wants to see the raw footage. Lydia had gotten a call from Michelle Bianco from the set who had nothing but glowing praise for Mica and stated that she had never seen a star react so comfortably to an interview in her career. And that got Lydia to wondering just what went on, on that back lot. Evol is not one to be messed with but Lydia Gray is, after all, the executive producer and calls the shots. Evol, of course, obliged but she is on deadline and not very happy.

There were two cameras and Lydia is as interested in the one on Mica as she is with the one recording Chad. But just what is she looking for? Both cameras showed playfulness and a willingness to answer all Mica's questions which seem comprehensive for a simple profile piece.

Evol shuttled through the B-roll and Chad dutifully took off his shirt after Mica goaded him. He even did a promo: "Hi, I am Chad Martin from *Divas*...Get the real 'skinny' on my life only on *Drop Zone*."

Lydia was nearly sated until she noticed the camera kept rolling as Mica approached Chad after the promo. It looked as if Mica reached out and touched Chad, in more than a familiar way as if Mica had put his hand on Chad's chest. In reality he tweaked Chad's nipple but mercifully he had his back to the camera, thereby blocking the action.

"Is camera two still running?" Lydia asked impatiently.

"Yes," Evol barked growing impatient herself at the apparent waste of time.

Camera two was focused on Mica's now empty seat but held the microphone taping of Mica's voice. "What did he say?" Lydia barked.

"I'll talk to you later." Chad's voice bled through on to Mica's microphone. "I have to get back to the set."

"What did he mean by that?" Lydia asked to no one in particular.

"Maybe, they just hit it off," B.J. interjected. "They are friends too, remember. They've met socially. That can only be good for the show. You are always asking, 'How do we become better friends with the stars so they will give us better access?' Well, there you have it." Even B.J. feels Lydia is overreacting.

"Did he ask Chad about his relationship with Suzy Chambers?" Lydia directed that to Evol.

Without saying a word, Evol found the place on the tape where Chad answered somewhat evasively, "Suzy and I have just begun a close friendship. Who knows where that will lead?" And then he winked at the camera.

"Make sure that is in the piece," Lydia directed, "along with the footage from that night they had dinner. Do we have any other shots of them on the town?"

"We have some red carpet shots and then some paparazzi footage of them coming out from club." B.J. stated.

"Good put it all in." Lydia demanded.

No one but B.J. would have the balls to ask, but clearly there is an elephant in the room. "Lydia, what the fuck is all this about? Mica did a good job. Michelle Bianco is clearly happy with the shoot. Chad Martin is now a friend of the show. And who knows what kind of access we are going to get with Suzy Chambers. You're acting like there is some sort of smoking gun to find."

"Is there?" Lydia asked indignantly, got up and walked out.

∘ ∘ ∘

A nondescript bungalow just on the edge of the Norma Triangle off of Santa Monica in West Hollywood houses Body Image, a private gym. Chad had made an appointment a couple of days ago to tour and maybe take a first workout if he likes what he sees. He is booked with Tommy.

Chad, who had heard about Body Image and Tommy Mercer in particular, from a rather buff stunt man on the set. His biggest recommendation is their discretion; you can literally book the entire place, just you and your trainer, and workout alone. It's not cheap but these days Chad is hardly worried about money.

Chad arrived in his new white Range Rover Sport, with its saddle interior and heavily tinted windows, precisely on time for their two o'clock meeting. Tommy opened the door for Chad and Chad did a double take. Tommy Mercer is well built, needless to say for a trainer, but had boyish good looks that reminded him somewhat of himself. He suddenly understood what Michelle Bianco said to him at the first meeting, about shedding his boyish looks and becoming a man.

Tommy Mercer grew up a thug who managed to beat the streets and a potential life in the system by hiding out—his words—in the neighborhood gym. With no real discipline from his home life, he found the routine of working out provided him the much-needed discipline lacking in his life, and more importantly, he found a role model in a boxer/trainer named "Sweet Louie" Ray. Sweet Louie taught him that strength and power were just part of the package but that poise, respect and manners were just as important. After a chance centerfold in *Playgirl* got him some attention across town with a couple of casting agents, his ability to act like a gentleman allowed him to move in Hollywood circles. The acting thing never worked out, but some stunt work did which lead to training work with some of the stars for whom he doubled. Within two years, Tommy Mercer was the trainer to the stars.

Tommy shook Chad's hand with both of his and Chad instantly noticed a wedding band and a wave of disappointment washed over him. It is probably better anyway, less distraction. Tommy, for his part, knows Chad is an actor but had not seen an episode of "Divas" and really has no idea who he is.

The windows of the entire bungalow were shaded, those inside could see out but those outside couldn't see in. As requested the place was empty of anyone except the two of them and an impressive array of state of the art workout equipment. Universal trainers in what would be the living room, weights in the dining room, aerobics in one of the bedrooms, yoga in another of the bedrooms, the kitchen worked as a snack or break room and in the walled back yard a wrestling/boxing ring. There is a casita, formerly the garage, which has been renovated to house the office space. It is all meticulously clean and more than adequate for Chad's needs.

"Impressive," Chad commented when they finished the tour. "But why the boxing ring."

"Kick boxing is very popular these days," Tommy explained in a rather matter of fact tone. "We also train a lot of MMA athletes. And I personally like to wrestle."

"Wrestle?"

"I'll get you into it yet," Tommy joked and gave Chad a slap on the back. "So do you want to give any of the equipment a try? See what I can do for you?"

"Ah, yeah I think so. I brought workout gear. Just need to know where I can get changed."

Tommy laughed a bit.

"What?"

"Well you can get changed in the bathroom which has an oversized shower stall and all the amenities. But you have rented this place out. You can drop your pants right here and it wouldn't matter. It is just you and I."

"Good to know. Let me get my stuff out of the car."

Chad left to get his gym bag out of the Range Rover parked just in front. While gone, Tommy took the liberty of replacing his polo shirt with a string tank top and slid out of his long pants and was about to pull up a pair of shorts when

Chad reentered. The sight of Tommy's muscular bare ass startled and pleased Chad. Clearly Tommy liked to go commando when he works out.

"Sorry," Chad muttered, apologizing for catching Tommy in the act.

"Don't worry about it. You should know we even have clients who work out naked, because they have forgotten their gear or just because they like to. Naked yoga is very popular. People like to look at themselves in the mirror."

"Of course they do. This is Hollywood." Chad shot back. "I may work up to that."

"No problem, I'm here to service your needs. You just tell me what you want."

Chad chuckled as he made his way to the spa like bathroom and proceeded to change. Once fully naked, he couldn't help but to look at himself in the full-length mirror. He is already in good shape but as Michelle Bianco told him, "you need to be in great shape." He slipped on the new jock strap, black, that Mica had bought him for other reasons than the gym and adjusted his penis to make a perfectly cupped bulge. After pulling on shorts, a tee and his shoes, he is ready for Tommy.

They started with some stretches. Facing the mirror in the aerobic room and sitting with legs spread wide, they bent over one leg at a time and down toward the middle. Each time Chad leaned over his left leg and faced Tommy, he could just see the tip of Tommy's penis exposing itself up the leg of his shorts. Chad had to stop staring.

That proved easier said than done when they began the weight training. As Chad lay on the bench with the bar bell weights suspended over his chest, Tommy is spotting—straddled across Chad and lightly holding the bar to make sure that he is able to complete the lift and the bar doesn't fall on Chad's chest. To get a good position to spot the bar, Tommy is straddling over Chad's face. Chad can easily see up the leg of Tommy's shorts and is staring at the dangling package. It is quite impressive. Chad is grateful he wore a jock, so his dick wouldn't spring to action by the sight.

"You shave," Chad blurted out accidently. It is what he is thinking; he just wasn't supposed to say it out loud. Shit!

"What?" Tommy was thrown and placed the bar back on its holder for safety. "Oh shit, I didn't mean to stick my dick in your face."

"No, no, I didn't mean to be looking," Chad countered.

"It's just that we are so carefree around here, like I said, no one thinks twice about being naked. Girls with girls, guys and girls and guys together...no one cares."

This all seems more than a little flirtatious to Chad, but what the hell. "Hey if you would be more comfortable naked, don't let me stop you."

"It is what you are comfortable with," Tommy corrected. But I will say, when I wrestle with some clients, naked is pretty good. They laughed.

"I bet."

"And to your observation, yes I do," Tommy added.

"Do what?"

"Shave." With that, Tommy pulled down his shorts to just above the penis base to reveal a silky smooth pubic area. But more to Chads interest are the pelvic muscles leading to the area.

"I want that," Chad said innocently enough, pointing to the muscles.

"My dick?" He asked with surprise and then winked. "I'm married."

"No those muscles," Chad corrected, although his dick is very tempting.

"We can definitely work on that. Do you mind if I see where we're starting from?" Tommy asked professionally.

"I don't know how well I can show you, I am wearing a jock." Chad, no stranger to being naked, just shrugged his shoulders and pulled down the shorts and jock, revealing his pelvis and primed but not hard cock.

Tommy walked over, took Chad's hand and placed it on his pelvis area and began to flex that area of muscles. "Do you feel that?"

Chad's cock began to twitch slightly. "Yeah."

"That's what I need you to achieve. Now you try it." Tommy reached over and laid his hand on Chad's pelvis. The more Chad flexed or attempted to flex, the more his cock jumped. "We'll work on that."

"Sorry," Chad apologized and cupped his cock. "I am rather sensitive."

"There is nothing to be embarrassed about, it's just guy stuff. People get hard around here all the time," Tommy dismissed. "Workouts can be very sensual. That is why I want you to know that what happens here, stay's here."

"That's good. I am all about discretion these days."

The two hours had flown by and, amid the obvious and subtle flirtations, a tough workout had taken place. Chad felt good about his new trainer Tommy and booked as many sessions as he could, working around his shooting schedule with *Divas*.

"This is going to be great," Tommy announced as he pulled off his tank top and started to wipe himself off with a towel. "Are you going to take a shower?" Chad shook his head no. "Then you don't mind if I do?" Again, Chad shook his head.

Having headed back to his car, Chad realized he had left his gym bag back and his clothes back in the bathroom. He came back into the bungalow and headed for the bathroom but could hear the shower running. He knocked cautiously. "Tommy, it's Chad. I've left my things in there."

"I noticed that...come on in."

Tommy turned off the water and leaned out of the glass stall covered in soap and semi-hard. Chad couldn't help but to be impressed with Tommy's very smooth, hairless body now that it is wet and glistening. "Sorry, I should have left them outside the door."

"No problem, sorry to bother you." Chad scurried over and busily got his things together.

"No bother."

When Chad turned to leave, Tommy had stepped out of the shower and was standing somewhat in the way. "Are you sure you don't want to shower. There is plenty of room and I can wash your back."

There was a pause and then Chad, not breaking eye contact with Tommy, put his things down. As Chad kicked off his shoes and pulled off his tee shirt, Tommy, as if to send a message, slipped off his wedding ring and placed it by the sink. "Now, I guess I am really naked."

But the message may have been the wrong message. Chad couldn't get past the ring. It is so small and yet it is like a beacon, pleading with Chad to not go there. It wasn't so much that Tommy is married, but the first time Chad felt he too had a relationship to protect.

"Look, I have a tight schedule," Chad lied. "I really have to get going."

"Sure thing," Tommy returned.

They both knew there would be other days, other times and other chances.

9

Ovation, the restaurant taken over by the owners of Michael's on La Cienega, Scott and Brian, opened to great success. The existing restaurant had already been considered gay friendly and so it was no great socio-dynamic pilgrimage to get the old clientele to the new location. It was the fact that the gays would actually cross town, some forty-five minutes in traffic, to leave the comfort of the two square miles of 'boys town' in West Hollywood to create a home away from home in Los Feliz. But they had.

Outside on his cell phone, Roger Keenan is getting the news he had hoped for—the resurrection of *The Other Brother.* He had been contracted to do the marketing for the film but back in its infancy. And at the time of the production, there was little to market. Three no-named leads hardly made a movie poster worth looking at. That was until Chad Martin had become a shirtless wonder on *Divas* and the focus of, certainly American, but thanks to syndication, worldwide audiences. Suddenly, this little sleeper, questionably acted, nothing of a film, has the potential of being a blockbuster and it's star, a star.

Inside, at the table for two situated in the dead center of the room, the table of choice, Mica sits drumming his fingers and nursing a second martini. They, he and Roger, had ordered their food so a second martini seems hardly decadent—more like a necessary. Chad's newfound popularity was playing on his and Mica's relationship. It's not like they weren't having sex and seeing each other, schedules permitting, as often as possible. But it seems Mica is working harder at this relationship than Chad.

Or maybe it is just paranoia on Mica's part. Who knows? But this choice of restaurant is a perfect example. If Chad didn't already have a meeting tonight, Mica is not sure Chad would have even wanted to join him and Roger—"too gay", he would say. What the fuck is too gay? It is a rhetorical question, as Mica knew the answer. But Mica is on television too and he can eat at a popular restaurant without brandishing it a gay mecca and therefore off limits.

Roger returned to the table just as the food arrived. Duck, Mica's favorite, which was chosen off the new selections on the fused menu, is placed in front of him. Meatloaf, a mediocre but crowd favorite that made it across town from the old restaurant and onto the menu of the new, is placed in front of Roger. Roger signaled for two more drinks. That would make three so far.

"Good call?" Mica questioned knowing that Roger would never have participated in the social disgrace of taking a call when entertaining a dinner partner unless it was important.

"You are going to know soon enough," he began and took a large and final swig from his glass. "That was Spectrum Studios. In light of Chad's overnight success, they are going to release *The Other Brother.*"

"That's fantastic!" was Mica's first reaction.

"Is it?"

"What do you mean?" Mica questioned with genuine intrigue.

"Well are you ready for you boyfriend to become an international sensation?" The crook of his eyebrow and the concerned look over his glasses indicated that Roger wasn't kidding.

"Oh come on," Mica dismissed, "we both know that script is not Shakespeare!"

"Don't be naïve, it's hardly the dialogue that people will go to see."

"So?" Mica asked, sort of defensively. He is proud to be the partner of a hot stud. Everyone should see what he gets to suck on.

"I am marketing this film. And don't for a second think we aren't going to market his cock in as overt a way as possible," Roger cautioned.

"Again, so?"

"Can your relationship hold up under the scrutiny of Chad becoming a sex symbol?" Roger grilled. "The bottom line is, the studio is going to throw a lot of money at this film. I know because I stand to take a great deal of it. And they are not marketing a faggot on film. They are marketing what every woman wants and what every man wants to be. And that is one hundred percent U.S. prime heterosexual. I wouldn't be surprised if they are rewriting his contract with decency—read no scandal—clauses as we speak."

"Your paranoia is duly noted," Mica dismissed, thankful that another Kettle One martini has arrived. But Mica isn't as confident on the inside. He already knows what life has morphed into since his success on *Divas* and it a legitimate question as to how the next phase of fame will affect them as a couple.

"So how are things between you two?" Roger pried, again looking over his very chic Oliver Peeples reading glasses propped ever so precariously on the edge of his nose—his signature look.

"Actually better than you would think," Mica began spinning. "I mean Chad is confused as to how to approach his new success and is, I will admit, questioning how to fit us in that picture. But for me, it is so exciting to see the birth of his success. He has wanted it for so long and now has it."

"So long? He is in his early twenties. People wait decades for success, he hasn't been alive for decades yet." Roger paused to let that sink in, took a swig from his own cocktail and continued, "I would like you two to come to Palm Springs, schedules permitting and let's talk. I have seen this scenario play out before and papa may just have a parable or two to bestow."

Mica patted his hand, thankful that someone in this town actually cares about something other than their own success and the casualties that result because of it. Perhaps a weekend away and some clarity of a plan is just what the doctor ordered.

∘ ∘ ∘

Chad pulled off Doheny, drove through the gate and into the bowels of the high rise across from one of the most prestigious condo buildings in Los Angeles— the condo building where Lydia Gray happens to live along with plenty of other talked about stars.

The penthouse of this particular building houses the members only London club—one in the international chain of British based, jet-set, A-list, havens where stars supposedly can let their hair down and be themselves without the prying eyes of the media. Chad is not a member but rather a guest of Sterling Lowe, the über agent from IMC—International Management Cooperative.

IMC recently merged with two other smaller boutique agencies, hence the word 'Cooperative' in the title, and moved into a glass atrocity of a building on Rodeo Drive in Beverly Hills and became what can only be referred to as the 'only game in town' when it comes to artist representation. Their client list reads like the phone book of A-List actors, directors, producers and writers. If it weren't for his own 'cocksure' self-image, Chad would have pissed himself on the way up in the elevator. But this is the big time and Chad can, and will, rise to the occasion.

Off the elevator and up the grandiose staircase that leads to the second floor above the private dining rooms, Chad arrives in the lounge, a too many thousand square foot living room of a place with a central bar and wrap around deck. The restaurant is behind him, but no one said anything about dinner. So he wasn't about to look back there. And the one thing Chad never likes is to look like a lost tourist in a room where everyone knows why they are there. He stops for a moment to take in the scene and quickly spotted Michelle Bianco, Lance Novak and some guy he doesn't recognize—presumably Sterling Lowe.

With purpose, he made his way toward their sitting area but not without passing supermodel Gretchen Howe who smiled his way, those sister tennis phenoms who it is rumored are being courted to act, and the lesbian comedienne Sarah Small.

Michelle greeted Chad first with a strong, slightly awkward hug, and forced kisses on both cheeks. "Welcome to the big leagues," she whispered in his ear and then introduced her drink-mates.

Lance he knew but they shook hands as if theirs was the first meeting.

It is pull-no-punches, time-is-money, Sterling Lowe that struck him as strikingly handsome in that preppy off-putting way. Not that he is aware of such things normally, but thanks to his recent education from the wardrobe people on set, even Chad took a double take at Sterling's look—a three thousand dollar Prada suit for sure, Brioni loafers and an Hermes tie. This guy is the real deal, thought Chad as he sat down to waiting champagne.

"We thought we would start with a celebration," Michelle began.

"What are we celebrating?" Chad inquired as he picked up his glass to toast.

"A couple of things," Michelle continued. "First, your new agent, Sterling Lowe of IMC."

Glasses clinked and sips sipped before Chad could process.

"You do know I have an agent," Chad choked before Michelle can go on.

"Had," Lance announced. "I have drafted papers to extricate yourself from ASS."

"ASA," Chad corrected.

"Says you," Lance rebutted to everyone's amusement and a muted laugh. Chad momentarily felt bad.

Sterling, with an already receding hairline, yet not much more than a decade older than Chad but world's wiser, leaned over to shake Chad's hand. "We, and I can speak for everyone and the vast resource that is IMC, are happy to have you with us."

Chad awkwardly thanked him and gulped from his glass in lieu of having to say anything. And then, "By the way, did anyone else see Gretchen?" Smiles indicated yes and that no one cared.

"Sterling has news," Michelle returned focus.

Chad leaned in to hear what was little more than a stage whisper coming from Sterling. "Good news! *The Other Brother* is coming out of mothballs and is going into wide release." Chad can't believe his ears. "Based on your success with *Divas*, Spectrum Studios thinks they have a hit on their hands."

Chad just sat their dumbfounded.

"And this is the part you should like," Sterling continued. "There was a clause in your then contract that rendered it null and void after a certain time period—a time period that has lapsed..."

"Are you ready for this?" Michelle interjected nearly ruining Sterling's moment. Chad still sat numb.

"We, on your behalf, with your lawyer's proxy..."

"You signed that in my office," Lance clarified.

"I did?" Lance nodded. Chad no longer knew where to focus but was drawn back into Sterling's announcement.

"...have renegotiated your contract. There's a pittance more upfront money, two hundred and fifty thousand dollars, but you will be getting ten percent of the gross."

There is a pause when everyone expected Chad to react. But there was nothing. Chad is simply stunned. "But I have an agent."

"Had," the trio chimed and again waited for a reaction.

After what seemed like forever, Chad lifted his glass to toast. "Here's to ten percent. If there is ever a time that we should hope that size matters, this is it."

None of the three having seen the film or even outtakes get that reference at the moment. But they will. Chad simply smiled knowing what they don't—if being shirtless is getting him this much attention, being naked should be a God damned sensation. And he is about to get ten percent of the frenzy.

"By the way," Lance interjected, "I have some business of my own." With that, he dropped a document the size of the phone book on to the glass-topped coffee table. It landed with a thud.

"What is that," Chad asked innocently enough.

"That is your employee contract," Lance clarified. "Basically, anyone on your payroll must sign this manifesto, which states how to behave, what is expected of them and lastly guarantees confidentiality."

"But I don't have any employees."

"Yet," Michelle jumped in. "It is just a matter of time before you have an assistant for instance."

"I did hire a new trainer," Chad mentioned in passing.

Lance sat up. "That is a perfect example of someone who must sign this document. God only knows what you will talk about while you're training. That is a variable we don't want. He signs this or he is fired. Simple as that."

"I hope you are hungry," Sterling said. "We have a reservation in the dining room." They get up to segue into dinner.

"Did I mention that Gretchen Howe smiled at me," Chad whispered to Michelle who had taken Chad's arm just in case anyone is looking. The excitement from Chad deflated anything she was personally trying to achieve being 'the girl on the arm of...' "Do you think I can get a date with her?"

Michelle dropped his arm. The rest of the night was all business.

○ ○ ○

Chad likes his workouts with Tommy. They're tough but exhilarating. He further likes the fact that it is just the two of them and they have the Body Image gym all to themselves. It has allowed them to become 'playful'—the slapping of asses and manly hugs, that sort of thing.

Chad stepped out of the shower, towel in hand, drying his hair as Tommy stepped in, still sweaty from a particularly aggressive workout. Again, Chad couldn't help but to notice Tommy's chiseled ass in the mirror and really can't stop admiring his smooth musculature in general. He found himself groping for conversation just to stay in the bathroom to watch Tommy shower.

"I still want to know how do I get those?" Chad said, pointing at the v-shaped muscles on either side of Tommy's pelvis, which eventually conjoin at Tommy's hairless pubic area.

"Oh, we can work on that," Tommy said. "Feel them, they are rock solid."

Chad didn't have to feel them to know they are rock solid. Everything about Tommy Mercer is rock solid. But Chad reached over and slid his hand down each side of Tommy's pelvis and toward his penis. He stopped just short of the prize.

"You don't have to stop," Tommy said, noticing the hesitancy, and took Chad's hand and put it on his growing penis. "It's just a guy thing."

Chad gave Tommy's penis a few cursory strokes and pulled his hand away before his own cock started to stir. "I have something for you," Chad said.

"Oh?"

"Yeah, let me pull on some clothes and get it from the car."

Tommy continued to stroke himself while Chad got dressed and ran off to the car, retrieving the employee handbook.

"What's that," Tommy asked, emerging from the bathroom wrapped in just a towel.

"Everyone I pay, including you, has to sign this. Lawyer's orders."

Without so much as a second glance, Tommy signed the back page and dated it accordingly.

"Now, what happens at Body Image, stays in Body Image," Chad teased.

Chad barely finished his statement when Tommy's towel hit the floor.

∘ ∘ ∘

Mica tosses in the bed. He doesn't like this bed; it's too hard—nothing like his own European pillow top king bed back at his place. In fact, Mica doesn't like much about Chad's place at all. Oh, it's beautiful to look at with a spectacular view of the basin of Los Angeles. But it is all so new. The furnishings, the art work, even the kitchen dishes are all so new. There is no history here, no sentimentality or memories. Besides, and more importantly, Mica feels Chad rented this place impulsively and is spending far too much money just to make a point. Did he really have to rent in the 'bird streets', the most desirable area for hot Hollywood, where past and present neighbors include Madonna, Leo and Toby? It is the curse of newfound money, it is spent as fast as it is made and the assumption is it is never going to end.

Mica tried to tell him past stories of over extension, foreclosures and bankruptcy by people just like Chad who got lucky and never saved for a rainy day and then got caught in a shit storm. But Chad rejects the notion that he is just 'lucky'. And Mica gets it. Again, the house is beautiful, if just a little cold, and Chad is making good money. But whom is he trying to impress?

The truth is, Chad is trying to impress himself.

They lay in bed, hardly having spoken. Chad mentioned that the film is back on and Mica said he knew. And then Chad mentioned he has a new agent, which made for another conversation non-starter. Although, Mica was quietly impressed with the addition of Sterling Lowe to Chad's team

Chad is exhausted, emotionally drained by everything he has been thrown at him—new agents, new contracts, and long hours on the set and the publicity for release of his film. Not to mention he has been working hard with Tommy his trainer. Between the physical and intellectual, he is rightfully exhausted.

Mica reaches under the covers and feels Chad's ass, which is hard as a rock. "My God. I don't know what you are doing with that new trainer but your hard ass is making me hard."

"Squats," Chad mumbled sleepily.

"Perfect," Mica continued. "How about squatting on my face. Now that is a hell of a workout!"

Chad rolled over on his back and stretched out, "Not tonight. I couldn't get it up if you paid me."

"Oh." Mica took that as a challenged, climbed under the sheets and began to suck on Chad.

Chad began to grow, surprising even himself. He had already cum today, but Mica wouldn't have known that. And there, again, was another reason to be exhausted.

o o o

At precisely the same time that a breaking press release is hitting the entertainment news wire services, a registered letter arrives at the offices of the Albert Switzer Agency and is signed for by Anthony. It is on the legal letterhead of the law offices of Dunning, Baker and Astin and signed by Lance Novak and Michelle Bianco of Regis and Canning.

The crux of the letter is simple; Chad Martin is no longer represented by ASA and will now be represented by the powerhouse IMC—International Management Cooperative. The press release basically told the same news to those who care.

Anthony presented the letter to Albert and as he read it, Anthony thought he saw a tear well in Albert's eye. Although, this departure doesn't nullify the contracts Albert, and Anthony, put together on behalf of Chad—meaning they would get their percentage of the first season of *Divas* and had already taken their slice of the seventy five thousand dollars Chad made on the movie—they would not be entitled to a chunk of the earnings renegotiated by Lance for *The Other Brother*. Albert Switzer had simply been screwed.

But what brought a tear to his eye isn't the price of business. This kind of shit happens all over town. The bigger issue for Albert is that Chad didn't have the balls to tell him, face-to-face, man-to-man. For all his quirky ways, Albert had, in fact, found, cultivated, invested in and created Chad Martin. Albert Switzer needed to mourn the moment as if it were a death. Anthony took it simply as a betrayal.

But Anthony saw this coming and had already done a little retaliatory damage.

o o o

Lydia threw the New York based rag down on Mica's desk with such force that the snap of the paper hitting the desktop actually scared Mica.

"Is there something I can do for you, Lydia," Mica droned, knowing whatever is up, Lydia is overreacting.

"I want to know who the fuck they are talking about!"

Mica picked up the paper, which is opened to the famed gossip section, where tit bits and salacious stories can get tongues wagging but, moreover, can make or break a career. Reaching over his shoulder and pointing to a segment known as a 'blind item'—an item assumed to be true because no names are mentioned in order to avoid a nasty lawsuit—Lydia simply said, "Read!"

The item reads: That regularly shirtless hot TV hunk who is about to drop his pants and reveal all on the big screen, has plenty yet to reveal about his personal life. What is the naked truth about the men in his life?

It didn't take much to connect the dots and figure out whom they are talking about. Mica momentarily had bile rise into the back of his throat and then had it settle into one of those pit of his stomach feelings hoping that maybe a few Hollywood insiders could add two and two, but the majority of the fan base would never see the item and never make the leap before the movie is released. But the bigger question for Mica is: who would have planted such an item? Chad couldn't be more discrete, even to the detriment of their relationship. And to Mica's knowledge, Chad has no enemies.

"So?" Lydia drummed her fingers against her folded arms. That is Lydia's favorite stance, arms folded—it makes her substantial cleavage even more prominent. And in Lydia's world, tits are power. "Who the fuck are they talking about?"

"How the fuck should I know?" Mica shot back a little too defensively.

"You should know because all you queens know all the shit on each other. Gossip is like an Olympic sport with you people. If you call yourself a reporter, you must have heard something."

"Even if I did know something, why would we pander to this sort of story?" Mica pleaded, again protesting too much. "This is the equivalent of outing someone who apparently has gone to great lengths to stay discrete and not be outed."

"You came to me and asked to do the hard stories and not just the entertaining fluff," Lydia shot back. "This is a hard story. Even if we don't run with it, it's a story. I want you to sniff around." Mica buried himself in his hands.

Lydia turned, took two or three steps forward and then turned back to Mica. And in a rather large voice, she asked Mica, "By the way, how's your friend Chad Martin doing these days? Hot on TV and has a movie coming out, I hear." Mica turned to face the accusation but had no real answer. She had her answer. "I'm just asking... that's all."

Again, Lydia turned and this time walked away.

○ ○ ○

Anthony Wright put down the paper and had a silent chuckle. This blind item is oh so very transparent. Anthony isn't one to hold a grudge but rather one to strike back immediately. And Mr. Wright is feeling very right about what he's done except he is surprised it happened so fast.

10

Another red carpet with it usual frenzy would have normally bored Mica. But instead, for the first time in a long time, Mica actually had butterflies. This, being located at the famed and former Cinerama Dome on Sunset Boulevard, may not be as prestigious an event as say if it had been located at the Chinese Theater, but this is a pretty good night for a movie that almost wasn't: *The Other Brother.*

Roger Keenan is a marketing genius to have been able to put this night together as quickly as he had once the movie was fast tracked. The big question now is: will there be a turnout? Stars are fickle and there hasn't been a lot of the usual hype surrounding this film other than industry buzz about Chad Martin's nude scenes. Will a swinging cock on screen, in a town full of swinging cocks, be enough to lure them in? Mica hopes so, for Chad's sake.

Mica hadn't seen Chad all day or even the night before. As Chad put it, "You are going to make me nervous." Fair enough.

As Mica made his way to his designated area where the crew had been allocated behind the rope, a hand landed on his shoulder. Joe, the cop, is back on security duty. "You haven't called."

"You're married..."

"Oh that," Joe joked. "Not for long, we're separated."

"...And I am seeing someone," Mica continued.

Joe smiled. "Well good seeing you anyway." Joe stepped back and was about to walk away but Mica stopped him.

"Maybe we should have coffee."

"Oh?"

"It's not that," Mica blushed. "I am just curious how much of this moonlighting work do you do?"

"A lot. I can use the money. Especially now that half of it is about to go to my soon to be ex-wife."

"Perhaps you could be one of our tipsters. You know get paid for what you see...or know...or find. That sort of thing."

"Like I said, call me." Joe walked off leaving Mica to wonder if he just insulted the man or hired the man. Like he said, he'd have to call to find out.

Roger had made sure Mica and the crew of *Drop Zone* had a large space in which to work, ten square feet, and that gave Mica room to breath but there is quid pro quo to such a gift. The expectation is that if *Drop Zone* is provided with the prominent spot on the carpet, the show, in turn, will air a significant segment on the night's events. No problem. Mica is more than happy to give as much coverage as he can to Chad—quid pro homo!

In so obliging though, it means that Mica would have to interview the studio heads and miscellaneous others the home audience couldn't give a shit about and wouldn't recognize if they sat on them. But that is the job, unfortunately.

The notoriously camera shy head of Spectrum Studios, Barry Stegman, stepped up first. "So good to see you." If he is speaking, clearly he believes in this picture.

His wife Diandra barely brushed Mica's cheek by way of an air kiss. "Zac Posen," she announced as if this were the Oscars and Mica would want to know who designed what she is wearing.

"Thank you for that," Mica began with a hint of sarcasm in his voice but moved on smartly. "Barry, let me ask you, why release this film now after shelving it for so many months?"

"Star power. Simple as that." Barry began with all the authority his title bestowed. "We always believed in this project except there was no real estate available to showcase the film at the time. Everything in the theaters was comic book heroes and sequel movies. Who knew that in the time it took to secure the right real estate, we would have a star on our hands. Chad Martin."

Mica couldn't help but to feel a twinge of pride. "What makes Chad Martin a star?"

"Look at him," Diandra nearly squealed.

Barry interjected, "But more than looks, he just has a natural ability to project emotion, pathos, humor...and...well, look at him!"

"We see a lot of him in this film," Mica prodded with a wink.

"You sure do," he winked back. "Audiences will get their money's worth."

"Thank you...both of you," Mica began by way of politely dismissing the studio head. "I know you have a big night ahead so I will let you get on your way."

Diandra kissed Mica on the cheek for real this time and they made their way to the next reporter only to regurgitate almost word for word what Barry had said to Mica.

The rest of the interviews went similarly, all praising Chad and virtually ignoring that there are other cast members in this film. That was fine with Mica who now beamed with pride.

Chad's co-stars on *Divas* had all shown their support by showing up with his cougar gal pal on the show, Gina Hamilton, having provided the best line and sight gag of the night. "We have all seen him shirtless. As his girlfriend on *Divas* I would like to know what I have been missing. So I have brought along two props." With that she pulls out binoculars and a portable battery operated fan. "The binoculars are in case I have to look closely to find his short comings and the fan is for the hot flash I'll have if what I hear is true."

A perfect sound bite for the segment, the kind of thing Lydia loves.

Ashley Beckwith, arriving with all the fanfare of a real diva, was less than accommodating with her interview. "All anyone is talking about is Chad Martin. I'm nude in this movie too but no one seems to care!" Ashley, who always reverted back to her Australian accent at times of stress, is clearly stressed

Just then a fan, who miraculously could hear her over the crowd, shouted, "I want to see you naked, Ashley."

"Finally someone gives a damn." Ashley's retort was an attempt at humor. "Honestly, it is like I am a co-star to a penis. I can see it now...*and the Oscar goes to another thirteen inch statuette!*"

The screams when Chad stepped out of the limo, better late than never, are deafening. Even Mica is taken aback. Chad hadn't come with a date by design but also coming out of the car is Michelle Bianco and a couple Mica didn't know.

Chad looked dashing in his Paul Smith bespoke suit and open shirt as he posed for the paparazzi. Despite the blinding light of the camera flashes going off, Chad barely blinked and flashed back a dazzling smile. He was born to be here, Mica thought. He had never looked more handsome.

After a fair amount of time, during which the entire cast was brought together to pose in front of the paparazzi, Michelle guided Chad to Mica. "Mica, of course, you know Chad."

Mica jumped right in. "Can you believe everything that has been happening to you these days?"

"It's a dream come true," Chad shouted back over the crowd.

"We've seen you out on the town with a number of hot dates as of late..." Both Chad and Michelle squinted with concern over where Mica may take this. "...Why no date tonight?"

"Just because I didn't arrive with somebody doesn't mean I won't be leaving with somebody."

In all reality, that was a great softball pitch Mica threw out to Chad. And Chad hit it out of the park. But it was too close for comfort for Michelle who took Chad by the arm and was about to lead him away.

"One second." Chad pulled away from Michelle and took a second to introduce the unknown man by Chad's side. "This is my trainer, Tommy."

"I've heard a lot about you." Mica extended his hand.

"It is great to meet you," Tommy shook Mica's hand enthusiastically. "This is our first time on a red carpet and it's pretty heady. Oh, this is my wife Suzanne. She's not in the business either."

Mica nodded a hello to Suzanne. Letting go of Mica's hand, Tommy leaned in. "I had no idea that you and Chad are friends. He's never mentioned it."

Mica paused for a moment to process what he'd just heard but there is no time for that. He has a job to do.

∘ ∘ ∘

Roger Keenan's idea of having a few people over to the house for an after party would be anyone else's idea of a small wedding—sixty or so of his nearest and dearest. Unlike the usual soirees here, there are no porn stars in the pool or fucking on a cake, just an industry celebration of what will clearly be a hit film. Mica was careful to arrive separately from Chad, which wasn't a difficult task as Chad had arrived in a limo.

"So how has your night been?" Roger asked Mica teasingly.

"Productive from a reporter standpoint but as you know this is not my night."

Roger brought his voice down to a whisper. "And overall, how are things?"

"Let's just say Chad has taken to his stardom very comfortably in public and uncomfortably behind closed doors."

At that moment, Chad walked in to a thunderous applause, which didn't sit well with Ashley Beckwith. "Here's the cock now, which just happens to be attached to Chad Martin." With that, she grabbed a glass of champagne from a passing tray and went through the motions of a toast.

Chad, too, grabbed a glass and, after a round of "helloes" and the occasional "nice to see you," made his way toward Mica.

"Congratulations," Mica began and, not thinking, leaned over to give him a kiss.

Chad pulled away. "Are you crazy. Here? Tonight? What are you thinking?"

Mica knew the kiss was a faux pas but didn't need the chastising that Chad was giving. "I was thinking how interesting it is that Tommy the trainer walks the red carpet with you but has no idea who I am. Where is he by the way?"

"He *and his wife* walked the red carpet. *They've* gone home. And why would he know about you. I told you I am trying to be discrete."

Roger, eyeing from a short distance away, interceded appropriately. "Now, now, ladies; we have guests."

Through clenched teeth, Chad spat, "Roger, I am not a lady!" With that he walked off to accept all the praise a little nudity would afford him.

"I thought you two are friends," Michelle Bianco began from behind Mica, "That looked a little heated."

"No nothing like that Michelle." Mica joked as best he could.

"Oh you know me, I don't like to see anything get in the way of a good segment."

"I think you will be very pleased with what we put together," Mica pacified.

A clinking of glassware indicated someone is about to speak. It took a significant amount of clinks to get the crowd to settle, but when they did, Roger began.

"First, thank you all for coming. And congratulations to the wonderful cast, the talented crew, the producers, director and studio for creating and championing what is inevitably going to be a hit movie." He paused for the applause. "Now we are all adults here. And anyone who has been to my house before will know I like to be a little cheeky with my guests. So to celebrate the theme of the evening...well not so much a theme as it is a topic of conversation...I felt the only way to stop talking about Chad's penis is to create a diversion. Boys..."

On cue, the waiters, some ten or so, ripped off their Velcro tuxedoes to become stark naked. And as if this was perfectly normal, they simply picked up their trays of drinks and canapés and continued to circulate much to the amusement and laughter of the crowd.

"I can count on you to not report that," Michelle cautioned Mica.

"What's the point without a camera crew to capture the moment," Mica reassured, sort of. "Besides this is not part of the event. I know where the line is drawn between personal and professional moments."

"Speaking of personal information. There was a certain blind item in the New York papers the other day. You wouldn't happen to know anything about it?" Michelle pried.

"I wish. I am getting shit about it too."

"What do you mean?" Michelle asked, rather concerned.

"Lydia is very curious," Mica explained.

"She'd better know when to back off," Michelle snapped. "And you can tell her I said so."

Duly noted.

Not everyone got the joke of the naked waiters or wanted to be part of it. A couple of dozen or so people saw the naked turn as an excuse to call it a night. And by the looks of things, so too is Chad. Mica raced to the door and pulled Chad aside.

"Where are you going?" Mica questioned.

"Outta here...home," Chad spat.

"What is wrong? This is all for you."

"Naked waiters? They're for me?" Chad seemed almost disgusted by the spectacle. "What's next? Blowjobs by the pool?"

"It wouldn't be the first time," Mica joked but perhaps the timing wasn't prudent.

"Look," Chad began passively, "Go have your fun. I have to be concerned about being associated with naked waiters, you don't."

"Barry Stegman, the head of the studio is here. I think you're protected."

"Mica, I'm going home, to *my* home by the way. Come over if you want but I have to get out of here."

After they stared at one another for what seemed like an eternity but in reality was just second, Mica pulled Chad into an alcove, away from the prying eyes of the mingling partygoers, and planted a kiss squarely on Chad's lips. Chad took it in for just a second or two, and pushed him back somewhat violently.

"See that," Mica pleaded. "Lightening didn't strike. You haven't been damned to hell. Barry Stegman didn't fire you. It's all okay."

"I'm going home," is all Chad could say and he walked out.

○ ○ ○

If there is one thing Mica likes about the house up in the 'bird streets' it is the infinity pool and, of course, the view it provides. It is a traditional rectangle shape, cantilevered out over the hillside, with polished concrete that continues out from the living room to surround the coping. The floor to ceiling glass doors, which make up the living room wall, recess into the side of the house to maximize indoor/outdoor living. On many a morning, Chad rolls out of bed, through the living room an out the already open doors for a early swim even before a morning piss. Such is the life on the 'bird streets'.

Chad too loves the pool and it's privacy as it affords him the luxury of an all over tan. For Chad the pool is just another excuse to be naked and Mica is all for that. The two lay there on their respective chaise lounges, cold drinks sharing the table between them, naked for the heavens to gaze down upon.

Mica reached over and took hold of Chad's hand. "Are we going to talk about last night?"

"There's nothing to talk about," Chad harrumphed and took his hand back. "Roger Keenan's parties are not where I am at, at the moment. I'm building something here."

"You don't have to tell me," Mica quipped. "I am trying to live within that construction zone. But Roger is just about good clean fun."

Chad sat upright and snapped at Mica. "Clean fun? There are people fucking in the pool, in the bathrooms, bedrooms, everywhere. There are porn stars blowing real stars and real stars snorting whatever they can. You call all that clean fun?"

"By Hollywood standards," Mica chuckled. "And let's not forget from clear up there on your high horse that we met at one of those parties and, as I recall, we had some fun in the pool. Roger's is a 'no tell' zone. For Christ's sake your studio head and your publicist were there and they were not shaken."

Chad took Mica's hand once again. "I guess you're right. But it all has to be on the down low for the conceivable future. Michelle Bianco tells me one scandal and I could be over before I have really begun."

Mica knows Chad is right but had lived too long in the closet to compromise now. They are clearly at a crossroads. "Speaking of fun in the pool...wanna have some."

Chad stood up, bent over and gave Mica a kiss. "Sorry, I have a gym session booked and at five hundred dollars an hour for a private booking, no fuck should cost that." Of course that is exactly what a fuck is costing him, there's just a work out first.

○ ○ ○

Chad drove off with more anger than afterglow.

Yes, he and Tommy worked out. And it was a great workout; today was chest and arms day so both are pumped. Yes, they wrestled. Chad is really getting into these wrestling sessions. Both are hot and sweaty from the workout. Rolling around on the mat, they tug at each other's wet tank tops and shorts. Chad had begun to no longer wear the jock strap underneath and loves when both their penises get pulled out and inevitably rub together. And yes, Chad got the requisite blowjob from

Tommy when the wrestling got heated enough. Chad had stopped reciprocating when he heard the movie was to be released. Again, he doesn't want to damage his image. Tommy is only too happy to give what he can't get. So win/win.

None of that is upsetting Chad. It was that paparazzi he caught snapping his picture on the way out of he Body Image bungalow. That has pissed him off.

11

This guy really has it in for this nobody actor, Joey thought. Chad Martin is hardly a nobody; he just hasn't crested. But then again Joey thinks all actors are nobodies—high paid snobs who haven't got a smart in their head and even less to say. He has some interesting ideas for a man who makes a living chasing them with a camera.

The paparazzi are a breed unto themselves. Chasing celebrities for a living, wracking up long hours to do so, fighting each other for the 'get'; it is no wonder people like the ironically named Joey Chase take on a freelance gig every once in a while. But knowing what he was able to capture, he wished he'd charged more than the twenty five hundred he did for this job. He could make a hundred times that if he sells these to the tabloids and if this Chad Martin guy is going to be as big as everyone says he'll be, perhaps there is a deal to be struck once the client sees the gold he's mined.

He has three good ones by the pool and one coming out of the gym. The first is of Chad laying naked on a chaise lounge next to another naked man by the pool. A palm frond has blocked the face of the second man but you can more than identify Chad Martin and his big cock. Nice pool by the way. The second photo is of the two men holding hands while lying by the pool. Again the second man's face is obstructed. And the third picture shows Chad bending over the second man, the back of Chad's head covering the second man's face. The inference, if one is to go there, is that they are kissing.

The final photo is of Chad coming out of his exclusive private gym in West Hollywood. He has his arm around the trainer and they are both laughing uproariously. Ordinarily you would simply think this is a fun 'buddy' moment. But who's to say that that man isn't the second man at the pool?

As the last of the four photos is making its way out of the printer, a text lights up Joey's phone: Where are you? Shit! He's late.

He quickly stuffed the four photos, plus a back up flash drive into a manila envelope and rushed out the door to meet his mystery buyer at what he referred to as 'the big gay coffee house on Santa Monica'. Joey knew the place; he had just never heard it referred to as that. Whatever. He just hoped he'd be able to figure out just who the client is. They'd only spoken by phone and all Joey knew is the guy is black and that the guy can spot Joey. Oh yeah and his name is Anthony something.

12

The click from the camera with the simultaneous pop from the flash bulbs is almost hypnotic. *The Other Brother* was an overnight success and so photo shoots like this have become routine in Chad's life. He has been hoping for some of the big covers—*GQ, Vanity Fair* and the like—and Michelle Bianco has been working overtime to make that happen. He seems more in contact with her these days than he is with Mica. And that has not done well for their relationship. But Mica seems willing to concede and understand without a lot of discussion about it, that this is really Chad's moment.

On this day, famed celebrity photographer Chuck Corman, has been brought in to a photo studio on the virtually empty second floor of 80's built storefront on Beverly near La Brea. A photo shoot with Corman is a coup—his work will get Chad on a cover faster than Chad's trajectory of fame.

Corman, who is not only internationally famous for intense star photos in exotic locations, but is also renowned for his male nudes. His coffee table books are highly desirable works of art unto themselves and sell for the hundreds of dollars. A signed copy can run in the thousands. And despite this being a style shoot—aptly named COCKSURE, which will be the title of the eventual article—Corman has a way of infusing a certain sexuality into a clothed man. For this shoot, Corman has styled Chad with very tight clothes, which, in some shots are soaking wet, and he has insisted Chad to go commando—no underwear—for this shoot. Thus a perfect outline of Chad's cock seems to creep into every shot. What the hell? Chad is now known for his big cock; why not exploit it?

But this shoot is going one step further. Chad has agreed to let Chuck photograph him candidly while he is changing clothes so there is a peek-a-boo aspect to the shoot. Anything too graphic or revealing will be reserved for another cocktail book in the works called STARS UNWRAPPED.

Michelle was a little uneasy with the concept at first but the combination of the gravitas of Chuck Corman and Chad's willingness to participate so eagerly put her at ease. She, of course, insisted on being at the shoot ostensibly to protect her client from anything going too far. Chuck Corman is notorious for crossing the line.

But in reality, she wanted to be there to see first hand the monster cock everyone's talking about.

For privacy purposes the crew is very small. Chuck, his assistant Dan, the clothes stylist Meg, hair and makeup artist Dawn, Michelle and Mica. Mica had been chosen, against Michelle's better judgment over bigger names in print journalism, to write the article that will accompany the photo shoot. Chad had chosen him and Michelle capitulated when Mica agreed that she would have editorial final say on its content. Besides, she knew that Mica and Chad have already become professional pals and it would keep Chad more comfortable.

Chad's comfort level was predetermined. He has no problem being naked in a room full of people. So within minutes of the shoot, Chad sat naked in the makeup chair getting worked on while Chuck snapped away. Those candid shots of Chad being prepped for the formal shoot are definitely more provocative than the fashion shots. Although, ironically, Chad's cock is more present and visibly styled in the wet pants than when he is naked and his cock is not seen. As the shoot evolved it was easy to see Chuck's vision come to life. The juxtaposition between the clothed but clearly outlined cock and the naked but revealing nothing candid pictures creates a reverse eroticism that is pure genius.

Mica busied himself taking notes about what he was seeing, the process of the shoot and the small talk between master and subject. He virtually stayed on the sidelines the entire time, readying himself for two very short interviews with Chuck and Chad when the shoot is over. His professionalism impressed Michelle and she made the mental note of using Mica again for 'delicate' shoots like this.

Michelle's professionalism is another story. Interjecting herself into conversations that had nothing to do with her and asking Chad innocuous questions in order to be close to him, she spent the day hanging out very close to the changing area where Chad would spend most of the afternoon naked.

Mica knew that his observations of the overly interested Michelle would never make it into the finished article, not while she has final editorial say. But it did amuse him.

Chuck, for his part, is all work and no play—even when he would call Chad over to look over the digital images and let Chad give his opinion. "Looking at myself, is going to make me hard," Chad joked.

Four hours later, almost to the minute, a champagne cork popping indicated the end of the shoot. Everyone clapped as if they had been watching some great theatrical performance, a ballet of sorts, and perhaps they had—a notation Mica would definitely put in the article.

Over champagne, Mica asked Chuck a couple of obligatory questions about Chad as a model and then asked Chad about the experience in general. After years of interviews, Mica was well aware that moments like these are simply love fests between the model and the photographer; neither was going to say a bad thing about the other even if the shoot had gone horribly wrong.

Mica is also smart enough to talk with Michelle about scheduling a follow up interview with Chad. The seriousness by which Michelle talked about Chad's tight schedule almost made Mica laugh, as he knew he didn't even need a second interview. He certainly knows enough about Chad to fill in the blanks in the article and anything else he needs to know, he can do over pillow talk.

"Call my office and we will set something up," Michelle concluded after exasperating herself over scheduling. And then Michelle ushered Mica to the door, reminding him that he was just a guest on this shoot and not an insider. Again, Mica had to stifle a laugh.

∘ ∘ ∘

Dressed in a pair of distressed but well fitting jeans that shows off his ass and his commando cock perfectly, scuffed motorcycle boots, a threadbare former dress shirt over a wife beater tank top, knit scull cap and aviator glasses, Chad Martin looks the epitome of today's hot hunks. Walking up Cahuenga Boulevard from a solo lunch at the counter of Kitchen 24/7, he thought he'd stop by the Orbit Newsstand and see what magazines are worth perusing. The shoot with Chuck Corman should be out any day now and Chad was very excited to see the choice of pictorial. He had read the article, courtesy of Mica but they both knew it would be the pictures that make the spread a hot commodity.

A couple of giddy girls giggled as he walked by. "Isn't that the guy from that television show?" one asked.

A second confirmed between giggles. "Yeah and he has movie out that my mother won't let me see."

Chad simply smiled at the girls and kept walking. He likes being noticed and it doesn't hurt that the maître ds and club bouncers also have come to know who he is and guide him to the V.I.P. areas without question. Not that he is a club guy per se, but it is nice to know that he can when he wants.

The Orbit Newsstand on Cahuenga has possibly the best selection of magazines and newspapers from all over the world. But these days, Chad is only interested in the publicity rags like the British magazines and the usual U.S. selections. He likes to bury the tabloids between a couple of more highbrow legitimate fare such as *Architectural Digest* and *U.S. News and World Report,* the latter of which will never be opened let alone read.

Hiding behind his aviators, he thumbs through the latest edition of the British celebrity glossy magazine *Gotcha!* while he surreptitiously eyes the covers to the gay pictorials. Hot but too hot to touch. And then he moved to what he came for.

Without saying a word, the man by the old fashioned cash register, tosses Chad a copy of *World View*, one of the more notorious tabloids. And there across the banner is the headline that almost made Chad choke: WHO ARE THE MEN IN CHAD MARTIN'S LIFE? And underneath the black bold of the headline is a full color picture of Chad naked, with a banner blurring his crotch, holding hands with another while they lounge, pool side, in the 'bird streets.'

Chad is too dumbfounded to speak other than to turn to the man who tipped him off and utter, "I'll take them all." He handed the guy a one hundred dollar bill for his kindness and walked off with the bundle under his arm.

Chad wished he hadn't walked up the street and that he could simply jump into the car, open the tabloid and read on. This is too public a place to be seen reading a story about himself. He ran down the road and handed the valet at Kitchen 24/7 his ticket and prayed the Range Rover is parked close by.

He wanted to call somebody—anybody—everybody and just scream after he read the rest of the article. Two other pictures poolside made it look as if he is kissing some mystery man. Then there is an inference that the mystery could be solved with the picture of Tommy Mercer, his trainer. This is a nightmare. What to do? What to do?

He drove for half an hour, trying to think rationally, before he could make the first phone call. When he pushed the phone button on his steering wheel, the first call would be to Mica. He managed to get his voicemail.

"Have you seen it? The article? It's in the fucking *World View* of all places. This is a fucking nightmare. Call me!"

Another similar rant was left on Tommy's phone with the stern warning to not talk to anyone until they are able to connect.

He didn't have to call Michelle Bianco; she called him. "It's me, Michelle. You're on speaker phone with Eddie Fielding."

Chad pulled off to the side of the road. He doesn't want to be distracted by Los Angeles traffic, not while Eddie Fielding is on the line. Chad has it already set in his mind that this has to be worse than even he thought if the boss, Eddie Fielding, is on the line and Michelle can't handle this on her own.

In Fielding's office at Regis and Canning, Michelle sat across the desk with a notebook in hand. This was hardly the first crisis she's found a client to be in, but this one, because of his recent positive publicity is potentially a powder keg ready to explode. Chad's career trajectory, having been mapped out by the best in the business, may just take a sharp turn in a direction no one wants to go.

Eddie, for his part, runs crisis like a military operation. You look at what is being presented, present an offense as a manageable defense and attack aggressively. Eddie will position Chad a victim here, never apologize and get the client out publically as much as possible to show there has been no harm or embarrassment.

Eddie has a booming bass voice over the speakerphone, which only makes the conversation sound that much more ominous. "First, how are you?" They assumed he's seen the article.

"I've been better," he choked as he began to get emotional.

"Kid," Eddie barked. "Everyone finds themselves compromised in one situation or another when they become as popular as you have become. People go gunning for you. There is no getting around it. The issue now is how to fix it. Now, first things first; is the trainer the same man who is next to you in the pool shots?"

"No," Chad mumbled back sheepishly.

"So the trainer we can explain," Eddie continued. "Now, I don't want to know who is in the picture with you. In fact, I don't even think we try to explain the picture. We go with the angle that it was an invasion of privacy..."

"And it was," Chad interrupted.

"...And that is the angle we take. The photographer was simply trying to get embarrassing nude shots of you and there just so happened to be an innocent friend with you, whom we will avoid acknowledging as to keep his privacy in tact."

"So what do I do?" Chad asked somewhat confused by the plan of action.

"Just be yourself," Michelle shouted down the speakerphone. She just had to add her two cents to the conversation. "Brush it off."

"Can't we sue? We can get Lance Novak on this," Chad pleaded.

"No we can't," Eddied explained. "They simply posed a question, which, granted, inferred there is something more to the pictures. But that is only inference and not a statement. If your trainer for instance stated that there was something to this, then we could sue."

Chad paused to process that new information.

"What we would like is to set you up on a date. Someone who is a paparazzi magnet, so that you can't help but be seen out on the town," Eddie explained.

"Who did you have in mind?" Chad asked cautiously.

Michelle dropped the bombshell, "Antonia Guest."

Antonia Guest would certainly be a paparazzi magnet. If she isn't dodging the media, she's dodging jail time, one probation after another. Chad at first rolled his eyes and then thought about it for a minute. He would certainly look like a 'player' by being seen with her. And chances are she has more to hide than he does. The paparazzi will be all over her, they won't even think of him and he gets daubed with the heterosexual paintbrush just by association.

"You still with us kid?" Eddie asked.

"Yeah...I think your right," Chad responded. "Let's set it up."

"I'll call you when we get date, time and place," Michelle confirmed, scribbling on the notebook as she spoke.

"In the meantime," Eddie interjected, "don't worry. This will blow over."

∘ ∘ ∘

Michelle Bianco did not get what she wanted when but better than she deserved. When she walked into Eddie Fielding's office on that Tuesday she wasn't sure what to expect. Since signing Chad Martin and some other 'new' faces to the agency, she had been working overtime to ingratiate herself with those clients to make her invaluable to them. The end result as she saw it would be the launch of Michelle Bianco and Associates and she would poach this cadre of newbies and branch out on her own. This was as dangerous but well honed formula for advancement.

Being summoned to Big Eddie's office could mean the jig was up. No one knew what she was planning but in Hollywood the walls have a way of talking.

"Michelle," he began with that baritone voice of his, "have you any idea of what this is all about."

"No sir."

"Well, I have been watching you. Closely."

She began to squirm.

"I know what you are doing with these new faces..."

"Look Eddie..." She was clearly taking a defensive tone.

"I like what I see."

"You do?" She was taken aback.

"Fresh faces. Young blood. The future. I want you to run with it."

She sat, mouth agape.

"To that end, I think it is time you get what is coming to you." He paused dramatically and she nearly vomited. "Congratulations. You are Regis and Canning's newest vice president."

"I don't know what to say," was all she could say, panting out her words.

"For now you will keep your office but we will work out the details of your pay raise. You deserve it. What you are doing with Chad Martin alone is worthy of this promotion."

"Thank you," she wasn't sure if she should laugh or cry.

Eddie Fielding is no idiot. He knew what was going on. Ordinarily he would fire someone like Michelle for mutiny but he saw something in Chad and he knew Chad trusted Michelle. This was simply a matter of 'keeping your enemies closer'.

○ ○ ○

Chad's date with Antonia Guest was nothing short of a disaster, personally, as Chad presumed it would be. But the purpose of the date was a big success. Hopping from one Hollywood hotspot to the next, being chased and snapped by the paparazzi was just what Michelle Bianco and Eddie Fielding had hoped for—buoying up that mythical playboy image.

Between club stops, Antonia snorted enough white powder to fill a sandbox. Chad isn't into that scene and it was making him completely nervous as the night progressed. All he needs is for a cop to stop them and he would be arrested by proxy. Fortunately, his heavily tinted windows prevented the paparazzi from seeing what was happening inside the car.

"You're such a party pooper," is all she could say about his repeated refusals to participate in her snort-a-thon.

"And aren't you on probation?" mumbled Chad in return.

"Fuck you," she snapped and then a smile came over her face.

Antonia reached over and started to rub her hand against Chad's crotch. He squirmed but he is driving and there is nowhere for him to turn. "Let's fuck," she suggested. "I mean I have seen your cock. Who hasn't seen your cock? And I would love for you to fuck me with that big thing."

He reached from the driving wheel, took her hand, pulled it from his crotch and placed it back in her lap. But she hung on to his hand, slipped it under her high cut skirt and placed his middle finger against the bald lips of her vagina. He tried to pull away but that was making the car swerve.

"What the fuck are you doing?" he shouted as she forced his finger insider her.

"Ooooh," she cooed and squirmed. "Finger fuck my cunt."

She shifted and he was able to free his hand and pull it back to the wheel. He could smell her juices on his finger and a little bile rose up in the back of his throat.

"Jesus Christ, it must be true," she continued. "You must be gay if you won't fuck me!"

Maneuvering smartly down Sunset Boulevard, he pulled a dangerous U-turn in the middle of the bend by Crescent Heights and skidded to a stop at the valet of the Chateau Marmont. The valet opened her door and in the moment when she stepped down from the Range Rover, he spat out, "It's not a gay thing. I just don't fuck drugged out whores like you."

With that, he skidded up the hill, around the back and out to safety, letting the door slam itself shut. More importantly, he left her screaming on the sidewalk. "Faggot!"

As luck would have it, bad luck at that, Joey Chase is right there, camera in hand, catching the whole thing. "Is that your official statement?"

13

"Damn it, I want to know who is in this picture," ranted Lydia in the conference room for the *Drop Zone* morning meeting. Everyone in the conference room this morning had a copy of the tabloid handed to them as they walked in. It wasn't as if the entire staff didn't know of the story by now, it is Lydia's way of shoving the story in everyone's faces. When Lydia Gray gets scooped, everyone is to blame. "We need to be on top of this story."

Mica noted that when Lydia is on a rant like this, she bleats like a sheep. Her voice raises an octave or so and the modulation is nothing short of bleating. He had been working on a good imitation of her to be used in most discrete of co-worker confabs. Now he knew to modulate with bleating at the next opportunity.

"How would you like us to proceed?" B.J., the voice of reason, chimed in, "we do the good stories here, remember?"

"What the fuck does that mean?" Lydia spewed as she paced—not paced but stomped—around the room. She tends to the wear the highest of heels and at a moment such as this, you know the craftsman at Manolo Blahnik and Christian Louboutin didn't craft thousand dollar shoes made for the punishment of her rants.

At any given moment, Mica thought nervously deflecting his own precarious situation being the other man in the photo, she is going to throw a shoe, snap an ankle along the way and we are going to have to put her down like a horse.

Lydia continued to stomp and spew—no bleat. "I just told you all that I want to know who is in this picture with Chad Martin. Is it the trainer? And who, by the way, is this 'celebrity trainer'? Just who are his clients?"

This is a bigger story than even Mica had foreseen. Of course, he knew Chad was becoming increasingly more interesting to the *Drop Zone* audience. And with the release of *The Other Brother*, Chad had become a bona fide sex symbol. But never did Mica assume that Lydia would be so obsessed with a gay rumor.

"Mica, what do you know?" Lydia demanded. "I put you on this story back when there was a blind item in *Page Six*. Now, it seems we know whom they were talking about. We *all* now know who they were talking about. My question to you is how come *you* didn't know who they were talking about?"

The entire room simply sat there, watched Mica squirm and waited for an answer.

"Or did you know?" Lydia drilled.

"Oh come on. It was a blind item," Mica attempted a defense. "Clearly someone has it out for Chad Martin. That might be the bigger story."

B.J., always a 'big picture' thinker, chimed in. "Maybe there is more than one story here. If we want to go down this track at all."

"What do you mean 'IF' we want to go down this track? Of course we do." Lydia is now incredulous. "Of course we do. Chad Martin is the hottest thing on two legs at the moment. And if you don't think this is a big enough story look at this."

With that one of the production assistants turned out the lights and montage of other networks' coverage of the story played on the big plasma usually reserved for viewing the days' segments for *Drop Zone*. In fairness to Lydia and her years of experience, she does know a big story. And if it is making the rounds of the late night talk shows, gets a mention on those daytime roundtable talk shows and, worse yet, is featured on a competing national news magazine show as it seems to have been; it is a big story in Lydia's eyes.

"And what are we trying to do? Destroy him?" B.J. shot back. "We give that car wreck of a talent, Antonia Guest, a pass time after time. What are we doing here?"

There was a silent gasp in the room.

"This is the business of show business," Lydia calmly explained—a calm before the storm. "If he wants to be a big sex symbol, out on the town every night with another 'IT' chick and expect us to pay attention to that side of his life and not pay attention to this. Forget it. This is the big league. It's not the gay thing; it's the hypocrisy behind it. It is no different than if he were caught cheating on a wife. We would report that too."

There is a logic in what she is saying, a distorted logic for sure. This is about being scooped by a tabloid and Lydia being Labia, it didn't matter whom she would bring down to get the big story.

"Mica, I want you on this story," Lydia punctuated. "We can meet in my office after the taping of the show and discuss how you will proceed."

○ ○ ○

Lydia isn't particularly listening. Her mind is made up. Mica is on the story.

"Lydia," Mica pleads, "we don't do these kinds of stories. Outing people. Why now?"

"Who said anything about outing Chad Martin?" Lydia responded somewhat aloof.

She had just uttered her question as B.J. walked into the office. "You did."

"I am just suggesting we find out the identity of the person in the tabloid photo," Lydia continued.

"You're not suggesting anything. You are insisting," Mica corrected.

"And to what end?" B.J. asked, knowing the answer. "To out him."

"Is this or is this not an entertainment *news* program?" Lydia shot back. "Chad Martin is news."

"Who cares about whether he is gay or not in this day and age?" Mica, again, pleaded.

"Clearly he does," Lydia pointed out. "Otherwise he would be seen with this guy on his arm on the red carpet rather than every C-list hooker of an actress he has been parading."

Mica couldn't argue with that. And moreover, he knew better. Chad does not want to come out of the closet anytime soon.

"Are you going to sit there and tell me when you were on the photo shoot with Chad and Chuck Corman, you didn't have an inkling that Chad may be gay?" Lydia quizzed with eyes squinted. "Matter of fact, didn't you introduce Chad to Michelle Bianco at Regis and Canning for P.R. representation. For Christ's sake you know this guy!"

"That is why I am telling you, there is no story here," Mica interjected, as Lydia is getting a little too close to the bone.

"Of course there is a story here," Lydia continued undeterred, "otherwise the tabloids wouldn't have printed the pictures or implied the innuendo."

Mica looked over at B.J. for support but only got a shrug of her shoulders. Lydia has a point; there is a story here.

"But chasing this isn't journalism. It's morally reprehensible," Mica declared.

"Look who's now a journalist," Lydia sniped.

B.J. quickly intervened to calm the escalation. "Look, you may find out the guy in the picture is his cousin or someone else equally benign. Let's at least do the job we've been assigned and find out who it is. Let's not jump to conclusions until then."

"You have your first test tonight," Lydia prodded. "There is some charity bull-shit event at the Beverly Hilton tonight. Supposedly *your friend* Chad is on the RSVP list. I want you there and I want you to ask the right questions, Mr. Journalist. I will screen the tapes tomorrow to verify you did your job. And let me tell you, your job is on the line if you don't."

o o o

No matter how many times they 'spruce' up the place, the Beverly Hilton still seems a relic to bygone Hollywood days. Still Mica likes the place. Whatever the event here, in the ballroom just off the lobby, it brings out just enough new Hollywood to be au currant and just enough of the old guard to be considered God's waiting room. A night like this, a black tie something or other for breast cancer, promises to entertain a nice mix.

"Mica?"

Mica turned toward the baritone voice and found himself face to face with his favorite police officer turned occasional event security guard and even more occasional dalliance, Joseph. Mica doesn't know what it is about this guy—he is so opposite in body type and demeanor from Chad. But every time he sees Joe, Mica feels his cock stirring.

"Joe, you get out to all the best occasions!"

"You look great Mica," Joe offered.

"Everyone looks good in a tux," Mica dismissed.

Then Joe got right up next to Mica's ear and said, "Maybe. But not everyone looks good enough to eat. And you, I would like to eat."

Mica stepped back and blushed.

"It's good to see you too, Joe. But I have work to do." Suppressing the want to give him a little peck on the cheek, Mica made his way down the line to find his designated spot behind the velvet rope.

As he was situating himself with his crew along the glass wall separating the circular drive from the main hotel lobby thoroughfare, Marilyn Lassiter emerged from the ballroom, darted directly at Mica and gave him a kiss on both cheeks. "Darling, I was hoping you would be here."

Marilyn Lassiter is exactly part of the old guard Mica still finds fascinating. She, Marilyn, is simply a society doyenne with no apparent means of support, who is famous for being famous—most notably for throwing lavishly over crowded dinner parties in her cramped high-rise condo at the top of Doheny. Coincidentally, the same condo building that Lydia Gray lives in.

It is at those parties that Mica loves to rub shoulders with those slightly forgotten, the kind of over the hill stars that Albert Switzer still represents. And it is at these parties that Mica likes to get a little cheeky—pointing out to an aging pioneer comedienne with a penchant for statement jewelry that Dorothy Hamill never skated on a piece of ice the size of the diamond she had on her finger. Another time, he told the 1950s sex kitten, who had long since abandoned acting to hawk beauty products, some suggestions as to what her lotions might be good for. And every once in a while, they'd snap back. Like the time he told a fading sitcom star, whom he had never met but was goading her for a reaction, by stating he was hurt that she never wrote or called him. To which she shouted, "Cause I don't know who the fuck you are!" She was a broad in every sense of the word, and that simply confirmed it.

A Lassiter party—or 'salon' as she calls them—is always filled with former supermodels, pop artists, singers, actors and actresses—all faces, no one behind the scenes. They are a dying breed for sure; to which Mica would joke that Marilyn Lassiter would have to read the obituaries to see who would not be coming to the next salon. But Mica simply loved the idea of being elbow to elbow with fading Hollywood—a time when stars were stars and not simply celebrities. For her part, Marilyn Lassiter loves the idea that Mica is part of the media and may, just may, mention her in one of his pieces.

"Aren't you early Marilyn?" Mica asked, to which she put her finger to her lips and shushed Mica. He knew she would inevitably loop around and walk the red carpet several times before the event officially began, each time next to a different member of the old guard, hoping to appear is some society column or another. Mica desperately wanted to tell her that society columns are like most of her friends, a thing of the past. Today, they are gossip columns and most likely she wouldn't want to end up in one of those.

"I have a crisis," Marilyn whispered as she slipped a ticket for the night's event into Mica's dinner jacket. "I only have nine at the table. I can't have an empty seat at my table. Please join us when you are done here." Not taking "no" for an answer, she scurried off.

With all the commotion with Marilyn Lassiter, Mica hadn't noticed Michelle Bianco making her way down the phalanx of media, passing out what appears to be a press release.

"Mica, here are the guidelines for Chad Martin," she directed as she handed him a sheet.

Mica glanced at the notice stating Chad Martin has just signed a deal to star in the next Conrad Barrington feature, *The River, Deep*. Mica was taken back to see the written word, not having heard it first from Chad. Chad had mentioned that he was us 'in talks' about some project or another, but nothing this formal or impressive. Conrad Barrington is one of those 'avant garde' producer/directors whose hits are huge and his misses are considered 'art house'. *The River, Deep*, as it states briefly on the press release, will star Chad Martin in the lead role of a young man who can't save the life of a drowning child and is subsequently haunted by both the attempt to do so and the afterlife of the boy himself.

"This is the story tonight, Mica," Michelle cautioned. "Do you hear me? There are no other questions. Again, let me make myself clear: there are no other questions to be answered." Michelle stared at Mica for a moment to punctuate her statement. Mica said nothing.

"Oh, and by the way," Michelle stepped back to announce. "Chad Martin will be here accompanied by Shawna Stevens who will be wearing a beautiful gown from Mon Atelier. You may want to mention that in your stories as well." With that she threw one more glance at Mica and headed back up the carpet to wait for Chad.

Charity nights are big events in Hollywood. Everyone wants to be seen as a giver. Mica, to his pleasure, interviewed the right number of has-beens all formaldehyde and Chanel #5, dressed as if it were the 1980's—sequined and bugle beaded by the likes of Bob Mackie and the late Nolan Miller. He wondered which he would be sitting with later.

And then there were just enough 'hot Hollywood' for Lydia to consider this an event, all teeth and tits, waxing on about how concerned they are for the cause du jour; ironically talking about breast cancer all the while flaunting their fake tits. Lydia considers yesterday's stars to be yesterday's news and not what she wants on *Drop Zone*.

Then, the lightening like eruption of paparazzi flashes, told Mica someone big had arrived. Angeline and Brad? Clooney or DiCaprio? No. Chad Martin. A flush of pride and then the wave of befuddled bemusement washed over Mica. How could this kid he picked up at a dinner party at Roger Keenan's house ever become this big, this fast? It truly is the American dream and Hollywood legend.

For all his hidden pride, Mica had a pit in his stomach. He wanted desperately to run up and give Chad a big congratulatory kiss; announce he, Mica, is the man poolside in the 'bird street' tabloid photo so they can live happily ever after as husband and husband as Chad's career grew exponentially. Instead, Mica has to watch his boyfriend walk the media gauntlet, smiling and lying, with Miss August and Hefner cast off, Shawna Stevens, knowing he has to ask the tough questions when it's his turn—despite the clear and present danger of Michelle Bianco.

"Two questions Mica," Michelle warned as Chad approached.

"Congratulations." Mica put out his hand to shake with Chad's but Chad stood firm with his arms around the set-up Shawna.

"Thanks, man."

There is a momentary pause, during which the handshake snub resonated in Mica's mind as to indicate that clearly Chad knows has a job to do and is doing it. But so does Mica. "In light of the good news with your new project, what is your reaction to the tabloid headlines this week?" Mica asked.

"Mica!" Michelle blurted out.

A wide-eyed Chad stared back at Mica and mumbled, "I am very happy about my new film and working with Conrad Barrington. I have nothing but respect for him."

"Everyone wants to know who your friend is in the picture."

"That is enough, Mica," Michelle spewed and grabbed Chad by the arm to lead him off.

"My dress is by Mon Atelier." Shawna shouted over her shoulder, as they were lead away.

"I didn't think you would do it," Jonathan, the cameraman, whispered to Mica and then patted him on the back.

"You did get all that on tape, didn't you?" Mica questioned, now ashen from what just transpired.

"You bet," Jonathan reassured.

Michelle Bianco had made her way back to Mica. He is not looking forward to whatever is coming next.

"What the fuck were you thinking?" Michelle spewed at Mica in front of Marilyn Lassiter, who as it happened was on her third trip down the red carpet looking for attention.

"I was thinking I needed to save my job," he defended half-heartedly. "If you have a problem with the direction of my interview, you need to take that up with Lydia Gray who gave me specific marching orders."

"Well you should have enough balls, to know when there is no story there and to stand up to that bitch. I will be talking to her but in the meantime, Chad is off limits to you and your show." And off she went.

Mica could see the shock on the other reporter's faces as he stepped back from the velvet rope. Michelle's vitriol was more than apparent, as was Mica's banishment.

"What on earth was all that about?" Marilyn not waiting for an answer continued, "You will have to tell us all about it at the table. You know I live for your stories."

"I don't know that I really want to stay for the evening," Mica returned.

"Oh but you must dear. You must. I can't have nine at my table."

"Of course you can't," Mica mumbled with all the sarcasm he could muster.

o o o

Halfway through the dainty but tasty crab Louis salad course, Mica could feel his phone vibrate. It is Lydia Gray. And rather than being overtly rude and answering it right there, Mica opted for the lesser, but still rude, option of excusing himself from the table to answer it.

Marilyn Lassiter doesn't believe a cell phone should be on let alone answered at an event like this, but shooed him off anyway to do what he had to do. She was already exasperated by Mica's deflecting of questions pertaining to the incident she had overheard between that shrew of a publicist and Mica.

Mica got as far as the bar on the upper level by the doors before he answered it.

"It's me," Lydia began. "I just had the most interesting one-sided explosion of a conversation with Michelle Bianco which leads me to believe you did your job tonight."

"You could say that," Mica returned. "I asked the questions but got no answers."

"But you asked the questions and that is important."

"But to what end," Mica questioned. "We, both me and the show, have been banned from access to Chad Martin."

"Says who?" Lydia dismissed.

"Michelle Bianco!"

"Fuck her," Lydia dismissed again. "She doesn't run *Drop Zone*. I do."

"But she does control access to the stars," Mica corrected.

"We'll talk about where we go from here tomorrow. In the meantime have a drink or several. Good work."

As Mica hung up and turned to go back to his table, he saw Chad heading for the bar closest to Mica. Mica thought for a moment and realized there would be no good time for this conversation. So why not now?

"Chad?"

"You have some fucking balls right now," Chad spewed through clenched teeth.

"I know. But hear me out. I had to ask. My job was threatened if I didn't"

That gave Chad pause but it didn't stop the distain over the situation.

Mica continued, "Look, I knew you were never going to answer the questions and because you didn't, it's a non-starter of a story. But Lydia gave me an ultimatum."

"Jesus Christ, Mica, I have a career!"

"And so do I, Chad. That's the part you don't seem to understand. It's always about your career."

They both stood and stared at each other for a moment, digesting what they've both been saying.

"I have to get back to the table," Chad mumbled. "Shawna's waiting."

"I'll be waiting too, later, at home," Mica choked, holding back tears.

"Not tonight," Chad waved him off. "I can't talk about this tonight. I'll be at my house. You stay at yours. Besides I have an early day tomorrow."

Mica nodded. "Roger Keenan invited us to Palm Springs to get away from the headlines and everything. Maybe we should go when we can. It'll be a good place to talk."

Chad simply nodded and walked away. And just in time.

"Isn't that that delicious Chad Martin?" Marilyn Lassiter said as she approached Mica at the bar. "Champagne." The bartender obliged. "Now do come back to the table and tell us what that was all about."

14

Mica had arrived the night before and was immediately whisked off to dinner, just Roger and him. Mica appreciated the fatherly side of Roger Keenan, not getting to see that often, except when a crisis is brewing. Roger has a unique ability to smell crisis in the air and fix it or at least manage it to some extent. Over dinner at Exotic, nestled in one of the high backed booths where people couldn't eavesdrop, Mica spilled to Roger the quandary of his new assignment.

"Oh dear, *that* is a problem," was all Roger could initially say. "Let me get this straight. You are expected to 'out' Chad and potentially damage his career. But to do so you have to admit you are the man he is seeing all along and potentially end your career because you have been lying to your boss. And Chad is aware of none of this? Again, that's a problem."

Palm Springs is the perfect little getaway, just far enough from Los Angeles in distance but a world away in terms of being able to decompress. Roger's home, in the Deepwell section of old Palm Springs, is quite literally an oasis within this oasis. Small, by the standards of his Hollywood palazzo, this three thousand square foot fully restored mid-century modern house is completely modernized with a period feel. He scooped up the place at the bottom of the market when white elephants like this needed more than their fair share of tender loving care and a good deal of cash to face lift their fading beauty. In those days, everyone screamed Palm Springs was dead. The high-end stores had all moved down to Rancho Mirage, Palm Desert and Indian Wells. The main strip of Palm Springs was lined with tee shirt havens, souvenir shops and empty storefronts. Until the gays saw the gold in the old and started buying up the real estate for pennies on the dollar. Today, Roger's barely six-figure investment is a healthy seven-figure gem. Mica loves coming here.

When they got back from dinner last evening, of course there were the requisite twinks in the pool, naked and cavorting. Six or so hotties picked up from the Warm Sands area where all the clothing optional, gay friendly hotels line what is little more than a sexual cul de sac. Mica liked what he saw, a show for late night cocktails. One in particular, Johannes, had a dick to rival Chad's and while it was on offer to Mica, Mica politely turned him down. Not to waste a good hard on, Johannes simply bent over and started sucking himself off. A Vegas act in the making. Forget Cirque du Soleil; this is purely Cirque So Gay!

Roger, to Mica's mind's eye, is slightly trapped in the pre-AIDS 80s with the constant decadence he surrounds himself with. Nakedness. Orgies. Drugs. As entertaining as it all is from an observers point of view, Mica is concerned that one day it will all go too far and Roger is going to wake up beaten or robbed or any number of other scenarios.

"When you've lost as many friends as I have to AIDS etcetera you adapt a "what the fuck" mentality. Life is too short not to have fun." Roger pontificated. "I don't advocate the behavior. I just provide a safe place for the inevitable to take place. No judgment here."

Mica nodded. He couldn't and wouldn't argue with that kind of logic.

"Besides, since AIDS has become a chronic illness and treatable, all this behavior is back. You think my house is the only spot in town?" Roger defended. "You should see what I have seen behind some of the more stately gates in Bel Air. Besides, don't tell me that you've never been to the Dreamland Spa and gotten fucked on occasion. Well, my house is a hell of a lot better setting to get fucked in than that shit house of a bath house."

Point taken.

Roger promised they all would be gone by the time Chad arrived the next day, sometime in the afternoon, traffic permitting. But, when Mica and Roger walked out by the pool with a morning coffee and two mimosas, two of last night's holdouts had stayed and were now lounging on the adjoining chaises, hung over presumably, getting an all over tan. It was a picture not unlike Mica and Chad's from the tabloids.

"Boys? What have I told you?" Roger began. "This is not a weekender for you. You now have about half an hour to get yourself together and get on your way. I have a guest arriving soon."

"Hate to see them go," Mica leaned in and whispered sotto voce to Roger. "But thank you."

Roger waved his hand in the air as if to dismiss the comment. "I promised you and Chad a quiet weekend. Besides neither of them is Johannes. If they had been you would have had a fight on your hands."

"These days I don't even think Chad would appreciate Johannes...but I did!" They share a chuckle and clinked their champagne glasses together. The boys made their exit and with one last glance over his shoulder, Mica could swear one of those cuties wasn't even of legal age. One of these days, Mica thought, Roger could find himself in real trouble.

"By the way," Roger said, "I loved the article you wrote for that magazine. Loved the title too, COCKSURE. Fantastic. And the pictorial spread by Chuck Corman was something else, so provocative and tasteful at the same time. Kudos to every-one involved. You should do more writing. You have a way with words."

"Thank you. Chad was really happy about it too, as happy as he can be these days. Since the tabloid thing, he is second guessing everything."

"Well he is certainly about town these days. Are there any no-talent bimbos left to be seen with?" Roger chuckled. "I think it is all too much."

"It is sort of overkill, protesting too much that sort of thing."

"Exactly," Roger again hoisted his mimosa high in the air and toasted. "Which brings me to your little dilemma."

"Little. I am being asked to out my boyfriend and in so doing would have to implicate myself as the other half. This no little dilemma."

"Well I think I have a solution."

As if on cue, out walks Chad dressed in a pair of jeans, white t-shirt and leather flip-flops. Dropping his Tumi leather duffle where he stands, he fanes ex-haustion. "Where can a guy get a drink around here. It's hot as hell out here."

Mica got up and got a peck on the lips and then Chad bent over to peck Roger on the cheek."

"So glad to have you here darling," Roger kissed back. "And as promised you have the place to yourself."

With that, Chad gives the backyard the once over. He had been here plenty of times but never, in the past, had cared about how high the perimeter wall is or whether there are sightlines for invasive cameras. Roger clocked the mini inspec-tion. "Fear not darling, it is completely private. If not, I would have been in some pretty deep shit by now."

"I am just a little paranoid these days." Chad pulled his tee shirt over his shoulders, kicked off the flip-flops and pulled down his pants, readying himself for a dive in the pool.

"You may be paranoid but if I had that body I would call every paparazzi I could find to show it off," Roger declared. "What the fuck have you been up to?"

He flexed jokingly for Roger, waved his dick at him and then dove in the pool.

"If he isn't on the set or on the town, he's in the gym. I never see him any more," Mica explained as they walked toward the bar area next to the kitchen.

"Ah yes, *that* trainer," Roger muttered, referring the picture in the tabloids.

Chad threw Roger a look as if to say, "back off". But there isn't much to say; the picture exists.

Chad proceeded to swim a few laps, pull himself from the pool and lay down on an empty chaise to dry by the sunlight. Roger returned from the bar with a tray of cocktails and fixings for more. Mica and Chad eagerly reached up when offered and took one of the fruity concoctions in the oversized martini glasses.

"You were missed at dinner. But we had a lovely time just the two of us. So for whom were we stood up? Who was last night's gal about town?" Roger asked.

"I was out with Michelle Bianco, my publicist," Chad dismissed. Mica and Roger groaned. "Can you believe this? She wanted to blow me in the car!"

"What?" Mica spat.

"She had a lot to drink. And I gather she has that sort of reputation with her clients. Supposedly she had a long affair with one client and it almost got her fired when he left the agency." Chad didn't think it was wise to let Mica know, she did blow him in the car.

"But the night was not a total loss. I have two solid movie offers, both eight figures!" Everyone raised a glass for a silent toast.

"When did that happen?" Mica questioned feeling even further distanced from Chad's life.

"This week. And that is why I was out with Michelle. She wanted to talk strategy. She thinks I should leave the television series and concentrate on my movie career. She sort of thinks I should go with a less-is-more strategy for publicity from now on as we create a movie star image." Turning to Mica. "She loved the COCKSURE article by the way." Of course Mica already knew that as Michelle had final say on the editorial content. She wasn't going to let anything out she didn't love. What he is saying is she loved the pictures.

"First, I get handed a press release on a red carpet about your starring role in *The River, Deep* and now this. Do we ever communicate?"

"Oh you had a lot to say on that red carpet," Chad unleashed.

"Is that what this is about?" Mica shot back. "I told you I had to ask those questions."

"Really?" Chad snapped. "What are you going to do next? Admit that it is you in those pictures?" No one spoke. "Of course you won't because that will jeopardize your career. But you don't mind fucking me up on a red carpet."

"And what about the tabloid issue," Roger introduced the elephant in the room. "There will be more stories you know. Mica will not be the only person to question what is going on in your life. The more famous you become, the more infamous you become. Mica was only doing his job. You have to be ready for it to come from all angles."

There was silence.

"I think I have a solution," Roger clapped as he spoke. "I think you should draft a statement and do an interview confronting this head on..."

"Michelle wants to pretend it didn't happen," Chad interjected.

"But it did happen," Roger hammered back. He winked at Mica, knowing Mica needed this solution for his own dilemma in outing Chad as much as Chad needed to quash the rumors. "Here's what I would do. I would draft a statement and follow up with an interview that I think Mica here could easily and expertly handle.

"The statement would read something to the effect of: I have gay friends. It's as simple as that. Now if you think that I am gay simply by my association, that's fine with me. My job is to create a fantasy figure as an actor, which brings you to the movie theaters or sits you in front of the television screen. If your fantasy says you think I am gay, that is fine as long as you are supporting my career. Having said that, if you see me hugging another man or even kissing another man, it is because I love and support my gay friends as much as my straight girlfriends. Life is hard enough and I choose love over hate."

"That is brilliant!" Mica exclaimed. "No one could ever question your actions because all you have to say is I love my gay friends. Simple and, again, brilliant. We can set up an interview on *Drop Zone* and the problem is solved."

Chad stood and put both fists on his hips, which created a bit of a surreal visual—he, being naked, in front of two gay men, and about to spout off in what could be construed as a genuine hissy fit. "I could never say that. Michelle Bianco would never let me say that. I am going to be a God damned movie star."

Everyone paused to let the hysteria of the moment pass. And then Roger softly but directly spoke. "I know a thing or two about stardom and publicity. You may not think you need to say anything now. But when the next pictures surface, and they will, mark my words. You will have wished you made that statement. And let's hope for your sake it won't be too late when you do." There is a pregnant pause and then Roger broke the ice. "More cocktails, anyone?"

15

Chad and Tommy sat across from each other, naked, dripping sweat, in the dry sauna attached to the guest house—the former garage turned office behind the bungalow that is the Body Image gym. Chad had taken to using the sauna after a workout hoping to shed non-existent extra pounds in order to lean up for *The River, Deep*. The sweat always turns Chad on, rubbing his hands over his moist hard body.

And of course, there is a stirring in Chad's cock.

"Just to let you know," Tommy began, "my wife left me."

"What?"

"My wife. She left me," Tommy restated.

"Sorry, I guess," Chad mumbled.

"Well, it sucks. But it does free me up."

"For what?" Chad sighed, not quite seeing where Tommy is going.

"This."

"What do you mean?" Chad suddenly connected the dots. "Why did she leave you?"

"Because of the picture of us," Tommy stammered.

"There is no story behind that picture," Chad snapped. "Unless, that is, you gave her a story."

"She's my wife. She knows what goes on when clients work out together, get sweaty, wrestle..."

Chad didn't let him finish. "What the fuck are you saying to me?

"It's not a problem..."

"It is to me!" Chad stood up and grabbed on to his own dick and started whipping Tommy in the face with it. "Did you get off telling her about this? Did you tell her you've sucked my cock?"

With his free hand, Chad grabbed Tommy by the neck and threw him to the floor. Before Tommy could react, Chad mounted him from behind and pounded his now hard dick into Tommy's ass. "Did you tell her how much you love this?"

The shock registered on Tommy's face. The pain is excruciating. "Fuck you are hurting me!"

"Like you hurt your wife?" Chad goaded as he pounded Tommy's raw ass.

His moans turned to groans of pleasure. Being dominated and raped by Chad Martin was a fantasy best kept secret. Before long Tommy gave in to the forceful thrusting and slammed his ass back against Chad.

"See you like it, you fuck!"

The pounding was relentless and seemed to go on forever. And just when Tommy thought he couldn't take anymore, Chad rolled him over, let out a loud grunt and spewed his hot cum all over Tommy's face. Tommy licked his lips and tasted a salty semen and sweat combination. He smiled up at Chad, satisfied and ready to cum himself. And just as Tommy let himself go and shot his wad all over his chest, Chad smacked him in the face just hard enough to snap him out of his after glow.

"You're fired you fuck," Chad stated as matter of fact and walked out of the sauna into the bright sunshine.

° ° °

"My key doesn't work," Mica began as Chad opened the door and let Mica in.

Mica is always impressed with the front door of Chad's house, an industrial chic frosted single pain of glass like the front door of an urban boutique, only milky opaque so you can't see in. One of Mica's favorite pictures he has of Chad, one of the few Chad's allowed Mica to take, is Chad's nude body pressed against the door. Through the opacity you can clearly see it is a man, clearly see that he is nude but have no idea it is *the* Chad Martin.

"Of course your key doesn't work," Chad replied as he walked back into the living area. He is uncharacteristically clothed. "I changed the locks."

"When? Why?"

"I have been thinking about it since the invasion."

"Invasion. You've been broken into?" Mica fired back, clearly upset.

"The invasion of my privacy."

Our privacy, Mica thought but decided it would be better not to split hairs on the matter.

"And since I have put a bid on the house, I don't want realtors or anyone else who might still have a key to have access."

"You bought this house!"

"Buying it," Chad corrected. "Semantics really. It's a short escrow for an all cash deal."

"So things are going well," Mica chirped with a hint of sarcasm. "You used to tell me when you had big news like buying a house."

"It's a business thing, no big deal."

"A multi-million dollar house in the 'bird streets' is kind of a big deal."

Chad waved off the idea and nestled himself in the corner of the couch underneath one of two matching Chuck Corman portraits of him.

"I haven't seen these before," Mica said as he gestured to the two large-scale photos. "I don't remember these from the photo shoot."

"They're not. Chuck had me into the studio for a sitting."

"Ah," was the best that Mica could utter. He is not the jealous type but he could feel some sort of resentment creeping from within. Chad's success has been nothing short of meteoric and good for him. But it is hard not to resent someone who has barely paid any dues, got lucky because he got lucky in the gene pool and has cashed in on his big dick and finally isn't sharing the spoils. When Chad was a nobody, Mica was more than happy to help out with everything from paying for dinners to introducing Chad to the right people. Now that he is somebody, everything is secretive and solitary.

Chad groaned, "I know you came all the way over here. But I am exhausted. I think I am going to have to call it a night."

The comment caught Mica completely off guard. "What? But I...do you have any idea when the last time I stayed overnight here? The last time we made love?"

"Yeah, when we got our pictures taken," Chad snapped. "As far as sex. I fucked you in Palm Springs."

"I know when we fucked. I was talking about making love."

"A fuck is a fuck. You can find it anywhere," Chad dismissed.

"Well I don't. I find it with you. I don't cheat." Mica paused for a mutual agreement but got nothing from Chad. "Do you?"

"I don't consider a blowjob from some horned up wannabe starlet to be cheating," Chad dismissed.

Well I do, Mica thought but didn't want to give in to Chad's clearly inflated idea of self. "What about your trainer, Tommy?"

"He is an employee. He works for me," Chad justified but didn't quite answer. "Or at least he did. I fired him."

Mica climbed on to the sofa and reached out to rub the inside of Chad's crossed leg but Chad brushed his hand aside. "I told you I am tired."

"You, who can get it up when the wind blows sideways, are tired?" Not waiting for an answer, Mica continued. "I miss you. I miss that cock of yours. I miss you being inside of me. I miss us!"

Chad sat stoic on the couch and then, "It's not you. It's me. There is just a lot going on in my life." The classic brush off.

"Yours is a life I thought I was going to share." Mica got up and headed toward the door. "Can we at least start over with a date?"

"Sure," Chad muttered noncommittally.

As Mica got to the door, he turned to Chad, "By the way, since you changed the locks I don't have a key."

"I know," is all Chad offered in return.

∘ ∘ ∘

Evol's edit bay is dark except for the glow of the monitors and one candle she burns continuously to ward off bad juju. Both Mica and she stare at the one monitor that plays the video in real time. Evol is dressed in her usual Goth meets punk attire and despite her intimidating piercings and tattoos, she is genuinely a nice person.

"So what is wrong," she began. "You are not your enthusiastic self."

"Personal stuff," he shrugged off.

They continued to watch the tape of Chad behind the scenes on the set of *Divas* on more than one red carpet and then the most recent debacle when Mica confronted him at the breast cancer event at the Beverly Hilton. Somehow, Mica is going to have to turn this perfectly harmless collection of video into some scandal mongering innuendo of a segment.

"Soooo?" Evol prodded.

"So what?"

"What do you want to do with all this?"

"Frankly I would like to burn it," Mica muttered back.

"Do you really think any of these gals Chad Martin goes out with really mean anything to him?"

"No!" Mica snapped.

"Well that was fairly emphatic," Evol shot back, somewhat surprised at the emphasis he is putting on an innocuous question.

"I've known Chad for a while. That's all."

"Is that why you got this assignment?"

"Probably," Mica huffed.

"So do you know who is in the tabloid pictures, next to him by the pool?" she asked innocently enough.

"The bigger question is: Who cares?" Mica shouted a little too defensively. "Lydia is like a fucking dog with a bone over those pictures. And I don't think it is anyone's business. And it is certainly not my job to try and out Chad Martin. Although, strangely that is exactly what my job has become."

Evol is taken aback by Mica's rant but continued on anyway. "I don't believe in outing either but that is what the news is fast becoming—chasing the motorcade of some fucked up young celebrity on their way to court, dodging their cars as they speed off from a club and occasionally turning a pool party into a sex scandal. And short of quitting, you have to do your job."

"I know but whatever happened to self respect? This show was conceived as the safe haven for stars to tell their sides of the story. We were the good verses the evil."

"Ha," she laughed. "The way I look at it is we didn't put them in their sticky situations. We are just holding them accountable...or so the new mandate goes. I have been told we are just giving the audience what they crave. And that is the only way to survive on television."

Mica knew there is something to that logic. He just didn't think it applied to his unique situation.

"Didn't you say sometime ago that you were dating some young actor?" Evol continued. "What would you think if he was caught in some compromising situation like the one Chad Martin is in?"

"There is no right answer," Mica answered. "I guess I would try to stand by him and let him make his own decision. The bigger question is can a relationship survive the decision?"

She hummed and nodded her agreement. He paused and thought for a moment and then the light in his head turned on.

"Evol, you may have just hit on the thrust of this segment: At what price freedom?"

"Huh?"

"Chad Martin," Mica began to explain, "is now a multi-millionaire with tens of millions more in contractual obligations. But those might just be handcuffs, tying him to a web of lies. Maybe it is not for us to answer the question but rather suggest the question: What is the price of freedom? How much does he have to earn in order to find happiness?"

Evol nodded, still not sure if she understood the concept but there is definitely something to it.

Mica would certainly have to run this idea by B.J. and then Lydia. But perhaps supposition will appease the need to accuse. Moreover, maybe then he can explain to Chad all that has been happening from his end.

°○°

"He fucked me over! Plain and simple. He fucked me over!"

The second martini is obviously the truth serum for which Anthony Wright was hoping. It is as if Tommy Mercer, trainer to the stars, had kept a lid so tight on what is a boiling cauldron of stories that he is about to explode. Tommy is a man's man and doesn't take well to being fucked over.

Anthony couldn't believe his ears or his luck, never thinking Tommy would give up or give in so easily. He had yet to use Chad's name in connection with any specific behavior but he knew that was just another martini away.

Anthony had invited Tommy for a drink just for this purpose. Anthony understood completely what it is like to be 'fucked over' by Chad Martin. Chad's defection from the Albert Switzer Agency to being represented by Sterling Lowe at International Management Cooperative was a devastating blow to Albert, the agency and Anthony's chances for partnership. Anthony wants his pound of flesh and has been working towards it with planting stories and pictures in the tabloids about Chad. But in Tommy Mercer, he may just have struck gold.

Anthony and Tommy decided on meeting at The Cathedral, a hot indoor/outdoor gay bar on Robertson just below Santa Monica Boulevard in the heart of West Hollywood. Because it is technically a gay bar, Anthony wasn't sure that Tommy would be comfortable here, even though it is just a stone's throw from Tommy's gym, Body Image, and therefore couldn't be more convenient. Tommy arrived still in his gym gear.

The Cathedral is hardly just a gay bar, it is a mecca for young Hollywood trying to look cool and older Hollywood trying to look liberal minded. Even Elizabeth Taylor used to hang out in the back of the courtyard on occasion, with her dog in her lap, sipping a cosmopolitan. Talk about your gay icon seal of approval! Not bad for a place that started out as a late night coffee haven for the under twenty-one set and is now one of the hottest clubs in the city, if not the country.

"This is such a cool place," Tommy commented looking around at the neo-gothic interior of the main bar area. There are, in fact, four bars in the one establishment, as it is bad business to keep a thirsty gay man waiting for a cocktail.

"I like it." Anthony agreed.

"I come here with my wife," Tommy began and then paused. "I should say soon to be ex-wife."

That tit bit of news startled Anthony. "I am sorry to hear that."

"I call it collateral damage."

"What does that mean?" Anthony pressed.

"That picture in the tabloid," Tommy muttered. "It was the straw that broke the camel's back."

"That picture was innocent enough," Anthony pushed.

"That's what I said. And I told her that I am not the man in the poolside pictures. But she knew that from my body type. It's just that I had gotten close to Chad over the months and she didn't like it."

"But to leave you over it?" Anthony figured it was time to roll the dice. "Just how close were you...or are you?"

"I don't talk about my clients, Tony. Do you mind if I call you Tony?"

"That's fine."

Anthony signaled the bartender for another round. The bartenders at The Cathedral are, ironically, mostly straight and are all wannabe actors of some sort. And this particular bartender, Dennis, Anthony has been eyeing for sometime as a potential client. If he is going to branch out on his own, with his own agency, Anthony has got to corral a stable of clients and Dennis could be one of them.

"Dennis meet Tommy," Anthony began. They exchanged a firm, body builder to trainer, handshake.

"You work out," Tommy noted. "Here is my card. I am a trainer just down the street. Come in I can give you a session and see what you think."

"Thanks," Dennis said as he looked over the card. "I think I've heard of you."

"Two more of the same," Anthony interjected, not to derail his conversation.

Dennis retreated back to the workstation and grabbed a big bottle of Kettle One and began to pour.

"I may need a trainer myself," Anthony joked.

"Well you too should come by the gym and see what there is on offer." There is another contemplative pause. "Actually, I could use the business." For all his bravado, Tommy seemed quite sincere.

"But aren't you the trainer to the stars?" Anthony queried.

"Since that picture ran of me and Chad, clients have been dropping off. They're afraid of me not being discrete. That is why I say I have been completely fucked over by Chad Martin."

Tommy's voice rose as the martinis arrived and even Dennis did a double take at the mention of Chad Martin's name.

"Speaking of that," Anthony cut him off with a low voiced warning to keep the comments on the down low, "that is why I've reached out to you."

"Oh?"

"Your story is worth money."

"My story?"

"For the lack of a better word, your relationship with your clients, especially Chad."

Up until then Tommy had been sipping his drink but the word 'relationship' resonated and he took a big gulp. "It was a relationship. It's professional of course. But a relationship for sure."

That was all Anthony needed to hear to confirm in his mind there is, indeed, a story behind the story.

"When you say my story is worth money...how much?" Tommy grilled.

"I believe I can get you fifty thousand dollars to talk about how you trained Chad Martin, that sort of thing. You can fill in the blanks from there." Anthony paused to let that sink in. "Of course my commission is...," He thought for a moment. "...Twenty percent."

"I'm not a rat!"

"That is not what I am inferring," Anthony clarified. "You are a contributor to Chad Martin's success. The body everyone wants to see, you created. People want to know how."

All Tommy can think of is the money. He has lost all of his best and highest paying clients thanks to Chad's defection. Why shouldn't he make a dollar or two off the deal? Chad is making millions off that body—the body he rightfully created.

"What do I need to do?" Tommy asked as his raised his glass to toast a done deal.

"I'll take care of it. I have already made some enquiries with a couple of European magazines who are very interested in hearing what you have to say."

○ ○ ○

Anthony had heard the expression 'three beer queer' but it seems three martinis is the winning combination to get Tommy Mercer out of his gym gear and his legs in the air.

The rather superficial tour of the gym, Body Image, happened after they downed the third cocktail, paid the bill and, on Tommy's insistence, walked the two blocks over to "the scene of the crime" as Tommy put it.

The bungalow was empty when they arrived and Tommy walked Anthony through the different rooms, encouraging him to try out the equipment as they went. Anthony indulged Tommy when it came to the bench press. Tommy egged Anthony on to see how much he can lift.

Anthony, athletic but on the skinny side, laid down as Tommy put on a guestimated amount of weight on each side of the bar. When ready, Tommy straddled his head in order to spot the weight bar as Anthony gave an almighty push. He was able to lift it, but just barely, as he was distracted by a glance up the leg of Tommy's gym shorts. And as it is Tommy's want to do, he is going commando. The impressive shaft of his penis caught Anthony off guard.

"That was very good," Tommy complimented. "I didn't think you would be able to handle that."

Catching Anthony off guard, he responded to the double entendre. "I have handled that and more."

They continued through the yoga room, past the kitchen and to the bathroom, which took Anthony again by surprise. "It is so spa like."

"Nice huh?"

Anthony walked into the oversized shower stall and jokingly made reference to the number of people who could use the shower at once. Just then in a tipsy moment of presumed frivolity, Tommy reached in and turned the tap causing the rain forest showerhead to pour down on Anthony. He turned it off as fast as he turned it on but the damage was done, Anthony was soaked.

"What the fuck am I supposed to do now?" Anthony squealed as Tommy threw him a towel.

"Sorry, I was just trying to be funny. I didn't expect it to rain like that. Don't worry; I have a clothes dryer in the back. Slip the wet stuff off and I'll take care of it.

"I can't," Anthony muttered. "I have nothing on underneath."

Tommy rolled his eyes. "We are guys, it is no big deal."

Anthony pulled off his shirt, revealing a well-defined mocha color torso, and handed the wet shirt to Tommy. He then pulled his belt free from his pants, emptied his pockets and wrapped the towel around himself. As he attempted to slip out of his jeans, the towel fell and revealed all. He scrambled to pick it back up but he realized it was out and on display.

"It's nothing I haven't seen before," Tommy joked. "I've got one myself. Let me dry the towel too."

Buck naked, Anthony handed it over. "Do you have any gym shorts or something I can slip on?"

"Yeah these." With that, Tommy pulled off the ones he was wearing and handed them over to Anthony. "There, now we are both in the same boat."

They eyed each other sheepishly and then Tommy reached over to give

Anthony a hug. "Hell, we're in business together. Now we really don't have any secrets."

As they hugged, Tommy's impressive cock rubbed against the mocha extension of Anthony's growing cock. It feels good.

"Ah, this is embarrassing," Anthony pointed out the obvious and tried to cup his growing member with his hand.

"It's okay," Tommy reassured. "It happens all the time when clients and I wrestle. Or when we do nude yoga or stretching."

"You work out in the nude?" Anthony was aghast.

"You're the client. We do what you want." Tommy shrugged. "Do you like to wrestle?"

Not waiting for answer, Tommy led Anthony to the yoga room where mats were already spread out. He grabbed Anthony, spun him around, locked his arms in a full nelson and pushed him to the ground. Anthony squirmed to put up a fight. All he was able to do was to flip over on his back only to have Tommy land on top of him, his cock and shaved balls resting on Anthony's face.

Tommy sat up, leaving the cock and balls nicely nestled and reached down under Anthony's butt and scooped him up with Anthony's legs wrapped around Tommy's neck. "That is called a pin and I win."

All that action and surprise had left Anthony flaccid but not so for Tommy, who had achieved a semi-erection as a result. "My turn to apologize?" he taunted Anthony with a couple of gentle strokes.

"As you said, we're just guys here," Anthony teased back.

Anthony reached over and playfully began to stroke Tommy, which caused both to get hard. With his other hand, Anthony ever so softly ran his fingers over Tommy's sculptured body. He loved the softness of his skin and the small tuft of a pubic mound Tommy had let grow back but obviously crafted to be neat and trimmed.

For his part, Tommy simply eschewed the foreplay and opened his mouth and took the majority of Anthony's long and wide cock, groaning with pleasure and leaving a significant amount of spit to trickle down to Anthony's balls.

As Anthony explored Tommy's body with his hands, he also began to explore with his tongue. First, the tip of Tommy's engorged cock, teasing it with little flickers, and then down the veiny shaft. As he settled down by his egg-sized balls, he took each in his mouth and massaged them with his tongue. Both Tommy and Anthony began to moan from their respective pleasures.

Tommy spread his legs apart to accommodate Anthony's head in his crotch as they both maneuvered into the sixty-nine position. As Anthony took Tommy's cock in his mouth and bobbed up and down accordingly, he reached underneath with his hand and let his middle finger glide down the crack of Tommy's ass, tapping gently on the tight button of his asshole. Tommy clenched and squirmed with delight.

While still pumping away in and out of Tommy's mouth, Anthony situated himself on his knees, astride Tommy's face, and pulled Tommy's legs into the air, exposing that pulsating asshole for which Anthony hungered. He spit directly on it and massaged the spit all around the opening as he slid first one and then a second finger in and out of the expanding hole.

After several minutes of teasing and taunting that wanting hole, Anthony pulled himself from Tommy's gulping throat and swung around to give him what he really wants. With a slow push, he inserted the head of his penis—a sizable insertion in its own right, which causes a usual initial gasp. And it did. Anthony paused as Tommy relaxed and then eased forward causing Tommy to squirm with pain and pleasure. Anthony, as he has learned to do, simply kept pushing. He knew Tommy would adapt and give in to the pleasure over the pain.

Tommy lay there writhing with a form of ecstasy only one man can give to another as Anthony let a big ball of spit trickle from his mouth and free fall onto Tommy's hard cock. Between the sweat and the saliva, Tommy's well-lubed cock was getting a firm hand job while Anthony pumped away on his ass. So rhythmic. So in sync. Tommy groaned with each thrust.

"Fuck me," he moaned. "Fuck me harder. Fuck me Chad!"

Chad? The Freudian slip wasn't lost on Anthony who now knew in Tommy he had indeed struck tabloid gold.

16

The headline in the *Hollywood Reporter* said it all: THE NAKED TRUTH ABOUT BOFFO BOX OFFICE. Clearly making your private parts public can turn into big-ticket sales. And it has for *The Other Brother*—the small independent film, never slated for release until Chad Martin became a shirtless wonder on the hit television series *Divas*—now has raked in a staggering half a billion dollars domestically. Who knows where it is going internationally and in ancillary rights for cable and DVD sales.

These days in Hollywood half a billion dollars is hardly chump change considering the film cost so little to produce and market, meaning most of that box office is pure profit with the exception of the ten percent Chad's agent, Sterling Lowe of International Management Cooperative, negotiated when the movie was going to be released, thanks to Chad's mounting television popularity. All of which has made Spectrum Studios very happy and Chad Martin very rich.

And that is cause to celebrate.

○ ○ ○

There was a commotion at the gate of Roger Keenan's house. Mica had decided to park his car on the street rather than to get in the fray of the valet when he would be ready to leave. He luckily found a space a block away that wasn't resident permit parking only. Mica always wondered where the valets stashed all the cars in a neighborhood like this and made sure no one got a ticket.

As he reached the gate, three men were going at it. The man in the distinguished dark suit with the clipboard was clearly from the studio, assigned to check for people on and off the guest list. There was officer Joe planted for security. And then there was a rather aggressive man in Joe's face. He was in a tight suit that showed off his distinctly built body.

"I am sure there is some mistake," the man nearly shouted. "Tommy. The name is Tommy Mercer. I was invited."

The man with the clipboard quickly interjected. "Maybe you were invited. But you are no longer invited."

"I am a good friend of Chad's. Chad Martin?" He pleaded.

"I am sure Chad has many friends," the clipboard holder calmly returned. "But they aren't on this list either."

"You are going to have to leave," Joe stated while he took the man by the arm and forcibly turned him away from the gate.

Suddenly face to face with Tommy, Chad's now ex-trainer, Mica blanched. He couldn't believe he was here and worse yet trying to crash the party. "That's Mica Daly. He knows me. He'll vouch for me," Tommy began in a panic.

Mica didn't know what to do, so he did nothing. Smiling at Joe and nodding to the clipboard holder, he simply didn't acknowledge Tommy and walked through the heavy wrought iron gate. But from over his shoulder he could hear one more desperate plea from Tommy, "Mica, I have to talk to Chad. Can you tell him I'm here?"

◦ ◦ ◦

Mica hadn't made his way two feet past the front door before he was grabbed and hugged by Barry Stegman, the head of Spectrum Studios and guest of honor for the evening.

"I don't know about you Mica, but I think half a billion in box office is a damn good reason to have a party," Barry Stegman chortled, putting his arm around Mica as if he was an integral part of the success of the movie. And maybe he was. Mica had done enough pieces on it and, along with Chad's profile piece, moved the marketing of the movie along nicely. As the famed head of Spectrum Studios, Barry Stegman has a reputation for being a cutthroat hard ass. But tonight all bets are off; Barry Stegman seems down right convivial.

Barry's wife Diandra leaned over to Mica as if to let him in on a scoop, "I am wearing vintage Badgley Mischka." Mica fought back telling Diandra that he wasn't there at the party in the capacity of a reporter. He is a guest. But he did want to ask her just when did a Badgley Mischka design fall into the category of 'vintage'? They've only been on the red carpet scene for two decades or so haven't they?

Mica actually likes Diandra and feels for her at the same time. It is hard to pity a woman perched atop a sprawling Bel Air mansion, reportedly purchased for fifty million at the height of the market from a notorious Russian oligarch who in turn wanted a piece of Hollywood history and then never set foot in the place. It was the former home of some pioneer studio head who had it created by the set design people from the studio back in the 1930's. The result was all giftwrap and no substance, meaning it looked pretty just like a movie set but was built to be torn down. And that is just what they did, tore it to the studs and rebuilt it exactly how it looked in the 30's. It was the talk of the town when the spread appeared in *Architectural Digest*. But for Diandra it is a gilded cage. She, like so many women married to powerful men in Hollywood, has little to do but shop and lunch, little to say, as their opinions rarely matter, and little to no interests, except the charity circuit. As a result, Mica always tries to engage Diandra, even briefly, just so she feels or knows that someone is aware that she, too, is in the room.

"I've got a piece of scoop for ya, Mica," Barry whispered in one of those stage whispers.

"Oh?" Mica played along.

"We're setting up Chad Martin with a three picture production deal," he glowed.

Mica didn't know what to say and couldn't conceal his shock. Chad and Mica may have taken a break for a week or so—maybe it's two by now, who's counting—but news this big Mica would have thought Chad would have shared.

"Don't look so surprised," Barry could register Mica's poker face had cracked. "Chat Martin is hot, hot, hot, and if I can cash in on that? Fuck it, you bet your ass I will."

"By the way," Barry cautioned. "This is still hush, hush. I know I probably shouldn't have told you, as you are a fucking reporter. But I would appreciate if you could hold off on any public announcements until we cross the 't's and dot the 'i's and get a press release together. But when the time is right, you will be the first with access," he added with that all too familiar Hollywood 'sincerity'.

"You aren't saying something you shouldn't, are you now Barry?" Lance Novak sidled up to the conversation stealthily but clearly close enough to hear enough. "Our contracts are confidential until we make them public," he cautioned to Barry.

"Mica here won't say anything," Barry defended.

"Mica here has already said enough in public," Lance pointed out.

Mica just smiled. He's learned as a reporter, as a journalist, that nothing makes people more uncomfortable than silence, especially when they want to make a point. Inevitably, they will show their hand, if you just stay quiet. Of course, in this case, the adversary is Lance Novak, the top gun lawyer from Dunning, Baker and Astin. There isn't a bigger question mark than a hungry, up and comer and you can only play the 'made you blink' game so long before you yourself blink.

"I hope that Mica knows better than to open his mouth," Lance cautioned.

"That actually sounds like a threat, Lance. Jesus Christ, how long have we known each other?"

"Calm down, let me buy you a drink." Lance guided Mica to the open bar while nodding their departure to the Stegmans. "We are preparing a template lawsuit on behalf of your friend Chad Martin. It's a slander and libel all encompassing package that can and will ruin the average person making unflattering comments including supposition and innuendo."

"And you are telling me this why?" Mica nervously questioned.

"You're not a stupid man, Mica. I just want you to avoid adding careless to the list of things you are."

Again, Mica chose to be silent. Nothing good is going to come from this conversation. And at this point, it is probably better that Lance Novak only knows that Mica is reporting on Chad and not cavorting with Chad as well. But the threat was duly noted.

With that, Lance stepped behind the bar and helped himself to a tumbler full of a 1926 Macallan scotch that Mica was aware of costing Roger tens of thousands of dollars. "Isn't that a drink above your pay grade? You're not a partner yet." Mica sniped and ordered a very large, very dry, Kettle One martini with a twist. You're nobody in this town without a threat hanging over your head, Mica thought. Let the fun begin.

° ° °

As Barry was saying, half a billion in box office is a very good reason to have a party and no one throws them better than Roger Keenan. Of course, Roger's parties are notorious for the debauchery sensibility to them. But on this night, it was all party perfect. Not a penis to be seen, nothing being snorted or lubed up. There is just the perfect array of the right faces in a setting of formality. Mica isn't sure if Roger had turned a new leaf or simply lost his touch. Of course the night is young.

"I got my hand slapped after the naked waiters from the last evening with this group," Roger ponied up an excuse for the staid atmosphere. "Nothing a little after party can't change."

"Have you seen Chad?" Mica asked over the din of the crowd.

"Didn't you come together?"

Mica chose not to answer and Roger got the point.

"He's here, somewhere," Roger answered, waving his hand across the room as if to reiterate 'somewhere'.

Mica stepped back and observed the room. Chuck Corman is talking to Conrad Barrington, the director/producer of Chad's new project *The River, Deep.* Between lively conversation nuggets between the two, Conrad is busy snapping pictures of the room for a pictorial spread in a glossy magazine. Mica knew this because everyone had to sign an image release before they walked in the door. He waved at the two of them, which was ignored, and made a mental note to congratulate Chuck on the photos hanging in Chad's house.

As Mica's shifted his gaze across the room, he spotted two throw back's to the Warhol factory days. Amazed they are still alive, Mica couldn't believe his luck in spotting the virtually unrecognizable duo—one now obese since her days as a model and the other, a debutant socialite, who is now broke and writing a book nobody will read about the days nobody will remember. Both had been intermittent stars in Warhol's artsy films as well as muses, respectively, to his silkscreen work. The average Joe on the street wouldn't be able to pick them out of a police line up, but Mica has always had a knack for this kind of celebrity spotting trivia.

Mica then went on to focus on the band in the corner, a mash up of Motown backup singers and second tier stars who were never fully or fairly compensated for the gold they spun back in Detroit all those years ago. A gig like this is as good as it gets these days.

Finally Mica rested in the sitting area in the back. There sits Chad and his co-star Ashley Beckwith, who somehow has been virtually forgotten as part of this movie—proving the size of a cock trumps the size of the role. They seem cozy, to Mica's eye but Mica passed it off as Ashley being bimbo du jour on a night celebrating *their* success in a movie that was never going to be seen. So what if they are holding hands?

○ ○ ○

Enough time had passed. Mica and Chad hadn't even acknowledged each other's presence, let alone talked. Mica chose to keep his distance out of respect and Chad was just being bitchy—the norm these days. But you can only stay apart, even in a crowded room, just so long. So it was inevitable that both, avoiding a tray of the passed lemon squares the rest of the room respectfully overlooked rather than looked over, they would collide.

"Fancy running into you," Mica began.

Chad simply smiled. "How are you?"

"Lonely," Mica began.

Chad nodded and then there was an awkward pause.

"Congrats, on the new deal with Spectrum," Mica offered neutrally.

"You know about that?" Chad asked cautiously.

"I am a reporter."

"I don't need to be reminded of that."

"Why? Is Michelle Bianco here?" Mica joked and thought twice that she could in fact be lurking.

"No," Chad blushed, "don't worry. Sorry about her by the way. I know she is crazy but she is just doing what she needs to do. But seriously, how did you know about Spectrum?"

"Barry Stegman is bursting to let the news out. He told me."

"Well, I can't shut him up," Chad said as a throwaway line but it wasn't lost on Mica. Is Chad or are his people trying to shut people up?

"You're friend is here by the way," Mica said nonchalantly.

Chad wrinkled his nose as if to ask, "who?"

"Tommy, your trainer."

"Ex-trainer," Chad clarified. "I fired his ass."

"Why?" Mica questioned and then caught himself. The tabloids, of course. "Don't worry they didn't let him in." There is yet another awkward pause. "Can we go somewhere to talk?"

Both glance around the room looking for a quiet spot, neither suggesting they should go upstairs to one of the vacant guest rooms. They settled on an empty spot on the patio overlooking the very pool they had frolicked in the night they met.

"I miss you," Mica started in immediately.

"Yeah, me too."

"Soooo?" Mica pressed.

"You know what," Chad countered. "I have been thinking a lot about life and choices and my career and us. There is no easy answer. I am on a trajectory I have dreamt of my whole life."

"All two decades or so of your life," Mica sniped.

"Don't bust my balls," Chad snapped back. "Opportunity is fleeting. You can always find a cock if you need it. But opportunity isn't always there. I don't need a cock. I need to fulfill my destiny."

Mica is dumbfounded by what he is hearing. "Is that all I am to you...a cock?"

"No. That is not what I mean. That's not what I mean at all. It's just there is too much at risk," Chad offered by way of explanation but Mica is having none of it.

"Kiss me," Mica said calmly.

"Are you kidding me?"

"We went through this once before here. We kissed when you thought you would be damned to hell. And you weren't hit by lightening, turned to a pile of ash and neither did anything of biblical proportions strike you down. But lightening did strike me as it did in this pool on the very night we met. I fell in love."

"Don't say that," Chad whispered.

"I have to say it because when else will I have a chance to say this. I love you."

Without thinking, Chad kissed Mica hard and deep, pulled away and then walked away. Mica instinctively knew that might well have been their last kiss.

Just as last time lighting may not have struck, no one was damaged...yet. But in that brief few seconds, while Chad and Mica were locked in passion, an enterprising young man snapped a photo on his smart phone. Then again, Anthony Wright, formerly of the Albert Switzer Agency, has always been enterprising.

17

As Mica pulls up to the gate at the former concrete factory that now houses the studio and offices for *Drop Zone*, the guard gives him a look and then radios that Mica has arrived.

"Is there something I should know about?" Mica asked half jokingly.

"Ms. Gray asked to be notified when you arrived," the guard returned stoically.

At that point, Mica knew he was in for a lousy day but is hardly prepared for the shit storm he is walking into. As he opened the heavy industrial door on the side, which serves as the formal entrance to the building, Lydia was standing there. Lisa at the front desk is wide eyed with anticipation and fear.

"Lydia?" he questioned by way of a greeting.

"Don't you fucking Lydia me. Don't even bother to go to your desk. Get to my office immediately," she barked with anger the likes of which he'd rarely seen.

"May I ask what is going on?"

"You may ask nothing," she snapped. "Wait for me. I will be there in a minute." With that she stormed off high atop those road weary Christian Louboutins.

Mica turned his attention to the only person present who may be able to shed some light. You can't get much past Lisa, so if anyone knows what is going on it is she. Lisa sheepishly handed Mica the latest rag tabloid. The color drained from Mica's face as he almost pissed his Pradas.

The headline reads: GETTING A 'MOUTHFUL' OF THE LATEST NEWS. CHAD MARTIN'S LOVER REVEALED. Below the headline is a large color picture of Chad and Mica kissing in what appears to be a passionate moment. Chad quickly jumped to the article inside to see two pictures leading up to the kiss: one, a medium shot of Mica and Chad talking and the second, a close up as they are about to embraced. The third picture is the same shot from the cover. Mica recognized enough of the setting and clothing in the first shot to know it was taken at Roger Keenan's party. But by whom?

"You'd better go to Lydia's office," Lisa cautioned rightfully.

Stunned, Mica managed to avoid his co-workers—or are they avoiding him—and made his way up the stairs and into Lydia's office with the big picture window overlooking the bullpen below. He is clearly on display.

He read the entire article, which reiterated the speculation of the identity of the man poolside in a previous article. And, of course, they had to run those pictures again. 'A source close to Chad has confirmed that Martin has been seeing entertainment news-mouth Mica Daly from the hit syndicated series *Drop Zone* It is an ironic twist as a source at *Drop Zone* has also confirmed Daly has been the reporter assigned to find out just who is the mystery man in the now infamous poolside pictures of a naked Chad Martin cavorting with another man.' A source at *Drop Zone*? Fuckers! Mica stood up, in full view of the bullpen below, and scanned the room to see just who could have been the Judas in the room all the while knowing it doesn't matter. The damage is done.

"Sit your ass down," Lydia snapped as she entered along with the shows' lawyer, Harry Levine.

"Do I need a lawyer too?" Mica asked nervously.

"Shut the fuck up," Lydia demanded. "I know you all call me a cunt...what is the name? Oh right Labia. Well you haven't seen anything yet."

At that point, Mica rightfully decided any word spoken by him would be ammunition for her. The lawyer is there to witness Mica hang himself.

Harry Levine is a quiet kind of guy. Young for a lawyer handling a client as big as *Drop Zone*, he sits in a corner office on the second floor and doesn't interact with the staff. He is all khakis and buttoned down shirts, penny loafers and ivy league— far from the L.A. look. His job is mostly to avoid slander suits and peruse talent contracts. In fact the only dealings Mica has had with Harry is when he negotiated his own contract—sans representation. At the time Harry complimented Mica on his negotiating skills.

"So you lying little shit," Lydia began. "Do you want to explain yourself?"

Mica could start a trail of denial but what would be the point. "Not particularly," Mica returned defiantly.

"How long has this been going on?" She asked in a dangerously quiet tone.

"What specifically?" Mica asked back knowing he would only raise her ire. But he needs time to think.

"You and your boyfriend! Are you the other person in the poolside pictures?"

"Chad, I am sure has lots of friends. Could be anyone," he dodged.

"And it could be you?"

Mica sat silent. And Lydia, in return, steamed.

"So let me get this straight, pardon the pun," she chuckled with sarcasm. "The whole time I had you on the case, you were the case?"

Mica again said nothing, which only pissed her off more.

"Do you have any idea how much you have jeopardized the reputation of this show and its relationships with the studios, publicists...the stars?"

"No I don't," he returned confident that he couldn't know what the fall out will be at this early stage. "And I dare say neither do any of us."

"They called you a God damned "*under the covers reporter*"! Do you think that bodes well for your reputation?"

"I was put in an untenable position," Mica shot back offensively.

"How so?" lawyer Levine questioned back, which threw Lydia off balance.

"He was not!" she spat but was waved quiet by Harry.

"I was told, in front of witnesses, that my job was on the line if I did not 'out' the mystery man in the pictures and de facto Chad Martin. So in order to keep my job I have to destroy my relationship. I would call that untenable."

There was a pause and then Lydia spoke up. "What witnesses?"

"Do I really have to point them out?" Mica asked sarcastically as he pointed out of the window at the entire bullpen.

"Yes," Harry said calmly. "I would like you to point them out."

"What the fuck?" Lydia grumbled.

"We have an issue here," Harry said vaguely. "I would like to meet with you Mica separately to hear your side of the story. Until then, I suggest you go home on a paid leave, talk to no one, including the staff here. And let's see what the fall out really is."

Mica stood to leave and, of course, Lydia had to have the last word, "Get out. There is no place for liars in journalism."

"There's no place for witch hunts either," Mica snarled and slammed the door as he exited.

Mica walked down the stairs, head held high, ignored the awkward 'HI's from his co-workers and headed right out the door. Lisa at the front desk knew enough not to say anything.

As he walked to his car, he could feel his knees buckle. He managed to keep it together long enough to drive through the gate and off the property before he burst into tears.

° ° °

Michelle Bianco got to the office earlier than usual in order to miss the obvious onslaught of questions she is about to receive from her co-workers. For once, in the modern glass edifice of an office that houses Regis and Canning, Michelle is happy to have a windowless center cube of an office. In there, blocked from the gaze of others, she can throw the requisite fit that accompanies news like this.

She knew it. He is just too pretty she thought. He had to be gay, right? Besides no one is that nonchalant when she gives a blowjob. Her throat is legendary and he barely uttered a moan. Gay!

She picked up the phone and called Chad Martin. It went straight to voice mail. "It's me. If you are screening your calls, I understand. But do not ignore me. We have got to talk. If you do not know the news, I strongly suggest you get your ass to a newsstand and find out what everyone is going to be talking about on the late night monologues tonight. You *must* get your ass in here today, so we can draft a statement and try to stem this *fucking* nightmare."

After hanging up, she thought twice about what she said and called back. "Hey it's me again. I know I sounded a little harsh a moment ago. I just want you to know you have a team behind you here and we are going to get through this. And you are going to be the star you are meant to be."

With that she hung up, cleared her throat and by way of catharsis, screamed "Faggot!"

∘ ∘ ∘

Roger Keenan was in the middle of his morning constitutional: a drive, top down, in the vintage 1983 Rolls Royce Corniche—butter cream with a saddle roof and interior—to the Sunset Plaza for breakfast at the French café and a read of the mornings' trades and news. He nearly spit his double espresso over the Euro-suave man sitting at the next table when he read the headline.

The first call was to Chad. And like all others this morning, his call went straight to voice mail. "Chad, it's Roger Keenan. Yes, I have seen the tabloids. Listen to me. You have probably already heard from your publicist. But I strongly suggest you make a statement like the one we discussed in Palm Springs. I know you were against it then but I don't think you have much of a choice at this point. If you re- member it went something like: Yes I have gay friends and yes I may embrace them from time to time as I would the straight friends I love and admire. That doesn't make me gay; it makes me open-minded. But if you think I am gay and that is your fantasy, then I have done my job. I am in the fantasy making business. I create char- acters and take on persona for you to fantasize about being, or loving or wanting. If that fantasy allows for you to like my work, so be it if you think I am gay. Anyway, it was something like that. Call me if you need me or if you just want to talk. Take care."

His second call mattered more to him. Mica and he have been friends for sometime and he has truly come to love and respect their friendship. There is always a fall guy in a situation like this. And Roger fears Mica will be it.

He called but like with Chad's call, Mica's phone went straight to voice mail. He didn't want to leave a message. He wanted to speak in person and hung up with the intent to do so later.

∘ ∘ ∘

Breaking the rules, B.J., the show producer from *Drop Zone*, reached out and called Mica. He wasn't sure if he should answer the phone when the caller I.D. told him it was she but he did.

"Hello," he sniffed as he held back tears.

"I knew you told me you had met an actor but...WOW!" The comment broke the tension.

"Where are you?" Mica joked back. "In your office with the lights turned off, hiding under the desk as to not be seen reaching out to the enemy."

"Something like that," she chuckled.

"This is so fucked up," Mica began.

"I know," she empathized. "I know basically what went down with Lydia because as a follow-up she ripped the staff new assholes trying to ferret out who the leak was from the bull pen."

"Any ideas?"

"I was hoping you had one," she half joked.

"How do you think this is going to play out?" Mica asked with a certain desperation in his voice.

"I don't know," she responded truthfully. "I would just take a couple of days off. Maybe go to Palm Springs and let the initial wave of bullshit blow over."

"Maybe you're right," Mica conceded.

"For what it is worth, I always thought you were getting a raw deal and were being boxed into a bad situation."

"Thanks, I will be sure to bring that up in court."

"Cute."

They hung up both knowing Mica wasn't being cute.

∘ ∘ ∘

Albert Switzer's office is littered with moving boxes—some taped, some half empty but mostly a lot are empty. And even though it is still the middle of a bright and sunny morning, the place seems slightly oppressive with its usual dank atmosphere. Albert is simply sitting behind his desk, reading the trades and waiting for the phone to ring—something that hasn't happened in quite some time.

Chad walked in to the outer office where there was no one to greet him. The place, oddly, felt like home. "Is anyone here?"

"Back here. Who is it?" came the cantankerous response.

He walked in on Albert blotting a tear from his eye. "It's me Chad."

Albert paused, gave him the once over and then rose to give him a hug. "I was wondering if you would come crawling back." Chad chuckled. "Well, it is too late. I am closing up shop."

"What?" Chad was startled. "Wait, where is Anthony?"

"Had to let him go. He didn't take that very well."

"What do you mean you are closing up shop?" It was at that point that Chad noticed all the boxes all over the place.

"Look, when you left, I got it. This is a young man's game. I couldn't hold you and you were the best thing I had going."

"I'm sorry."

"Don't be. You had to do what you had to do. And now I know that I have to do what I have to do."

"So what are you going to do?" Chad asked.

"Don't really know yet. But I will figure it out."

"Yeah..."

There was an awkward but contemplative pause between one at the start of his career and the other at the end. "So, what are you doing back here?" Albert quizzed.

"I don't know frankly," Chad admitted honestly. "Shit is hitting the fan and I just needed to talk to someone who has my best interests at heart and not all wrapped up with what they stand to lose."

"And I am the best you could come up with?" Albert asked genuinely concerned for his former client. Chad's non-response was enough of a validation. "I see. What about this boyfriend of yours?"

"We are not boyfriends," Chad snapped defensively.

"Well, whatever you guys call it these days, I am not judging. I would think you should be talking to him."

Again Chad said nothing.

"Look kid, it's great you have all this success and from what I read some big money coming your way. But in the end you can't curl up in bed at night with a resume. At what price happiness? Take it from a lonely old man, of all the things you will be able to buy with your new found wealth—houses, cars, stuff—you can't buy happiness."

"I am going to be a star," Chad mumbled like a mantra.

"Be careful what you ask for. Stars burn brightly and then they burn out. Trust me, I've represented a lot of them."

Albert could see that Chad was hearing but wondered whether he was listening. "I would imagine today of all days, you have some business to attend to," Albert said. "So get on your way and let me get on mine. I have some packing to do."

Chad nodded. They hugged again. "I am sorry I left you," Chad said.

"No you're not. It's just business. I know that." Albert gave him a wink and shooed him out the door.

The Albert Switzer Agency is now officially closed. And Albert, for his part, now had closure.

∘ ∘ ∘

"I don't want to know if this Mica Daly is the other guy by the pool. I don't want to know if you are taking it up the ass by this guy either." Chad was about to interject but "Big Eddie" Fielding shot him down by simply raising his hand. Eddie Fielding is an intimidating guy. "Like I was saying. I don't care. But other people do."

"Just whom are you talking about?" Chad questioned hesitantly.

"Like Spectrum Studios who are just about to release *The Other Brother* to DVD. They're worried about sales. Conrad Barrington who is paying you twenty million dollars plus a percentage for *The River, Deep*. Those, and people like them, who wonder if you are played out are the people concerned."

Chad squirmed in his seat. He would much rather have had this meeting in Michelle's windowless office than in here, the all-glass enclosure corner office of Eddie Fielding. Chad felt exposed and vulnerable here where all the support staff can walk by and inevitably pass judgment. Everybody knows why he is there.

"First we have drafted a statement," Michelle, whose hair is tied in one of those knots that frantic women style when they have lost control of their day, broke in. "It is of course a classic denial."

"Denial of what?" Chad questioned.

"That you are gay," she continued. "We are stating that the incident was Mica Daly's doing. That he, being openly gay, attacked you."

"But..."

"There are no but's, Chad," Eddie instructed. "We have to deflect."

"What about the poolside pictures?" Chad questioned.

"We are not addressing those. Just the kiss," Michelle continued.

"Look, can't we just say that I have gay friends and my association with them is meaningless to my career. And that I am just a good, loving, friend who is not afraid to show affection?" Chad suggested, having listed to Roger Keenan's phone message earlier.

"NO!" Michelle snapped.

"We are deflecting," Eddie reiterated. "We need to get you past this as soon as possible. You have to understand, you are contracted for a lot of money. You do not want to be sued by film companies, etcetera. We will figure out your relationship to your 'friends' once we are legally in the clear. Do you want what's coming to you or don't you?"

"Of course," Chad chimed in.

"So throwing some overzealous fag friend under the bus is the price you are going to pay," Eddie declared.

"We will see each other again. He is a reporter for Christ's sake. It is not like you can eliminate him from my sphere."

"Let us take care of Mica Daly," Michelle fired back.

Chad slumped in his chair, defeated and somewhat confused by all that is happening. He loves Mica but there is no coming back from this.

"And let me tell you body language matters," Eddie spat at the deflated Chad. "Sit up in your chair. You never want passers by to think anything is wrong or even challenging. You have the world by the balls is the answer to everything and standing tall is the first step of showing it."

Chad sat erect with a combination of motivation and denial. He had crossed the line—selling out his boyfriend for an eight-figure salary, he sat up and embraced his newly unencumbered star trajectory.

"Now there is a second reason to call you here," Michelle began to explain as Eddie dealt a handful of pictures out like a deck of cards, each with a pretty young starlet emblazoned on the front.

"You are going to pick one. Right here, right now," Eddie explained. Chad knew the drill. They had been setting him up on 'dates' since he signed with Regis and Canning.

"But I have been out with each of these gals," Chad noted rather perplexed by the choices.

"And now one of them is going to be your girlfriend," Eddie further explained.

"We think it is time you look a little more settled and little less playboy."

"You mean gay boy," Chad shot back sarcastically.

There was a bit of a stare down and then Chad took another look at the pictures. He pointed to the picture of Ashley Beckwith, his co-star from *The Other Brother.*

"Perfect," Michelle squealed.

Ashley's career had gone nowhere since the release of the film and Chad felt bad about that and that was the motivation for his choice. But moreover, she, out of all the ones on the table seemed the most stable, been out of the tabloids and gave a great blowjob from what he could remember from their encounter on the set.

"It is perfect P.R.," Eddie said. "Their attraction began on set when they were both filming naked together. We'll come up with something more flowery than that but, suffice it to say, it is perfect. We can run with this. Good choice kid."

Eddie and Michelle dismissed Chad with a handshake and a kiss on the cheek, which seemed very smarmy even to Chad. He wanted to take a shower and thought about stopping by Body Image gym, which is conveniently located between this Century City ice palace and his home. And then he realized there is no more Body Image in his life. There is no more Mica in his life. He needed a drink.

18

It didn't take long before the niceties of the air kissing and mutual, if not patently insincere, compliments on each other's choice of ensemble wore off. For the record, Michelle Bianco is in her usual publicist's black skirt, top, black tights and to the knee boots despite it being ninety degrees outside. Lydia Gray, on the other hand, wore a knockoff of a Diane von Furstenberg wrap dress that left little to the imagination. She's got tits and likes to show them off.

The two met at the mutually agreed upon Hugo's on Santa Monica for breakfast. As Lydia hates to be late for the rundown of the show, let alone the taping, they agreed to meet at 7:00 am much to the displeasure of Michelle. Still this is neutral territory and a place to see and be seen if you are on the 'power breakfast' circuit. As they sat in the far end booth by the window, Lydia instinctively looked around for a familiar face—star or otherwise—she could brag about having been seated better than. Michelle, in turn, scanned for cronies. And despite the sea of raised copies of the days trades and heads buried within, both were disappointed at the lack of 'names' and within minutes were simply forced to face each other.

Michelle began first. "You know I love you. I love the show."

"Yes," Lydia responded with appreciation and waited for the 'But'. She knew it was coming and she knew what it is about. That damn kissing picture. She could kill Mica.

"But it is the picture," Michelle served up. "It is inexcusable."

"Inexcusable?" Lydia questioned as she motioned to the waiter that she would like a cappuccino—something she is loathe to drink as the acid in the coffee mixed with the bile in her stomach from having to eat crow in front of Michelle Bianco is more than she would stand for, but likes the pretense of cappuccino over an ordinary coffee which would be no less an enemy. "What was inexcusable? The lighting?"

Michelle knew she was being baited but jumped for it anyway. "The subject matter," she snapped.

"And you think I had something to do with that?"

"No," Michelle spit. "And you can cut the coquettish bullshit. You've got to be as blindly furious with Mica as we are."

Lydia continued her thinly veiled coy routine. "We were surprised, if that is what you are getting at." Lydia knew she was being cornered, hated it, and figured she might as well drag out Michelle's anger as long as she could by trying to appear nonplussed.

"Mica has been given unprecedented access to Chad. We have been great in giving you exclusives and first opportunities. And this is what we get in return..."

"I can't help it if your client is gay," Lydia calmly shot back. "Nor can I help it if he has questionable taste in men."

"First my client is not gay. And we will be making a statement regarding the friendly and accepting nature he has with gays around him. Also, Chad has a girl-friend who can vouch for his heterosexual proclivities. That too will be news very soon. But it won't be on your show. You are officially banned from all Regis and Canning projects, events and clientele."

"What?" Lydia spat. "That is outrageous."

"Oh come on," Michelle spat right back. "What did you think our reaction would be? Your reporter misrepresented himself if nothing else. And we have to think of our clients and wonder what and who else is misrepresenting the agenda of *Drop Zone.*"

"You can't just ban us from the town. We are a legitimate news source."

"Without access you are neither legitimate nor a source. You were supposed to report the news not make the news. Mica crossed the line." Michelle is feeling a little full of herself, getting the upper hand of the infamous Lydia Gray. "But we are not unreasonable. Even we can believe that Mica duped you as well. We can work together. We will keep you at arms length but that is better than nothing. But you have to fire Mica Daly."

"You can't force me to fire one of my reporters," Lydia squirmed.

"But we can force you off the red carpets."

"You couldn't do this over the phone?" Lydia mumbled, internally defeated.

Lydia had already made up her mind about the fate of Mica Daly. She just didn't want Michelle Bianco to feel that she had twisted Lydia's arm to come to the same result. Again, Lydia could kill that damned Mica Daly. How dare he put her and the show she had worked so hard to build, in this position. He deserved his fate.

With that, Michelle stood to leave.

"Are you not having something to eat?" Lydia questioned by way of a set up. "I have to assume that will save you the embarrassment of having to throw it up later." She paused, as Michelle grew wide-eyed, "Oh that's right, my mistake. You're the one everyone says has no gag reflex. But that is a story for another day, I suppose. Let's deal with one cock sucker at a time."

Michelle, stunned, simply turned on her heels and retreated. Lydia knew her words were nothing more than a Pyrrhic victory. But, then again, she never assumed she'd win this war.

∘ ∘ ∘

Mica sat in his chair, staring at nothing, alternatively sipping and then swallowing a big gulp of a Kettle One martini. He jokingly calls what he makes a martini as it is poured into a traditional martini glass. But for all intents and purposes, it is simply a glass of vodka straight up.

Mica never got into the housing market. He was always content with his vintage and rent controlled Hancock Park apartment. The plan, eventually, is to buy a place in Palm Springs and keep this apartment as a city pied à terre. Now that he was out on his ass, he would be putting off buying anything, let alone a house in Palm Springs.

He loved his cool, deep colored walls—walls he called museum colors. His eclectic but impressive art collection popped off the saturated colors behind and the whole atmosphere is cocoon like. The furnishings were a smart collection of a few pieces picked up at the Pacific Design Center sale and classics from the Mitchell + Gold collection—a favorite among the stylish gay set who chose their own tastes over that of an interior decorator. At times like this, when things aren't going so well—and being fired certainly constitutes a 'time like this'—he loves curling up in his club chair, drink in hand, contemplating life.

Ordinarily, Mica wouldn't answer numbers without caller I.D. But at this point he didn't give a shit who was on the other end of the phone. All news has been bad news, whoever this is might as well pile it on. He debated letting the call go to voice mail and thought otherwise. On the fourth ring he answered, "Hello?"

"It's me," Chad answered.

"Ah," Mica began, "Funny, I've tried to call you and couldn't get more than a busy signal."

"I've changed my phone number," Chad explained.

"So what is the new one?" Mica scrambled for something to write with but couldn't find anything by the time Chad responded.

"I am not giving it out."

Mica paused for a gulp assuming that was some feeble attempt at humor on Chad's part. But there was nothing more said.

"You are not giving it out?" Mica questioned. "To anyone? Or just to me?"

"Anyone...for the most part."

Again, there was an awkward pause. Chad didn't really want to have this conversation; he just knew he needed to. He sat naked in the Jacuzzi, jets turned off so as to not muddle the sound, lit by just the glow of the underwater lights. He too has a drink in hand—a scotch, Dewar's, ice and just a splash of water. He for some reason has taken to scotch as of late. It makes him feel more mature.

"You aren't speaking," Chad prodded.

"What would like me to say to that," Mica began. "You've changed the lock on the house and I don't get a key. You've changed phone numbers and I am not privy to the new one. You apparently are dating women. Effectively, you are cutting me out of your life."

"It's not like that."

"Oh, how is it like?" Mica asked indignantly.

"It's just my career..."

Before Chad could go on, Mica quickly snapped, cutting him off. "Your career! Your fucking career! I am fully aware of your career, as I have just lost mine to protect yours. A thank you would have been acceptable but instead, for my loyalty, you have chosen to cut my balls off."

"I didn't mean to..."

Again Mica cut him off, "Didn't mean to what? Fuck me over? I have effectively lost my job and now my boyfriend in the same week. Thanks for the support. Let's not forget, I was an integral part in helping your precious career along. Now when I am in need, you just run."

"It's not like we were real boyfriends," Chad justified.

"What?" Mica spewed. "What would you call us? Fuck buddies? Friends with benefits?"

"Don't say that," Chad said with a knot in his throat. "I have genuine feelings for you."

"There is nothing genuine about you," Mica spat. "You are gay—one of those self loathing gays who fucks in secret and denies in public. Eventually you will not be able to run or hide from who you are. You will be found out."

"You can't..."

"Not by me," Mica assured. "I'm not pulling you out of the closet. The recent press has done that for you. All you look like is a liar. And you may be able to pull that off for the foreseeable future..."

"My lawyers are working on protecting me."

"Do you have any idea how ridiculous that sounds?" Mica fired back.

Again, there was a pause and on both ends of the phone both grabbed for their respective drinks. After a few minutes of calm silence, Mica spoke first.

"Why did you call?"

"Well," Chad stammered. "I did want to say that I am sorry about what happened with your job. Roger Keenan explained to me what your assignment was and how you tried to work around having to speak up. I genuinely appreciate it."

"Well, thank you. I guess." Mica sighed.

"And..."

"And?"

"And I just needed to tell you that I can't do this anymore. I have to move forward with everything that is happening to me and I can't have you in my life."

"It's as simple as that for you, isn't it?" Mica questioned, defeated.

"Not really. It just is what it is."

"I like spending time with you," Mica confessed, with a slight desperation in his voice he couldn't hide. He could feel the tears welling in his eyes.

"We are linked in the media. My publicist said we shouldn't associate."

"That's just great. Michelle Bianco has successfully destroyed my professional and personal life all in one wave of her hand. Perfect. It's so Hollywood. Does your publicist wipe your ass too?"

After yet another awkward pause, Chad realized there was no reason to carry on. "Good bye, Mica."

"Good luck, Chad." The subtlety of the dig was lost on Chad.

Chad paused one last time and then hung up the phone. He reached over and turned on the jets for the hot tub and leaned back to contemplate what had just happened. It's okay. I am a star.

Across town, in his comfortable chair, martini in hand, Mica Daly cried.

∘ ∘ ∘

There is something called plausible deniability, which is why Anthony Wright set up the interview and then chose not to be there during the actual interplay. If anything really slanderous comes up, he would always have the ability to deny knowledge not having been there. His commission of the fifty thousand dollar payday is good enough. And frankly, even Anthony was impressed with how much he was able to negotiate out of some benign European magazine, *Der something or other*, he didn't really know the agenda of the article. All he knew is the check cleared; he had taken his twenty percent; had a hefty remainder to present to Tommy and at some point in the course of the conversation the name Chad Martin would come up.

When the German reporter showed up, he was given the usual tour of the Body Image bungalow and an explanation that emphasizes the discretion of the place and its clientele. Good background information but for fifty grand there would be no discretion. Tommy Mercer is going to have to tell all.

The interview began innocuously enough, with the reporter asking about Tommy's training technique and then moved on to some of the more famous clients he has worked with. As Tommy explained his workout routine, they walked from machine to equipment to the different spaces in the bungalow.

"What happens here?" The reporter asked as they approached the empty room lined with mats.

"Yoga mostly," Tommy explained. "But I like to use it, along with the ring outside, for wrestling."

"Wrestling?"

"Yeah, I am really into it and several of the clients like to wind down with a roll around."

"Oh," the reporter prodded. "Like who?"

"Well some really get into it," Tommy began innocently enough.

"Like Chad Martin?" the reporter asks.

Tommy had opened the door and admitted that Chad Martin was, indeed, a client and the reporter ran with it. "Tell me how you developed Chad's incredible body."

Ego inflated and tens of thousands of dollars now in his pocket, Tommy spilled all about Chad and his workouts—which equipment, which exercises, how many, how long. And all the while, the reporter took copious notes.

As the interview wound down, the reporter took out his cell phone, called his photographer who apparently been waiting patiently outside to come in. Tommy was more than happy to pose for pictures—stripping shirtless and pumping up with weights and on the machines.

After a good half hour of various poses, stretches and lifts, the reporter was sated...almost. Tommy asked if they minded if he jumped in the shower and the reporter, in turn, asked whether they could take a picture of Tommy in his towel. Tommy, naively, obliged. "Hell, I don't care if you see me naked." And they did.

Tommy, letting his sensual ego get the best of him, let them shoot while he showered. He kept his back to the camera for the most part. But when he turned around the reporter couldn't help but notice a large geometric tattoo on Tommy's hip. "How long have you had that?"

"A while. Why do you ask?" Tommy asked as he toweled off.

"He's not the man in the poolside pictures for sure," the reporter noted to the photographer. "He didn't have a tattoo."

"No, that's Mica Daly," Tommy offered up. "Or at least that is what everyone thinks since the new pictures."

"Have you had sex with Chad Martin?" The reporter asked nonchalantly but directly.

Tommy paused, thought for a moment about the money in his pocket and then spoke.

19

Marilyn Lassiter always surreptitiously takes care of the bill. You never see her do it, so it is never an embarrassment. So when she invited Mica to lunch, he was more than happy to accept. Not that money is so tight, he did get a sizeable settlement from *Drop Zone* which paid off the rest of his contract plus a considerable extra for the libelous nature of his assignment in the first place, but Mica is out of work officially and on a budget. But there would be a price to be paid. In Hollywood, there is no such thing as a free lunch. Marilyn wants to know all the gossip and right now, Mica is the subject of plenty.

As Mica pulled up to Spago in Beverly Hills, the lone paparazzi—Joey Chase, a guy he had come to know on the red carpet circuit—snapped a few shots of Mica.

"What's it like to be the news rather than report the news," he goaded. Mica just walked inside.

Marilyn chose to meet at Spago, naturally. It is such the 'ladies who lunch' place. Marilyn arrived in Bulgari. It was that kind of day, chunky Bulgari jewelry and a classic Chanel jacket over a white blouse and black pencil skirt. A sensible three-inch heel and the look was chic, expensive, but right for lunch.

"Oh look, there is Candy," she giggled and waved. "And Barbara. It's so good that she is getting out more these days. All that time in mourning...enough already."

Marilyn hugged Mica tight and gave him a big kiss on the cheek. She had deliberately booked a middle table so that everyone would see the display. "I don't care what anyone thinks, I am always on your side," she opened with.

"There is no side to be on," Mica corrected but with no effect.

Wolfgang, who always seemed to spend more time circling the dining room and romancing the ladies than he does in the kitchen supervising the staff—or cooking for that matter—made his way to the table in a shot. Kisses and something inaudible later, Marilyn was back and in an eye-lock with Mica.

"Now tell me everything. How are you doing?"

Before he could answer, a bottle of champagne arrived at the table. Marilyn was notorious for not drinking anything at lunch but a carbonated water of some sort. She liked to be the one in control. But occasionally, she will imbibe with costly champagne and rarely still a martini. Today it would be champagne. "Oh dear," she said to the waitress who is busy pouring two flutes, "could you also bring me a sparkling water?" The waitress nodded appropriately, placed the champagne in front of each of them and then darted off.

"A toast?" Marilyn asked, raising her glass.

"To?"

"Us. Surviving, Mica. We are nothing if not survivors."

"I'll drink to that," Mica agreed and tapped glasses.

"Now, do tell. What has been going on?"

"Not much," Mica confessed truthfully. "Since leaving *Drop Zone* I have been laying low. I really have to get back on the horse and start looking at what my options are. But everyone at the moment is obsessed with the picture and no one is letting me talk about anything else."

"Well, speaking of that picture..." Here it comes. "What was that all about?"

"You too?" Mica questioned naughtily. He knows why he is here and what she wants to talk about. She is Marilyn, Goddamn, Lassiter after all.

"What?"

"Oh Marilyn, I knew you would ask. It is no big thing."

"Well?"

"Well, Chad and I are...were...friends. I have been a big supporter of his career since we met at a party at Roger Keenan's house."

"I know what goes on at those parties, Mica." Marilyn winked as she spoke and took a dramatic sip of her champagne. "So friends? Or were you *'friends'?*"

"Now Marilyn!"

"Oh please...were you fucking or what?"

"Marilyn!" Mica blushed. It was as if his mother had asked that question. "I am going to excuse myself to the restroom before I say something I may regret." It was his turn to wink at Marilyn.

Weaving his way through the tables on his way to the back corner, a hand grabbed his arm. It is Gina Hamilton, Chad's cougar love interest from *Divas.*

"So you got the prize," she purred loudly for her tablemates to hear.

"I beg your pardon?"

"I'm Gina Hamilton," she said.

"I know who you are Ms. Hamilton. And I assume you already know I am Mica Daly."

"You got my prize," she reiterated.

"Again, I don't know what you mean," Mica returned awkwardly, looking around the table for help but there is not a familiar face in the crowd.

"Chad Martin. It is no wonder he rebuffed my advances. He had you. All the while I thought we could have had a great, publicity making, affair. Would have done the show wonders." She laughed with her cohorts at the table. "I always wanted to be a real life cougar."

"I am sure you will get your chance, Ms. Hamilton."

"Gina, please. After all you are sleeping with my co-star."

"No I am not," Mica rebuffed honestly. He is no longer sleeping with Chad. "But don't you mean former co-star. Just as I refer to him as a former friend."

"Well...I..."

"Ms. Hamilton I would have thought idle gossip is beneath you. But I guess, just like your co-stars, nothing is beneath you."

The double entendre was not lost on the table who collectively "ooh"ed and "ahh"ed as Mica started to walk away. And then he looked back, "I do hope you get a good fuck one of these days but that would mean someone would have to be beneath you."

One at the table actually applauded. It was a good moment for Mica.

Once back at the table, Marilyn grilled Mica as to what happened with Gina Hamilton, which Mica reiterated with great relish.

"I just love being in your company," Marilyn said. "You not only have good stories but you are making good stories." Apparently Mica had just earned his lunch.

Just then, the waitress arrived with a martini and placed it in front of Mica. He looked at Marilyn who just shrugged her own curiosity. "It is from the lady three tables over," the waitress said.

"You just have admirers all over the room," Marilyn chortled. This is her idea of the perfect lunch.

Mica looked over and saw the unholy duo of Conrad Barrington, the producer/director of Chad's latest film, the just wrapped *The River, Deep,* who had a scowl on his face as he looked over at Mica, and, of all people, Lydia Gray, Mica's now former boss. She rose her glass to acknowledge her gesture.

"Send it back," Mica instructed the waitress.

"What?" Marilyn snapped. "Never waste a perfectly good martini. I'll drink the damn thing."

"Send it back," Mica repeated firmly and the drink was whisked off the table. Mica turned to Marilyn, "As the late, great Bette Davis could have, would have, should have and probably did in a movie say: I can't be had for the price of a cocktail!"

"Damn you gays and your standards," Marilyn huffed. "Was there a note at least? In my day, there would have been a note."

Mica noticed that was the first time ever that Marilyn referred to her age as anything but contemporary with the people around her. He liked her more when she is little liquored up.

Lydia made her move to the table, extended her hand to Marilyn and introduced herself, "I am Lydia Gray."

"Marilyn Lassiter."

"I've heard your name," Lydia gave back graciously and then looked directly at Mica. "Can we have a word?"

"No. You've said enough to me."

"It's just that I believe, despite everything, that we can still be friends."

"You mean you want to use me for my friends. If I am fucking somebody that you want to have access to, that sort of thing?"

Bested and knowing it, Lydia decided this would devolve into nothing but a catfight. Without saying another word, she turned on her heels and went back to her table.

"Well played," Marilyn complimented.

"Now I need that martini."

"Dammit I knew it," she muttered half jokingly. "Now it's on my bill." She may have been a woman of means. But by no means is she wasteful. She would go on to box her lunch to go causing Mica to wonder, who leaves Spago with a doggie bag?

o o o

Mica poured himself another martini, Kettle One in a fancy glass, and settled into his favorite club chair readying himself for a night of pay-per-view. He has fallen behind on his movies now that he doesn't go to screenings for free. But as he put down his drink on the glass coffee table, he instinctually picked up the magazine he'd not even cracked open yet.

Leafing through the *Vanity Fair* that he had bought at the newsstand on Beverly Boulevard after his lunch with Marilyn Lassiter, he came across a BEHIND THE SCENES one-pager on the progress of the filming of *The River, Deep*. It isn't an article on Chad, per se, but of course the only picture was of the director, Conrad Barrington, directing Chad in a scene.

That short blurb would have been bad enough but a few pages later in a regular section called OUT TO LUNCH wherein one celebrity is interviewed for, again, a short one pager, the subject du jour is none other than Chad Martin. Clearly Michelle Bianco is working overtime to earn her retainer and 'straighten' things out in Chad's life.

A quick read through, and he realized that, again, Michelle must have had editorial control. The article was all very jovial and there wasn't a mention of Chad's recent travails in the tabloids but rather painted him as quite the Hollywood lothario with a string of ladies and broken hearts all over town. It's cute but bullshit.

Mica had to stop feeling sorry for himself. Part angry over the firing and more hurt by the dismissal from Chad, Mica had spent too much time making others feel better about what has happened and leaving himself an empty shell when he comes home.

He shifted the pile of magazines on the glass coffee table in order to put down the current issue. It is that or he would throw it across the room in disgust. But the worry about damage to his own room caused him to think better of the idea. Mica has always been more of a pragmatist than a tantrum thrower. As he moved the magazines to make more room for his beloved cocktail, he noticed the personal business card of Joseph Tomasso. He gave it a little though and then picked up his cell phone.

"Detective Tomasso."

"Detective?" Mica questioned out of surprise.

"Who is this?"

"Oh sorry. It's me...Mica Daly. I hope I haven't caught you at a bad time."

"Well, well," Joe began. "And no I am off duty at the moment."

"I didn't realize you've become a detective," Mica shot back awkwardly. "Congratulations. I guess."

"Thanks." There was a pause. And then it grew longer than usual. "Are you okay? Is there something wrong?"

"No. No," Mica snapped back. "I just came across your card and thought... well...it would be good to see you."

"Oh?" Joe teased.

"Don't make this difficult," Mica pleaded somewhat jokingly.

"Well I can tell you I am officially divorced and on the market, if that will make you feel less naughty."

"Oh?" Mica teased back.

"Touché. So what can I do for you?"

"It's more like what you can do *to* me."

"Now that is intriguing."

"Feel free to use your detective skills to deduce what I have in mind."

"My nightstick is already out," Joe groaned.

"I know this is last minute," Mica began to explain.

"And fortunately it is my night off," Joe continued.

"Perhaps..."

"I am on my way," Joe punctuated.

Mica fortified himself with another martini while he waited for the doorbell.

∘ ∘ ∘

They kissed hard and passionately, Joe and Mica. Joe's beard of two days, scratched on Mica's face. And that seemed a badge of honor more than an irritant. After the smooth body of Chad, the course hair on Joe's chest, stomach, pubic area and ass, gave Mica a sensual charge. He rolled his tongue around Joe's nipple, bit on it lightly and then dragged his tongue across to the other. Somehow the taste of his recently showered skin and the roughness of his hairy chest gave Mica a raging hard on. Joe reached down and started to stroke it.

Joe gave back too. He too began to suck on Mica's nipples. He rolled Mica on to his back and lay on top, pressing his heavy weight on Mica's more slight body. As they kissed, Joe's hand roamed over Mica's body, hooking up underneath Mica's leg and lifting up on his shoulder. Mica writhed with anticipation.

Joe ran his hand across Mica's ass stopping to flick his middle finger against Mica's asshole. The flicking made Mica's hole pucker and flex, pucker and flex. Joe slid down, grabbed underneath Mica's other leg and rolled him up on to his shoulders. Mica's ass is high in the air and splayed wide, an invitation for Joe's tongue, which he buried deep inside. Mica groaned with pleasure. Joe's beard scratched the sides of Mica's ass and the pleasure/pain combination only added to the eroticism.

Sufficiently lubricated by Joe's tongue, Joe rolled Mica back down and slid him on to his stiff cock. The piercing as Joe's engorged dick head entered his tight hole made Mica wince then groan with pleasure. There was no hesitation. The combination of vodka and lust invited him in. Mica slid down the shaft, both creating a rhythm of pumping and grinding, pumping and grinding. Mica stroked his own cock as he is being fucked.

Just as they found their ecstatic rhythm, Joe pulled out, gave Mica a gentle kiss and then climbed up and straddled Mica's pelvis. He positioned Mica's rock hard cock against his own puckered hole and slid down on it. He bounced up and down sending Mica into spasms of joy.

As much as Mica loved getting fucked, he never had a chance to fuck Chad and, as such, never felt that theirs had been a mutual love. Chad needed to dominate and with that beautiful body and huge cock, Mica was more than willing to be dominated. Today, in the throws of fucking Joe, Mica suddenly understood his and Chad's relationship as little more than a hole and a pole.

The bouncing turned into Joe slamming up and down on Mica's lap. The sound of his balls slapping against Mica's skin made Mica even harder. Joe stroked his cock faster and faster. "Aaaaahhhh," Joe let out an almighty groan and shot his load all over Mica's chest and on to his face. Mica licked his lips and tasted the salty, acrid taste of Joe's cum and that was enough for Mica to reach his own climax.

Mica pulled out just in time and blew his wad all over Joe's ass. Joe rolled over to suck the last of Mica's juice out of his still stiff cock and straddled Mica face. Mica could see the thick cream caught in the hair of Joe's ass crack. Mica reached up and rubbed it into Joe's skin. Ordinarily this would have made Mica feel dirty. But this time, all he can feel is sated.

○ ○ ○

Anthony Wright is nothing if not opportunistic. So when he contacted Mica Daly to set up a meeting, he was ready with the pitch of a lifetime. They decided to meet at The Cathedral, the same gay bar Anthony used to woo Tommy Mercer into giving that interview to the European magazine that netted both of them a pretty paycheck. And now, once again, if Anthony has his way, another set of Europeans are going to step up.

Mica loves The Cathedral. He could never get Chad to come here even though plenty of less homophobic stars had been there time after time. In fact, for a gay bar, the crowd is usually mixed and there is none of that 'guilt by association' moniker that goes with frequenting this place. It is just a hot spot.

Anthony, who had gotten to The Cathedral fifteen minutes early by design, marched right up to Mica when he arrived. "Hello there, I'm Anthony Wright," he began, hand extended and ready to shake. Mica shook it. "I have a table in the back."

"If you don't mind, I like to sit at the bar," Mica suggested.

"That's fine too. I just wanted to make sure we could be more private, so that people weren't all in your business."

"I'm Mica Daly," he corrected. "These days I have very little left to hide."

Anthony laughed.

The bar side facing the courtyard was relatively empty despite it being another beautiful Southern California day. And despite the earliness of the afternoon, Mica decided on his usual martini. Anthony ordered a diet coke.

"Oh no," Mica corrected. "Unless you are in AA, for which I apologize in advance for the following but if I am having a drink and we are having a meeting, you must also have a drink."

"Fair enough," Anthony capitulated and ordered a margarita.

"So Anthony, have we met before?" Mica had been desperately trying to place Anthony's name since he'd called. He sounded familiar but the face wasn't so.

"No we haven't met but we have someone in common," Anthony said.

"Who would that be?"

"Chad Martin."

Mica rolled his eyes, no longer sure if he is being set up or not. "Look, I will not talk about Chad Martin if that is what this meeting is all about."

"No, not at all," Anthony quickly retreated. "I don't mean to make you uncomfortable. I used to work for Albert Switzer. We represented Chad."

"Now I know where I have heard your name."

"And now I want to represent you," Anthony declared.

"Represent me?" Mica took a big swig from his over-poured martini. "I have always worked alone."

"And how is that working for you today?"

"Smart ass," Mica snapped back indignantly.

"No, that didn't come out right," Anthony corrected.

"Damn right it didn't."

"What I mean to say is, I don't think you realize there is opportunity out there for you that you are either not hearing about or not taking advantage of."

"Opportunity?"

"Like for instance Great Britain."

"I am going to need another martini for this," Mica mumbled sarcastically. "What the fuck are you getting at?"

"Like it or not, you are big news these days because of that picture." Anthony would never admit that it was he who took the now infamous shot nor was he going to admit that he and Mica had met before, at Roger Keenan's party where he took *that* picture. Clearly Mica hadn't put two and two together. So why force the issue? Besides at the moment of the picture, Mica and Chad were embroiled in their own drama. Anthony would hardly have expected Mica to realize the connection.

"I am not news," Mica corrected. "I am little more than road kill along the trajectory of a star...a star who managed to run over said speed bump and continue nicely on his way, I might add."

"Nevertheless, there is interest in you because there is interest in everything about Chad Martin."

"Perfect."

"No, this is a good thing," Anthony scrambled to make his point before losing Mica to Chad Martin overload. "I know a number of outlets who would be interested in hearing your story."

"I am not interested in telling my story."

"There is significant money to be made here and a short window of opportunity to cash in."

"How do you know all this?" Mica questioned.

Anthony wasn't about to confess that he had brokered the yet to be published Tommy Mercer story with the Germans. "Suffice it to say, I do my homework."

"You have balls, that's for sure." Mica hoisted his glass in a mock toast. "How old are you, kid?"

"Old enough to know how to use my balls."

Mica took a moment to study Anthony. He trusted his gut, which is why he never went with any sort of representation before—it never felt right. "What's in it for you?"

"Commission," Anthony returned. "A standard fifteen percent."

Mica stared at him.

"Hell I get twenty percent from other deals. But I don't think you understand fully. I don't want to make a one time deal. I want to represent you for your career."

"And why would I do that when I have never had an agent in my life."

"Two reasons," Anthony began. "One, you aren't working and not hearing about opportunity. I make opportunity. And two. You already said it. I have balls."

Mica squinted. There is something conniving about this kid and Mica's gut is saying to go with it. It is about time he stops being played and becomes a player.

"Well I have two things to say as well," Mica shot back. "One, let's take it slow, see what you can do and if I don't like it we both walk away. Second, the drinks are on you. You can write them off as a business expense for your client."

They shook on the deal and ordered a second round.

20

An always fashionable and usually stunning Ashley Beckwith stepped out of the car and on to the curb with all the impression of it being a red carpet—so deliberate, so choreographed. Despite a career that has gone virtually nowhere, she has managed to become famous for being famous just like those hotel heir sisters and that Armenian family. She is the darling of the media these days and the paparazzi, along with the ever-present Joey Chase, went to town, flashbulbs blinding both her and her equally dazzling date. They are "IT" at the moment and know how to play it.

Chad Martin and Ashley Beckwith are what Hollywood yearns for: young, beautiful and just talented enough for us to care—the whole being greater than the sum of the parts, for sure. Coached by the diligent team at Regis and Canning, under the watchful eye of Michelle Bianco and "Big Eddie" Fielding, they had been told less is more when it comes to the media. Show up, smile and say nothing. And that is what they have been doing for the last several weeks, showing up at all the right places, looking deliriously happy and saying nothing about their presumptive relationship. If there is anything that gets the media salivating is no response to the on-going question: what's going on?

Tonight it is the Tower on Sunset for an intimate dinner. Up until now, at all the right hotspots, they have been seen arm in arm and holding hands. It is has all been very coy but done the job of getting tongues wagging all over town. Tonight, for Joey Chase and company, they will throw the 'paps' something bigger—a kiss. It's just a little peck on the lips to keep the buzz alive but it's the kind of the thing that will make tabloid headlines around the world.

"Is kissing Ashley better than kissing a man?" Amid the clicking sounds from the cameras and continuous flashes, the question floated out there for just a second. Neither could identify who threw out the incendiary question.

"He's the best," Ashley deflected back as they turned and walked through the doors. Perfect. They had done their job for the night and now it was time to relax with a good drink and dinner.

○ ○ ○

Joey Chase dropped off the pictures from the night before at Michelle Bianco's office in the Century City glass tower offices of Regis and Canning in an unmarked manila envelope and picked up a similarly unmarked envelop with his check for five grand inside—a good nights work.

Michelle, in turn, would be distributing those pictures with discretion. The kiss shot from outside the Tower on Sunset, gotten by all paparazzi present, would go worldwide. But it is the exclusive inside shots, taken by a waiter on Chase's payroll, that show the happy couple holding hands at a candle lit table that will only go to select outlets that will give favorable coverage, such as *Drop Zone* who owe Michelle and Chad a considerable favor.

Despite having been cautioned to say nothing to the media, Michelle is very happy with Ashley's little quip from the night before: "He's the best." It will go nicely into the freshly drafted press release ordaining Chad and Ashley's 'friendship' as a 'relationship'.

FOR IMMEDIATE RELEASE

HOLLYWOOD, CA

Contact:
  Michelle Bianco
  Regis and Canning

ASHLEY BECKWITH SAYS, "HE'S THE BEST" AS CHAD MARTIN CONFIRMS RELATIONSHIP WITH AUSSIE HOTTIE

The much talked about 'are they' or 'aren't they' coupling of Hollywood heart throb Chad Martin with his former co-star, Australia's Ashley Beckwith has been confirmed as: THEY ARE! The couple, who first came together as a steamy love interest in the much talked about and highly reviewed independent feature, *The Other Brother*, have ended weeks of speculation as to the nature of their relationship.

Having been seen on the town on a number of flirtatious evenings out, Chad sealed the deal with a kiss last evening at the famed Tower on Sunset with Ashley confirming, "He's the best," to the surrounding media.

Chad, who is looking forward to shedding his much earned playboy image, states he's "a one woman man at heart" who is "looking forward to balancing a crazy career with a old fashioned romance."

Ashley, who has taken Hollywood by storm but is never far from her Australian roots, "can't wait to bring Chad home and have him meet the family."

Now all there is to wonder is: are Chad Martin and Ashley Beckwith today's Elizabeth Taylor and Richard Burton or the next Angelina and Brad? From fan response, this is certainly the next "IT" couple.

Any future official announcements, comments and notifications regarding this matter will come from the offices of Regis and Canning. Any other source material regarding Chad Martin and Ashley Beckwith distributed without the specific authorization of Regis and Canning will be considered slanderous. The publication or broadcast of such material in the media on any platform may be subject to legal action.

21

All Anthony would say was for Mica to think of this interview as a paid audition. But the pay wasn't much—a thousand dollars, which after Anthony's commission and taxes was just enough for a night out at any one of the hot steak houses in Los Angeles. But it was not about the money. It is all about getting back on the horse from which Mica had fallen off before paralyzing fear takes over and destroys his career.

Mica circled the block three times before he decided to look up and realized the space ship shaped studio on the second floor of a non-descript building in Culver City is where he needed to be. Fortunately, he was there within plenty of time for his one o'clock in the morning interview with the number one rated British morning news magazine show, *Rise 'N Shine*.

Anthony was already there when Mica walked through the door and nervously started firing details of what is about to happen in Mica's face.

"You are going to be talking to a Scottish woman, Corrine, who is the anchor woman for this hour of the show. She has an accent you can cut with a knife, so I say if you don't understand her just keep talking. You are the guest after all and they want to hear from you not her...."

"Breathe," Mica instructed as he put both hands on Anthony's shoulders. "If anyone should be nervous, it should be me. So for Christ's sake...or better yet, for my sake, calm down. Now, how much time do we have?"

"Half an hour," Anthony said, much calmer.

"Good, plenty of time for me to put on my face. Is there some sort of dressing room here?"

"Right this way, Mica," a voice boomed from over his shoulder. "Hi, I am Greg, the technician for tonight." As they moved toward the restroom and alternate makeup room, Greg went on. "First may I say that I am a big fan of your work on *Drop Zone* and I think your sensibility is perfect for *Rise 'N Shine*."

"Thank you and how so?"

"It's a serious news show. But they like to have fun in the segments between the newsbreaks. I do a lot of satellite feeds from here to this show, so I have gotten to know what they like."

"Good to know," Mica chirped, already more comfortable than when he walked in. "Now if you will excuse me, I just have to spackle my face to be camera ready."

Mica and Anthony stepped into the room and shut the door. It was B.J., his precious B.J., the producer of *Drop Zone,* who first told him to learn how to apply makeup. "No two makeup artists will do it the same way and only you will know what looks good on you." To this day, Mica prays at the alter of B.J. for that advice because whether it is in the studio or in the field, Mica can paste it on and look better than he does in real life.

"So what do you mean, audition?" Mica shot over to Anthony as Mica applied the base cover.

"All I know is that they are interested in your story..."

"You mean the Chad story..."

"Get over it. It is getting you back on the air," Anthony snapped. "Anyway. I hear that they are looking for a Los Angeles based correspondent to do a number of segments a week on a contractual basis. It is the first time a British news show would contract out to a non-Brit in British television history. You could make history if this goes well."

" Let me know when I am a question in the game of Trivial Pursuit and I will let you know when history is made." Mica may have been joking but even he knew this was a prestigious opportunity and, at the very least, a job to be had.

There was a knock on the door from Greg. "Five minutes. I need to get you in the chair to check the lighting, audio and the feed." It suddenly seemed like old times.

Mica, sitting in the chair of the cramped studio with the cheesy backdrop of downtown Los Angeles behind him, suddenly realized this interview is live. Despite the fact that *Drop Zone* was always taped as if live, if anything went seriously wrong they could always stop tape and start again. Sitting there now, Mica felt just a little vulnerable as there is no turning back.

"Anthony, this is live," Mica stage whispered to Anthony sitting just out of camera range.

"I didn't want to worry you."

"You have."

Greg talked down the earpiece, which would Mica's only communication with Great Britain when all begins, that and his microphone. "I must say you look great on camera."

"Thank you," Mica blushed. "It's the makeup."

"Then you know what you are doing?"

"Greg, I am just curious," Mica changed direction. "Will I be able to see who I am talking to?"

"No," Greg pointed out nonchalantly. "We don't have that capability."

"So if you don't understand her accent," Anthony piped in, "just keep talking. How often have you done live television?"

"Never," Mica confessed but was interrupted by a voice in his ear.

"Mica Daly, this is the control room in London. I am Nate, the director of the show."

"Hello Nate," Mica said with trepidation.

"First of all, thank you for being with us this morning...or last night for you. We are two minutes away from your segment with Corrine. We are going to switch you to the live broadcast. I will give you a five count before your introduction and then a ten count when you need to wrap."

"Got it," Mica said with all the false confidence he could muster. "But I have a question."

"Yes."

"What is Corrine wearing?"

"A green dress. Why?"

"Just wondering," Mica said and then they turned the live broadcast on in his ear.

Within a too short amount of time Nate began to count down Mica's segment and with that there was no turning back.

"Today we have a rare treat indeed," Corrine chirped in a lyric accent straight out of a Scottish version of a Lucky Charms commercial. "Mica Daly has the envious position of being a Hollywood insider with all the gossip of the day. Helllloooo Mica."

"Hello Corrine," Mica began, sitting upright and staring directly into the camera lens. "And may I say Corrine, green is your color."

Knowing she knows he can't see her, from nearly six thousand miles away Mica managed to throw the anchor of the number one rated morning show a reason to blush. "Ooooh you are a flirt Mica Daly," she fired back. "And flirting has gotten you a headline or two these days. We have all seen the picture of the kiss. Do tell, how did you end up kissing Chad Martin?"

"Well, I have to answer your question with a question. Have you never kissed a friend before?"

"On the cheek," Corrine answered quickly.

"Which cheek Corrine? There are four to choose from..."

"Ooooh you are wicked," Corrine fired back and then burst into laughter.

○ ○ ○

The interview with Corrine for *Rise 'N Shine* was quite literally an overnight success. By the time Mica had risen the morning after his late night sojourn on British television, there were two-dozen emails requesting interviews and several phone messages from Anthony.

"They loved you," was the simple voice mail from Anthony. "I have been on the phone all night with the executives," was the crux of the second voice mail.

By the sixth voice mail, Anthony had sealed the deal and Mica Daly was the newest contributing correspondent for *Rise 'N Shine*—details to follow. Mica sat stunned.

What had he really done? He gossiped with a girlfriend, one he'd never met nor seen, on live television. This was hardly journalism. Mica quickly got over that notion and settled into the idea that he was the voice of the people. He would just tell it like he saw it and he liked the freedom that gave him.

The other interview requests were from radio and print. What Mica had no understanding of, is that the Brits would pay to interview Mica—so different from America where you do interviews for publicity. Six of the dozen or so requests turned into real money—not big money, but money nonetheless. All of them wanted to know about Mica's relationship with Chad, which he was careful to couch as a very good friendship. Every one of his interviewers seemed to take that as enough and quickly moved on to Chad's relationship with their Commonwealth sister, Ashley Beckwith. Chad knew little to nothing about the details beyond they co-starred together in *The Other Brother* and had been seen on the town flirting. Interjecting a little 'wink and a nod' innuendo and Mica looked like a bona fide expert on that and all other Hollywood romances. He barely had a fact to go on and suddenly, Mica Daly is the go-to guy in Hollywood as far as Great Britain is concerned.

A career is reborn. Mica made a mental note to send Anthony some champagne.

○ ○ ○

Lance Novak is a charmer when he wants to be and a shark when he needs to be. This is one of those days when he will start out as one and become the other if need be. But even he doesn't believe it will come to that.

At just thirty-two years old, Lance has achieved what few have had the honor of having at Dunning, Baker and Astin—a corner office, which generally means he is a lifer and on the fast track to partnership. His décor is airline VIP lounge sleek with mid century modern furniture and chic period piece art works bought from his favorite gallery in Santa Fe, the Matthews Gallery, whose proprietor has his finger on the private collections the world over and can get what he needs from whom he knows for those who need it and where there is none of that Beverly Hills bullshit and price gouging. The small but significant Fernand Leger that hangs next to his desk is the newest acquisition and a favorite piece.

Nothing in the room was bought for comfort, although some pieces in spite of themselves prove to be comfortable. The room makes a statement, grays and whites with the occasional splash of color. It is meant to be a power palace and is designed not so much to distract people as it is to keep them on edge. It works.

Darcy at reception knows to keep Ms. Beckwith waiting at reception for an uncomfortable amount of minutes before escorting her to the office. Lance's assistant has already gotten the word she's arrived and let Lance know it is time to tighten his Burberry tie and throw on his suit jacket. Calvin Klein is the designer of the day.

After approximately eight minutes of waiting, Caroline, Lance's assistant, gave a gentle wrap on the door, opened it and introduced Ashley Beckwith to one of the most powerful, up and coming, lawyers in the entertainment industry.

"Ms. Beckwith," Lance stood but remained behind his desk, "please come in and make yourself at home."

"Please call me Ashley," she said.

Ashley, dressed in a suitable pencil skirt and silk shirt—her idea of business chic—is clearly having a hard time figuring out just where to sit. The chrome and white ostrich leather chairs in front of the desk seemed so cold and a formal presentation for a chat, as this meeting had been billed as.

"Can I get you anything to drink? Coffee? Water?" Caroline asked as Lance simply stood behind the desk watching Ashley weigh her options.

"No...thank you," Ashley muttered.

"Why don't you sit here at the desk," Lance suggested. "I have some papers to go over and it just might be easier."

"Papers?"

"I am a lawyer. We always have papers."

The laughter broke the ice and Ashley sat.

"So how are things going?" Lance began.

"Great...I mean depending on what things you are referring to."

"Well, specifically, with Chad." Lance leaned back in his ergonomic desk chair and waited.

"Oh that," Ashley giggled, "Chad is fantastic. We are having a really good time."

"Is it fair to say things are getting serious?" he questioned as if in court.

"Fair to say? I guess it is fair to say. But that is an odd choice of phase. Am I on trial here?"

"No, of course not. It is just an occupational hazard. I am always trying to protect the client."

Despite the previous "no", Caroline walked back in with a tray of coffee and pastries as if Ashley Beckwith would dare to down a cheese danish and risk altering her well maintained body weight. There was a reason for this well scripted interruption. She delivered what could only be described as a manuscript thick contract and laid it on the desk.

"Coffee would be nice, thank you," Ashley capitulated. "What on earth is that?"

"A contract," Lance began, turning the document around and pushing it toward Ashley. "It is for you."

Lance looked up toward Caroline and indicated they should now be left alone.

"For me? I have bought houses and made movies with less paperwork involved," Ashley quipped.

"That maybe true. But none of those changed your life like this does."

Lance paused to let that sink in for a moment."

"What is it?"

"A marital arrangement, pre-nup and child custody agreement all wrapped into one," Lance declared rather as a matter of fact.

"That can't be for me."

"Oh but it is. I may be letting the cat out of the bag but Chad Martin will propose to you and you will marry him."

"What? Why would I do that...I mean right now...this is all a bit early." She slumped in her chair a little as having been hit on the side of her head with the contract rather than having had explained to her. "How do you know he is going to propose?"

"He will. It is in both your interests."

"How is it is my interest? Unless I am in love with him..."

"Are you?"

"I don't know."

At this point, as if well orchestrated and choreographed, Lance stood and indicated that perhaps they should move to the sofa or chairs to make themselves less legal and more human.

"I know it seems like a lot," Lance began. "But you are an ambitious woman. You came here to conquer Hollywood but let's face it, that hasn't gone so well."

"I beg your pardon!"

"You're more famous than accredited. That is not a career and it is certainly not a future. I am about to change all that. That contract is the key to your future. For the next ten years, contractually, you are going to be Mrs. Chad Martin. For that privilege, we have arranged everything for you right down to the size of the diamond—no smaller than six carats and no larger than ten designed by Cartier, Van Cleef, Harry Winston or Tiffany; your choice."

"Oh I actually have some choice in this do I?" Ashley shot back flippantly.

"Calm down, it gets better. For each of the ten years, you will receive two million dollars in compensation that is yours to keep. Spend it, stockpile it, give it away...but if you are smart you will have twenty million in the bank at the end of ten years. At the five year point there is a bonus of five million. After ten years, should you decide to get a divorce, there is a flat twenty five million more."

"Where are you getting these numbers from? How is Chad Martin worth this much money?" Ashley is more aghast at the numbers than the audacity of the proposition itself.

"I am his lawyer," Lance explained slowly and carefully. "We are negotiating five years out already. His salary alone at these early negotiations more than covers these numbers. And then he is in the fifteen to twenty percent of the gross profit club."

She took a moment to catch her breath.

"If there are children, they will be appropriately taken care of financially and an egalitarian arrangement has been spelled out in terms of custody."

"Children?" she nearly whispered.

"But there is even more in it for you. Chad's production company, which is being underwritten by Spectrum Studios as we speak, will produce no less than three movies in which you will star. If they do well, who knows, there could be more. But that should jump start your career."

"I don't know what to say." At this point Ashley was numb. The verbal strafing is one thing. But the numbers, the details, and the children—it is all too much for her to process. "I have to think about all this. Perhaps my lawyer should read this."

"We would prefer that the 'arrangement' is kept in as tight a circle as possible. But of course you can do what you want. But I am going to warn you, this offer has a shelf life. You will agree or Chad will move on."

"That seems a bit cold…"

"That's why it is me who is telling you this and not Chad. He doesn't want to taint the beauty of what you have with these minor details."

"Minor details," Ashley scoffed as she stood. "You are asking me to change my life for the next ten years."

"This is the forward trajectory you are already on. This would be the same arrangement if you had been dating for a year or two already. The difference is no one wants to wait a year or two."

"Like I said," she said, "I should think about this." She reached for her Birken bag as if to indicate a leave.

"Tick tock Ms. Beckwith. If I were you I would sign now." Lance scooped up the contract and headed for his desk. "If you were so righteously indignant about this proposition you would have gotten up and walked out some time ago. But here you are. Is it really so abhorrent to marry the hottest man in Hollywood, get rich and famous in doing so? It is so much less of a contract and more like a life insurance policy."

"You haven't said what happens if I don't sign," she shot back—her attempt at a cross-examination.

"Yes I have. Needless to say, Chad will move on. But I can assure you, you won't. What do you think? Can you still make a career for yourself in Aussie soaps? Because there won't be anything for you here."

The standoff seemed to last an eternity but in reality it was just under a minute.

"I trust you have a pen?" she asked as she made her way to the desk.

22

It should surprise no one that Lydia Gray is a carnivore of the first order. Why wouldn't she be? She eats people up and spits them out—mostly out of competition and sometimes it's her wrath on a wayward employee. Mica Daly is a case in point. So if she is that way with people, what she can do to actual meat? Lydia loves a good Kobe steak and loves even more the most expensive steakhouse in the city, Cut, another in the collection of the famed celebrity chef Wolfgang Puck.

Cut is an industrial chic minimalist room in the back of the Beverly Wilshire Hotel. It is designed on two levels in order to make every seat in the house a good seat. Every month, having starved herself on half eaten salads with lemon instead of dressing, Lydia craves meat and insists on Cut and its over one hundred dollar a la carte steak. B.J. is the lucky invitee for this go around.

Lydia likes the second tier, looking over the crowd. B.J. is more the 'seeing' rather than 'being seen' type and the second tier is a perfect vantage point. Tonight, there were the usual suspects—society folks, Wolfgang groupies and a smattering of the old guard—that is until *she* walked in.

Ashley Beckwith arrived with very little fanfare with a couple of nobody girl-friends in tow. She had become somewhat known for traveling with a posse of old Aussie friends she had remained close with from back in her soap opera days. And, as luck would have it, Ashley and company are sat just below Lydia and B.J. At the lower level, the acoustics in Cut are atrocious and it is killing Lydia that she can't hear a thing from the table just three feet below hers. But that didn't mean there isn't a story to be gotten from this little outing. After all, it was hard to miss.

The massive diamond ring on Ashley's left hand said it all. This was the kind of rock a woman dreams of having but would never buy for herself. Could it be true that the "IT" couple of Chad Martin and Ashley Beckwith are going to tie the knot? This is new information. No one has this story. And Lydia is now salivating for an exclusive. Lydia discretely pointed to her own left ring finger and indicated to B.J. to glance over the railing at the table below. Even B.J., who is notoriously nonplussed about most things, let her jaw drop. The ring is just that impressive.

"What should we do?" B.J. asked.

"I am calling a crew to wait outside," Lydia began.

"There is a problem with that," B.J. shot back. "The valet is off the street and therefore on private property. The crew won't be able to get close enough."

"We could be ballsy and ask her for a sound bite for our camera when she is ready to go."

B.J. wrinkled her nose at the notion of ambushing Chad Martin's girlfriend. "Wait I have an idea." With that, B.J. stood up, darted across the restaurant and out the door.

Lydia took the moment to text the assignment desk their instructions and then took a second moment to text her favorite paparazzi, Joey Chase, to get a close up of the ring if in fact Ashley wishes to avoid the *Drop Zone* crew. By the time Lydia was through with her marching orders, B.J. was back.

"Where the hell did you go?" Lydia asked.

"The Valet. I told them I was with the Beckwith party and we thought Ashley had left her cell phone in the car. So I asked if she had valeted the car with them. And she hadn't. So no matter what, she has to hit the sidewalk in one direction or another when she leaves."

"Brilliant," Lydia squealed. "I should order two camera crews—one for each side of the building. This is our lead story tomorrow."

∘ ∘ ∘

Lydia slipped the waiter three hundred dollars to let B.J. and her sit for another two hours as Ashley and company enjoyed their dinner and nursed a drink or two before they decided they were done. When the bill arrived at Ashley's table, Lydia impulsively signaled to the waiter to bring it to her.

"What are you doing?" B.J. whispered as the waiter made his way over.

"Just a hunch."

Lydia handed over her black American Express card and stood.

Ashley and her friends met up with Lydia and B.J. at the halfway point between the tables.

"That was so kind of you and so unnecessary," Ashley gushed as she extended her hand.

"I am Lydia Gray, the executive producer of *Drop Zone* and this is my senior supervising producer, B.J." Lydia said as they shook hands. Ashley didn't pull away, which Lydia took as a good sign. "And frankly, it is your other hand I am interested in."

"You mean this?" Ashley blushed as she wiggled her glistening finger in the air for all to see.

"Isn't it gorgeous?" one of the nameless nobodies blurted out. Lydia simply threw her a look.

"It is," B.J. appeased but meant it.

"I was wondering," Lydia began in a sort of syrupy sweet way she could turn on when she wants something. "We have a crew outside and I would like for you to show the ring off. It will be our lead story tomorrow." It's rare to see this 'kill 'em with kindness' approach over her usual snapping of fingers and demanding her way or no way.

Ashley, with more aspiration than sense, agreed and Lydia walked her out the door and right to the waiting crew and Joey Chase.

Once settled in front of the camera, B.J. took charge. "Ashley, tell us about the ring."

Without missing a beat, Ashley Beckwith turned on her star appeal. "Well, it is a cushion cut, just shy of eights carats in the center and has a carat and half on either side. Harry Winston."

"Now, it sits on your left hand ring finger. Most people would have to assume that is an engagement ring," B.J. prodded using Lydia's sugary approach.

"Now a girl can't just kiss and tell," Ashley returned coyly.

Both B.J. and Lydia stood quiet, letting an awkward pause settle in. It is an old journalist's trick. Inevitably the subject being interviewed will start to talk and fill the silence. And it worked again.

"Yes, it is from Chad. But that is all I will say. I am sure you will be there when we are ready to make an announcement." With that Ashley and the nobodies were on their way.

Clearly, she had just made the announcement in Lydia's mind. The lead story is a done deal.

"How much for the photos Joey?" Lydia snapped. No need for syrup with Joey Chase.

"Are you kidding me? On the open market, the first pictures of that ring..."

"How much? Remember Joey, you wouldn't have gotten those pictures if I hadn't texted you. I am running with the exclusive and I want to know how much for the pictures?"

They settled on ten thousand dollars—nowhere near what he could have gotten but not bad for a night's work and an on-going relationship.

° ° °

Award season is a dizzying three months at the beginning of the calendar year in Hollywood where glad-handing and back slapping rise to the equivalent of Olympic sports. It is the time if the year when awards as big as the Oscars, as questionable as the Golden Globes and as self-serving as the Producers, Directors, Writers and Screen Actors Guild Awards are served up to a wanting audience and sometimes a deserving nominee. This year, so early in his career, Chad Martin had done well this award season, at least as far as nominations are concerned and the world's media all wanted a piece of him because of it. This was a perfect excuse for Michelle Bianco to invite the salivating media to an unprecedented one-off opportunity to talk with Chad, one-on-one, about his reaction to award season. But that was only part of her plan.

The space was beautiful. It should be. Michelle Bianco had bypassed the normal catering at the hotel and brought in Mighty Oak Productions and the impeccable taste of Shari Somerset at the last minute. Normally, Shari and crew would not take on something this small—she is the party design guru behind big premieres, big award shows, big film festivals game and not some poolside cocktail bash. But as this is Chad Martin's evening and the theme is award nominations—not to mention the fifty thousand dollars of a budget—Shari threw together some props from past galas and made the place look spectacular. Not bad for a two day notice. Shari and Chad had come along way since he'd pissed in her centerpiece and gotten fired as a cater waiter way back when.

The press conference was hastily put together, ostensibly to applaud Chad Martin's number of award nominations this season—a Golden Globe, two SAG awards and numerous critics choice awards. Could an Oscar nomination be next? Not a chance but that is the supposed question on everyone's lips for this press conference. After all, Golden Globe and Screen Actors nods can usually indicate where the Academy of Arts and Sciences—the people who give out the Oscars—are thinking. But in this case, everyone knew the Golden Globe is in recognition of Chad's big dick. The SAG award nominations are for 'ensemble cast' for his work on *Divas* and 'best actor'...for showing his dick. Who really cares what the critics tout?

Michelle was apoplectic when she saw Ashley Beckwith's interview and ring displayed on *Drop Zone*. Lydia couldn't have been more pleased when Michelle called to bitch. Lydia had bested her and it felt good. This press conference is a pre-emptive strike against that scenario playing out again. Everything with regard to Chad Martin and his career is to be orchestrated by Michelle Bianco and Regis and Canning. *Drop Zone* will pay a price and part of that starts here and now by not being invited to a soiree that would have become their lead story for the next evening.

'Here' is the poolside at the Tower on Sunset—apropos, it seems, as this was where Chad and Ashley declared they were "happy". What better spot to announce the future of their relationship? Yes, Michelle, slightly reluctantly, has called the world's media together to announce Chad and Ashley would be tying the knot. Ashley is ensconced in a room upstairs, just waiting for the right moment.

Until that time, it all seems like a fun cocktail party. Michelle paraded Chad around the patio giving each and every reporter, be it print, radio or television, a couple of minutes with the star. This sort of access is unprecedented but nothing short of brilliant in getting as much exposure during award season.

The sight of Mica Daly stopped Michelle dead in her tracks. "What the fuck are you doing here?" Michelle spit through clenched teeth.

"Working."

"For whom?"

Rise 'N Shine in Great Britain. I am their new Hollywood correspondent," Mica announced triumphantly.

"You are not on the list," she fired at him as her assistant frantically thumbed a clipboard full of papers.

"We confirmed through our London office. You will find me in the foreign journalist list." Mica smiled and lifted his cocktail in toast.

"Don't fuck this up, Mica," she huffed and stormed over to Eddie Fielding who'd put himself between Chad and Mica, obstructing Chad's view.

They concurred that it would make more of a scene to throw Mica out or even discretely asking him to leave. The media in the room, so far miraculously, had not tried to change the game plan and make the story about Mica and Chad. Neither Michelle nor Eddie had seen the paparazzi snapping Mica's picture as he walked in. And Mica, to his credit has said nothing to any media who had made the connection. Inside, Mica was left alone. No one wants to piss off the host and end up in the entertainment equivalent of Siberia.

"It is best to let sleeping dogs lie," Eddie said. And with that Michelle pulled Chad over for Mica's moment.

Chad flinched when he saw Mica and Mica, in turn, tried not to tear up.

Mica broke the ice, "How are you?"

"Get to it, Mica," Michelle snapped. "One question."

Mica looked at Chad, expecting him to slap Michelle down but Chad remained stoic.

"Well, the obvious question of the day is: with all these peer award nominations, what do you think your chances are for an Oscar nomination?" Mica dutifully asked.

"Well I certainly appreciate the recognition but it is really up to my peers to decide. I couldn't dream of speculating," Chad returned professionally and unattached—his best acting to date.

"Thank you," Michelle announced and pulled Chad away. The interview was over.

While Mica stood stunned, he too had mustered some of his finest performance skills of his life just then; Chad and Michelle made their way to the pool's end and to a waiting microphone. Michelle spoke first.

"I want to thank you all for coming today. And thank you more for your kind words with Chad and the support you have given him, not just during an exciting award season, but from the start of his career. We wanted to have you have a moment or two with Chad to let you see just how appreciative he is with all that has happened to him over the past year and then some. But I have to confess; I brought you here for a second reason. And with that I give you Chad Martin."

There was a smattering of applause as Chad took the microphone from Michelle.

"I can only reiterate what Michelle said and offer my thanks to all of you for being here today. And like Michelle said, there is a second reason to bring you all together. I want to introduce a woman without whom these award nominations wouldn't have happened but moreover the reason for my happiness. Ladies and Gentlemen, my fiancé Ashley Beckwith."

Ashley emerged from a French door leading from the dining room high atop her Louboutins, wearing a pink wrap dress, large pearls and *that* diamond—the very picture of the bride to be.

They kissed for the applauding media and fielded the obvious questions of dates and plans—neither of which were answered. Mica, who hadn't seen the *Drop Zone* piece with Ashley didn't see this coming. All he could do was stand there, dumbfounded. Only one of the paparazzi had the good sense to aim his camera not at the happy couple but in the direction of the jilted lover. And that man is Joey Chase. "And what do you think of all this," he asked.

"What are you getting at?" Mica asked.

"I know you are the story," Joey probed.

"I know that is a lot of speculation and not a lot foundation," Mica said excusing his cameraman by instructing him to shoot some of the party and then call it a night. He then pulled Joey aside

"Why are you holding back on this guy?" Joey asked.

"Moral high ground."

"Can I quote you on that?" Joey pulled out a pad to start taking notes.

"That is not a quote, just an observation."

Mica knew this would not go well and decided to extricate himself from the situation and began to walk away.

"Nice cock by the way."

Mica turned back with steam rising, "I beg your pardon."

"Nice body. Do you work out?"

"How would you know about my body?"

"I know you are the man by the pool," Joey stated and baited.

"I saw those pictures," Mica stepped forward and got in Joey's face. "No one knows who that person is. If you did, I would assume you would have cashed in by now."

With that, Mica turned and headed for the door.

"If you tell your story, you could make a fortune," Joey shouted over the din to the disappearing Mica. "You do it...or someone else will," he mumbled to himself.

                              ∘ ∘ ∘

"Mica? That's Mica Daly," the man yelled as Mica headed to the valet. A beefy bald with an earpiece and a tailored suit—straight out of central casting—held him back.

Mica loves the convenience of valet parking but is always astounded as to how much time it takes. It is the Hollywood equivalent of watching the microwave and waiting for a potato to bake—it's faster on paper.

"Mica...it's me," the man shouted and Mica instinctually turned to see who it is. Tommy Mercer.

"What are you doing here?" Mica asked and signaled to the security goon that things are all right. "Tommy right?"

"That's right," he turned to the security guard and nodded with that 'I told you so' look.

Mica simply paused and waited for him to speak.

"Look, is Chad in there? I need to talk to him."

Mica still said nothing.

"I think I did something wrong. I need to explain."

"Look, Tommy, can't this wait until you see him at the gym."

"He doesn't train with me anymore. No one does. Not since the picture."

Tommy's voice is cracking with emotion. "I did it for the money Mica. He has to know that. And I can fix it if it is bad."

"What are you talking about?"

"I need to talk to Chad."

"I don't think that is going to happen."

As he finished his statement, Mica's car arrived and he simply turned and walked to the open door, paid the man and drove off. Mica has his own problems and no time to listen to another sob story from someone Chad Martin simply dismissed.

o o o

Only one magazine *World Beat,* which ironically wasn't invited to the press conference, ran a story using acquired pictures and stringer sound bites focusing on Mica as the jilted lover having to endure the announcement of Chad and Ashley's engagement. Mica expected there to be more coverage about his being there but it seems the mainstream media stuck to their 'best behavior' sensibilities and stayed clear. No one wanted the wrath of Regis and Canning or ostracizing by Michelle Bianco.

Although, Mica was surprised to see his picture run in the article in *Gotcha!* magazine. It was just one picture with a tag line that read: All is forgiven. Mica Daly, the reported 'close friend' of Chad Martin was there to hand off his man.

Mica though that was a little ballsy of such a star friendly magazine but Mica is now a fixture on British television and all is fair game for their media.

23

Mica couldn't believe what he was seeing. Chad Martin is making a spectacle of himself on live television.

Chad's career had skyrocketed. Nothing seemed to happen to his existing contracts as a result of his brush with infamy in the tabloids. He had wrapped production on *The River, Deep* and gone straight into production on *Fire Power*, an action adventure that promises make Chad the next action hero. Between having been naked on screen in *The Other Brother*, the poignancy he will show in *The River, Deep* and the testosterone he will pump in *Fire Power*, Chad Martin is fast being positioned as the man women want and men want to be as was prophesized some time back by "Big Eddie" when Chad signed with Regis and Canning for publicity.

Now, with the announcement that he is getting married to Ashley Beckwith, he...they...are the darlings of the media. And clearly his publicist, Michelle, and the fine folks at Regis and Canning are working overtime to promote that image.

So it didn't surprise Mica that Chad would be booked on *Chatter*, a women-centric daytime talk show hosted by a four women panel consisting of a journalist, a comedian, a former politician and an author turned social commentator. Mica tuned in just to see how Chad would do. He is not used to appearing on live television and as charming as he can be during an interview, he could be thrown by just the right...or wrong...question when it is live.

Fortunately for Chad, the whole interview consisted of softball questions about his being nude on screen, his career trajectory and his relationship with Ashley. And when they got around to Ashley is when Chad lost it.

He explained how they had met on the set of *The Other Brother* to which the comedian quipped, "There wasn't much left to the imagination after that."

And then he explained how his publicist set up the first date to which the author joked, "Another Hollywood contract!"

Even though she had no idea what she had said, that comment hit too close to the bone and Chad began to feel that he had been exposed. So by the time the journalist asked, "When did it become love?" Chad was ready to explode.

"I love her. I love her!" he screamed and got up, jumped up on his over-scaled club chair and starting jumping up and down. "Have you ever felt like a kid in a playground...felt that kind of love," he exclaimed. "That is what I feel for her."

The women panelist weren't sure what to do. Was he losing it on the air or was he simply in a childlike smitten state? All anyone knew is that one of the highest paid actors in Hollywood is jumping up and down on the furniture like a six year old, declaring his love for Ashley. It was more than awkward, it bordered on the psychotic. The women panelists giggled but couldn't hide their stunned expressions. In the middle of the spectacle, they broke for a commercial.

Mica was sure this would be the clip seen round the world and prepared himself for the phone to ring. He assumed this would be the next subject for his appearance on *Rise 'N Shine*. Mica had to hand it to Chad. If this was the plan to get people talking about Chad Martin in a different context than the tabloids, this was certainly going to do it.

∘ ∘ ∘

"Chamtini?" Chad offered to Ashley as he walked into the bedroom with a tray of the makings in hand.

"What is that?" Ashley giggled at the sight of a naked Chad with tray in hand.

He set the tray down on the nightstand and explained. "I came up with this drink, a champagne and vodka martini, and only make them for special occasions."

"And what is the special occasion?" Ashley purred as she reached over and started to stroke his manhood. "Saw your display today on "Chatter"."

"I meant it," Chad muttered, slightly embarrassed by it all.

"It was sweet. A little weird," she chuckled, "but sweet. Is that why we are celebrating with the celebrated chamtini?"

"I have something special in mind."

Up until now their sex life has been sparse and rather unimaginative. Ashley had always chalked it up to his work schedule and being tired. She had seen the tabloids and heard the rumors but chose not to believe what they said, completely. It never occurred to her that he was simply not into her in that way, maybe just bi-functional in a sexual way.

He concocted two chamtinis and handed one to Ashley. His, he began to let dribble over her pert breasts before he started to flick each nipple with his tongue. He used to do the same with Mica. She moaned with pleasure.

He took a big gulp of his drink and began to kiss his way down her tight stomach, past her belly and down to her Brazilian cared for mound. This is uncharted territory. He had never gone down on her before.

He slowly spread her legs and caressed her inner thighs. No wham bam thank you ma'am. Slow and steady. Again he took a fortifying swig and leaned in.

"I'm Australian and I have finally gotten you to go down under," she joked

He first let his fingers explore; touching, pressing and rubbing. Ashley arched her back and moaned again with pleasure. She began to spread open ever so slightly, inviting him in.

Chad lay on his stomach and leaned his face in. He first licked all around, getting a taste of her juice, feeling the soft texture and getting in rhythm with her ever so subtle gyrations. He probed his tongue in and out of her opening, her lips sealing around him. He aggressively pushed his face further down and in. He is a master with his tongue.

Chad inserted his finger deep into her pussy as he made his way up and discovered her engorged clit and began to work on that; flicking and sucking, flicking and sucking. The wet softness of Ashley's inside and the now puffed lips of her labia are a curiosity to Chad. He looked upon this mission as a science experiment more than lovemaking and that distraction intrigued him enough to continue on. There was no emotion, just pure exploration.

There was a gush of wet as she screamed lightly and bucked wildly. As she came, he pulled himself up and rammed his hard cock into her begging pussy. She screamed loudly this time. He slammed against her. His big balls, slapping her ass making a rhythmic clapping sound. They were in sync as he pushed and she thrust. He continued slamming harder and harder, just shy of being violent, and then rolled her over.

Doggie style is his favorite position. It let his mind wander to where he needed it to be. As he calmed into a more flow, he gently fingered her asshole, wishing he could be in there. As much as her fleshy pussy served his purpose, he missed Mica's tight ass and his ability to tighten his muscled hole around Chad's big cock. Just thinking about that got Chad hot again, and he began to slam hard into Ashley. She groaned from pain not pleasure and he eased off.

A few more hypnotic minutes later and Ashley was reaching her second climax, her bucking backwards only made Chad hotter and he too was soon ready to release. He bent over her and cupped her breasts, squeezing her nipples. He too liked to have his nipples played with but she would never have known that. The sweat coming from Chad's face, dripped on to Ashley's body and he began to lick it off, the way he did with Mica. Only she wasn't his sweaty equal and the co-mingling of salty manliness wasn't there.

He pumped away as she groaned and then squealed one more time as he pumped his hot spunk into her. He thrust a couple of times, pulled out, rolled her over and pushed his meat toward her mouth.

"Eeeiiiwwee," she screeched.

He suddenly realized it was Mica who loved that post climax taste and he pulled back. "Sorry, I just got caught up in the moment."

"Cum tastes like bleach," Ashley grimaced. "I don't know why anyone would want to put that in their mouth."

"I remember a time on the set when you didn't mind swallowing."

"That was work," she said. "Besides what did you think?" Ashley asked, reaching for her cocktail.

He did the same, taking a large gulp to wash away the taste of her vagina. "About what?"

"You've never gone down on me before. How was that?"

"Great," he lied. "It's not like I wasn't going to. It's just that I consider that something special and, well, was waiting for a right moment."

"Speaking of something special," she began as she got up from the bed and walked over to Chad's highboy dresser. She reached up into the highest drawer and pulled out a rather substantial dildo. "Did you get this for me?"

The dildo, larger than the average, was made of a type of flesh feeling plastic and was designed to be more naturally correct than a vibrator with a veiny shaft and balls attached to the bottom end.

"What the fuck are you doing?" he snapped. "Have you just been going through my things?"

"So it is not for me?" she asked curiously.

The truth is Chad had been experimenting. He knew that Mica had always wanted to reciprocate and fuck him but he never seemed ready for it. He had been mildly curious and then very curious about what it would feel like. The courage it took to buy that thing took him weeks to work up. And since then it has become a fun toy, which will one day ready him for the real thing.

"That's disgusting," he said. "It was a gag gift when all the shit was going down in the tabloids." That was the first time he even acknowledged the tabloids in her presence.

"Where there's smoke, there's fire," she prodded as she swung the thing around with a certain precocious sarcasm.

He grabbed it from her hand, grabbed the bottle of vodka in the other and stormed off. "Fuck you. You can sleep alone." And he stormed off to the guest bedroom.

Ashley began to tear up as she curled up in the bed wondering whether she should just leave. She fingered her impressive diamond, decided to stay and apologize in the morning.

After a few good-sized swigs from the vodka bottle, Chad calmed down. He fondled the dildo, stoking the edifice up and down as if trying to make it harder than it already is. He licked the tip and then began to suck the head. To erase the taste, he took yet another swig. His own cock is getting hard and he reached down between his legs and tapped his smooth asshole. In the guest bathroom, in the back of one of the drawers, Chad found the lube he had been looking for. He stroked the silky liquid up and down the dildo and inserted it slowly. It felt good.

24

The magazine is German with a name no one can pronounce and is one of those gay rags so obscure, it is not even found on the racks of America's newsstands. And yet, it has published an article being talked about the world over. Trainer to the stars, Tommy Mercer, is the first person to come forward and say they have had sex with Chad Martin. Explosive.

Mica had been quickly propped up for a reactionary interview with *Rise 'N Shine* during which he said he was shocked at the revelation and had to wonder if it is true. Mostly, Mica internally questioned its validity because, if it is true, the affair would have had to have been going on while Mica and Chad were together. And Mica didn't want to contemplate that.

Mica pointed out to the deeply intrigued anchorwoman, Corrine, that there would have been nothing in it for the trainer to say those things other than money. And there couldn't have been enough money to sacrifice his career with other celebrity clients, which accordingly he has. Moreover, it was even less likely that the magazine reporter had anything more than a fishing expedition in mind when he sat down to interview Tommy. As such, it would have been Tommy who gave up the information rather than having been asked specific questions about Chad Martin.

He went on to say that Hollywood is a strange place and people grasp for fifteen minutes of fame anyway they can. The interview was all very perfunctory, as Mica hadn't really seen the entire article, just the passages emailed from the show. And Corrine was careful not to ask about Mica's own 'friendship' with Chad, which Mica had been ready for but not looking forward to. He breathed a sigh of relief when the director counted down the segment, it was wrapped and he got the all clear.

Reaction wasn't so convivial around town. In the offices of Regis and Canning, Michelle Bianco was combustible. She hadn't been able to reach Chad who is on the set of his latest film *Fire Power*. She did, however, reach his lawyer Lance Novak.

"We're on it," was the crux of the conversation.

° ° °

Chad hadn't seen the magazine, just a rewritten tabloid version of the story which one of the makeup people had brought to the set. There it was in black and white, with a repurposed version of the original picture of Chad and Tommy from tabloids past and a series of new shots of Tommy done at the Body Image gym.

Chad had that makeup person summarily fired for ostensibly spreading gossip—something he would reconsider and make good on when he is thinking more clearly. But it is just eleven o'clock in the morning and he is well into a bottle of Jack Daniels. He doesn't even like Jack Daniels but it was a gift left in his trailer and the only thing available.

Chad's trailer, a four hundred thousand dollar behemoth of a bus, is hardly some primitive sanctuary. It is state of the art, complete with a bedroom in the back, a kitchenette, full bathroom with shower and a living room area. If he is going to hide out, this is hardly roughing it. And hide out he has, shutting down production on *Fire Power* for at least the day.

First the director and then the producer and even co-stars tried to intervene. Chad simply remained silent behind the locked door. He took only one phone call, from Lance Novak, who spelled out a fairly ironclad retaliatory plan of action.

o o o

"I want to see Chad. I want to explain to him."

"That won't be happening," Lance Novak explained to a clearly agitated Tommy Mercer.

Tommy is out of his element and he knows it. Sleek corner offices in Beverly Hills are not his domain. He is a gym rat at heart. Even in an upscale personal gym like Body Image, he is still a gym rat.

"This is not the story I told." Tommy pleaded his case.

"What is the story you told?"

"They asked me about how I work out. You know, what is my regimen and training advice. They wanted the Hollywood secrets to a better body."

"And of course they asked about your celebrity clients."

"Well, yeah..."

"And you named Chad Martin?" Lance is clearly leading Tommy down a path. "Yeah..."

Without saying another word to Tommy, Lance reached over and buzzed his outer office and told Caroline, his assistant, to bring in the contract. Tommy squirmed in his chair.

Tommy is looking rough. Most of his celebrity clients had long left him after the initial tabloid story and picture put him and Chad Martin together. The overall reasoning was a breach of discretion. Suzanne, Tommy's wife, left him because of his 'obsession' with Chad and moreover, left him broke. He's begun to drink and that has left his ultra-toned physique bloated and out of shape. Even his face is less chiseled and puffier. Today, in the offices of Dunning, Baker and Astin, he is trying to look his most professional. And for Tommy that means a now ill-fitting suit jacket over a starched white button down shirt and clean jeans. But he hasn't shaved in a couple of days and looks simply tired.

Caroline walked in with something the size and weight of a phone book and placed it on the desk equidistant between Lance and Tommy.

"Do you remember this?" Lance asked.

"No," Tommy answered honestly.

"This is the confidentiality agreement you signed with Chad."

"I did? When was that?"

"It's dated, you can check." But that question sparked a thought in Lance's mind. "For the record, let's check something."

He opened the impressive document and flipped to the correct page and pointed to the signature at the bottom. "Is that your signature?"

Tommy looked over and hesitated to answer. "Yes. I suppose so."

"Suppose? Or know?"

"Yes, it is my signature."

Lance nodded to Caroline. She had done her job for the moment as witness and it was now time for her to leave them to the business at hand.

"Could I have a glass of water?" Tommy asked nervously. Caroline dutifully obliged and then shut the door behind her as to punctuate there would be no more distractions.

"So," Lance began again, "let's talk about the article. Just how did it come around to sex? You said that the article was supposed to be about your workout strategy."

"Well," Tommy began and then took a large gulp of water. "They asked me about wrestling. I told them a lot of my clients like to wrestle as a warm up or cool down to the their work out. I mentioned that because it is a private gym, we can wrestle in the nude, even work out in the nude. It was meant as a joke, something provocative to say."

"Did you mention anything about Chad in context with wrestling."

"Maybe..."

"Maybe?" Lance was too smooth to lose his cool but Tommy was testing him mightily. "It says here in print that you specifically said that you and Chad wrestled in the nude."

"I don't remember saying that," Tommy snapped defensively.

"What do you remember saying?"

"I am not sure. They took things out of context."

"Did they take things out of context when you said, and I quote: Yeah Chad and I have fooled around. Working out is a bonding moment. Sometimes we just got carried away. Exploring each other's bodies is just a natural thing after working up a sweat or wrestling. Or was it taken out of context when you said, quote: Of course we shower together. Guys do at the gym all the time, that is nothing new. But what is different is Chad's body. He is extraordinary and that gets me going. And when I get going, Chad gets going and then it is just good clean fun."

"We were talking about male bonding," Tommy stammered. "Fuck, they were foreign. Maybe they didn't understand."

Lance sighed and leaned back in his chair. The silence is deafening.

"Let me tell you how it is going to work from here." With that, Lance pulled out three envelopes. "In this first envelope is a retraction that you are going to sign. It is has been written for you and all you have to do is agree to what it says. We will have it distributed to the media. You will say nothing from this point forward." Tommy nodded almost overly enthusiastically.

"To guarantee that, I present you with envelope number two. Inside this envelope is a check for five million dollars." Lance paused to let that sink in. "For this money, you are going to never speak publically again, about anything. I suggest you change your name, but I insist you get out of town. Your association with Chad Martin is officially and irrevocably over." Again, Tommy nodded.

"And to guarantee that, again, I present another envelope. This third envelope contains a one hundred million dollar lawsuit, which I will be filing tomorrow. Let me make this perfectly clear, we are going forward with this lawsuit. In it are numerous pages listing the damages that your article has caused Mr. Martin, including and notwithstanding, loss of income derived from his gross percentages lost from disappointed fans not going to his movies, etcetera." Tommy looked numb. "After a lot of legalese you will get to the second to the last page and there it will state how we will win this lawsuit. You are in breach of contract. You signed this confidentiality agreement stating that you would never speak publically about Chad Martin and you broke your confidentiality. Bottom line, we win."

Again, Lance leaned back in his chair and let the moment hang in the air. Tommy appropriately squirmed.

"I don't have one hundred million dollars," Tommy mumbled as tears welled in his eyes.

"No you don't but you do now have five million. Simply follow the directions I have just spelled out for you and you are a rich man. We won't collect on the suit. Break the rules and I assure you, we will go after the five million and then the one hundred million and break you."

Tommy reached for envelope two and peered in. There is a five million dollar cashier's check with his name on it. Tommy began to weep openly.

"I just have one question," Lance asked with a seriousness that stopped Tommy's tears. "Do you understand everything I have said to you?"

Tommy nodded.

Lance pushed the button on his phone. The door opened from behind and Caroline lead a burly security guard borrowed for the occasion from the office building reception.

"Mr. Mercer, I need to escort you off the premises."

∘ ∘ ∘

Mica loves being in Palm Springs and loves even more being the recurring guest of Roger Keenan whose home is spectacular and every need is met. He drove down the morning after his broadcast for *Rise 'N Shine*. The atmosphere is so much different this visit, the tension between Chad and Mica is no longer hanging in the air like a dark cloud. But that doesn't mean Chad's presence didn't still linger.

The subject hadn't come up over dinner. Mica and Roger were the guests of another for once. Octavio, an Argentinian painter and long time friend of Roger's, and his Croatian boyfriend boy-toy of over a decade, are in town from their adopted Miami to scout galleries to represent Octavio's work. Fortunately for Mica, Roger had no idea they were in town. If he had, he would have invited them to stay at the house. Instead, they were ensconced in a suite at one of those chic boutique hotels, gems from Palm Springs past restored lovingly by some newly minted, fresh faced, interior designers—the ones with their own shows on cable television. Mica was relieved. He wasn't sure he could have taken two full days and nights of Octavio and the Croat.

Most of the conversation at the table revolved around the globe hopping adventures of the international couple, the state of the art market, what either or the other is working on currently and then the smattering of old time remembrances between Octavio and Roger. Finally, "And what is it you do?"

Roger answered for Mica, "Mica Daly is quite the rising star on British television."

Mica blushed. "I report on Hollywood for the British television morning news magazine show *Rise 'N Shine*."

"And what is the news from Hollywood?" Octavio asked rather uncaringly.

"The odd sex scandal," Mica answered vaguely.

"You American's are all so hung up on sex," Octavio returned. "The rest of the world not so much. I personally believe there is no such thing as a sex scandal. Just sexual adventure." With that, he let out a hearty laugh and turned to Roger. "If there was such a thing we would all be guilty just having attending one of your Hollywood soirees."

Suddenly Mica's contribution was dismissed and the conversation took a left turn back to memories of the adventures of Roger and Octavio. And Mica was just fine with that.

The next day, sitting by the pool sipping Bloody Mary's—Mica getting an all over tan and Roger draped in a caftan and panama hat—Roger apologized for Octavio dominating the evening.

"There is nothing to apologize for. You two are old friends and it was great hearing about your past indulgences."

"Well, you are quite the conversationalist yourself," Roger said. "And I just got the impression that you weren't getting a chance to say much."

"It is fun to take a night off once in a while and not have to be 'the Hollywood guy.'"

"We did brush past the biggest story coming out of Hollywood."

"And that was fine too."

"Is everything okay?" Roger sat up and asked with genuine concern.

"Yeah. I mean, its bad enough about this marriage to Ashley Beckwith—who from what I hear should be named Ashley Beenwith. But I hate the idea that Chad was fucking around when we were together," Mica returned half-heartedly. "The first thing you have to wonder is, is it true? Only two people know. One isn't ever going to admit to it and the other could simply be down on his luck and looking for some sort of payout."

"How much do you think he got for his story?"

"Enough to have him tell it. Everyone's price is different."

"What is your price?" Roger prodded.

"Excuse me?"

"Have you ever thought of telling your story?"

"Why would I do that? What would be in it for me? A single picture nearly ruined my career," Mica pointed out.

"And gave you a new career trajectory," Roger countered.

"I don't want to be forever known as 'the other man' in another man's story of ambition."

"But that is just what makes this story so interesting," Roger grew excited. "The lengths to which people go to follow ambition."

"Chad is too powerful. It is a game of he said/he said. And Chad had the machinations in place to disavow with a powerful team to back him. I would look as pathetic as Tommy Mercer. But if I had to have name a price, it would certainly be in the seven figures...enough to be ruined over."

Mica stood and walked over to the pool's edge, dipped his foot in to feel the temperature of the water and just before he dove in, turned back to Roger. "We haven't seen what will happen to Tommy Mercer yet. That may be it's own cautionary tale."

25

Drop Zone was the first to break the story of the one hundred million dollar lawsuit by Chad Martin against his former trainer, Tommy Mercer. It is a staggering amount of money designed to put the fear of God into anyone thinking about saying anything negative about Chad Martin. It is a big story.

Lydia had been handed the exclusive from Michelle Bianco as a sort of olive branch reward for toeing the P.R. line as of late—favorable stories about Michelle's clients and, of course, the previous dismissal of Mica Daly. And in return, Lydia sent a massive bouquet of flowers over to Michelle and a muffin basket for the staff at Regis and Canning—five hundred dollars well spent.

Despite having been handed the story, Lydia strutted through the newsroom as if it was her investigative journalism pedigree that sniffed out and broke the story. Hardly, but that is quintessentially Lydia being Labia.

To her credit though, Lydia quickly contracted the number one mouthpiece on the subject in an exclusive deal for five segments over a 'to-be-determined' number of weeks. The spokes-mouth is none other than Chad Martin's chief council, Lance Novak.

The question for Lydia was where to do the interview? She wanted to set Lance apart, almost as a reluctant witness, who, thanks to *Drop Zone* is finally able to tell his story. It is all very dramatic, but that is what the show has become. Lydia nixed the idea of doing it at his office, as he would look to be in control. She didn't want to do it at the desk on the set as he would come across as too willing. She settled on a corner of the studio cloaked in heavy black drapery.

"He's not in the witness protection program for Christ's sake," B.J. blurted out when she walked on to the stage and saw the clandestine set up.

"Shut the fuck up," Lydia snapped. "I don't want this to look like some sort or premixed interview that anyone could get. I want this to appear like we have something special and that only we were able to pry this information from an unwilling participant." These were the kinds of subliminal tactics Lydia had become know for as the executive producer of *Hot Type*—her television tabloid previous incarnation. And as much as *Hot Type* was ridiculed and pilloried for its sensationalist form of journalism and eventually went off the air because of it. And yet, that is fast becoming the model by which *Drop Zone* is heading.

Despite sitting in the studio, with lights a blaze, and a camera uncomfortably close, Lance Novak is remarkably collected and confident. There would be no flop sweat or unintentional weeping on the horizon—not from this cool customer. B.J. was chosen to conduct the interviews. It speaks volumes about Lydia's confidence in her reporter staff in that when the big interviews come down it is always B.J., a producer, who conducts them. Ordinarily an interview like this would have gone to Mica but fuck it, he's not there.

"One hundred million dollars? Why such an extreme amount of damages?" B.J. began, pulling no punches.

"We don't think it is a lot of money, when you consider what Chad Martin is worth as a commodity and if that commodity is damaged what the dollars and sense of that means," Lance defined. "Now having said that. We know the average person is awestruck by that monetary amount. But that is by design as well. It is supposed to scare people."

"So the idea is to ruin a person?" B.J. continued.

"No, we want people to see the light as it were. We gave Mr. Mercer a chance to recant and he took it."

"In light of being ruined he changed his story," B.J. clarified. "How are we supposed to believe him when he changed his story because he had a monetary gun cocked to his head."

"That's nonsense. Nobody has cocked a gun to anyone's head, monetarily or otherwise. As I said, that number is based on actual damages we can calculate and the court specifies the need for that calculation when it comes to a civil suit such as this one. It is unfortunate that Mr. Mercer took on a big fish."

"Do you think this is the only lawsuit you will be filing?" B.J. prodded. "Or do you think there are others out there who may come out of the closet?"

"I would be careful how you phrase that question," Lance chuckled but wasn't joking. "We are looking into suing the magazine who published the interview as well as the America tabloids that excerpted the salacious passages."

"Does that mean this show is in the cross hairs? We ran with the story as well."

Good question, Lydia thought, sitting in the control room. It hadn't occurred to her that they could be being set up.

"No," Lance reassured. "This show is allowing Mr. Martin, via me, to state his side of the story and therefore showing balance. Do we wish you hadn't run the story initially? Of course. But we understand that sometimes entertainment news comes from the bottom of the barrel."

The dig was duly noted.

"But to answer your previous question," Lance began. "No. We don't believe there are others out there with similar claims."

"I have one last question." B.J. toyed with not going here but she couldn't help herself. "Do you seriously believe that Chad Martin, as big as he has become, would be harmed if people think he is gay?"

"Yes."

The answer hung in the air for a moment and then Lydia, the voice of God from the control room, stopped the interview. "Thank you Lance. That is all we need for today."

Lydia sat back in her chair and let out a squeal, which startled the control room staff. She got what she wanted.

∘ ∘ ∘

Mica could understand retaliation, certainly when it comes to Chad Martin, but a one hundred million dollar lawsuit against a man who is virtually penniless is simply over the top. And of course Tommy retracted his quotes as misquotes when faced with that overwhelming lawsuit filed by the most powerful entertainment lawyers in Hollywood.

Mica combed through the damages section of the lawsuit, the part that was released with the press release. It stated, among other obscene and outrageous damage claims, was that people would not go and see a Chad Martin movie if they thought he was gay. De facto, Chad would lose actual money as owed to him by contractual gross box office percentage participation. And that got Mica to thinking. Could there be any truth to that?

Mica contacted the producers of *Rise 'N Shine* with a story idea. Mica wanted to simply walk the streets of Hollywood, say in front of the Chinese Theater, where there would be a good mix of tourist and not just industry savvy locals, and ask one hundred people: would you go to see a Chad Martin movie if he were in fact gay? He would televise the results as an informal poll but meant to question the validity of the damage claim as asserted in the lawsuit that have Chad and his lawyers chosen to make public.

"No!" The answer was resounding. "It's not that we don't think it is a good story, we are just afraid that we too will be sued. We, of course, would win the lawsuit but it would cost us a fortune in legal fees. And we don't want to alienate a A-list Hollywood star anyway."

"But it is not like I am going to ask if they think he is gay," Mica said in his defense. "I just want to see the validity of his own damage claim in his own lawsuit."

"We understand your premise. But we have run it by our lawyers and the answer is 'No.'"

Mica hung up the phone in disgust. He always thought the British had bigger balls than that. At least the tabloids do. It seems that Chad Martin may no longer be fucking Mica, but Mica is certainly getting fucked over by him.

∘ ∘ ∘

Anthony Wright, Mica's new agent, is quite the dealmaker or so it seems to Mica. He managed to concoct a situation like no other Mica has experience in his entire career. It came to Anthony's attention that Suzanne Mercer's story is up for grabs and no one had figured it out. Anthony is banking that hers is a story worth hearing.

Suzanne Mercer is the estranged wife of Tommy Mercer and is she angry. Suzanne found out that Tommy had made the better part of fifty thousand dollars to tell his story to that European magazine and then hid it from her in the divorce negotiations. It is her turn to cash in—her story to the highest bidder. Little did she know what Tommy has really pocketed. But he has disappeared and presumably no one knows.

The German magazine wasn't interested in paying again for a story they already reported and got plenty of worldwide recognition in return. But they did turn Suzanne on to Anthony as the man who brokered the deal.

Anthony, not one to miss out on a commission and yet not wanting to screw his best client, came up with the ultimate compromise. He contacted the tabloid *World Beat* to pay Suzanne twenty five thousand dollars for a first option but not an exclusive. In other words, they would publish her story first and then Mica, who will have taped the interview but not have conducted the interview, would have the television rights. Win/win. Surprisingly to all parties, *World Beat* went for it. They had no idea that Mica put no money up.

They met collectively at the *World Beat* offices on Wilshire Boulevard—a surprisingly sleek bee hive of a complex with far more staff that Mica would have imagined and not the sleazy back alley dungeon Mica presumed for such a sleazy, back alley, publication. The only homage to the product they produce are the framed covers and headlines lining the common hallway—everything from AN ALIEN ATE

MY BABY to I SLEPT WITH BIGFOOT and of course a plethora of unflattering photos of wayward stars like Antonia Guest.

"Coffee?" some nice assistant asked as they made their way into the conference room where the interview was to take place—not the nicest of settings for a television camera but Mica had been warned to say nothing. This was a gift to him.

Suzanne arrived slightly late but completely put together. Mica remembered seeing her, along with Tommy, when they were Chad's guest at some premiere or other. And she was thrilled to see Mica.

"Hello, you," she said and planted a kiss on each of Mica's cheeks. "It is so good to see you again. How do I look...you know...for television."

"Fantastic."

"Thanks, now that I don't have a trainer anymore," she winked, "things can go shit."

"Don't worry, you look great."

Suzanne turned to the rest of the room. "Always trust the gays. They are fucking honest."

The interviewer is a smarmy Brit, Ian Thomas, who, for the most part, spoon fed Suzanne with leading questions and just let her speak. And she was more than willing to speak. She spewed her side of the story with both venom and lust and couldn't get it out fast enough as if she was ridding her body of a poison.

"Our sex life? Fantastic...well at the beginning...before he was too tired from his 'workouts'," she chortled. "My husband...er...ex-husband, has a great cock. He loved showing it off at the gym under the guise of 'guys just being guys'. I suppose I can't blame anyone for falling for that piece of meat."

She continued. "And his body. Christ, you could chip a tooth on his ass. Trust me, I nearly did."

Mica had to work hard at not laughing out loud. Suzanne, the woman scorned, turned out to be quite the comedian.

"Tell me about Chad Martin," Ian asked without looking up from the notebook he had been continuously scribbling in.

"It is all true," she stated emphatically. "Now mind you, I never saw them together. But I know it is true, everything my husband...ex-husband, said."

"How do you know?"

"A wife knows when her husband cheats. First, he is no longer interested in sex on the days he worked out with Chad Martin. And believe me my Tommy was one horny motherfucker. It was sex every day, sometimes twice, except on Chad

Martin days. Second, my husband wasn't a liar, except when it came to our divorce assets and now with the denial or...how do you put it? Retraction. But if he were paid to give an interview he would never lie. And in that interview he said he had sex with Chad Martin. Hell, he let us get divorced based on that interview. That would have been a perfect time to say he had made it all up."

"I see..."

"And one more thing," she interrupted. "I don't think he could lie legally. He signed some big form that Chad Martin makes all people he pays sign. I think he had to tell the truth."

"Form?"

"It is something or other about the way employees have to act," she mumbled, somewhat unsure of herself.

Ian turned to Mica and smiled. Both knew Suzanne may have been confused about the foundation of the 'form' Tommy signed but she had now confirmed the presence of a smoking gun.

"We've tried to contact your husband..."

"*Ex*-husband," she corrected.

"Ex-husband. And it seems he has fallen off the face of the earth. Do you know where he is and why he is so silent after dropping such a bombshell?" Ian prodded.

"I wish I knew. I can't find him either. And the bastard owes me money."

"Why did you choose to do this interview?"

"That bastard got paid to do an interview which ended up ruining my marriage and then hid the money from me in my divorce. And now he has the balls to deny everything. Fuck him. I deserve to earn a little something from all this too."

"Thank you," Ian said, ending the interview.

Suzanne looked over at Mica, "How'd I do?"

"You were great."

"What did I tell you? Listen to gays!"

As everyone started to disband and the assistant took Suzanne by the arm to lead her out, Mica spoke up. "Suzanne can I ask you one question?"

Anthony threw Mica a look. No questions was the deal.

"It is not on camera. It is just a curiosity," Mica explained to Anthony and then turned to Suzanne. "Do you happen to know where that 'form' Tommy signed is?"

"Not a fucking clue," she declared and then kissed him again on each cheek.

∘ ∘ ∘

Mica stopped by Ovation for a cocktail. It is a little out his way but the atmosphere is great and he inevitably he comes across a familiar face to share a barstool with. And, of course, he has. Sitting at the bar alone is Lance Novak.

The bar at Ovation is actually in the back of the restaurant. It is a newly built architectural add on, which, to get to, you must enter from the rear of the building or come through the entirety of the restaurant and out through a courtyard and into the freestanding bar. The walls of glass open to the courtyard with its own outdoor seating and huge mature oak growing up through the middle. It makes for a great indoor/outdoor experience.

Mica noticed the Prada suit before he noticed the man wearing it. There is nothing like being able to spot the cut of a great suit, even from behind, Mica thought. And of course then it takes the right man to wear the right suit. All that ran through his mind before he saw the right man is Mr. Novak.

Mica had always thought of Lance as handsome in that slick way. Well groomed with product in the hair to keep it in place. He never thought much more beyond that. And of course, once he signed Chad as a client and the tabloids intervened, he hadn't thought of Lance at all. But somehow, sitting alone at the end of the bar, Lance has a certain vulnerability that is attractive to Mica.

"Buy a boy a drink?"

Lance laughed. "Hi Mica, how are you?"

"Good." Mica sidled into the seat next to Lance. "What brings you to this part of town. It's a long way from Beverly Hills."

"I wasn't at my office. I was at your old office in the valley, doing an interview for *Drop Zone*." Lance signaled to the bartender for another of the same, a martini, and one for Mica.

"You are becoming quite the media darling. And I must say, you look good doing it. You are a natural."

"Well, I don't know about that. But I am wracking up quite a bit of airtime," Lance acknowledged. "Sorry I couldn't throw you a bone on this whole lawsuit thing but I am contracted to *Drop Zone* for a number of segments."

"A bone? I thought I was the enemy."

"Not to me. It is just business."

"I understand. No one knows better that I do just how territorial Lydia Gray can be," Mica sighed.

"Off the record. She is one piece of work." They both laughed and raised a glass to toast. "Lydia!"

"Off the record. We called her Labia because she could be such a cunt," Mica confessed.

Again, they raised their glasses, "To Labia!"

"I never thought I would hear myself say that," Lance chuckled.

Mica paused for a moment and the conversation went dead as he thought carefully about his next move.

"Something on your mind?" Lance asked as only a litigator can.

"As a matter of fact there is a bone you can throw me," Mica said.

"Careful now," Lance joked back. "I can't be sleeping with the enemy." Mica filed that away in the back of his mind.

"I have just one question. Why didn't you sue the wife?"

Lance stopped cold, squinted his eyes and said nothing. Mica clearly knew something he shouldn't or, at the very least, was putting two and two together. "I can't discuss that at the moment," Lance declared with a clear punctuation that that conversation isn't going any further.

"Well when you can speak of it that will be my exclusive." Mica and Lance shook on the deal. Both knew the other knew more than they were saying.

"Perhaps we could have something to eat, unless I am still considered the enemy," Mica suggested.

"Let's eat," Lance returned and then winked at Mica.

∘ ∘ ∘

The knock at the door startled Mica. Mica had been sitting around in his underwear, drinking a morning coffee, wondering what story he would come up with for his usual slot on *Rise 'N Shine* when the messenger arrived. Mica signed for the envelope with a little trepidation. Information coming in this form is never good news.

Inside is a press release from Lance Novak.

FOR IMMEDIATE RELEASE

HOLLYWOOD, CA

Contact:
     Lance Novak
     Dunning, Baker and Astin

CHAD MARTIN SERVES WIFE OF FORMER TRAINER, SUZANNE MERCER, WITH $100 MILLION LAWSUIT

In keeping with the previously announced aggressive approach to stopping any and all vicious, malicious and unfounded rumors and accusations surrounding Chad Martin's supposed 'sexuality', the law firm of Dunning, Baker and Astin has moved forward with a one hundred million dollar lawsuit against Ms. Suzanne Mercer.

Ms. Mercer, the former wife of Thomas Mercer, a previous litigant in a similar lawsuit, has made public defamatory, libelous and/or slanderous comments about Mr. Martin that could result in actual and emotional damages (as spelled out in the attached excerpted lawsuit) which include but are not limited to diminished income due to confused or upset fans turning away from Chad Martin movies.

"We take this extremely seriously," says Lance Novak, chief council for Chad Martin. "People are not allowed to simply make outrageous and defamatory accusations against a public figure. This one hundred million dollar lawsuit will be imposed on anyone who makes a similar accusation and will aggressively be pursued in the courts."

Recently, Mr. Martin, star of *The Other Brother, The River, Deep* and the upcoming *Fire Power* has become engaged to his former co-star, Australian actress Ashley Beckwith. The date of the upcoming nuptials—what the media is already calling "the wedding of the decade"—will be announced shortly.

"Anyone who knows the couple in any capacity can see the love between them," says Mr. Novak. "This is why we are being so aggressive in pursuing and putting to an end any vicious rumors so that the soon to be Mr. and Mrs. Martin can get on with a very happy time in their lives. To them we say congratulations. To the rumor mongers out there, we say: watch out."

Any future official announcements, comments and notifications regarding this matter will come from the offices of Dunning, Baker and Astin. Any other source material regarding Chad Martin and Ashley Beckwith distributed without the specific authorization of the publicity firm of Regis and Canning will be considered slanderous. The publication or broadcast of such material in the media on any platform may be subject to legal action.

Mica had almost forgotten his throwaway line to Lance Novak the other evening at Ovation, as he never did get an answer to 'why didn't you sue the wife?' Well, he got his answer now.

Attached to the press release is a note card, hand written, from Lance. *Thanks for the heads up. I owe you. Would you like a sound bite?* .

Mica has his story for *Rise 'N Shine.*

26

Finally, it was Mica's chance for a genuine scoop. He knew that Lance Novak would give him an interview or a least a couple of quotes, which he would have to use judiciously. And he knew that he had the previous interview with Suzanne Mercer on tape and could more than likely wrangle a second one out of her for clarification. His entire story rested on just a couple of questions.

A meeting was set up on Monday morning with Lance. Lance had become a little full of himself and become a bit of a media whore in a world where sometimes less is more. But Lance had promised Mica his turn after Lance's exclusivity with *Drop Zone* had lapsed. Mica turned up early, in order for the cameraman, Jonathan, who Mica had poached from *Drop Zone* as a 'fuck you' to Lydia, to have time to set up. They chose Lance's sleek office as a backdrop.

While Jonathan set the camera and lights in place, Lance and Mica had a chance to speak.

"So what are we talking about?" Lance asked as he poured Mica a coffee in the firm's lounge area.

"Who else?"

"How much more is there to say?" Lance joked.

"Oh, I want to talk about Suzanne Mercer," Mica clarified.

Suzanne Mercer was nothing more than a bit player in this whole theater of the absurd in Lance's mind. The lawsuit was simply a tempest in a teapot, follow-up on precedent set with the client—anyone who talks gets sued. What could he possibly be fishing for? Lance thought as he made his way to the waiting camera.

"How do I look?" Lance lightheartedly asked as he sat. "Hair? Makeup?"

"You look guilty," Mica joked back and signaled Jonathan to fire up the camera.

"What is the basis of the lawsuit against Suzanne Mercer?" Mica began. The conversational tone is over; Mica is very direct and professional.

"Well Mica," Lance returned with a decidedly informal tone. "We are suing Ms. Mercer for slander and liable."

"A one hundred million dollar lawsuit for a woman who was ostensibly defending her husband's credibility," Mica fired back.

"She made claims of her own."

"Which were?"

"She said her husband had relations with my client." Lance began to squirm ever so slightly.

"No," Mica corrected. "She said that she believed her husband didn't lie when he said he had relations with your client. She also said that her husband signed a form. Please take a look at this."

With that, Mica pulled out his laptop and played a snippet from Suzanne's interview where she states that her husband signed some 'form.'

"Do you have a question?"

"Yes, Mr. Novak," Mica said. "What is that form her husband signed?"

"All employees of Mr. Martin, and I will clarify employee as anyone who is paid by Mr. Martin directly or indirectly for services rendered, signs a standard employee understanding contract which spells out expectations of performance and privacy."

"A confidentiality agreement?"

"In part."

"One last question Mr. Novak. Did Suzanne Mercer sign one of those 'forms'?"

"Ms. Mercer was never an employee of Mr. Martin."

"So your answer is no?"

"Correct."

Mica signaled Jonathan to turn off the camera. The interview is over.

"You should think about being a lawyer," Lance said to Mica as he reached to shake his hand. "And I trust this issue is over."

Later that day, Mica arranged to meet Suzanne Mercer at her house. Anthony had set it up. Lance had promised it would just be a couple of questions for clarity and therefore there would be no payment for the interview. She agreed.

The house, a Spanish bungalow not far from the Body Image gym, is small, quaint and tastefully done. The 'For Sale' sign out front said it all. She isn't going to be able to keep it as, as she puts it, Tommy has already proven to be a deadbeat and has provided no alimony. The house is the only asset and she is going to sell. The twenty five thousand dollars, minus Anthony's commission, she got from the last print interview with Ian Thomas at *World Beat* only went so far.

"I am only doing this for you, Mica," Suzanne said as she opened the door and let he and Jonathan in. Anthony, expectedly, was already there.

In the few minutes it took Jonathan to set up the camera, Mica had gotten an earful from Suzanne on the fact that Tommy has not returned any of her calls, "He's moved out but to God knows where? The few remaining clients he has, haven't heard from him and they are calling me. And the fucker isn't paying me." Clearly, she will have no problem talking. But ironically, Mica only needed her to say two things.

They sat in the living room where the light and the backdrop were the most conducive for the interview.

"I am going to make this very easy for you Suzanne," Mica began. "My first question is: did you ever see or read the 'form', as you called it, Chad Martin had your husband sign as an 'employee'?"

"No," she said.

"Have you ever been asked to, or in reality, signed a form provided by Chad Martin or any of his representatives?"

"No."

"Thank you, Suzanne. That is all I need."

"Really?" she quizzed.

"Really?" Anthony asked.

"Really!" Mica smiled as he spoke. He had his story.

∘ ∘ ∘

"How did this happen?" Chad slammed his fist on Lance's desk hard enough for Michelle Bianco to flinch.

"How?" Lance leaned and snapped loudly. "How? You know how it happened. It's up to us to fix it. Do not shoot the messenger. This is what is called damage control."

"But I thought it was over with Tommy's settlement," Chad snapped back. "You know, back when he recanted."

"Look Suzanne Mercer is small time. We will take care of her silence and hope that is the last of it. It is the last of it, isn't it?" Lance looked at Chad, imploring him to let them know now if any similar scenarios are out there waiting to come forward. Chad shook his head no, knowing otherwise.

"Look I have to get back to the set. What do we do from here?"

"Same as last time. She'll sign the papers and we buy her silence."

"When is this going down?" Chad asked.

"As soon as you okay the plan."

"Then you have my okay. Make this shit go away!" Chad demanded.

"The terms of Suzanne's deal will be significantly less than that of Tommy, but suffice it to say Suzanne will be happy to shut up."

Chad nodded, got up and walked out of the office, slamming the door behind.

Lance and Michelle simply looked at each other, and then Michelle spoke. "Do you believe there are more?"

"It is my job to believe my client," Lance said, clearly instructing Michelle to do the same. She nodded. "Now, I need you to call one contact and we plant the story."

"The New York tabloids. Everyone will see it and some won't believe it. It is win/win," Michelle said.

"No paper trail," Lance said. "Can you do it by phone now?"

"Sure."

The tabloid is on speed dial on Michelle's phone and within moments is on to the right person. "Write this down. There will be no press release."

Lance slid a pre-written statement across the desk and over to Michelle.

"Ready?" Michelle asked and then began to speak. "A settlement has been reached between Chad Martin and Suzanne Mercer over the one hundred million dollar slander and liable lawsuit filed by Mr. Martin. Martin, having a private meeting with Mercer, understood her to be apologetic for her outrageous statements and has learned that they were simply retaliatory as a result of an emotionally charged divorce from her husband Tommy Mercer, who has also retracted his claims of a 'friendship' with Mr. Martin. Understanding Ms. Mercer's personal and financial issues arising from her divorce, Mr. Martin has offered Ms. Mercer an undisclosed settlement in return for neither speaking of this situation again, publically or privately. Representatives for Mr. Martin have said the matter is closed and there will be no further statements."

There was a pause and then Michelle spoke again. "Correct. That is the only statement. You have it. I expect it to be printed in its entirety and there will be no formal press release or further comments." Pause. "No, thank you!"

"Done," she said to Lance.

"Great," he sighed. "Now there is one more thing." Lance slid a second document towards Michelle. "You're turn."

"What's this?"

"Your confidentiality agreement."

"That's outrageous. He is a client of mine. I would never say..."

"You are not a lawyer. There is no client privilege here. You are, in fact, an employee. Sign it or you won't be an employee. This matter is too delicate. It is your choice."

"You are questioning my professionalism," she growled as she signed.

"I am simply obstructing temptation."

∘ ∘ ∘

As luck would have it, the New York tabloid story ran on the same day as Mica was to present his own interview with Suzanne Mercer and Lance Novak on *Rise 'N Shine*. Believing his interview had somehow motivated this settlement, made him proud. He has a genuine scoop.

Corrine was riveted by the report. More than she loves Hollywood gossip, she loves the intrigue.

"So you're saying..."

"Suggesting," Mica clarified.

"Suggesting," she giggled and clarified. "I love the legal tightrope we have to walk. So you're suggesting that because she, Suzanne, didn't sign the legal employee document they gave her money to keep her mouth shut from here on."

"It does point to that," Mica said.

"And you feel you had a hand in that," Corrine said leadingly.

"I do, Corrine," Mica said. "Both interviews had been conducted before this settlement. As you can see from my taped report, the statements back up the hypothesis from both parties. And, may I just say for the record, these were exclusive interviews just for us and our viewers of *Rise 'N Shine*."

Of course that self-congratulations was meant to put punctuation on this report. *Rise 'N Shine* is part of a media and news outlet which sells it's product on to other media outlets through out the world. It wouldn't surprise Mica if Lydia Gray and *Drop Zone* were on the phone making a rebroadcast deal as Mica was delivering the report.

He felt good.

∘ ∘ ∘

The knock on his door woke Mica up. His reports from Hollywood to London happen at 1:00 am in the morning in order for him to be live in the morning, London time. By the time he gets home, showers, let's the adrenaline that live television creates subside and goes to bed; it is the wee hours of the morning. And last night was a particularly late night as he detoured on the way home to drive by Suzanne Mercer's house on a hunch. He was right. The 'For Sale' sign is gone. She has taken the house off the market—presumably because of a new infusion of cash.

A knock at the door at 9:00 A.M. isn't welcome.

The bouquet is enormous and had to have cost a fortune. Mica could not imagine from whom it came and even questioned whether the deliveryman—a hottie, by the way—had the right address. Mica fumbled around in his jeans for a few dollars to give the guy before he tore open the attached card.

Tipped and on his way, the deliveryman had placed the massive arrangement in the center of Mica's dining room table—the only space open enough to carry such a spray of flowers. Mica stood and stared for a moment and then reached for the card.

Fuck You...Love Lydia.

27

Suzanne Mercer glowed as she stepped out of her new Mercedes S-class and handed the keys to the valet at the Beverly Hills Hotel. As it happened, Mica, her lunch date at the Polo Lounge is in the car right behind her and beeped to tell her to wait for him.

The valet pulled her car away and Mica proceeded forward and in turn handed his keys to the classically beautiful man in the pink shirt. All of the valets seem to have aspirations in this town and those at the Beverly Hills Hotel appear to have come straight from central casting.

"Nice car," Mica joked as he gave Suzanne a big hug and a kiss, again on both cheeks.

"You know I can't talk about that," she cautioned.

"You can't talk about your car?"

"I guess I can talk about the car itself...just not how I got the car."

"I get it," Mica laughed, took her arm and they headed under the striped awning and into the lobby of the hotel.

It was Suzanne's idea to have lunch—a sort of 'thank you' for all that has happened. She knew that Mica had set up Lance Novak in such a way that she would be exonerated at the very least. She never expected the payout she received. But, of course, she too has signed the 'form' and cannot speak of the details. This was going to be a simply lunch.

"You look great," Mica said as they reached the maître d' who was somewhat startled to see Mica. The reservation was under Suzanne's name. "Is there a problem?"

"Of course not," he returned. "I just have to check on the table."

The Polo Lounge employees, and in particular the maître d's at the Polo Lounge, are particularly versed on the news of the town. They go to great lengths to avoid placing warring sides of an argument, who just so happen to have the conflicting reservations, at opposite sides of the restaurant to avoid an obvious scene or even mild discomfort. It works nicely for divorcing couples, film negotiations, contract disputes, television rivalries and all sorts of other petty, personal and profession feuds. So when the maître d' walked away, Mica grew cautious.

"That was odd," Mica said to Suzanne. She hadn't noticed anything.

They were on their way to their table out on the patio when a figure leapt from the far booth along the windows in the main dining room and darted for them.

"You are not supposed to talk," Chad said, getting right up into Suzanne's face. Lance Novak and Sterling Lowe were just behind Chad and pulled him back. Suzanne was startled by the attack.

"What?"

"Let's calm down here," Lance said to Chad and stepped between the star and Suzanne.

"And what the fuck are you doing with her?" Chad spit through clenched teeth toward Mica.

To the rest of the room, this didn't look like much more than two couples greeting each other but, nevertheless, they were drawing attention.

"We are simply here to have lunch," the now composed Suzanne said indignantly.

"Suzanne, we have an agreement," Lance said.

"This is not an interview," Mica stage whispered as to not be overheard. "We are simply having lunch."

"You fucked me," Chad whispered back to Mica.

"Like you fucked my husband?" Suzanne snapped back.

"That's it," Lance interceded. "Enough! This conversation is over. Chad, let's get back to our table. We have business to discuss."

"I have another big back end deal coming my way," Chad lauded to Mica.

"Chad!" Sterling cautioned Chad to shut up.

"I bet you know a lot about 'the back end'," Suzanne sniped at Chad and then headed toward the maître d' to be escorted to her table.

Mica could hardly hold back a snicker when he caught Lance's eye. Lance squinted his anger and Mica simply winked in return, which caught Lance off guard. Lance smiled back.

28

The smell had permeated through walls, something rotting with a hint of sweetness to it. The neighbors had been the ones to call it in, reluctantly as this wasn't the kind of place where the police were regularly welcome.

The building is on the lower end of Whitley Avenue, above Hollywood Boulevard and below the famous Heights—the former chic retreat for such past tense notables as Barbara Stanwyck, Marlene Dietrich, W.C. Fields, Gloria Swanson, Jean Harlow, Rosalind Russell and Tyrone Power. Today, Whitley Avenue is just shy of the gentrification taking over Hollywood and where the down and out can still find affordable housing.

Apartment 226 was down the hall and toward the back, looking out on to the wall of the next building. The hallway itself smelled from the well-worn carpeting lining the hall and the deep steeped smoke in the walls so desperately in need of fresh paint.

As the officers approached 226, they too could smell the sickening scent. It is the kind of the scent that gets into your nostrils and stays there. Even raising a handkerchief to their noses was not going to help.

The name on the mailbox is Mercer and according to the neighbors who barely peaked through a chained crack in their door, Mercer is a man. That's all they know.

"Mr. Mercer?" The first officer spoke loudly and clearly as he knocked on the door. The second officer had already retreated to find a manager with a key. "Mr. Mercer? It's the police."

No answer.

The second officer returned with the manager who was visibly surprised by the smell emitting from beyond the door.

"Didn't you know there was a smell?" The second officer questioned.

The man shook his head without speaking and handed the key over to the first officer.

"Some fucking management they have here," the second officer said to the first and then turned back to the manager. "We should take you in for gross negligence."

The opened door let out an invisible cloud of stench, nearly unbearable. And there inside the junior one bedroom—a studio with a sleeping nook—hung the naked body of Tommy Mercer, dangling from a Hermes tie looped around a ceiling light fixture in the center of the room. The body is blue and bloated from having been there a significant amount of time.

° ° °

On a bluff above the shores of Malibu, at the French Chateau inspired home formerly owned by a music pop star, some two hundred guests were starting to arrive. The invitation said arrivals and cocktails at two o'clock. The ceremony would begin promptly at four o'clock. The dress code is cocktail chic, the ladies to wear hats and the men in suits and ties. Nothing too formal as it was to be the essence of an English garden party. And, under no circumstances, would there be cameras or cell phones allowed.

No detail was left unattended to, thanks to the party prowess of Shari Somerset and her Mighty Oak Productions. Estimates for the day's budget ranged from two hundred thousand to just over one million dollars. But everyone was being tight lipped about the money involved—gauche talk. But money was not an issue. Pictures of the day have already been presold to the English glossy celebrity magazine *Gotcha!* for two and a half million dollars. Suffice it to say the extravagance was not lost on the attendees.

Guests were instructed to park in one of three locations in Santa Monica, where a phalanx of limousines would whisk them the twenty odd minutes to Malibu. Inside each limo, for each ride, a fresh bottle of Crystal champagne was furnished.

At the house, an array of blush colored cocktails—lightly infused cosmopolitans, pomegranate martini's, Cape Cods with just a whisper of cranberry juice and, of course, pink champagne—met each guest as they stepped out of the limo and walked the long tiled trail through the house and out into the tented back garden. The day was hot but a nice breeze blew off the shore, across the yard and into the house. Throughout the house's main living areas were selections of canapés and hors d'oeuvres—everything from Russian caviar to Australian lamb Wellington. This being a Hollywood affair, virtually no one touched the food—a crushing blow to Scott and Brian, the geniuses behind the success of Ovation, who have become the caterers to the stars thanks to the constant endorsement and employment from Shari Somerset

A series of string quartets dotted both the inside home, outside patio and pool area where the ceremony will be held. Each has synchronized their playing as to start precisely together, playing the same tune. In that way, no guest is ever out of earshot of the music.

The yard has been tented to protect against the prying eyes of paparazzi, which will most assuredly be just off shore, pointing telephoto lenses out of the side of chartered helicopters. Again, Mighty Oak Productions thought of that scenario and secured a no-fly perimeter forcing any and all helicopters to be significantly off shore so that noise won't be a factor during the ceremony.

What they couldn't prevent was the paparazzi standing across the Pacific Coast Highway, slightly above on the hill, getting shots of celebrities and guests stepping out of the limos as they pulled up in a steady stream. And it is there that Joey Chase has staked his claim. So far he's managed to get a side view and even a few smiles and waves from the likes of Mr. and Mrs. Barry Stegman from Spectrum Studios, Suzy Chambers, Gina Hamilton and some beefy boy toy on her arm, the super agent Sterling Lowe, Chuck Corman the photographer, directors Drew Peters and Conrad Barrington, British action star Sean Jones, actor Rod Stevens and the occasional socialite such as Marilyn Lassiter who is there as the guest of marketing guru Roger Keenan.

Marilyn Lassiter is the perfect 'plus one' for an event such as this. She inevitably will find a way to talk to every name worth talking to. As a result, Roger, who is the perennial host will be forced to play the role of the guest and mingle accordingly. It will be a 'hoot' for him to simply trail her and her non-stop nattering. As soon as they entered the doorway, Marilyn grabbed at two drinks—pink champagne for her and a Cosmo for him—and she was off.

Along with the staff of Mighty Oak, both Michelle Bianco and Eddie Fielding planted themselves just inside the doorway, out of the camera's eye, ostensibly to greet the guests but moreover to make sure of no gatecrashers, cameras or cell phones.

As the guests made their way to the back garden, they had already experienced an explosion of pink. Some two hundred and fifty thousand pink roses filled every nook and crevice with five different centerpiece arrangements strategically placed on the twenty tables of ten, which surrounded the pool. Hanging over each table, a substantial Baccarat crystal chandelier strung together by garlands of the same roses making a canopy of fresh flowers. In the center of the pool is a stage where the nuptials will take place and later still, when the pool is covered over, the pool will act as a dance floor.

Marilyn Lassiter, who had already swiped her and Roger's place cards from being trapped next to some name she didn't recognize, Lance Novak, at a table she felt the floral centerpiece was too high for her to have a clear view of all the goings on, is frantically looking for a place to sit. Within minutes, she decided to place she and Roger with their backs to the ocean, on either side of reality television star, Suzy Chambers, banishing the Stegmans to her former seats.

° ° °

The cause of death: auto erotic asphyxiation—accidental suicide by strangulation during a sexual act. There would be an autopsy performed, but the cause of death seemed fairly obvious to Detective Joseph Tomasso—the body is naked, his left hand grasping his penis and, after the forensics team is through, there is likely to be semen in the carpet below. Of course the porn shot of two men fucking, paused on the television screen certainly only added to the conclusion.

So the cause of death was not the puzzlement, the reason for the location was. Tommy Mercer, to Joe's recollection, was a successful 'trainer to the stars' in West Hollywood and had been linked to Chad Martin recently. Surely this was not the place where someone with those connections lives?

But Tommy had been in a downward spiral since the scandal of Chad Martin, the loss of his marriage and his business falling off to virtually nothing. This dingy little place on the questionable end of Whitley Avenue is, indeed, where Tommy had ended up. But it wouldn't have been for long, not since the check arrived. Five million dollars, made out to him drawn on a holding account with the law firm of Dunning, Baker and Astin. The check, which sat on the table next to the overturned chair Tommy had used to place himself inside the noose, was covered with the remnants of lines of a white substance, the consistency of powder, as noted by Detective Joe Tomasso.

Scattered all over the floor are legal documents, pages and pages haphazardly strewn as if someone had taken a pile and thrown it in the air. Detective Tomasso instructed the forensics team to photograph everything. But, then, he took out his own cell phone and began to do the same—the body, the check, the papers on the floor—he wanted his own record of the scene.

He knew it wasn't long before this scene would be messed up or cleaned up by the shear numbers of people that had to trample through the tight room. So once he and the forensics team were through with the papers on the floor, he began to gather them up and put them in numerical order, snapping a shot of each page as he went. It appears to be some sort of lawsuit, drafted from the same law firm as the five million dollar check.

He handed off the task of locating and notifying the next of kin to his partner Bobby. He had a notification of his own to do.

° ° °

A semi-circle of chairs had been placed just before the bridge that will take the bride and the groom to the waiting nuptial island in the middle of the pool. The chairs are for immediate family—mothers, fathers, maid of honor and best man. The rest of the guests would sit at their assigned seats for the reception.

About three thirty, Chad, in a cream colored Ralph Lauren bespoke suit, made his way out to the guests and around the yard, greeting and thanking everyone for being there. He glowed partially from the attention but mostly from the nervous tension he was feeling. There is no turning back now. Close at his side, the best man, Lance Novak.

At five minutes to four the string quartets sounded and the respective mothers made their way from the house to their seats. The maid of honor, some Aussie school friend, came next and exactly at four, the bridal march began.

Ashley Beckwith had never looked more angelic. Draped in a form fitting, elegant and appropriate Stella McCartney gown of duchess satin—a design you could easily see on the Oscar red carpet—she floated forward grounded only by her father's arm. He father, a hard assed retired army Lieutenant was teary eyed for the first time in as far back as anyone could remember. And the crowd sighed with emotion.

"Getting any ideas?" Gina Hamilton whispered to her boy toy du jour.

"No," he quickly returned. It's bad enough I have to fuck you. But a fuck is a buck, he thought.

"Wouldn't you like to get married like this?" she pressed.

Not to you old lady. "Someday." About the time you will be collecting social security.

Chad collected his Ashley from her father and led her over the bridge to the waiting minister.

The ceremony was short, mercifully short. It began with the usual "We are gathered here..." notations and quickly went into the personally written vows from each other, to each other.

"Chad, I can't believe we met on the set of a Hollywood movie because ours has become a script, a love story, I could never have written. It has been filled with, drama and romance, action and adventure, and as I turn the page to see where the story goes I am always excited by the idea of what's ahead. And the one thing I am sure of is ours is a story that can only continue *happily ever after.*"

"Ashley," Chad began. "In a world that just keeps spinning faster and faster for me, you are my center, my anchor. You remind me, every day, that there is more to life than chasing a dream, that with you I am living a dream. And if this is just a dream, I beg the angels around us to not let me wake. You are my dream, my center and all I hope is that I can be and continue to be that for you."

There wasn't a dry eye as the couple exchanged rings, hers a eternity band of emerald cut diamonds set in platinum from the fine craftsmen at Harry Winston— classic, but just showy enough. His is a simple platinum band with a channel of baguette diamonds all around.

Let the party begin.

○ ○ ○

Mica was going to ignore the texting that was humming across his phone. He knew this was the day that Chad was getting married and he didn't want to know the details from those who are there or get condolences from friends who aren't. But the texts were relentless and he knew he would have to face them one time or another.

Have story for you. The number didn't immediately compute to a person, Mica read on. Tommy Mercer is dead.

It suddenly hit him as to who was sending the messages. Joe. OMG, Mica wrote back. Do you have details?

On the scene now. Accidental suicide. Have pictures of scene. Gruesome. Have some questions you might be able to help with. Can I send pics?

Yes!

○ ○ ○

As it turned out, Marilyn Lassiter had done the Stegmans a great favor by moving their seats to sitting next to Lance Novak. Barry Stegman had been trying to set up a meeting with Lance for weeks to negotiate Chad's next two projects with Spectrum Studios under Chad's overall production deal with the studio. Now, he had his captive ear. Diandra knew enough to excuse herself when Barry began his shtick. And she was smart enough to know who Barry's next target would be. So she set off to find Chad's agent, Sterling Lowe and guide him back to their table.

Marilyn herself had been thoroughly intrigued by her seating companion, Suzy Chambers, as the whole reality television craze has become a kind of obsession with Marilyn.

"Tell me, dear, do you mind all those cameras? It seems they are in your life twenty four seven."

Suzy, who was thrilled by the attention as she is never taken very seriously and considered a circumstantial celebrity with no real talent, jumped into the conversation. "It isn't long before you forget they are even there. The producers and the crew are instructed to not interface with us, ever. So eventually you let your guard down and life goes on, for millions of people to see."

Marilyn, who is just a little jealous as she too has an idea to turn herself into a reality star, was so engrossed she didn't notice Roger Keenan had left her side and was working the party, talking to the directors Barrington and Peters about their next project and pitching himself as their marketing answer.

As the early dinner—a surf and turf of Maine lobster tails and Kobe beef—segued into an evening party, Chuck Corman surreptitiously snapped hundreds of candid shots of the event. Chad had chosen Chuck because, as Chad believes, those earlier shots of Chad had really helped him become the star he is. And, as such, is incredibly grateful. Besides, Chuck is quite simply the best.

After Chad and Ashley posed for the more traditional shots of newly weds by the sea and those group shots with friends and relatives, Chuck and his new assistant Danny made their way into the house to set up some rather unorthodox shots for the bride and groom to approve.

Ashley, in the meantime, introduced Chad to now fellow action star, Sean Jones. They had met on a British talk show, which led to a few inconsequential dates and a long-term friendship. And Chad, in turn, introduced an old pal of his, Rod Stevens, who was accompanied by the requisite and nameless big-titted bimbo.

"You're a lucky man," Sean congratulated Chad with a robust handshake. His thick Welsh accent threw Chad for a moment, who had only heard him speak with an American dialect on screen.

"Thank you," Chad returned and then glanced up to see Chuck signaling him from a window above.

Ashley and Chad walked into the large master bathroom to find Danny lying naked in a bubble bath. It was set up to show the couple what Chuck is envisioning. Ashley, in her wedding gown will be sitting on the tubs edge, leaning over to kiss a naked Chad in the tub. Interesting. They agreed and Ashley stepped out to avoid getting water splashed on the silk of her dress leaving just Danny and Chad to swap places.

Danny stepped out of the tub to reveal a cock to rival Chad's and Chad could not hide his surprise. Danny stood dripping in front of Chad and let him take it in. Chad could feel a stirring in his own crotch. "Excuse me," Danny said as he reached past Chad to retrieve a towel.

"Sorry," Chad mumbled. "I am in your way."

"You're turn," Danny said as he pointed to the bath beside them. "I should get out of your way, so you can get undressed."

"No!" Chad snapped. "It would be helpful if you make sure my clothes don't get wet." And Chad began to get undressed.

As Chad pulled down his Calvin Klein boxers and handed them to Danny and Danny bent over to place them in a corner, Danny's towel slipped off revealing a semi-erect hard on. He blushed but wasn't quick to pick up the towel. "Sorry," he excused.

"Nothing to be sorry for. It is quite impressive."

Danny smiled.

"You did sign one of my contracts before you got here today. Lawyers...go figure. Everyone I employ has to sign a confidentiality agreement."

"Oh, yes, I signed it back at the office and Chuck sent them on to someone named Lance."

"Great." And Chad stepped into the tub 'accidently' losing his balance and grabbing on to Danny. His hand brushed against Danny's cock, which made it jump. "Sorry."

"No problem. It is your day. You can do whatever you want," Danny teased and wrapped his towel back around himself. "If you don't mind me saying, Ashley Beckwith is one lucky lady."

It was Chad's turn to blush.

Chuck walked into the room, camera in hand, followed by Ashley, "I see you are ready."

Thanks to digital photography, both Ashley and Chad could see the results through the viewfinder and were awestruck as to how beautiful the composition turned out.

"I have to say, I had my doubts," Ashley confessed. "But you are a true artist, Chuck."

"Good. Because I have another idea."

It was Ashley's turn to get naked. She stood next to the glow of picture window, overlooking the sea, with one hand across her breasts and the second holding her bouquet in front of her nether regions. At her feet lay her wedding dress. It was all beautifully angelic.

A second set of pictures were taken from behind the naked silhouette of Chad as he stood in the door looking at his nude bride and the dress at her feet.

Chuck promised unorthodox wedding photos and that is clearly what they would be getting. But all concerned knew this series of photos was what the British magazine paid two and half million to publish.

o o o

Mica didn't really think he would get Lance Novak on the phone—not on a Saturday evening for sure. But he did. Ever since that awkward meeting at the Polo Lounge, they had become somewhat friendly, even flirtatious—exchanging teasing texts and emails for the most part.

Lance figured Mica wanted to pump him for details of the wedding when he got Mica's call. Mica suggested they meet for a drink at The Cathedral but Lance, not wanting to do anymore drinking before, yet again, getting behind the wheel to head home; suggested that Mica simply come over to his place for a nightcap. Mica, for his part, hadn't realized Lance had gone to the wedding. He had Tommy Mercer on the mind.

Mica arrived at the first of the two twin towers just off of Holloway in West Hollywood and dropped his car off with the valet. In the lobby, the concierge called up to the Novak condo to announce Mica's arrival.

"Twelfth floor," the concierge instructed. "Twelve-o-one. Mr. Novak is expecting you."

Inside the elevator, Mica remembered this high rise was the former home of wild child Antonia Guest back when she was just beginning her wild ways. He camped out here once waiting for her to be pulled out by the police for the first of what would have been many drunken or drug infused infractions with the law. He is so glad that *Rise 'N Shine* isn't the same sort of show bordering on the sleazy that *Drop Zone* seems to be morphing into and therefore is not given assignments like another Antonia Guest 'perp walk'.

He knocked on 1201 and was greeted by a scantily clad Lance Novak, wearing nothing more than short jogging shorts and a tank top.

"You shouldn't have dressed for me," Mica joked as he walked in. "Are those your legal briefs?"

"Cute. I have been in a suit all day. I just wanted to get comfortable." Mica had never seen Lance in anything but a suit. His legs are beautiful, Mica noted, runners legs. And from what he can tell, a swimmers torso—not overly built, just taut and compact.

"A suit? On a Saturday?" Mica queried.

"There was a specific dress code for the wedding," Lance explained as he led Mica into the living room.

Wedding? Mica thought and then he realized that, of course, Lance would have been a guest at his client's wedding, let alone being his best man.

"That is what I assumed is why you wanted to have a drink. To get the scoop on the wedding."

"Actually no," Mica corrected. "Unless some great faux pas took place, I am not sure I ever want to know the details."

"Fair enough," Lance said in that way lawyers can shut down a topic of conversation without emotion or curiosity. "Now, what can I get you to drink?"

It was then that Mica took in the room before him. Dimly lit with in-ceiling lighting and plenty of candles, the room, with it's two walls of windows, has a panoramic view of the basin of Los Angeles—from downtown to the sea. With the lighting low, the city lights sparkled. Mica gasped.

"Is everything okay?" Lance asked.

"I forget sometimes just how beautiful this city can be considering how much time we spend wading through the shit in it." Mica explained. "And I will have a vodka."

Lance moved over to the bar to pour. Mica continued to take it all in.

"The candles are a nice touch. But you didn't have to go through this trouble for me," Mica teased. Lance looked over and their eyes locked for just one uncomfortable moment too long and they both blushed.

"I like an atmosphere when I come home," Lance handed over the vodka on the rocks as he spoke. "My office is kind of sterile and this is warm."

The room is decorated in shades of beiges, mossy greens and greys—earthy, grounding colors. And the taste in which it is decorated is nothing short of impeccable. The contrast of the over-scaled contemporary art with the sleek lines of the nicely upholstered furnishings created kind of urban chic, the decor you'd expect in New York, not necessarily Los Angeles. Mica is impressed.

"Sit," Lance suggested.

Lance sat first on the couch giving Mica the option for the chair next to him or to join him on the sofa. There was a sort of awkward chemistry happening here, which made the sofa verses chair choice a conundrum. Mica chose the sofa.

"So to what may I attribute this visit, if not for wedding details?" Lance asked.

"I guess I should ask," Mica cringed as he spoke. "How was the wedding?"

"Beautiful, if not slightly over the top."

"And those are the details that I am better off not knowing."

They clinked glasses, signifying a Chad Martin détent.

"Did you know that Tommy Mercer is dead?" Mica asked disarmingly.

Lance clearly had been taken by surprise with that news. "Really? When?"

"They found him today. Suicide. Of a sort."

"Of a sort?"

"Accidental."

"Ah. That is shocking to me," Lance mumbled and took a big sip from his glass. "I would think he had a lot to live for."

"Five million reasons that I can think of," Mica goaded.

"And what do you know about that?"

Mica took out his phone, pressed the photo button, quickly scrolled to the picture of the check that Detective Joe had sent him and presented it to Lance. "And now you know why I am here."

"That is attorney client privilege," Lance began.

"Ex-client. He's dead."

"Tommy Mercer is not the client I am talking about."

"And that connects the dots," Mica leaned back satisfied. He raised his glass to thank Lance for his unwitting response.

"Stop! That is a conflict of interest," Lance, not used to being out smarted, pleaded playfully.

"Maybe it is confluence of interest," Mica returned teasingly.

"How so?"

"I haven't figured that part out yet. But I will."

"You intrigue me, Mica Daly."

"Ditto!"

Both locked eyes once again and stared at one another for a long moment—studying, tempting, and waiting for one or the other to make the obvious move. Lance took the option, leaned in and gently gave Mica a kiss. Mica had gauged correctly on the sofa verses chair conflict. The kiss never would have happened if he were in the chair.

"I have more pictures," Mica whispers.

"I bet you do."

"More questions too."

With that, Lance got up and left the room. Mica simply waited, sipped his drink and waited some more until he heard from the other room. "Are you staying?"

Mica got up and walked down the hall to the dimly lit room on the end. There, the naked and beautiful body of Lance Novak peaked out from underneath the covers of the tufted kings sized bed. "Well?"

"We have a lot to talk about."

"Well if you stay, I don't want you to be rude," Lance cautioned. It was his turn to tease.

"Rude?"

"You said you have a lot to talk about. Well, it is rude to talk with your mouth full. And I fully intend to keep your mouth full."

Epilogue

Ironically, Tommy Mercer's obituary ran the same day as the release of Chad and Ashley's wedding pictures in the glossy British celebrity magazine *Gotcha!* in much the same way Tommy's hanging body was discovered on the same day as the 'IT' couple's wedding. Tommy's write up was slightly longer than it should have been as the paper found it necessary to rehash the details of the scandal that lead to his death—infamy, from beyond. Tommy may have even liked that!

Mica chose not to talk about the irony of Tommy Mercer's obituary during his segment on *Rise 'N Shine*. The buzz this day was the borderline scandalous nude shots that Chad and Ashley chose to release as "wedding" pictures.

There was no argument they were beautiful shots. Chuck Corman, yet again, showed why he is considered the best. But the choice of shot is what has everyone buzzing. Again, Mica tipped his hat to the publicity onslaught this would inevitably cause and talked about how this very stunt is what keeps some celebrities on the top of the A-List.

"I know for a fact Corrine, that Ashley Beckwith will get work because of these pictures and it will have nothing to do with whether or not she can act."

"Are you saying you don't think our beloved Ashley is a good actress," Corrine teased.

"I am saying that before the marriage and before these pictures you would not have used the word 'beloved' when talking about Ashley Beckwith," Mica teased back.

"You are probably right there," Corrine admitted slightly embarrassed. "But you have to admit, they are a strikingly gorgeous couple."

"Oh, most definitely."

"So what were they thinking?

"Well, they selected Chuck Corman as the official photographer. And Chuck is known for his provocative and evocative work. Now, he had been snapping all day the candid shots you see in the magazine. Supposedly there are hundreds of those. And of course, there are the traditional shots of the family and the wedding party posed lovingly by the view of the ocean. But as you have pointed out Corrine, it is the images in the bathtub and by the window that are going to keep people talking for some time. As a publicity stunt, this is a pretty good one."

"Do you think it is a publicity stunt," Corrine asked.

"Well two things come to mind. They met on the set of *The Other Brother* in which they both appeared naked and as lovers. So these pictures harken back to that moment in their lives. Secondly, and I have heard this but can't confirm it, that they are thinking of releasing their wedding photos as a coffee table book. So the question is: are there any more provocative photos like these?"

"Oh I don't know if I would want my wedding photos out there as a coffee table book," Corrine shuttered. "My Aunt Lily passing out from too much sherry is hardly a work of art." One of the appeals of Corrine is her motherly sensibility that resonates with the audience. They count on her to make these kinds of value judgments.

"Really? Word has it they have been offered a five million dollar advance," Mica declared.

"But he is now being called the billion dollar boy because his movies have grossed over a billion dollars faster than any other actor in Hollywood history. Does he really need another five million dollars?" Corrine giggled as she spoke. "Can you believe I just asked if anyone needs another five million dollars? I would love to *have* five million dollars."

"You've hit the nail on the head Corrine," Mica explained. "With his backend deals, Chad Martin is already worth over one hundred million dollars. And with five pictures in the pipeline, the dollars keep adding up. Your answer Corrine as to why is the same answer that motivates every deal in Hollywood. Ego." Mica paused and then, "There are people who die in this town because they get in the way of damaging someone else's ego."

"We are going to have more with Mica after the break," Corrine said and the sound in Mica's ear went to an innocuous commercial.

"We're extending the segment," the director said in Mica's ear.

o o o

Across town in a darkened studio, Chad is face down in a pillow being rammed in the ass by Danny, Chuck's handsome and well-endowed assistant.

"Do you like that?" Danny demanded.

"Fuck yeah," Chad moaned. "Let me have it. I love it."

All around them, scattered on the floor, are pictures from the wedding shoot. There are in fact, many more provocative images not released to the media. And among the pile are the test shots using Danny as a model. That is all Chad had to see.

He had come over to look at the proofs. Or that was the plan. He and Ashley had been sent four by six inch versions as samples so they could pick the ones for the magazine. They promised the magazine ten of the candid shots, three friends and family, four romantic shots by the sea and, of course, the provocative shots. The magazine was thrilled and sales were expected to go through the roof. But when the parent company of the magazine, a book publisher, saw the nude shots everything changed. They were quickly approached about a cocktail book, for which they would have full editorial control, an advance and the requisite royalties. They jumped at the idea.

Danny had set up a meeting for Chad to see larger eight by ten and eleven by fourteen versions of the pictures at Chad's request. He wanted to see them before Ashley had a chance to put her two cents in, or so the premise was. But really, Chad wanted to see Danny, alone—no Ashley, no Chuck.

When Chad arrived, the studio was dark, almost ominous. One light by a work desk far on the other side of the cavernous room was the only beacon from which Chad had to navigate. Chad came out from the back, dressed in a tee shirt and jeans.

"Do you want something to drink?" Danny offered, giving Chad a hello hug. "Good to see you again. The pictures are amazing."

"Aren't they? What do you have to drink?"

"Well I know there are bottles of champagne..."

"Do you have any vodka?" Chad asked, provocatively.

"I'll check but I don't think so."

"Damn, I could have made you a chamtini."

"What?"

"Nothing," Chad caught himself. "Champagne will be great."

"Are you warm?" Danny shouted from the back just before the familiar pop sound told Chad the champagne was opened.

"Kinda," Chad said, now that he noticed it is, indeed hot in the place.

"It cost a fortune to air condition this place so we don't unless there is a shoot. But on a hot night like this, this place is like an incubator," Danny explained as he came from around the back, bottle in one hand and two glasses in the other. "Do you mind if I take off my shirt?"

"Take off whatever you want," Chad encouraged.

"Don't tell Chuck, but there are plenty of nights I am checking proofs completely naked.

"Don't let me stop you," Chad teased. "It is not like you haven't been naked in front of me before."

"And you in front of me," Danny shot back and they exchanged a charged look. This was going right in the direction Chad wanted it to go.

Pouring both a glass of bubbly, Danny started to squeal with excitement. "You know your wedding was the biggest...well, most important...shoot I have been on. And I just want to thank you for your letting Chuck bring me along." With that, they clinked glasses. "And by the way, I meant to tell you. I looked at the previous shoot you did for that magazine where you let Chuck shoot you getting dressed. Those shots are amazing!"

"Thank you," Chad said, surprisingly humble and appreciative of the compliment. "But I am surprised Chuck has not shot you. You are very attractive in your own right."

"Oh he has," Danny quips back nonchalantly. "Oh my God, I would love your opinion."

There is a pause and then Danny collects himself. "I am so sorry. That is completely inappropriate."

"Don't be ridiculous," Chad comforted. "I would love to see your photos."

Danny pulled out a portfolio—some headshots, some nudes and some, more or less, erotic. Danny blushed as Chad came upon the erotic shots. "You don't have to look at those."

Chad thought Danny's cock was large flaccid but engorged is another story. "That is some weapon you are carrying," Chad joked. "You should do porn."

"Don't think I haven't been asked," Danny dismissed.

"Well, the collection is very nice and I think you have a future in modeling," Chad said.

"You think so?"

"I am no expert."

Chad swigged down the rest of his champagne. And as Danny refilled his glass, their eyes met.

"You're sweating." Chad noticed the beads forming on Danny's forehead. And as he pulled back, he noticed the rivulets streaming between his pectorals. "Do you need a towel?"

"I'm sorry," Danny apologized. "I just find this studio stifling when it is hot like this. What I need is shower. Do you mind if I take two minutes and excuse myself?"

Danny dropped his jeans just beyond the lit area of the stage, just in front of the bathroom with, as Chad remembers, a large show stall. Chuck had it installed for models that had body painting and makeup they needed to remove after a shoot. And as promised, little more then two minutes later, Danny emerged into the light with a towel wrapped around him and wet hair. "Thank you. I feel so much better."

Without saying a work, Chad simply reached for Danny's towel and it slipped off. Again, their eyes met but there was no talking. Danny reached for the buttons of Chad's shirt and pulled. The shirt gave way. Chad felt Danny's well-developed chest, afraid to look down at the real prize. And Danny, still locked on Chad's eyes, reached down and undid Chad's belt, unzipped his pants and pulled. They were naked.

Chad was reluctant to let Danny kiss him, so Danny buried his face in Chad's neck and he began to nuzzle. He pushed Chad to the table and the wedding pictures spilled across it and on to the floor—an ironic display.

As Danny's tongue traveled down Chad's chest and torso, Chad began to get hard. Danny was already there. He started to suck Chad, softly and exploring at first and then decisively and rhythmically soon after.

Danny took control. He reached back to the one sofa and grabbed a pillow and threw it on the floor. He pulled Chad down to the pillow and hoisted Chad's legs in the air, for which he was able to bury his face between Chad's ass cheeks and lick. His tongue sensually probed the area, darting in and out of Chad's sweet ass. Chad, slightly stunned by the turn of the events, simply moaned with anticipation.

In one quick move, Danny flipped Chad over, pushed his face down into the pillow, spread his cheeks and asked the question that would change Chad's life, "Are you ready?"

Without waiting for an answer, Danny plunged himself into Chad. Chad screamed deep into the pillow. Danny was well aware that his size and girth was difficult for most men to handle. But this is Chad Martin and when would he ever have the chance to fuck a superstar again. Tears filled Chad's eyes.

Danny slowed his rhythm. "You must relax."

Chad caught his breath and did just that. And Danny continued—slow and steady and then harder and harder. Chad screamed for more. Danny pounded the tight hole and Chad squealed the same way Mica had time after time. Danny had gone where Mica could never but maybe he should have tried harder.

"Fuck me Mica," Chad screamed. "Fuck me."

° ° °

"There is other news today," Corrine began, changing directions. Mica had heard in is ear from the director back in London that they were extending the segment and he wondered if it was because of the last line he spoke, "that people die from getting in the way of others ego."

"It seems, Los Angeles police found the body of Tommy Mercer, who was the weight trainer who was sued by Chad Martin for one hundred million dollars," Corrine continued.

Mica hadn't had wanted to go there but Corrine opened the door. "That is correct Corrine and a sad end to a very sad story. Tommy Mercer, who was know as the trainer to the stars had many more clients that just Chad Martin. But it seems Chad Martin was his obsession. In an interview published not long ago, Mercer claimed that Martin and he were more than just client and trainer, more than just friends. For legal reasons, I won't elaborate. But his accusations met with the first of what is now the standard response from Martin's camp, a one hundred million dollar lawsuit."

Mica began to fiddle with his cell phone. "Please understand I wasn't prepared to talk about this tonight. But if you will indulge me and my technician here in the studio can download the following pictures to you," Mica turned to the technician who took his camera and went back into the control room and quickly downloaded a number of pictures into still store where from the London control room could access them and put them on the screen.

"What I have here is evidence that there is more to the story than meets the eye. First, you will see a picture of a five million dollar check made out to Mr. Mercer from an account with Mr. Martin's law firm. The next picture is of the scattered pages of the one hundred million dollar lawsuit. Why would there be both a five million dollar cashier's check and a one hundred million dollar lawsuit? The answer is in this next photo."

The photo on the screen displayed the passage by which Tommy Mercer pledged confidentiality. "You will see that Mr. Mercer breached confidentiality. Cut and dry. The lawsuit stands."

"So why the check?" Corrine asked impatiently.

"Because he may have been breaching confidentiality but he may also have been telling the truth. How do I know that? Well in a story we reported exclusively on *Rise 'N Shine* the wife of Tommy Mercer confirmed he was telling the truth. And subsequently, when a lawsuit was filed against her, she too was given a settlement."

"Let me ask one more question," the now spellbound Corrine chimed in with. "If the lawsuit was cut and dry and Mr. Mercer was guilty. Why pay him at all?"

"Good question with two answers Corrine," Mica responded. "First, the one hundred million dollars was a benchmark to scare anyone else from opening their mouths. They knew that Tommy Mercer could never pay that off over his lifetime. But second, they needed to buy his silence. If you are faced with an overwhelming legal judgment against you, the only way to retaliate is to talk. They effectively bought his silence and scare any others with salacious accusations away."

"Mica Daly, you never cease to amaze me," Corrine squealed. "You know so much about Hollywood, maybe you should write a book."

There was a pause on the Hollywood end, as Mica processed what she just said. "Maybe I will Corrine. Maybe I will." With that, he winked into the camera and was counted down by the director.

And while he still thought of her suggestion, seriously thought, he heard the familiar voice of the director in his ear. "All clear."

CPSIA information can be obtained at www.ICGtesting.com
Printed in the USA
BVOW04s1811260215

389261BV00003B/242/P